A Cry for Rodney

II

True Reparation

JEW

Dedication

I Dedicate This Book to My Best Friend Don Niedie. The reason why I dedicate this book to him is because of two major reasons. One, he was around when I first started writing this story over twenty years ago, and now, sad to say, may he rest in peace. He knew the message I wanted to convey to the American people, and being an Italian man, he understood the need to kill this thing called racism, while he encouraged me to finish my work. Two, because as a friend and a brother to him, I wanted to give him something even though his flesh is not here with me, his loving spirit deserves more than I can give, which is not a comparison to what he did for me when he was here on Earth as my best friend. He taught me that there are still good people in this world, but his death taught me that life is too short. So, love the ones that love you back and don't waste time on those who don't. In this lifetime, we as humans are so far from God that we are lucky to have one true friend and one true love. God, please lift up my brother to the heavens for his light to shine on the world so they can see what I witnessed being his best friend.

CONTENTS

Chapter 1

Inmates are lined up in shackles and chains, waiting to board the bus that awaits them. Rodney noticed that the bus he was about to board looked brand new. It appeared freshly painted sky blue with white letters that read, in small print, something illegible, "New Jersey Correctional." Rodney scanned his surroundings and, for the most part, he noticed mostly Black males of all ages, a few men of Hispanic descent, and a small number of White males. One by one, the men entered the bus, which already had a dreary feeling of being caged or trapped due to its metal fencing protecting the glass windows. Many of the men seemed accustomed to this as they calmly sat quietly during the journey. There were a few first-timers who looked nervous, with jitteriness running through their bodies. Rodney, at that time, looked scared to be around the savage men, and those who noticed saw the tears of fear running down his face.

The Correctional Officer on the bus noticed Rodney almost immediately. He was the power-hungry authority type who thrived on seeing a weak individual. The guard noticed a familiar habitual convict sitting next to him. He bent over and spoke jovially into the man's ear, "Oh, looks like we got a Sissy Boy on our hands." He glanced over at Rodney to make it clear that his words were referring to him. Sweat began to run down Rodney's face, even though it was the middle of winter.

The ride upstate meant traveling down into the valleys, which seemed to have come way too fast as they arrived at the entrance of the correctional facility. The bus stopped at the front gate so they could be let in, and when the gate opened, Rodney and the others were ordered to stand while the bus driver opened the door to let the C.O.'s off the bus first. "Ok, you worthless pieces of shit, get the fuck off my bus now!" he ordered. One by one, they struggled to walk, trying to find a rhythm among themselves to make their departure smoother and ease the pain a bit from the modern slave shackles on their wrists and ankles.

Rodney noticed the inmates standing at the gates inside, waiting to see what the state had to offer. The minute Rodney's feet stepped off that bus, it was as if the spirit of an unwilling slave had been trapped in his soul. He impulsively began to scream out, "No! I must go home! Please, somebody help me!" The C.O. smacked his hand with his billy club in anger and shouted, "If someone doesn't get ahold of that nigger and his emotions, there are going to be some harsh consequences and repercussions." The men closest to Rodney were telling him to chill out for his own good, but Rodney's ears went deaf as he fought a losing battle. He began swinging his arms and kicking his legs, causing the men in front of and behind him to fall to the ground.

Now the C.O., even more aggravated, had seen enough. He ran up to Rodney and hit him in the gut with his nightstick, making him vomit all over himself. However, that didn't stop him from screaming for help; it simply made matters worse. The C.O.'s face turned bright red, and beyond furious, he irrationally took his nightstick and smacked Rodney across the temple, rendering him unconscious and resulting in a trickle of blood running down the side of his face. "Now you two niggas help this pussy to his feet so we can get this show on the road." He walked to the front of the line, not caring one bit about anyone's thoughts on what he'd done; in his heart, he felt he did what was needed.

As soon as they entered the building, Rodney was awakened by the sound of other inmates welcoming the new fish. The smell of the prison gave his nose a malodorous welcome to the joint. His ears were assaulted by caged men shouting at the newcomers, using all types of words to see who was the weak one of the bunch. A few noticed the fear surrounding Rodney's aura, and one man shouted out to him, "Hey pussy! We have plenty of clothes to be washed and some heads that need massaging from a pretty light-skinned thing like you. As soon as you make yourself at home, come see me, you hear." Rodney instantly urinated on himself, noticing that all the other inmates couldn't help but notice as well.

After being humiliated by the prison's inhuman protocol strip search, Rodney and the other inmates made their way to their assigned rooms. Rodney walked into his room, feeling the cold bouncing off the steel bars and the thin concrete floors. His cellmate was sitting at his desk on his side of the room, reading a book. He didn't say a word to Rodney, as if he didn't exist. Rodney walked into the room slowly, unsure if he should speak first or just play along with his cellmate's mutism. Rodney could tell that he was granted the top bunk by the display of sheets needing to be put on his mattress. He was caught off guard by the display of a cupcake resting on his bed. He picked it up and looked at his cellmate, wondering if he should thank him or ask where it came from. "Excuse me, is this cupcake yours, sir?" His cellmate, feeling a little agitated, never lifted his head from the book he was reading. "If you want it, you can have it, but you must know that everything in this joint costs."

Rodney heard the man's words but thought to himself about what kind of price he would have to pay for such a small thing as this cupcake. He ate it without caring about any debt that might be owed. An hour later, the C.O. who had put the gash on his head walked into his room. Rodney's cellmate knew that whatever was about to take place was no concern of his, so he gathered his things and slid past the guard and out of the room. The guard smiled at the inmate, letting him know that he was thankful for his understanding of the need for privacy with Rodney. Rodney's heart was beating fast because he wasn't sure what was coming next. "Did you like the sweet cupcake?" the guard asked. Rodney wasn't sure if there was a right or wrong answer, so all he could think to do was shrug his shoulders. "I guess," he answered. The guard moved further into the cell, closed the door behind him, and grabbed the only seat in the room. He turned the chair around and sat down. "Well, I hope it was good for you because I sent it hoping you would like it. One good turn deserves another. At the end of the month, I'm going to need you to give me something that would make me happy." Rodney didn't understand what the guard was trying to say, so he asked, "What do you mean?" The guard stood up quickly, kicked the chair aside, and moved in close to Rodney's face. "Are you stupid or something?" he said, rubbing Rodney's face gently. He then raised Rodney's chin to lock eyes with him before backhanding him across the face. "If I come in here at the end of the month and your mother or whoever you have on the outside doesn't give you something that I want, well, I guess I'll just have to take something else from you that would be so sweet to me." He smiled at Rodney, noticing how scared he had made him. The guard walked to the door, looked out the small glass window to see if anyone was being nosy, then opened the door and walked out. Right in front of him was Rodney's cellmate, sitting on the railing, waiting to return to his cell. The guard passed him, not worried if he had heard what was going on, knowing that he was trained to keep his mouth shut and his eyes closed to things that didn't concern him.

Rodney's cellmate walked into the cell, noticing that Rodney looked like he would rather be dead. For the first two weeks, Rodney stayed in his room, not coming out to eat, shower, or shave, except for roll call, which was becoming a problem for his cellmate. James Jackson was sitting on the toilet and wasn't sure what smelled worse, his shit or the funk of Rodney not showering. There were only a few sheets of toilet paper left for him to use. "Yo! Do you have anything I can use to finish cleaning myself up?" Jackson asked Rodney. Rodney didn't have anything, so he just shook his head no.

"I see the only way you would say a word to me is when your ass needed me. I don't even know your name," said Rodney. Jackson thought that was kind of rude of himself not to have said a word to him, but it wasn't personal; he just kept to himself, knowing that was the best way to survive in the joint. "I'm sorry, I'm Jackson, James Jackson. I don't talk much in here because words have so much power that they can make you or break you." Rodney wanted to understand. "What do you mean?" he asked.

Jackson had an Afro and was somewhat on the heavy side. He stood in the only mirror in the room, picking his hair. "If you say the right things in here, it could lead to peaceful times. Say the wrong thing, and it could lead to your worst nightmare." He stopped for a second and turned to face Rodney. "And man, if you don't wash your ass, you're going to give others a reason to fuck with you. You're making matters worse for yourself, and I don't care for the way you've got this room smelling." Jackson had a lighter in his hand and lit the butt of his cigarette, hoping to kill the smell of his lingering shit while Rodney kept contributing in his own way by not showering. Rodney was scared to leave the room because he wasn't sure what he was going to walk into, but he knew he needed to use the phone to call his mother or Michelle to hopefully bail him out. The next morning, Rodney got up, took his long-needed shower, got dressed, and mustered the courage to head to the café for breakfast. He stood in line to get his food, then glanced around to find a place to sit. He found an empty seat way in the back, walked over to the table, and started to eat. While eating, he could feel people staring at him as if he had done something wrong, but he kept his head down and took his time eating.

The guard who had it out for him noticed that he finally came out of his room and went over to an inmate with whom he had a great understanding of how things ran in the prison. "You see that scared fish over there in the corner?" The bald-headed, dark-skinned man looked into the guard's eyes to see whom he was referring to, then turned to look and noticed Rodney looking uneasy. "You mean that kid back there looking like he's from the 60s or something?" The guard nodded. "You got it. What about him?" the inmate asked. "I don't want him to be able to use the phone, you hear me?" The inmate, with a mouth full of food, said he got it. "What's in it for me?" he asked. The guard thought for a minute. "You do this for me, and when you need a favor or whatever you want, I will see to it that you get it." That was all that needed to be said. The guard walked away, thinking about how it wouldn't be long before he had his way with Rodney. Rodney noticed the inmates who finished eating were going to the phone to make calls, so he quickly finished his food and went over to the line to use the phone. He waited and waited for the line to move but noticed that people were letting others use the phone who hadn't been waiting as long as he had. By now, he would have gotten closer to using the phone if the other inmates hadn't started butting in front of him, daring him to say something about it. Rodney couldn't fight if he tried, so he just let the men have their way. He thought to himself there must be someone he could talk to about this problem. When it was time to leave the café, he realized that the only one he could talk to was the guard who had it out for him, so he just went to his room wondering when he'd get his chance to use the phone.

Another week went by, and this time Rodney made his way to the phone. Just as he picked it up to use it, the inmate the guard had spoken to yelled out, "Did I say you could use that phone?" Rodney looked at him, not knowing what to say. He was speechless. To Rodney, the inmate heading toward him looked like he had been eating the weights. His biceps were twice the size of

Rodney's, and his chest looked like two bowling balls under his shirt. He held the phone in his hand until the man came over, nicely took it out of his hand, and hung it back up. "To use this phone, you gotta pay me." Rodney was baffled. "I don't have anything to give you," he told the muscular man. "Oh, well, that's cool for now, but since you don't, stay the fuck off my phone!" He turned and looked at the C.O. and smiled, letting him know that Rodney was indeed a bitch and had nothing to offer to use the phone. He went back over to his crew, watching Rodney walk away like a dog with its tail between its legs. Later that day, Rodney was in his room listening to what his cellmate was playing on the radio. It was some good old Dru Hill, bringing back that R&B sound that seemed to have been lost in today's modern music. There was a tapping sound on the door, and then it opened. Just as before, Rodney's cellmate got up and removed himself from the room. The guard walked in slowly and looked around the room. "So, it's been a full month now. What do you have for me?"

Rodney quickly answered, "I don't have anything because, for one, I haven't been able to use the phone. I can't even call home to let someone know that I'm in here." The guard was happy to hear that not a soul knew his whereabouts. "Oh, is that right? So you're basically saying, 'Fuck me!' right? Ok, you little shit." The guard unzipped his pants, pulled out his manhood, and held it in his hand. "Well, I guess I will get the next best thing from you." He grabbed

Rodney by the neck, feeling him shake. Rodney noticed the man getting a hard-on and tried screaming for help, but the guard quickly covered his mouth. He put his finger up to his lips to imply that Rodney should be very quiet.

Rodney became quiet but wasn't trying to play along with the guard. The guard grabbed Rodney by his hair, forcefully trying to push his head down to his hip area for oral sex. Rodney forcefully lifted his head up, hitting the guard's chin and making it bleed profusely. Blood was leaking from the guard's chin so much that what he'd come for would now have to take place another time. Rodney was scared, unsure of what would happen next. He sat there, watching the guard try to stop the bleeding with his hands. The C.O. looked at his hands a few times and knew right away that he was going to need a few stitches. He looked over at Rodney and said, "You're going to pay for this, nigger!" After saying that, he deliberately coughed up phlegm from his throat and spit right in Rodney's face. Then he turned his back to him and left the room to get his chin looked after.

An hour had passed, and by now, everyone on Rodney's pod knew that someone was in big trouble because the guards came to their pod in full gear, ready for war. When they came up the stairs, passing the rooms quickly, it sounded like a group of soldiers. They reached Rodney's room, opened the door, grabbed the inmate who was in the cell with him, and tossed him onto the floor.

10

The mob of C.O.s stepped over him, entered the room, and closed the door behind them. Without saying a word, they started beating Rodney with anything and everything they had. They beat him so badly that the floor turned red from all the blood he lost. They stomped and kicked him until his body couldn't move any longer and his crying went mute.

The inmates on his pod knew what the outcome would be when the C.O.s arrived, but they hadn't seen anyone get beaten as long as they beat Rodney. After they finished, they sent the medical staff to his room to get him because they knew he wouldn't be able to walk, let alone talk. When they arrived at his room, they put him on a stretcher and brought him out with the inmates standing around, looking at his body. They thought he was dead. Rodney was ordered to stay in the infirmary room until he was able to move his body around in bed and eat his food without the machine feeding him through a straw. As soon as he was able to do so, he was sent straight to the hole until the warden was ready to see his face. Rodney found himself shaking in the corner on the floor in the small cell that he was going to be staying for the next few months which every second of the hour seemed as if a year would have passed by. He was so much in pain and needed nothing more than rest but most of the time all he could do was try and find rest on a small slab of metal connected to the brick wall they considered a bed.

The cell was cold and dirty, with rat droppings all around the room as if no one had cleaned it in years. The aroma in the air was a mix of mold and rodent piss, and the only light that entered the room came from under the door, from an old room down the hall where the light was occasionally left on. Every day, Rodney was given breakfast and dinner, which consisted of stale bread and tap water that tasted like rusted pipes. What he didn't eat, the big roaches that shared his new home made sure to finish.

After sitting in the cell for the first month, Rodney did nothing but wait for his pain to go away. Once he got over that, he started talking to himself, repeating, "It's going to be ok, it's going to get better, I will be free." There was no mirror in the cell; he was surrounded by brick walls and an old gray steel door, so the only way he could look at himself was to close his eyes and imagine. He started feeling his face and his facial hair, which had grown into a full-blown beard that badly needed combing. His hair was as knotty as a man who had been to war and back without a care or need for a haircut. His hair began to lock together like he was a dreadlocked Rasta.

Rodney couldn't take a shower or brush his teeth, and if he did, the water the state had to offer was so dirty that it would have defeated the purpose. His skin was so filthy that he could scratch the dirt on his skin and write words or draw pictures if he wanted to. He had smelled himself for so long that he had become immune to it. Each

12

day, it felt as if he were becoming uncivilized, like the Europeans during the Stone Age. He masturbated every chance he got until he had no sperm left nor any rags or toilet paper of any kind, so when he ejaculated, his sperm went on the wall or the floor, matching the remnants of others who had done the same in the past.

Some light made its way into the room, making his eyes focus on its source. Rodney dove down to the floor with his head at the foot of the door. He tried adjusting his eyes to the light as best he could, but having no light in the room whatsoever made even the smallest bit of light hurt his eyes. In the dark room, for the most part, he kept his eyes closed and envisioned what the room would look like with the lights on and in better condition. All he could do was run in place, do a thousand sit-ups and a million push-ups, all while having an all-out conversation with himself.

After six months in the hole, due to the fact that he was granted two extra months just because they truly wanted to break him, two guards went to get him. One of the guards was a short, stocky Black man and the other was a chubby redheaded White man. The chubby redheaded guard put the key in the doorknob and opened the door, stepping into the cell and smelling something close to death. They quickly covered their noses with the insides of their arms and noticed Rodney on the floor in the corner, sweating as if he were truly in hell. The guards were in the room for less than five minutes and started shedding pounds due to the heat.

Rodney's lips had a white ring around them, badly chapped from the lack of water. They picked him up off the floor, surprised at how much weight he must have lost because he felt lighter than a sack of potatoes. They helped him down the hallway to the room that occasionally gave him a little light at night. Rodney instantly frowned when the light invaded his face, lifting his arms to shield his eyes from the irritation. Sitting at the desk, waiting for Rodney to come in, was his worst nightmare: the guard David Hunt, the man who had it out for him since he arrived at the prison. Hunt stood up, leaning against his desk with his legs and arms crossed, enjoying what he had done to Rodney, but now feeling the need to put a cherry on top of his wish list.

"Take his stinking ass to the shower down the hall and bring him back when he's good and clean," Hunt ordered the two guards. Rodney's body got chills at the sound of his voice. Hunt sat at his desk, smiling at his own devilish thoughts. The two guards pulled Rodney to the shower room in handcuffs. The short Black guard went in and ran the water, not too hot but just right. The chubby redhead guard stood back, admiring Rodney's body even though he looked like a stick to most inmates. His eyes were locked onto Rodney's ass cheeks, making him gain a hard-on that clarified his preference.

Rodney got in the shower and slowly washed off the dirt from his body, almost forgetting what it felt like to have water running down it. He washed his body a few times while thinking about what his grandmother always told him: "You can only get close to God if you're clean, in body and soul." They didn't even offer him a towel before walking him back to Hunt. Rodney could feel the devil's presence in the air and he could smell it. As they walked him down the hall, he tried to stop himself from going to the room by reaching out to grab something, but two against one was too much for him to fight off.

Hunt was presented with Rodney's naked body in front of him, soapy suds of water running down his skin. Hunt had already made sure that not a soul would be coming to his secret office, plus he had shielded off every window the room had. "Well, inmate, do you understand now that I can do what I want to you? And when I ask for something, I expect returns?" Rodney didn't say a word because he was trying to make out if this was all just in his head or if he was having a conversation with himself, or if it was truly Hunt's voice playing on his mental.

Hunt asked him again and got the same reply, so he became angry and took it personally, as a sign of disrespect. He looked over to the short Black guard and nodded. The young C.O. knew what that meant, so he did as he was told. He backhanded Rodney in the face, and before Rodney could react, he punched him in the stomach

15

while Hunt kept saying in his ear like a drill sergeant, "Am I clear?" Rodney remained quiet. Hunt nodded at the short Black man again, only this time he wanted to draw a little blood. The short man smacked Rodney across his back with a nightstick, sending him down to his knees, then punched him a few times in the face and stepped back to see what damage he had done. Rodney's lips had trickles of blood coming from the corners of his mouth.

"Pick him up!" Hunt ordered, as he stuck his hand down his pants to feel his dick, confirming to himself that he was ready for what he came for. "Jordan, go and check the stairs and then come back," Hunt told the short Black C.O.

Jordan went on his way to the stairs, making sure nobody came down to this Hell Pit. "Take the cuffs off him," Hunt ordered the other C.O. The fat redhead scrambled through the keys on his key ring until he found the right one, then uncuffed Rodney. As soon as Rodney felt his hands were free, he started to throw a few blows himself, but he couldn't see what he was trying to hit, so for the most part, he was swinging at air, which only delayed Hunt's mission.

Jordan walked into the room and noticed Rodney going off, so he got behind him and grabbed him. Rodney tried to scream for help, but Jordan placed his hand over Rodney's mouth to silence him.

Hunt enjoyed watching others take another man's manhood as much as he loved doing so himself. He turned and looked at the fat redhead and said, "Go in the top drawer and grab the duct tape and tape that nigga's mouth shut so you two can break him in for me." Rodney tried to bite the C.O., but the short C.O. helped close his mouth by holding his jaw shut for a second.

"Who's going first?" Hunt asked. The fat redhead couldn't wait, so he dropped his pants quickly while his short partner undid his. Rodney was scared, but he had learned one main thing from being in the hole: the power of the mind. His body started to feel pain, and he stiffened up, unsure of what he could do to help himself. Hunt moved his seat to the back of the room in the corner because he liked the view better from there. The redhead was stiff and ready to open Rodney's rear end while the black C.O. stood close to make sure Rodney didn't resist. As soon as the C.O. grabbed Rodney's right ass cheek and moved it aside to make his way into his rectum, Rodney felt his stomach bubbling and let out the biggest, silent but deadly fart.

The fat redhead C.O. started choking, and then his partner did the same. The toxin from the fart was like a miracle for Rodney, but he himself didn't understand what was going on until the two C.O.s hit the floor and started going into convulsions, foaming at the mouth. The redhead C.O.'s convulsions started slowing down as he took his last breath, and soon after, the same happened to his partner. Hunt was so shocked that his body paused; he didn't know what to do. Rodney noticed that the two men were dead or just passed out, but he knew the best thing to do was to break out of the room before Hunt snapped out of his shock. He slid out of the room and took off running down the hall and up the stairs, only to notice that the other side of the door had chains on it. Rodney felt helpless and leaned up against the wall, sliding down to the floor in tears, hoping he would make it out alive.

Hunt had to think fast about how he was going to explain two dead bodies to the warden. He reached into his back pocket and pulled out a shank he had confiscated from an inmate earlier that day. He went over to the two dead bodies, pinching his nose closed with his left hand because they had taken their last shits. He quickly stabbed the two guards in the heart a few times and then ran off looking for Rodney. He ran up the stairway and noticed Rodney on the floor. "Nigga! You fucked up now. You're in big, big trouble." Rodney held his head up, looking at Hunt, wondering why this man had it out for him so much and how it had turned his life for the worse within that year. Hunt walked over to Rodney, grabbed his hand, placed the shank in it, then took it back from him and turned around, walking in the other direction.

Chapter two

"Life changes"

Hunt made his way to meet with the warden of the prison, Tom Bradford. At his desk, the warden was on the phone having a happy conversation with whomever was on the other end. When he noticed Hunt walking into his office, he saw that Hunt had a serious look on his face. Without saying a word to the person on the phone, he hung up and waited for Hunt to deliver the news. Hunt walked over to the warden's desk and placed the shank on it.

"What's the big deal with this?" the warden asked, as he had seen plenty of them over the years.

Hunt cleared his throat. "Well, sir, this here is the weapon that has been used to kill two of your guards."

The warden stood up from his desk. "What the fuck do you mean?" he asked, his face turning bloodshot red.

"Well, the new inmate, 478903, Rodney something—I'm not sure of his last name—but sir, this man has been a problem since he arrived, and he's only been here a little more than six months. I sent the two guards to get him out of the hole, and they were taking so long to bring him to his pod that I went looking for them to see for myself what was taking so long. When I got down there, sir, I noticed the old vacant office door was open with the lights on, so I went in to see why. To my surprise, I found Officer Jordan and Officer Bates on the floor, almost covered in their own blood."

The warden couldn't believe what he was hearing, but nonetheless, he had to take action. "Call out to the staff for a Code Blue and go get that shit-for-brains and bring him back to me alive."

Hunt nodded his head to confirm he understood the order. Bradford hit the alert button to inform the other C.O.s that it was time to suit up. The alarm went off, and the guards geared up, ready for whatever. Hunt told the guards where Rodney was and ordered, "Bring him to the warden alive." He walked slowly behind the men who were rushing to snatch Rodney up.

Without any question, when the guards reached Rodney, one of them grabbed him by his hair while two others dragged him by his armpits, one on the left side and one on the right. The other guards beat his back with sticks, and some kicked him in the ribs, cracking two of them. They dragged him to the warden and dropped him on the floor in front of his desk. Most of the guards wanted to kill him for the two officers because, to most of them, they were friends and considered family.

The warden spoke, "Pick that piece of shit up." The officers roughly placed Rodney in the seat in front of the warden's desk. The warden looked Rodney over and was very surprised that he didn't look worse than he did. Rodney could hardly breathe, and moving any part of his body brought so much pain that he would have preferred to rest on the floor.

"Well, well, the second time I get to meet you, and instead of you just asking to stay here for the rest of your life, you decided to take out two of my overseers. What do you have to say for yourself?"

Rodney couldn't believe what was happening to him, but he mustered up the strength to say, "Sir, you have a crooked faculty, and this place is very inhumane." Then he coughed and spat a small amount of blood onto the floor.

The warden didn't like people telling him how to run the place and could care less about the living conditions. "Well, I tell you what, since it looks like you will be staying for a while, I'll try to make you feel a little more at home." He gave Rodney a fake smile and then ordered him to clean the blood off the floor.

"May I have something to clean it with?" Rodney asked.

"Use your fucking tongue," the warden replied.

Rodney couldn't believe how people in charge of this place could be so cruel to a human being. Rodney didn't move fast enough, so Hunt pushed his face to the floor until Rodney licked his own blood up. Bradford looked at Hunt. "Take this animal out of my office and send him to his new cage." Before Hunt did as he was told, the warden walked over to him and whispered into his ear, "Make that nigger suffer the same as Jesus did." Hunt knew just what to do. He smiled at Bradford and escorted Rodney to his new room.

Hunt didn't know much about the lifers' side of the prison, but he did know a handful of inmates who understood that he could make matters worse or smoother while one was doing hard time. He stopped Rodney at his door. "Open! Cage 345!" The door opened, and Hunt tossed Rodney into his room where he was again all alone. The door shut behind him, and Hunt looked at him, reminiscing about how the two deaths really occurred.

Nighttime hit, and lights were ordered to be out by 9 PM. Some inmates struggled in the dark to read a book while others let their minds drift. Some couldn't wait for the night to come so they could jerk off to release some testosterone, but it was hard for them this night because every time Rodney breathed in, his lungs felt like they were being stabbed all over again. When he moved to try and ease the pain, he only made matters worse by moaning and groaning loud enough for the inmates to hear him.

One by one, the inmates asked, "Yo! Who's that fool crying like some bitch in here? He must be a new fish because you know that's a no-go in this piece. Shit, why ain't nobody put a radio on? With his crying ass." One inmate said out loud for a few to hear, "It's the new person on board making all that noise." Within a few minutes, they all knew who the new resident was but had no clue what he looked like. Hunt could hear Rodney crying out, so he sent a guard down to his room to tell him that he better quiet up or else he'd give him something to cry for.

After the night was over and morning struck, Hunt felt it wouldn't be a good idea to see Rodney in the café. When he entered the café, he noticed an inmate from years ago that he once made a good accord with, named Hammer Jack, government name Frank Hendrix. Hammer Jack made his name in the prison by pushing plates of weight like it was no tomorrow. He had a small clique that he ran with to make things go right when they could go wrong. Hunt liked his style of moving in silence without getting himself dirty with the dirty work. Hunt sent a message to him that he needed a favor for a favor. Hammer loved favors from C.O.s because he knew then that whatever he wanted out of the deal could gain him a little power on the inside.

Hammer got the word that Hunt wanted the new person named Rodney beaten down to the point that he'd wish he were dead. He asked the messenger how he would know who he was if he never got a chance to lay eyes on him. Hunt knew that could be the case, so he let Hammer know that he would hear him crying out at night. Hammer was doing a nice bid, but he wasn't trying to stay there for the rest of his life, so he knew not to go overboard by killing the man. Hammer put the word out to his goons about what to do when the time came. Later that night, it was déjà vu all over again with Rodney crying out. Inmates shouted out loud, "Shut the fuck up!" just before lights out and doors closed shut. Hammer and his crew were let out of their cells by a guard, and then they were off to give Rodney a visit.

It was déjà vu once again, but Hammer noticed that Hunt and the guards had already done enough damage that he didn't press too hard on him. However, he did want to make sure it was known that his job was handled. They took Rodney out of his room and dragged him to the lounge area for everyone to see who was making all the noise at night. All Rodney could do was think to himself, "Lord, please forgive them, for they know not what they do."

The next morning, when the inmates were let out of their cages, they noticed Rodney lying on the floor. Little by little, they walked over to him, standing around thinking how messed up it was how badly he was beaten. Rodney's best friend Rob from high school was one of the last few inmates to look at the body left on the floor. Rob glanced at Rodney's body but couldn't make out who it was. The closer he got to the body and focused on the face, despite the blood and scars, the more familiar it became to him. Rob wasn't sure if his mind was playing tricks on him because, to him, there was no way in hell Rodney, of all people, would be in jail, let alone on his pod with the rest of the lifers.

"Rodney, is that you?" he asked. Rodney looked up at him the best he could with his eye almost closed shut and recognized Rob's voice despite his knotty dreads. "Rob, is that you?" Rodney asked, his voice muffled. Rob dropped to his knees and gently touched Rodney's body to see how bad off he had been beaten. Tears ran down his face because he could feel the pain his friend was enduring. "Help!" he yelled out. "This is my friend! Please, someone help me!" Inmates were just standing around looking as if they only knew how to mind their own business. Hammer Jack walked over to Rob, feeling a little bad, but he knew he had to let him know there wasn't any hope of getting his friend any help.

"Man, your boy here is on his own. He's been pointed out." Rob knew that meant only two things 1. He was going to pay the price of an ass whopping or 2. Death, one or the other and lucky for Rodney they spared his life. "This is my people from the outside. I don't want another person in here to lay a hand on him. Do I make myself clear?" Hammer knew that Rob's words carried a little wait in the joint being as though Rob was going to spend the remainder of his life behind them bars, so he had a little more say on what they wanted and how things went down more so than anyone else who was in prison on borrowed time. "Look! as you can see, what has been done has been done and the best thing for you to do for your Homie is to clean him up and wait on his wounds to heal." Hammer said to Rob while he walked off feeling a little bit sad for Rodney, but he knew if it wasn't him who gotten the job done it would of, been the next man. Rob helped Rodney up from the floor trying his best not to cause him any pain. Rob and Rodney slowly made their way to Rodney's room trying to help Rodney onto his bed was a great struggle for Rob and when he got him fully onto the bed Rodney held onto Robs arms tight as he could not wanting to let him go.

"Thank you, please help me in here I fear for my life." Rodney said to Rob before letting his arm lose. Rob looked at him and with all the truth in his heart, he told him "No one in here will harm you ever again, you hear me? No one! And that's my word." Rob's words touched Rodney's soul making him feel a smidge better, more at ease. He turned and walked out the room wanting to go to war with whomever did this to his friend, but he knew it was bigger than what he could handle do to the fact that the order of the beat down came from a higher place and that's the closes thing in the joint to politics there was. He went to his room and grabbed his note pad and began to write his uncle Wisdom to inform him on what he just witnessed. Rodney didn't leave his room because his wounds wouldn't allow him to so Rob came by his room every day to check on him making sure that he eat Breakfast, lunch and dinner even though he knew the consequences of getting caught doing so. Hunt knew what Rob was doing because it wasn't anything he didn't know that was going on in the prison thanks to the snitches who ran their mouths like Bitches, hoping that it would make them have brighter days while doing their time, so Hunt turned his back to what Rob was doing because he knew two things for sure and that was, if he wanted to Blackmail Rob in the near future, a Trump card if need be for 1. and 2. just the smear fact that he was going to enjoy seeing Rodney's face for the remainder of his life. He was happy to see an inmate doing life because his thinking was if one is doing life, he knew having a job wasn't ever going to be a problem. Time was moving slow making sure that one should learn to appreciate every second of their lives. Rodney was in his bed staring at his court papers that were resting on his desk, he was thinking about opening them up and trying to make out what it read. Being as though he couldn't read much it was a struggle, it made him feel what it had to have felt like if he was born a Slave and had the determination and desire to learn to read, he struggled night after night and day after day, but every struggle was a prospering moment for him.

Chapter 3

Knowledge is Power

Rodney made his way to Rob's room and tapped on his door. "Yo! You decent?" Rodney asked, making sure he didn't just walk in while Rob could be getting dressed.

"Yeah, you good," Rob said. Rodney entered the room with an angry look on his face. "No man, I'm not," he replied.

"Why? What's the problem?" Rob asked, sitting upright in his bed to give Rodney his undivided attention.

Rodney tossed his papers to Rob. "Man, I've been in this place for a year now and they still can't give me a court date. They're talking about being sorry, but they're severely backed up because of COVID-19. What the fuck does that have to do with me? It's my life they're playing with." Rob could see the frustration on his face, and even though he himself was looking at life in prison, he still understood how Rodney felt.

"Look man, I know it sounds fucked up, but you have to be a little patient."

Rodney wasn't trying to hear that. "Man, fuck patience!" he said and then took a seat in Rob's chair that he used to sit in to read his books. Rodney looked around his room, noticing on the other side of the room a wall full of books.

"Never say fuck patience in here again because you're going to learn real fast that's the only way to make it in here." The look on Rodney's face after hearing that statement said "Whatever" and Rob noticed it.

"Let me explain something to you. There's time on the outside and then there's time in this fucking place. Two things are for sure: on the outside, they say time flies, and there aren't enough hours in a day. On the flip side, the only time time goes slow is when you're paying child support and doing time in this shithole, and that's a fact." Rodney changed his whole demeanor after he digested what Rob just laid on him. His eyes started scanning the books on the wall, which made him think of Rob's uncle Wisdom.

"Yo, how's your uncle?"

Rob and his uncle were still very tight, and because of his uncle, Rob was still getting a little work in selling a little of that Happy he used to push before his incarceration. He noticed Rodney looking at his books a little dumbfounded because some of the books on his wall were about law, and the majority were about Black history, whether it be Black American history or African history. He walked over to his books and scanned the rows with his eyes, trying to key in on something that he felt would be some knowledge for Rodney. His eyes passed by books like "A Message to the Black Man," "The Autobiography of Malcolm X," and "Booker T. Washington," among others. Rob grabbed a book for Rodney to read called "We the Black Jews" by Yosef A.A. Ben-Jochannan. He handed Rodney the book and then pulled out a beginner's book for chess players.

Rodney took the books and looked at the one about the Black Jews. "What's this crap about Black Jews?" Rob looked at Rodney and almost forgot that he lacked knowledge of self, remembering the great words of Malcolm X who once said to never pass judgment on others when at one point in time in your life you didn't know what you know now. So, he just gave Rodney a side eye and spoke, "Boy, you have a lot to learn, my friend."

Rodney knew it to be true, so he laughed it off and then asked, "What's up with this chess book? I've never played the game and have no concept of what it's about."

Rob shook his head at him. "You play chess every day, only thing is you don't know it because you don't know the game yet."

Rodney wanted to understand what he was talking about. "What do you mean I play chess every day?"

Rob went under his bed, pulled out the board with the 64 squares, and set the pieces up. "Alright, look, check it. This board right here is like them streets out there, and the squares are the blocks on the streets. Each spot that has a piece on its square runs the block, and just like a person running the block, it needs protection. Now as for the pieces, you have these little motherfuckers right here." Rob picked up the pawn and showed Rodney what it looked like. "Now these pawns, I look at them as if they are friends and family, so never just give them up freely, because we all need someone in our lives."

Rodney was really intrigued now. "Now these pieces in the back row are more powerful. Let's start with the king. He's the piece with the cross on top of his head, and that's you, my nigga. And every king should have what? A queen, and that's the one next to you but a little smaller, and if you notice she has a crown on her head. Then you have the piece that looks like a horse, which is called the knight. The knight is like a thief in the night; you'll understand why when you learn how to use it. Next to that, you have the bishop, and I like to refer to that as a bishop in the church because it goes across the world to serve its purpose. And these two on the end are what a king and queen need, and that's a castle. Now take that back to your cell and get back with me so I can show you how the game works. Oh, one more thing, the key to winning in this game is to be patient and to think more moves ahead of your opponent, and the most important thing is to make a sacrifice for the greater cause." Rodney walked out of the room feeling as if he had his hands full of food for thought.

Two weeks later, Rob and another inmate were sitting in the rec room at a round table in the center of the room, playing a few games of chess with a little wager on it for some commissary. "Man, it's election time again, and I hope those Republican motherfuckers don't win again. Those niggas on the outside gotta get out and vote. Shit! I wish I had the chance," said Heart, a light-skinned brother who they called Heart to Heart because he would always keep it real with you when it came to asking for advice or if you just wanted an intelligent conversation.

Rob kept his eyes on the board. "Why, nigga? They're two of the same kind." Heart disagreed, and that was okay because what made Rob and him click together so well was the fact that they could disagree and that be it, no animosity whatsoever among each other. "Man, if Black people don't get out to vote, then they can't complain when shit don't go their way or when laws get put in place that have their asses fucked up, and then they be up in here with us."

Rob made a move on the board and then sat back in his seat and looked at Heart. "You think that if Black people go and vote, whoever they put in place of any political stature will change things for Black folks here in America? Nigga, think again. The system wasn't designed for Blacks to get a fair share from the jump, and if you think that placing a Democrat in place is going to do that, then why is it that since you and I have been able to vote, a Democrat has won and shit is still the same? Now answer that."

Heart pondered for a second on Rob's words. "I hear you, my brother, but I do believe in time we will see a change." Rob smirked at him. Heart could tell that Rob wasn't trying to hear him out. "Look, we never thought we would see a Black president," Heart said while he focused on the move Rob made.

Rob crossed his arms and leaned back in his seat once again. "Again, look at us now. Man, can't you see the game that's being played? They put one party in office for four to eight years, and if it benefits the rich, they keep their mouths shut because they're happy their money is good. And if it's in favor of the poor and middle class, they become thankful and hope that things have gotten somewhat better and stay that way forever. Man, this goes on so the rich can stay rich, the poor stay poor, and the middle class get in where they fit in. Now, if a low-income person comes up a class, then that's great, and if a somewhat wealthy person drops down a class, that's even better. What I'm trying to say is, if everyone had a fair chance to be rich, then what would taint the value of wealthiness? If you have an old item from over a hundred years and there are thousands of them circulating, it doesn't have much value for profits. But if it's only a few in circulation, depending on its demand or one's interest in its value, it will determine its worth."

Heart couldn't say anything on that note, but he fixed his mouth to have his last word heard. "It's bigger than money," he stated, and then made his move.

Rob anticipated the move he was about to make and then made his own move. He leaned back into his seat again with a little smile. "Okay then, let's just say that for some reason or another, the American dollar's value was to drop substantially. What would this country be worth if it ain't about money?" Rob said, nodding his head at Heart.

Heart smacked his hand onto his forehead. "Fuck!" he yelled out because he knew the move he just made would likely cost him a few packs of smokes. After looking over the game, Rob himself knew it would be over in a few moves, so Heart tipped his king over, giving Rob the win. "Man, good game. Run it back," Heart said, holding out his hand for them to shake on it, and then they set the pieces back up for a fresh new game.

Rodney walked into the rec room and noticed Rob and Heart playing chess. He was happy to see them doing so, so he could learn a few pointers about the game. He had one book in his hand, "We the Black Jews." He grabbed an empty seat from the table next to Rob's and then took a seat, placing the book on the table next to Rob. "Done," Rodney said with pride.

Rob took his eye off the game and glanced over at Rodney. "So, you ready for some more knowledge?" he asked, then returned his focus to the game.

"Yes, I am, Rob. Man, reading that book felt like something got into me, I just can't explain it."

Rob moved his queen to f4. "Check," he called out to let Heart know he was in check.

"Word, that's what's up. I got more where that came from. When this game is over, we'll go back to my room, and this time you can pick the books out for yourself."

Rodney couldn't wait for that chess game to be over, but at the same time, he was enjoying watching every move the two were making. Heart couldn't move his king because he was trapped but not checkmated.

"Why couldn't the king go next to the other king?" Rodney asked. Rob explained why the two kings aren't allowed next to one another. "No homo, man and man are not to be together on this board or in the eyes of the Lord God, which means a man shouldn't be close up on another man." Heart smiled at the scenario and said, "True that." One move later, Rob won the game again. "Checkmate," Rob said as calm as one could be.

"Man, I'm done. You got yours today, but you know, same place, same time tomorrow."

Heart got up from the table, thinking about where he went wrong and what move would have been better. Rob gathered his board and pieces, and the two of them headed to his cell. It wasn't long before Rodney made his way over to those books. He picked up the books "A Message to the Black Man," "As a Man Thinketh," and "Before the Mayflower." Rodney was so interested in the books he chose that he headed for the door before saying goodbye.

"Hold up, Star, what did you grab? I at least want to know what you're taking from my cell." Rodney revealed the covers of the three books.

"Those are three good ones, Star. What's on your agenda for the day?" Rodney stopped at the door and wanted to know what was up with him calling him Star. "Yo, what's with you calling me Star? I think I'll go to my room and try writing another letter to my mom or Jim."

Rob smiled and said, "When I call you Star, that's because that's what you are. You're Jah's light that he placed in this world to shine your light among us. Your mom didn't send you a kite yet?"

Rodney had a sad look on his face and shook his head no. "No, man, she hasn't even tried looking for me, but she did send the drum your uncle gave me way back."

36

"Man, that's cold, but at least you have the drum. Keep your head up and don't lose focus. Guidance, my Lord." Rob's wordplay was strange to Rodney, but that was just Rob being Rob with a little Rasta background. Rodney sadly went to his room, leaving Rob to his thoughts. Rob picked up the letter from his table that his uncle wrote him, so he opened it and started to read it.

"Rob, I received your letter and I'm so, so sorry to hear about brother Rodney, but I had a vision on these circumstances, and we know, Rasta, that everything happens for a reason. Truth is he's placed in there to save those who want to be saved. You will see what I'm talking about when the time comes. Just don't let him forget what I told him a few years ago about listening out for the sound of the drum. Oh, your little brother is doing well; he's getting bigger as we speak, and your father told me to tell you to be strong. Your mother said not to worry yourself too much because she knows in her heart that she's going to see you again without those bars holding you back."

Rob shed a tear at that moment, placed the letter back on the table, then got up, stretched his body, and did an easy two hundred push-ups. It was so ironic that Rodney went back to his room and soon after was surprised to see another inmate standing in front of his door. The inmate was an unfamiliar face, and Rodney wasn't sure if he was coming to do harm to him, so he wasn't sure if he should have been at ease or ready to endure pain. But the inmate handed

37

him a letter that was from his mother. "This came to me today by mistake, and I knew it was yours, so I brought it by," the inmate said.

Rodney thanked him and looked at the date on the letter. Sadly, it was at least six months old. That didn't matter too much when he noticed it was from his mother. He couldn't wait to read what she had to say. While he was reading, he had tears running down his face. He couldn't believe the things she was telling him about how she felt about him as a person and his new living arrangement. She basically told him that he was a disappointment to her and to all that Jim had done for him. She went on to say that he shouldn't have been dealing with Michelle because she warned him about those Black hood bitches in the first place, and how he would have been better off with someone outside his race, and dealing with Mike and Matt was the same as dealing with a Black nigga because they wanted so much to be Black. If Rodney would have read that letter six months ago it might have held a little more weight on his input of how her feelings meant but not now, he was ashamed of her thoughts, but the pain of her saying that he was a big disappointment was a big blow to his Gut. After reading the letter he decided not to write back, the thought of writing back to see how Jim was doing only lasted a few seconds and his mind was made up not too, because in the back of his mind he wondered if Jim was the one believing that he was a great disappointment.

Instead, Rodney rather skip pass the pain and focus on those three books he'd just gotten from Rob. After reading page by page, he began to feel something inside his body changing, he wasn't sure what it was but for sure something that he never felt before. When the morning arrived Rodney woke up out of bed and got up to use the toilet and while he was pissing, he looked down to make sure that he was aiming his piss right into the toilet but that's when he noticed that his feet were no longer of light skin, they had turned a few shades darker. He shook the piss off his little head and then sat back down on his bed looking down at his feet trying to figure out what was wrong with him. He wasn't sure if he should tell anyone or keep it to himself or should he go to the infirmary. He touched his feet and they even felt different, they were smooth as if he never walked on them. A knocking sound at his door took his focus from off his feet. "Yo!" Rob called out from outside the door while he dapped a few other inmates up that had respect for him." How's everything? You good right?" Rob questioned one of the men that he had moving a little Happy on the inside. The man smiled at him to let him know that everything was kosher. Rodney quickly grabbed a pair of socks and slipped them on before Rob entered the room.

Rob walked into the room with his bright white jail suit on and a brand-new pair of white and blue Bo Jackson's sneakers and a book under his arm pit. The black numbers on his suit and his black long dreadlocks stood out by resting on his white state issued uniform. "Man, your dreads are long almost like your uncle." Rodney said. Rob smiled at the statement. "That's why I get wiser and I'm strong, solid as a rock." Rodney always thought that the dreads were cool looking but didn't have a clue of why anyone would want the type of dreads that Rob and his uncle have. "You every going to cut them or twist them like how I see some other men have them? I mean the only person I know to have dreads looking like yours is images of Bob Marley." Rob looked at him as if he was crazy, but he understood that he and many others don't understand his culture, nor have they been to bigger cities to have possibly come across someone with his image. "Na! I will never cut my hair. If I do that then I will lose all my strength and besides I love the way my hair looks, it looks like a Lions Main and a Lion is for sure the king of his jungle." Rodney thought about when he used to go to church with his grandmother and he learned the story of Samson and Delilah, he understood the part of Rob referring to his hair as being his strength. "Rob man, why you don't have them neat looking?" Rob had a feeling that question may come up. "I believed that every one of my dreads look great, and unique and besides that look where we're standing at. I'm not the one who be setting in between another man's legs trying to get my hair done." Rodney never looked at it that way, as he saw it as if it were the same as a barber until he redirected his thoughts at that very moment to some of the men in the prison who were getting their hair done by another man. "My hair, I love it, but the hair doesn't make the man. It's what's in my heart that matters, and from the looks of it, your hair looks like it's on its way," Rob said, feeling the need to elaborate.

Rodney investigated his image in the only mirror in the room that rested over the bathroom toilet. From the looks of his hair, it wasn't far from knotty dreads forming. Rodney shook his head at the sight and said, "Shit, I might as well go all out and let them look like yours." Rob stopped him before he could say anything else.

"Yours," Rob said, looking at the small number of books Rodney had lying on his desk.

"What do you mean?" Rodney asked.

"Just that. Your hair will never be the same as mine because they are mine and yours will be yours, and no other shall be like it," was Rob's response.

"Oh, well, is there anything else I need to do? Because I'm sure learning right now about your philosophy on hair, what else you got for me today?" Rodney said with a smile on his face.

"Well, for one, stop eating that shellfish and meat altogether," Rob said, then handed Rodney a book to read about the Rasta culture.

Rodney took the book from his hand, and almost instantly, his body made that weird feeling come over him again the minute he read the cover, "Rasta Way of Life." The feeling made him feel a little awkward, so he thought of a way to be alone for the time being. "Yo man, can I have this time to myself? I think the food from the café isn't sitting right with me," he said, holding his belly while making his way onto his bed.

Before Rob walked out of the room, he turned to him. "Oh, leave that dairy alone as well." The minute he was out of sight, Rodney quickly pulled up his pant leg and noticed his skin had gotten darker in the area that already had changed its pigment and somewhat darker in other places on his body. He thought to himself at that moment he was going to have to learn how to truly love himself with this new image that was taking over him. Knowing sooner or later he was going to have to say something to somebody about it, he started feeling his hair because it felt as if it was tightening up on him, not in a painful way, but one could say it was forming a strong bond, "Dreadlock bound."

Chapter 4

A Year In

It was the crack of dawn, and Rodney just finished the last page of the book. To his surprise, Rob had placed a joint of Happy in it, rolled up in toilet paper, ready to be smoked. It had been a year since he had taken a puff, so he went through desperate measures to find something to give him fire to burn the herb. After a few hours of thinking about what he could do, he realized that the only thing that might work would be the lamp cord, its wires, and the socket. He unplugged the cord from the wall socket and began stripping the black rubber off the cord with his teeth, just enough to see a little bare wire. Then he broke a piece of metal off a spring inside his mattress. He plugged the cord back into the socket, picked up his government shower shoes, and took a piece of rubber from the bottom of one, then jammed the piece of spring into it to hold it. He held the cord in his left hand and the joint in his right. He kept tapping the bare part of the wired cord onto the spring until a spark caught the tissue paper on fire. A spark was all he needed to make it do what he had yearned for so long.

After digesting every word he read in the book, he got a whole new perspective on what smoking herb was all about. He realized that in the past, he had been smoking for all the wrong reasons other than just getting high. He learned about its healing powers and the

43

spiritual aspect of it. He went to the only window in his room that revealed the yard, hoping the smell he made would make its way out of the small piece of broken glass in the corner of the window. He took a hard pull on the joint, released a good amount of smoke, and then snatched it right out of the air with his hands and rubbed it all over his face to wash away any wickedness. He remembered seeing Rob do that in the past, so he figured he should do the same. He stood there in his boxers, looking down at his body, revealing his two-toned skin, but no longer ashamed of the dark complexion that was taking over his body at the cost of learning the knowledge of self. The darker he got, the more he wanted to read, and Rob alone didn't have enough books to feed his brain. So before taking the next step of getting more knowledge of "each one teach one," he read most of the books over and over until they were embedded in his brain as if he had written them himself. After reading about sixty books, his body gained sixty percent darkness, melanin, or whatever you want to call it. The only places still light, bright, and almost white were his hands and face.

The smell of nasty-tasting breakfast was being cooked, and it wouldn't be much longer before Rob came to his room so they could go eat. Quickly, he got dressed so that he wouldn't have to explain to Rob what was going on with him. Just as he slid into his government jumpsuit, he heard two knocks from Rob's knuckles at his door. "Yo Yo! Star, you ready to go to the shithole to eat?"

Rodney noticed Rob holding out another book for him to read. He took it out of his hand, and they headed to the café.

The cafeteria was noisy from the inmates talking. It almost seemed as if the seats were assigned to the inmates since every clique in the place took their section. Rodney and Rob got their food, which wasn't much due to the fact that eating an only-green-food diet was slim to none. Just as they took their seats, it wouldn't be long before the meat eaters came over to ask for a trade-off. "Yo Rob, I'll trade you my mushy broccoli for your chicken," an inmate asked. Rob didn't want the bird near his food anyway, so he gladly accepted the trade-off. Rodney wanted so badly to eat his chicken, but after reading those books along with the Bible, he knew those days were behind him. The inmate's friends noticed the trade taking place and wanted in on the deal. "Yo Rob, how about your boy over there? Is he trying to part with that chicken as well?" Rodney waved the inmate over to the table and slid the man his tray. The inmate took the chicken and slid the tray back to him. Rodney was looking at him and his tray, wondering where his veggies were, but the inmate wanted to keep his food and test Rodney's manhood. He walked back to his table, sat down, and started eating. Rob had a look on his face that showed he wasn't for the foolishness. "Yo! You just going to let the man walk away with your food without giving you anything in return?"

A lot had changed about Rodney except for the fact that he never could fight and standing up for himself was never a fact of the matter. Rodney just put his head down to Rob's response. "Yo my man, if you don't say anything to that man, he's going to think that you're a pushover as well as the people you roll with, and I ain't having that." Rob got up from the table and stood over the wrongdoing man. "My man, you're not going to play my man like that. You're going to have to come off with something in return." The man looked at Rob and then at Rodney. "Oh, that's your man? Y'all on that homo shit?" Rob looked at him as if he wanted the man to get up out of his seat to fight. "What the blood clot! Rasta man don't get down with that, but I will stand strong and fight for what's right." The inmate had not long ago come out from being in the hole, so he didn't want any smoke with Rob. "Tell your man I got him later with a few packs of cigarettes." Rob didn't say a word, but his stare spoke volumes. Rob walked back to his table, began to eat, and then tossed Rodney his baked potato. "Time's up!" the C.O. yelled out loud. Everyone got up to toss their trash in the garbage, and then one by one they headed outdoors for an hour of rec time. When Rodney hit the outdoors, he instantly held his hand up to his eyes, trying to block the brightness of the sun. The prison yard was more segregated than the Whites and Blacks in the fifties. They walked around the yard slowly, trying to spare every minute of the hour they had. Rob led the way to his spot where he chilled every day, checking out the scene that the yard of inmates had to offer. The yard was paved in dirt, smoothed out by the millions of inmates who walked the grounds, except for the basketball court that needed to be redone many years ago. Like many others, Rob's chill spot had a picnic table that had many inmates' names carved into it from the past and present. Rodney scanned the yard, trying to make out who was who, and noticed that some inmates were doing the same to him. "Don't be looking too long and too hard. Inmates don't like that much around here. It's like saying you have a problem and want to get something off your chest," Rob said to Rodney. That was Rodney's first lesson. Then he asked Rob, "Why is it I notice most cliques in here seem to have more people around them than you?"

He asked the question because if he knew one thing for sure, it was that Rob was one of the coolest brothers he knew, and for sure if he knew it, then most likely other inmates would notice the same about him. "Well, let's say this: you will learn real fast that the Rasta man stands alone for the most part, simply because most people haven't the faintest idea of who we are and what we are about unless they are from the Caribbean." Rodney looked over and nodded his head in the direction of what seemed to be the minority of the prison. "Oh, them, the White boys? Some of them are racist pieces of shit, but a few of them get in where they fit in, being as though the last place a White man needs or wants to be is in this place by themselves, surrounded by a bunch of— and you know I hate to use this word—but, niggas." Rodney totally understood what it was like to be an outsider. He looked across from the White boys' crew of people and asked, "And them?"

. "Ok, I'm going to run it down to you. Over there on the west end of the Yard is your Israelite's. You see they have them things hanging off their waist and they always keep their bible with them at all times. That set of people over there with the dark circle in the middle of their foreheads are your Muslim's, now many of them get up in here and need some protection so now they want to be a member of the faith, but for the most part it changed many of men to be the better person they've become today and that's what matters for the most part. You can say, they probably have the most people in there click than most others do in here and those few over there are a few old heads from the Nation and it's a small amount of Youth in the Nation of Islam nowadays. They were top dog in here at one point in time." Rodney asked, "Well what happen?"

"I just think that they're the Nation of the old and now the younger generation has more option of religion to choose from and I also think it's a big question in many Black people's mind today if they killed brother ElHajj Malik Shabazz." The look on Rodney's face was saying he hadn't a clue of whom he was referring to. "Who's that?" Rob smiled at him. "To most people he's known as Brother Malcolm X. Then Rob shifts his eyes in the direction of the man who looked as if he was the strongest man in the prison. His dark

48

complexion hid most of his Tat's except for the ones on his face. Rob shook his head at the thought of the man's lifestyle. "That's Bill Jenkins but the people in here know him as Buck." Rodney was curious so he had to ask. "Why Buck if his name is Bill?" Rob knew that anyone that was a newcomer to the prison system in the states wouldn't understand until they reached such a place. "Take a look at them and tell me what you see." Rodney looked at Buck and the people surrounding him. "What am I supposed to see other than the norm of a bunch of men in a click." Rob shook his head at Rodney for being so naïve. "Look at that…" Rob didn't want to use the word Nigg'a so he paused for a second hoping that Rodney could fill in the blanks of his lost words. "You don't see something out of place over there?" Rodney still didn't have a clue because his mind had been clogged due to the ways of thinking in this western world. "Look at that…He's getting his hair Braided by his Bitch." Rodney took notice but it was going to take time to retrain his thinking of homosexuals. "Yo that's crazy because if I didn't know that I was in a male prison I would of, thought that his Bitch was really a Chick." Rob nodded to him that he was right on that. "Yes, they are Wooden Nickels." Now he lost Rodney on that one. "What you mean Wooden Nickels?" "Well just think for a minute, is it such of a thing? No! it's simple, it's just not supposed to be, point blank. Now as far as how he got his name well let's just say that if your soft, on the feminine side and decide to play spades with that Wooden Nickel and lose and can't pay up, then you'll

49

become the victim of Buck rearranging the way a man once walked, next they would learn their new way of feeling what's it like to take a shit unexpectedly." Rodney understood without anymore of Rob's inconsiderate description. "You see the young men over there and over there? They are the Bloods, and they are the Crips and all you need to know is stay out the way when it comes down to them because the two of them have the mind frame of not giving a fuck about this world and anything in it that's not Blood or Crip. And last of them all is that little old man way in the back all to his lonesome." Rodney could see who he was referring to but wasn't for sure if it was the little old man that was sitting Indian style on the ground with his eye's closed and one hand placed in the middle of his chest with his fingers pointing up right and in the other hand, he's rotating two stress balls. "That's Chin Chow, No one fucks with him, the word has it that his hand and feet are deadly weapons and that's the cause of him being in here with the rest of us lifers." The loud noise set off in the Yard to let the inmates know that the fresh air of their enjoyment has come to an end and straight to their humiliating cells. After a few weeks Rodney finished a few more books and yearned for more. Rob was delightful with lending them out to him for the greater cause of him getting the knowledge that most family and schools lack to teach. Rodney sat in his cell again until every page was read and comprehended. A few months passed by, and no one heard a peep from Rodney, but to Rob it wasn't unusual for him knowing the reasoning of it. Book after book that Rodney read, he found himself looking at the new man in the mirror. His skin was now completely Blue Black, and it wasn't anyway he could hide it any longer. Within those few months he learned how to fast which caused him a great deal of weight loss and the time had come for him to head to the café. When he stepped into the café one by one the stares came from every inmate and guard that was there. Mostly everyone thought that it was a new arrival until he walked to his normal seat next to Rob. The new look had Rob wondering what the fuck was going on. When Rodney was just about to take his seat the head C.O. walked over to him looking him up and down to make sure that it was him. He stood face to face and toe to toe with him and then he lifted Rodney's chin up a bit while moving his face around slowly. "What do we have here Gents? This Boy looks as if he went to a cookout and barbecued himself and now, he looks like burnt chicken." C.O. 's started laughing at his raciest joke along with the other White inmates that could relate to the corny ass joke. Rob stood up from the table and yelled at the C.O. "I've had just about all I could take from your raciest ass!" He punched the man right in the nose causing a trinkle of blood to appear. The C.O. took the punch like a G and then laughed it off just as he pulled his nightstick out from off the side of his waist and then struck Rob in the Gut causing him to bind over for the next blow to the middle of his back sending Rob to the floor and before he could get himself together the other guards came and

51

snatch Rob up from off the floor. "Put that Boy in the fucking hole! And finish the job." Off Rob went to the hole and they beat him so bad that his load screams of pain faded away into silence do to the fact that he was knocked uncinches only for him to awake to a six-month sentence into his new cell, The Hole. While Rob was knocked out cold his mind was revealing visions of who Rodney has become and he couldn't wait to see Rodney again. The one thing that his mind brought to him about Rodney was his birth date 7-23 the same day as the great Negus, Emperor Hail Selasssie.

Chapter 5

Chin Chow

Rodney finished his food alone again by chose, for the last four months and now he wanted to post up in the yard for the first time without Rob by his side. The minute his body touch ground in the Yard fear entered his heart for a second and other inmates could grasp his energy of fear that he was giving off by the way he walked, the look on his face along with the sweat running down his cheek bone and he hadn't even been in the sun five minutes. He made his way to the Picnic table that Rob posted up most of the time. This time it was a few new faces at the table, and they didn't look inviting, so he walked a little pass them and stood along the gate that housed them in the yard. He looked and noticed Chin Chow in motion making out what looked to be a three-step motion into a Horse stance that he did every day. He sat in that horse stance as if he was sitting in a seat for a half hour and Rodney was amazed at the mans will power to be able to do so. Chin reached into his back pocket and pulled out his six-inch homemade piece pipe and placed it into his mouth and then he pulled off the side of the pipe a matchstick and then he took his two fingers and snapped the tip of it hard and quickly making the fire he needed appear. Rodney couldn't understand how he did it, but he also wanted to see what the six-foot pipe was made from. He started to make his way over to Chin and couldn't believe what he was seeing and wondering if the other inmates ever taken noticed of Chin, and they may have but it was just all new to him. The closer Rodney got to Chin he noticed he was an old man, almost ancient. Chin's skin was wrinkled and much expected from a 91-year-old man who had been doing time since the age of 20. Rodney took a good look at the pipe hanging out Chins mouth and noticed that it was made of cut up plastic straws melted together piece by piece. Chin had a long dual black and white Goatee Beard and didn't wear anything on his feet. On the top of his head, was a hat that looked as if he or someone had made it. It was white and the brim of the hat rested around his head down by his temples with a tiny knot at the top. Chin's eyes where closed as he meditated. Rodney stood in front of him and stared at him for a minute not sure of what to say.

"Yes, my son?" Chin asked once he noticed Rodney's presents hadn't moved on. "I'm Rodney." Was all he could think to say. "You have come." Chin replied. Rodney hadn't a clue of what Chin was referring to. "What?" Chin removed the pipe from his mouth. "I've been waiting for you for some time now." Rodney was still lost. "I'm not…" Chin opens his slanted red eye's a little bit and looked at Rodney." Many years my son, I been waiting on your arrival. I wasn't too sure when, and many years passed me by but now is better than never." Rodney just knew Chin had to be old and senile and just talking." I think you have me mistaking for someone else." Chin took a deep breath and slowly released it. "I could be, but I saw this day coming over 20 years ago and besides I knew that the chosen one would come to me, and I've been in here over 40 years and not one person has come to me and said one word, so I'm pretty sure it's you, my son." Chin normally would stay in that horse stance the entire hour, but he peacefully and slowly got out of the stance and then pulled out those stress balls from out his pocket and then put them to uses. "Walk with me." Rodney walked a little behind him noticing that Chin's hair looked to be a part of an old fashion custom. The top of his head under his hat was bald and the back of his head was a long gray braid that reached his lower back. "I need you to come and see me every day until the day I die, we have much work to do and I'm not getting any younger and we're running out of time. I most likely won't be around when the time comes."

Rodney heard every word and just decided to use what God had given him ears for. "I will have you to the point that you will be one with nature and your skills of combat will be as strong as Chaka Zulu's nation. Your Hand-to-Hand combat would be remarkable in many ways. Your mind will be impeccable and witty." Chin said. The load warning sound roared out into the yard and the inmates took their place in line to head back to their Pods. "Tomorrow same time same place, oh and it's great that you learned to play chess and loved to read books on knowledge of self." The look on Rodney's face questioned how he knew these things about him, so he asked. "How did you know this about me?" Chin modestly said to him. "I can see years before they come my son and soon you will be able to do the same."

Rodney entered his room and sat down on his bed replaying the talk Chin had with him. He couldn't wait for the next day to come just to see what Chin had to offer him. Rodney looked over at his desk and on top of it was a thick book that rested on the corner of the desk all alone with a sticky sheet with a few words on it. He got up from his bed and walked over to the book and picked it up and read the note. "This is a book from Rob, he asked me to make sure that you got it. Rob also said don't leave this book out in the open because Nigga's keep stealing it and the book is very hard to get. He also said to take your time with it, and he'd get it whenever he gets out from the hole whenever that could be." Rodney was sad to hear that. He picks the book up and reads the title. "Behold a Pale Horse" he skimmed through a few pages to try and get a gist of what the book was about, and it wasn't long before he made himself start from the very beginning. The next day he took the book with him to the café and when he finished his toast and a glass of water, he and the rest of the inmates headed out to the yard.

When they all reach the outdoors, it must had rained while they were asleep being as though the ground were wet. Rodney notice Chin at his normal spot doing his regular routine. The only thing that stood out from his normal look was a brown bag that was hanging from his hip. It looked as if it was the bag that the liquor bottle Crown Royal comes in. Rodney greeted Chin "Good morning" Chin just gave him a head nod. "Stand here" Chin order. He pointed to the slab of concrete that once a picnic table resided on it. Rodney did as he was told while he fixed his eyes on what Chin was doing. "What are you doing?" he asked. Chin ignored the question while he kept pulling out hands full of rice from out the brown bag from his hip and placing them in front of where Rodney stood. Chin stood side by side next to him and then he smacked his hands together. Rodney was caught off guard after hearing the load sound, he jumped a little. "Do! as I do." Chin ordered. Rodney was looking for a place to place the book down but the only place that he could, was on the ground. Just as he was about to place the book on the ground Chin raised his arm out across Rodney's body stopping him from doing so. "No need for that, you may need that to help take your mind off the pain." Rodney started to wonder what he meant by pain, and should he bail out now knowing that he has very low tolerance for pain. Chin shuffled his feet into their proper position needed for them to form their horse stance. Rodney copied the steps. "Bend those knees as if you're sitting in a chair." Chin pushes down on Rodney's shoulders until he was in the right position.

After the first two minutes of being in that stance Rodney could feel his legs becoming weak. He opened the book up and started to read it hoping it would take his mind off his troubled legs. Chin closed his eyes and began to meditate. Rodney stopped reading for a second looking over at Chin wondering if he could stand upright for a quick second, so he tried his luck and stood up. "Cheating on yourself I see, but you must understand it's all in your mind." Chin said to him calmly. Rodney was thinking that, this was some bullshit being as though his legs were saying the same. He tried to man up and remain in the horse stance a little longer but the strain in his legs made him come to his knees, right on top of the pile of rice. He was confused about what was more painful the horse stance or his knees on top of the rice for a long period of time. This took place every day from that day on until he could remain in the horse stance for hours so the rice wouldn't be needed. A few more months passed and Rodney practiced his horse stance every day and could tell that his mind and legs had gotten much stronger. He was proud of himself but what was most important to him on this day was Rob's return to the Pod. He finished the book, and it opened his eyes up to the conspiracy of the U.S. government. He knew without a doubt in his mind that the author of the Pale Horse, William Cooper most likely was dead do to someone murdering him. But he couldn't wait to see Rob so they could converse over the theory of the book. The one thing that stood out to him from the book was how a lot of what he read was on the lines of what

58

brother Malcom X was saying about the U.S. government. It was ironic to him that a man such as Malcom had so much wisdom on how they planned to keep the oppression on the Black man in America's back without dwelling much in the information of the Free Mason organization.

The word got around that Rob would be back to his cell after everyone returned from the courtyard. Rodney was outside in the cold without realizing how brisk it was due to him being able to use his mind control. He was in his horse stance without any shoes on his feet and not a thought of worrying about breaking down and giving up. Chin walked around Rodney's body, looking him over. He pushed Rodney a few good times trying to knock him down to the ground, but that didn't work. Chin began giving him blows to the body trying to steal Rodney's mental focus but that didn't work. He punched Rodney's body until he knew most parts of his body were black and blue. He did this to toughing his skin, making it a body shield. While Chin punched on his body, he was talking to him. "You will be tough on the outside like nails and your spirt and soul will be peaceful from within. You will be in tune with mother nature and all it has to offer along with being able to humble the deadliest beast that walks the face of this earth. You my son, will need to learn the principles of the Ying and the Yang." Rodney's mind tried to phantom what Chin was teaching him, while he remained getting beat. After a half hour Chin stopped beating on him. "Do you have any questions my son?" Rodney couldn't wait for him to ask. "I sure do, how is it that a man of your stature ends up in here?" he noticed a few tears coming down Chins face. Chin blanks out for a second from the question, thinking of the days he was living as a freeman and then he snapped out of it once his thoughts drifted to him being incarcerated. His words were muffled, choked up until he came to grips with explaining what he never shared with anyone else. The only thing people knew of him being locked up was he killed a man with his bare hands. "When my father was a child, he was raised in a Shaolin Temple in China. His father had been a Monk from birth and raised his only son my father in the Temple until my father got of age to venture out and that's when he met my mother who was a Black China's woman who was an outkast because of her skin being black complected, but that didn't stop my father who thought the world of her and in his eye's she was the most gorgeous woman he'd ever seen so they started running around together until the two of them had been seen and then shunned. My mother suggested they come to the western world, America. So they came and my father got a job on the railroad in the U.S. and a year in he found out he couldn't escape the racism the country had to offer. The White men that worked along with him had it out for him. They didn't like the fact that a man from a foreign land could come over to their country and land a job that could have been given to one who looked like themselves. They felt that it was a White man without a job to feed his kids because of my father. Day after day they picked on my father, and he took the abuse. My mother had just given birth to me and those White men that he worked with didn't like the fact that my father had a son because they figured it wouldn't be long before I would be needing a job as well. They did all they could to run him off but what he did was raised me up to learn Kung Fu but without the humble and peaceful aspects of it, I was raised to protect myself and kill if need be."

The tears started to run down his face once again. "One night my father was walking home, and these two White men followed him home. They stood outside our house and threw rocks at it until my father came outside. He didn't want any trouble he just wanted them to leave. My mother came out the house and that was all those two White men needed to see. "You, Nigger! Nigger Bitch!" My father stood there with the principal belief that sticks, and stones could break his bones, but the names could never hurt him. But that wasn't the case for my mother, she was in rage and went up to one of the White men and spit right in the man's face. The man's instinct was to kill her that very moment but instead he reacted by punching my mother in the face knocking her unconscious leaving her with a tab bit of blood dripping out the corner of her month. My father used his Kung Fu on that man until the man couldn't breathe any longer while the other White man didn't wait for his turn to come, he quickly pulled out his gun and shot my father in the head leaving him for dead. My poor mother never forgot those men faces and from that day on I trained to get revenge for my father's death and then years later my mother and I were out in the downtown area, and I guess it was the other White man's turn to die that day because she pointed him out to me and the minute, I laid eyes on him I couldn't wait to kill him. I lived for that day, so I killed him by using my Kung Fu. But what I learned my son is that you can kill a man because he's a racist but that won't stop racism and it for sure won't make them change on how they feel about the color of the brown man's skin all over the world. You my son can see it on the news for yourself and one thing is for sure." Rodney couldn't wait to know what that was. "What's that?" he asked. "Well, it's going to get worse before it gets any better and you my son, you will be the one that will make a change." Rodney didn't understand how he was going to play out in such a roll.

Chapter 6

Game changer

Rodney got out of his horse stance after hearing his cell door being knocked on. He opened the door, and Rob stood in front of him, looking as if he had been doing push-ups every minute of the hour he spent in that place that resembled what a shithole would be like. "Wah Gwaan, my brother," Rob said as he stepped into the cell, noticing that Rodney himself had been occupying his body structure. The two of them hugged each other with a bond that was unbreakable.

"Yo Rob, man, I miss you. We have so much to catch up on." Rob agreed. He looked around the room, seeing that Rodney had been introduced to another avenue of knowledge. He saw some pictures and notes taped to his wall.

"What's this Kung Fu shit all about?" Rodney pointed at the pictures. "What this? Oh, it's another way of seeing things, that's all. You should look into it." Rob reached behind his back, pulled out his shirt from his pants, and pulled out another book, handing it to Rodney. "Here, I know you finished the other books I gave you, and now I think you're ready for a new one. This one here is going to make you think, and for sure you'll need to grab a dictionary." Rodney looked at the small book that had powerful information in it. The title of the book read "Black Skin, White Masks" by Frantz Fanon.

"So, what's this book about?" Rodney questioned him while taking the book from him. Rob thought of what to say before speaking. "Comprehension in depth of a single instance will often enable us, phenomenologically, to apply this understanding in general to innumerable cases. Often what one has once grasped is soon met again." Rob looked into Rodney's eyes, trying to see if he grasped the words. "That's just a smidge of what the book has to offer. Look, I'm out. We'll link up later." Rob went off to his room, leaving Rodney standing still, thinking of the meaning of what Rob read out of the book. Not long after he retrieved the understanding of it, he laid down on his bed, crossed his legs, and began to indulge in the book.

The next day in the rec room, a few inmates were conversing about the Black race here in America. Rob and Rodney just entered the room, catching the tail end of the conversation by an inmate named Banks, but the streets knew him as Bank. "It's the White man's fault!" Then he noticed Rob and Rodney walking into the room. "Ain't that right, Rob?" Talking about the Black race and its problems here in America is a serious matter in Rob's eyes. It wasn't the first time he indulged in that type of conversation, and it probably wouldn't be the last.

"Well, it's a lot that plays into it." Banks agreed with him, and he always admired Rob's intellectual insight on things. "What do you mean, brother? Talk to me, run your knowledge, homie." Rob stopped and stood in the mix of the group that had been conversing over the matter while Rodney stood back a bit to listen in on Rob's words.

"The number one reason is our youth trying to be grown before their time. Not all, but most are having sex before they hit high school, when they shouldn't even be thinking about anything other than finding a relationship with the Most High God and learning all they can from what the schools and their parents teach them. Then I must say also how the powers that be have mastered their plan on how to split up the Black family structure." One of the young inmates was listening and loved to hear what his elders had to say because he knew, for the most part, he would gain some kind of wisdom.

"Elaborate," the young man said as he grabbed the empty chair next to him, picked it up, and spun it around to have a seat. Rob already got the engine running, so he fixed his lips to continue. "Check it, it's more women out here in the world than men, we all know that. Now you take most of those Black women who either went to school and got out and received a good-paying job, whereas most young Black males have gotten lost either in the government system or due to poor education, which leads to jail

65

for the most part. Now hear this, if one man makes it out of the stumbling blocks and does well for himself and he's not a gay man, he will be looking for a Black woman who he hopes fits her high standards of femininity in all aspects, especially financially, which can be a good chance that she may have him beat in that field. If not, she can also go the sucker way out and use the government as security for them when they feel the Black man has failed them and then use the law of this land to make sure that the Black man will have to lower himself to comply with her wants and needs, which means she, in return, has no problem thinking she doesn't need a Black man."

Buck and his he-she walked into the room. Buck led his man and himself over to the only table in the room. His jailhouse bitch held onto the back of his shirt while sucking on his thumb. They took a seat and listened to what Rob was saying. Rob noticed them taking a seat and he hated seeing them or anything gay for that matter. Rob stopped what he was saying and gave Buck and his bitch a smirk. "Now without a man in the household, you are having young girls out here not having a clue of what type of man she should date, or she may find herself thinking it's alright to have relations with other women. As for the man that's gay, she wouldn't have a problem with his lifestyle. I feel it's an insult to the humanity of men. I mean, how the fuck do they think life can go on if man is with man and woman with woman? Oh, that's right, unless those wooden nickels lie to our queens about being a straight man until they get what they want. That shit works the same when it comes down to two women wanting a baby; they'll use a young man quick because I sure don't see dykes having sex with gay men making babies."

Buck's bitch didn't like what he just heard and sucked his teeth and rolled his eyes at Rob, and Buck felt he needed to say something. "Yo, nigga, I got your wooden nickel," Buck said to Rob like he wanted to "lock in" and put the towel over the window of the cell door so they could give each other some mean body shots. Rob knew what he said was going to offend them, but he felt he was standing on truth, so in his mind, he didn't give a fuck. In this country, we are supposed to have the freedom of speech. Another inmate understood what Rob was saying and noticed that Buck was getting into his feelings over it, and out of the blue, he shouted, "Damn! That nigga is just like a bitch, he's got to have the last word."

Buck got up from the table and held out his hand for his man. He locked eyes on Rob, hoping his eyes could talk so they could tell him how he wanted to try to beat the manhood out of him and turn him into his new bitch. Buck and his man did just as the devil would do if he was called out in the house of the Lord; they removed themselves from the truth and left the room. Rob gave them a wave goodbye with his backhand. "Fire! Shall burn the wicked! And may the fire bring forth purification." He sucked his teeth at the thought of the two of them like a true Yaadi.

"Like I was saying, with the White man on our backs keeping a brother down the best way they can through schooling and not giving the Black man enough jobs to house themselves, along with having to struggle to feed his children and not a piece of dried-up dirt to stand on to call his own, and with Black women surpassing us in many aspects. When the Black men start feeling like society and its women have given up on him, he starts to feel helpless. When he feels helpless, he won't respect himself or know his worth and what he could be giving to the universe. Without fulfilling his dreams and not being able to be the provider that he desires to be, it makes a man walk with his head down, leaving the youth to question his future and hopefully not his manhood. There are many more things I could elaborate on, but if there's one more thing I can think of to wrap up this depressing reality, it's that we need to stop pointing a gun at another Black man and hating on each other, especially towards your family."

"And it's a must that we stop trying to get over on one another. If we can do that, we just might be able to move forward even with obstacles in our way. One thing is for sure: if we don't change these things on our own, we'll feel the wrath of it when we're made to by someone else." Rob had everyone in the room thinking to themselves, realizing he made some sense. That's when Rodney thought he could teach the inmates who wanted to learn some of the knowledge he'd gained from the books he read.

Rob and the rest of the inmates on his pod went to eat lunch and then out to the yard. Like the rest of them, Rodney was thinking about how beautiful it would be if they came together as a race of Black people whose main purpose would be love. "Rodney, did you know your Earth Day is the same day as the great King Haile Selassie?" Rob asked. Rodney shook his head, indicating he didn't. "Man, I see the greatness in you, and being born on the king's Earth Day puts the cherry on top of your devised entity." That went way over his head, and Rodney broke out into his horse stance.

"Ok! Black Monk, I'll leave you be while you and Mr. Bruce Lee do what y'all do. I'm out, hit me if need be, I'll be in the gym." No more than a second passed when a boom erupted, sounding like lightning had struck something. The noise shook Rodney, reminding him of the day he went out with Matt and Mike to the beach and got struck by lightning and was resurrected from the dead. The rain came down fast and hard, and the guards were just about to call the inmates in until Rodney used his mind and focused on the sun coming back out. Just like that, the sun reappeared. Rodney shocked himself because everything Chin was teaching him about mind power was coming forth. Everyone in the yard was looking into the sky in disbelief, wondering what the purpose of the quick change from rain to sunshine was. Rodney held his hands up to the sky, embracing the rays the sunlight was giving off, enduring all the vitamin D it had to offer. Rodney humbled himself at that very moment at the sound of lightning striking again.

Chin had just walked back into the yard from using the restroom. While he was walking towards Rodney, a quick burst of wind came through the yard, causing Chin's hat to fly off his head. Chin moved quickly to retrieve it, but it was unnecessary, as in a matter of seconds, everything was still, like the universe was on pause. Chin picked his hat up from the ground while looking at Rodney. A flash of lightning struck, hovering over the inmates, and the daylight went out for about forty seconds. Rodney was really shook now and wanted to dart out of the yard because he didn't like the flashbacks he was having from the night he was struck by lightning at the beach. When the sun revealed itself again, a big, beautiful butterfly that was black and yellow with a white trim around its wings fluttered right in front of him. Rodney put his hand out, and the butterfly landed in the palm of his hand. He slowly cupped his hand and brought it closer to himself, captivated by how beautiful the simplest things could be. Next, a few birds landed on him while others surrounded him, embracing his humbleness. Everyone saw what was happening and really started to think things were weird when a few spiders started coming down from the sky on their silk webs. The only thing the web could have been attached to was a miracle in the sky.

Rodney started walking around the yard with God's creatures following him. The inmates were walking back into the prison, looking back at Rodney amazed at what they'd just witnessed. Rob wanted to come close to him along with the birds, bees, spiders, and squirrels too, but the minute Rob got a little closer to Rodney, every insect and bird vanished in many different directions. Rob stopped in his tracks, a little upset that he scared them off, and then pointed his finger at Rodney. "Brother Rodney," Rob said with a genuine smile on his face. "People said it, and at times I may have thought it. Yes, you are a little weird and a little strange, but what I, and all of us, have witnessed with our own eyes could only be done by someone who is divine or something. Star, I almost forgot to tell you that my uncle Wisdom said to remind you of what he told you some years back: to have a keen ear for the sound of the African drum he gave you when the time comes." Rodney didn't think much about some African drum but wondered what Wisdom was talking about. Once his life had been forced into incarceration, he forgot all about what he was told way back then, but now he took the words and stored them in his memory bank.

That was a day that those inmates and guards would never forget, and if they told anyone what they witnessed, they would be looked at as liars to the eyes of the unknown. A couple of days went by, and Rodney was in the yard doing his normal routine, but he became a little worried that Chin hadn't come to the yard nor the café. So, he walked over to one of the guards. "Have you seen or heard a word about Chin?" The guard was a tall 6'7" young White male who couldn't be much older than Rodney. "Sorry to say, my man, but the old man isn't doing too well. You know he's past being up there; he's there, if you know what I mean." Rodney could feel in his bones that something wasn't right. "Please, can I go see him?" The guard knew he wasn't supposed to do so, but he knew that Chin didn't have any family or friends who ever came to visit him. So he figured that the right thing to do for the old man was to at least let the only person the old man would let get close to him see him, just in case he was going to pass away. He looked around the yard to see which guards or inmates wouldn't be minding their own business.

He slid past Rodney, and Rodney went to Chin's cell for the first time. When Rodney got to Chin's cell, he heard Chin coughing, but it sounded like he was choking on something. The door was slightly ajar, so Rodney helped himself in. Chin was lying in his bed, either resting or meditating, as his eyes were closed. Rodney pulled the desk chair close to the bed. "Chin, how are you? Do you need anything?" Chin opened his eyes to see that it was someone other than the prison nurse. Chin held out his hand for Rodney, but his hand was shaking as if his nervous system was being bombarded by Tourette's. Rodney took hold of Chin's arm, and it was cold as if he were dead. "Chin, you're cold. Tell me what I can do for you." Chin coughed a few more times. Rodney didn't like the look of Chin and wanted to get help for him, but Chin took his other hand and grabbed Rodney's wrist. "My son, all I need from you is to fulfill my dream." Rodney was never told what that was. "And what may that be?" Rodney asked. "Never mind that because what will be, will be. What I need from you is to master the principles of life, understand the nature of the human spirit, know the understanding of time, and understand that you must be spiritually connected to the earth so that we can live a harmonious life. Know that everything is spiritual, and everything has a spirit because we are made up of energy. Be one with the trees because if they breathe, you breathe and live. You and the trees, my son, are the same when it comes to the need for oxygen. So you need to become one with the understanding of yourself and the trees and take time out to hug them to receive their energy. Know where you come from, and I'm not talking about your racial background alone. I'm talking about knowing that God created you and formed you from the Earth. To serve, you must do these things because if you choose otherwise, the spirit within you will self-destruct, as well as the universe. If all else fails, my son, follow nature. If the wind blows left, you go left. If the birds, bees, and other wildlife go south, you go south." Rodney's mind drifted for a minute, thinking to himself how he had to remember two important things: the sound of the drum and to follow nature. When Rodney snapped out of his thoughts, he looked down at Chin, and his eyes were

73

closed. He shook Chin's body. "Chin! Oh no, please… Chin." Rodney said, fearing the worst. He grabbed Chin's arm and noticed it was dead weight. Rodney began crying and sobbing. "Chin, I'm going to miss you, and I will do everything that you taught me and more." Rodney got up from the chair and headed back to the yard to inform the guard that Chin had passed.

Chapter 7

God Sent

Almost five years after Chin passed away, Rodney had learned more about knowledge of self than most, and his humbleness reflected the ways of Christ. He became second to the wisest man that ever walked this earth, "King Solomon." Rodney was becoming his own person, but the foundation of his person was built on the great Black scholars he read about over the years. He studied the opinions of those scholars and their viewpoints, cherishing their wisdom so much that it lived on through him.

Many men in the prison started to call him by the nickname "Black Monk." Those who wanted to hear him speak knew the time and place, while the other inmates, who didn't desire to hear what he had to say or teach, went on living the only way they knew how to survive in prison. Those who wanted to learn seemed to catch on like fire connecting to grease. Inmates who practiced this became very peaceful yet didn't take any shit, demanding respect while mastering the art of defending themselves by all means. Most of the Black inmates, along with a sprinkle of White and Hispanic males, gathered in a circle around Rodney while he spoke his own words of wisdom or elaborated on the problems that this country had manifested on its own due to negative thought processes. Sometimes, inmates would come to him for his wisdom on their own personal matters to the point that the inmates made him the man of peace, helping keep some order in the prison. The words he spoke were so powerful that they echoed throughout the air, quietly reaching every prison across America. The inmates didn't know that his mental power had them translating his every word subconsciously through a third party.

"Black Monk! Black Monk! Black Monk!" The inmates yelled out loud after Rodney spoke his piece on his point of view on Western medicine versus old African holistic medicine. "Teach on, Monk!" an inmate way in the back of the crowd listening shouted out. Rodney was just about to elaborate some more, but the prison alarm was sounding off so loudly that it was hard to hear what a person was trying to say while standing next to you. The inmates knew something was seriously wrong because when that sound goes off, the whole prison goes into lockdown. Rodney and Rob were walking onto their pod, and out of the blue, a young dark-skinned inmate started snapping, yelling out loud, "Fuck this shit! Fuckin' punk-ass, pussy motherfuckers!" The inmate then kicked the chair in the rec room to the other side of the room. The guard on duty, a cool young White male named Tom Landing, who had not long started working there, walked into the room trying to talk with food in his mouth.

"Yo! Chill the fuck out, my man, because if you don't chill the fuck out, them boys that are dressed like me are going to…" Before

76

the guard could finish his words, the young Black angry male quickly ran up on him, punched the C.O. in the nose, and then jumped back, dancing in a fighting stance like he was Ali. He was waiting for the guard to react, but he didn't notice the two other guards who saw the whole thing on their TV monitors running to their fellow worker's rescue. They ran quickly down to the pod before the young inmate could brace himself for the beatdown he had coming.

The two C.O.s beat him so badly that one had the sense to stop while the other remained beating the man to death. They stood over the dead body, slumped over with their hands on their knees from being out of breath. They looked at one another, knowing that shit was about to get ugly. The inmates noticed that the man had gotten beaten to death, and they wanted answers immediately. The news in the prison spread faster than prostitutes opening their legs to a paying trick. The word going around in the prison was that the inmate was the first to have heard about a Black man being shot to death by a cop in Delaware. A mob of C.O.s ran down on the inmates quickly, forcing them into their cells while the C.O.s nervously ran back to their conference room to discuss what had now become breaking news across the country.

Chapter 8

"This All Takes Place In The Same Day."

Wilmington, Delaware, is the place they called at one point in time, "A place to be somebody." On May 22, two young Black males, who looked to be in their mid-thirties, were hanging out downtown in the center of the city at Rodney Square. James Snow and his cousin Jimmy Dollar were hanging out, hoping to see a few young ladies walking by so they could spit game, hoping to add a few more numbers to their phones. Lunchtime at the square had all the nice-looking ladies one could want. Some were walking at a fast pace while others found a place to sit and eat their lunch. At the top of the hill, a traffic light was broken, causing the lights to flash on and off while two police officers controlled the traffic of cars and pedestrians. One officer, a somewhat tall and clean-cut White male who looked to be no more than 21, was named Bobby Gopher. He was waving his arms fast, yelling at the lead car that wasn't following his direction. "Move it!" he shouted, anger evident on his face. The other officer, an older White male, was 58 and had gray hairs in his mustache to prove it. He stood at the other end of the corner, controlling the foot traffic.

James and Jimmy noticed the two young White ladies the older officer was smiling at. The ladies were attractive, and James and Jimmy got themselves hyped up about trying to talk to them. "Yo, bro, you see these two White girls the cop is talking to? Bro, I'm telling you, if I give that girl some of this long dick, she'll never want another White man again," Jimmy said out loud, holding onto his crotch, not caring that the cop could hear him. One of the young ladies had black hair while the other was a redhead. The cop and the black-haired girl shared the same suburban neighborhood but didn't know each other's names. The redhead smiled at Jimmy, showing she was interested. Jimmy walked over to her. "Just give me your name and number, and we can go from there. No need to beat around the bush," Jimmy said, pulling up his pants and reaching for his phone. She took his phone and began to type her name. "Heather is your name," he said, gently grabbing her ass. She smiled harder.

Heather's friend and the cop noticed what was going on. Heather quickly gave the officer a smile and joined her friend and Jimmy. James confidently waited for the black-haired girl to follow suit. They introduced themselves, and the energy was high. The officer, now red with anger, approached them. "Ok, keep it moving," he ordered. The four ignored him. "I said move it, or I will move you," the officer said, eyeing Jimmy and James. James waved off the cop. "This guy is tripping," he said. They continued talking, ignoring the cop. Anger turned to rage as the cop forcefully grabbed Jimmy by the back of his shirt. Jimmy snatched away, and the officer stepped back, pulling out his weapon. "Pop! Pop!" Two bullets entered Jimmy's chest, leaving him dead. James watched his cousin's body shake for the last time and dropped to his knees, crying over him. Heather and her friend, Jamie, stood in shock, tears streaming down their faces.

The scene quickly filled with onlookers. All James could think of was revenge. He thought about how deep his family and his cousin's family ran in their city. He stood up, soaked in tears. "I'm going to…" An older Black man from the crowd grabbed James. "It's okay, little brother. I got you," he said. James tried to break free, but the cop was ready to fire another round if needed. The other officer, Bobby, called for backup and shouted for everyone to disperse. Most people followed his direction, but the image of what had just happened stayed with them forever.

Women were standing around in tears covering their faces in disbelief while many of the men had become angry and wanted answers. "Why! Just why?" a White male shouted out. "We're sick of this shit! I want to talk to whoever is in charge." Yelled out an older Black man who'd seen this situation on the news way too many times and now he needs to know the meaning behind this madness. While the officer they were yelling at didn't have anything to say to them at all and the most they could get him to

80

say was that he had to do what he had to do. The Captain on the police force pulled up to the scene and parked his car and chilled out in it for a few minutes to peep out the seen, trying to make out the temperament of the crowed. The tall clean shaved White Officer got out his car dressed in his black and white uniform that was military pressed and the bars that rested on his collar shined with pride. He walked slowly through a few on lookers heading towards his deputy. "O.K. Klosowski, what going on?" Deputy Klosowski stood in front of the Captain with a calm demeaner and said. "Sir, the young Black male moved away from me quickly when I was trying to apprehend him. Sir I didn't leave a second between my life and his. You understand the fact that we don't have a second to give when it comes to reacting, one second can cost you your life, I'm from the old school, I shoot first and ask the dead man the question later." Captain James had his head down listing and then he nodded his head up and down to confirm that he bit the story Klosowski stated. "Look, did he have a gun or any kind of weapon on his person?" Klosowki never gave an answer because he knew that's where he fucked up but hoping and kind of knowing that his Captain would make matters all in his favor. "Klosowski, you have to do better." Klosowki quickly agreed. "Yes Sir," he replied. The older Black man in the crowed that wanted answers was listing in on the Captain and Klosowski conversation, he became overly heated. "What? that's all you have to say to him?" the Black man shouted out to the Captain. The

81

Captain started walking back to his car. "Yo! you fucking pig!" someone yelled, causing the Captain to stop for a second. The angry Black man felt disrespected when the Captain turned his back on him, so he looked around and picked up the closest thing to him, which was an empty beer bottle. Without thinking, he threw the bottle at the Captain, hitting him in the face. The Captain grabbed his face where the bottle hit him. "Fuck!" he shouted while checking his hand to see how much blood was leaking from his forehead.

Officer Klosowski fired his gun at the man, hitting him in the shoulder. The heat from the bullet gave off a burning feeling that made him humble himself, keeping quiet and wishing the pain would go away. He fell to the ground and rested against a parked car, hoping the officer wouldn't come to finish him off like he did Jimmy Dollar. Rodney Square was being surrounded by more people interested in what was going on. The more chaos the Devil had going on at that moment, the more evil entered the minds of the onlookers. The younger kids arrived before their parents heard about what was happening. Many parents went looking for their kids to protect them and bring them home safely, while other parents went looking for trouble and were angry at their children for not informing them sooner.

Klosowski walked toward the car to finish the job with his gun. Just as he started to cross the street, bottles and bricks came flying at his head from a group of young Black teenagers. The more bricks and bottles were thrown, the more others joined in like it was a high school food fight. Klosowski and Captain James took cover by getting into their cars, immediately locking the doors. They were locked in the back seat, wondering how they would get into the driver's seat without having to get back out of the car. All they could see was a mob of mostly Black people coming towards the car. "Help! Oh Lord, they're going to kill me!" yelled the young officer, Bobby Gopher. The Captain and Klosowski could see his body in the middle of King Street, rolling around on broken glass and pieces of brick. His skin was almost beaten off him by sticks, stones, hands, and feet with deadly intent. Every time Gopher tried to get up, he was hit everywhere on his body. He realized that being on the ground was better since at least whatever side of his body rested on the ground was safe. It didn't matter because after his head was stomped into the ground by two Black males, his body went into convulsions, moving around like a fish out of water.

Bricks were being thrown at the cops' cars, but the windows seemed to have some type of glass that could only break after numerous hits. However, the breaking point was nearing. Klosowski and the Captain had to think about life or death. Seeing Gopher's condition, they had to ask themselves what they would want if the roles were reversed. The Captain couldn't stand seeing it anymore, so he dug deep into his soul and got out of the car to help Gopher. The minute he opened the car door, he was attacked by more young Black teenagers like ants finding sugar. He was hit by anything and everything, knocking him out cold so fast his mind didn't have time to register. His body hit the ground, and the focus that was once on Gopher shifted to him.

Klosowski's car was being rocked back and forth by people on both sides, trying to tip it over and force him out. Klosowski looked at the gun in his hand and counted the rounds in his head, knowing the odds weren't in his favor against a mob of angry Black people. He got out of the rocking car with his gun pointing at the nearest Black person. "Bang! Bang! Bang! Bang!" His gun went off, piercing a few more young Black youths before the rest beat him to death. Out of nowhere, the streets were covered with candy-cane lights from cop cars flooding the area. Without questioning what was going on, the cops got out of their cars and took cover behind their doors with their guns out. Gun smoke filled King Street once the police realized three officers were dead. The police called for more backup, making sure every bullet they had was used. The more cops arrived, the more young Black youth from every part of the city came out to continue the madness.

After hours of this, ambulances couldn't make their way through the streets, and the cops didn't have enough ammo or deputies to overcome the mob. The cops called the fire department to drive through the traffic and the mob, not caring who or what got in their way. Once they arrived, the fire officer asked what they needed to do next. The cops weren't sure, so the old fire chief suggested using water hoses to disperse the crowd, reminiscent of the tactics used in the sixties. They ordered the hoses, and water was forcefully used on many people, slamming bodies to the ground or pinning them against walls, causing water to enter their noses and mouths, leading to drowning. The water for the most part cooled off the Devil's work by sending those who could back to their homes, leaving King Street littered with the bodies of mostly Black people.

Chapter 9

It Takes a Nation of Millions to Hold Us Back

Rodney and the rest of the inmates were standing in a line, cuffed in chains, waiting to go outside. The prison had been on lockdown since the young man struck the CO, and now grown men were waiting to smell the so-called fresh air. "Something just feels strange to me. I just can't put my finger on it," Rodney said to Rob. "What are you talking about, Monk?" Rodney sucked his teeth, and Rob began to laugh at him. "What's so funny?" he asked, giving Rob a side-eye look. "It's you sucking your teeth like you're a true Jamaican."

The CO opened the door to the yard, and the fresh air was greatly appreciated by the inmates. It was the early hours of the morning, and everyone following Rodney was waiting for him to start his workout regimen. They all wondered what was up with him as he stood at attention, looking into the sky as if seeking answers from God. Rob looked at Rodney and could tell his mind was elsewhere. "Yo, Star, you alright? I mean, you over there daydreaming and shit." Rodney snapped out of it for a minute as soon as he heard the word "dream." "Dreams, my man, are something that almost seems to have been forgotten within the minds of the young Black youth. It almost seems as if they're the ones daydreaming." Rob understood what Rodney was saying, but for him and many other inmates, it was different. They learned to embrace their dreams, whether it was false hope of reality or a dream in the making. "That's crazy, Star, because I dream every day. That's right, I dream of one day getting the fuck out of here. I know you be dreaming." Rodney started reminiscing for a minute about those crazy dreams he had over the years. "Yeah, I dream, and when I dream, I dream big." Rob said in a sarcastic way. "Oh, I see you on some MLK 'I have a dream' type shit. Well, if you have a dream, Star, then shine your light."

Rodney's mind played back the dream 'I have a dream' that MLK spoke on, and then he thought about his own dream. "I have a dream!" Rodney shouted out for the whole yard to hear. "I have a dream!" He shouted out two more times, causing everyone to surround him. He stood there looking at the inmates for a few more minutes without saying another word, then began to clear his throat. "I had a dream that one day my Black brothers and sisters would love each other unconditionally. I want to see my race of people show the world that we are the gods of the earth and let us become so humble that the laws of the land could no longer make money off us due to crime, and the devil would hate that we never told another lie." As he continued about his dream, the inmates started looking at him strangely because the more he talked, the more his voice began to emulate MLK. The people listening couldn't believe what they were hearing. He stopped for a second to swallow his spit and then started back talking. "Oh! Now, my brothers, we need to check ourselves. We, as a race of people, still have the problem of hating on a man being lighter or darker than the next man." The older men in the yard started to tear up as they listened to what he was saying, and the more he talked, his voice became stern and rightfully so, as his voice was taken over by the voice of Malcolm X.

"Our Black sisters say we ain't shit, that's right, that's what they say, but huh, my Black brothers have been saying the same about them. Oh! Now that's two shits, and when you have come to that state of mind, only two things can come of it. One, they will pass down to their kids the same thinking process, or two, by all means necessary, do whatever it takes to clean that shit up." The older men who caught onto his voice changing into Malcolm walked over to him in tears, almost second-guessing if it were truly Malcolm's voice because Rodney's physical presence was saying the word shit. They knew Malcolm's vocabulary would have been insulted to stoop so low, but this day was different, you could hear the pain in his voice.

"First thing first, I want to be understood that I am not a racist, and as a matter of fact, I despise it. The time has come for us as a people

88

of the human race to understand that dividing people by the color of their skin is nothing but the devil using us to destroy humanity with its unloving heart and wicked mind frame of how to conquer and destroy." Rodney noticed a good number of Black inmates looking at any White person as if they were the devil he was referring to. "I know you all think I'm referring to the white man being the devil, but that would be foolish thinking. The devil isn't the color of a race, the devil is an evil spirit that wanders throughout the universe, waiting on one's free will to choose evil over the loving spirit of God. The spirit of good and evil controls the air we breathe and the flesh of man and beast. When it's all said and done, humans have free will to choose which spirit they want to be connected to. I must say if one chooses the spirit of love and not evil, he must love himself enough to defend himself no matter if it comes down to life or death."

Rodney paused for a second to think of what to say next while the crowd was deep in thought on what they heard. It was almost as if it was embedded in their brains and their ears grasped every word with a K9's keen sense of hearing. Rodney started pacing back and forth, holding onto his chin, then he pointed out to the inmates, shaking his finger at them before he began to speak again. "Repeat after me, Black Power!" The inmates proudly repeated the words, Black Power. Rodney's mind tapped into saying the words of the great leader Huey P. Newton. "Black Power is giving power to determine their destiny, and with that being said, you must have the mindset of thinking that a person can take your life, but they can never kill your soul, for your soul is everlasting."

"Now, every last one of us in here has committed a crime, and I can probably bet a good amount of that was due to the crimes committed against us. When we were young, we passed through schools without learning how to navigate the loopholes created by the powers that be. We were forced to look for employment in a biased job market, and that's if any jobs were available. We would go home at night wishing for morning to come because breakfast, which costs less than dinner, was the next meal we could afford. To overcome this problem, we need proper education and self-determination to learn all we can on our own through factual information. Read, my brothers! Reading will change the course of your life. Reading is the blueprint of life through other people's vivid imagination and true experiences. Now, repeat after me: Knowledge is power!"

The inmates shouted out loud, "Knowledge is power!" One young Black inmate, around 22 years of age, felt the power in the air at that moment. He was curious about who the voice of wisdom was coming from, so he looked at the older Black inmates pumping their fists in the air like revolutionaries. "O.G., whose voice was that coming out of his mouth?" he asked the brother closest to him. "Those are the words of Huey P. Newton," the old head replied.

The young man had heard of him but never cared to learn about him until now. "Can I find him in the library?" he asked. The old head looked at him with a little disgust and said, "What did he just say? Go and read, little brother, before it becomes against the law for Black folks again." The young man gave the O.G. a look as if to ask what he meant by "against the law again." Rodney now wanted to share some wisdom from a true prophet. He began to talk, but his words were distorted to most, except for those with a Caribbean background. When he spoke this time, his words were hard to understand, so Rob answered anyone who had questions until their ears adjusted. "You can find me in the whirlwind or the storm. Wake up, mighty race! Accomplish what you will. We must liberate our minds as men, and from doing so, you will liberate the bodies of men. We, as humans of the Black race, must honor honesty and respect to the tenth power of fair play."

Rob stepped in front of Rodney, held up his hand for him to stop talking for a minute, and then faced the inmates with his chest out and his head held high. "The dialect of words you're hearing comes from the Honorable Prophet Marcus Garvey. R.B.G., you hear me?" Rob had a proud smile on his face, born from the same place of struggle that Garvey came from. He moved aside for Rodney to continue. Without losing focus, Rodney went right back to where he left off. "What has happened to us as a race of people who have no problem taking the life of another Black man? Why have some of us taken the bait when it comes to selling drugs? I know many of you are here on some type of drug charge. If you are, I want you to think about this question: If the Black race isn't the one bringing the drugs into this country, but we have no problem getting work out of it, then ask yourself two things and decide. One, who and how do you believe the drugs are getting into the country and into the hands of the Black community? Two, if you ever picked up that drug and sold it to make a dollar, then ask yourself, who do you work for?"

Rodney stopped speaking and began to cough, trying to conquer his dry throat. "I need some water," he asked anyone who heard his request. No one had any water, and the one water fountain in the yard had been broken for many years. An inmate from way in the back of the crowd sneakily pulled out some of his homemade wine and passed it from one inmate to another until it reached Rodney. Rodney took the plastic sandwich bag that had the wine in it and opened it, the potency hitting his nose instantly. He really wanted water, but the thought of wine reminded him of going to church with his grandmother and having communion with grape wine. The thought of that made him feel like he was about to take part in communion. He put the bag up to his lips, drank what he needed, and then asked, "What's the time?" An inmate yelled out, "It's time for you to keep on preaching and teaching." Rodney could feel they didn't have much more time in the yard, so he thought about what to say next. When he began to speak, his words were faint but heard by the inmates who had adapted to hearing what was being said like a blind man gaining heightened hearing. Rodney couldn't remember the speech he wanted to recite about racial discrimination, but he held onto the great Emperor Haile Selassie I's speech he had copied down word for word on a piece of paper. He pulled out the paper from his pocket, unfolded it, and instantly felt like he was crowned Negus. He looked at the speech and began to read the words of the king.

"I have to say that until the philosophy that makes one race superior and another inferior is finally and permanently discredited and abandoned; until we no longer see first and second-class citizens of any nation; when the color of a man's skin is no more significant than the color of his eyes; until every human right is equally guaranteed to everyone without regard to race; until that day comes, the dream of peace and world citizenship and the rule of international morality will remain but a fleeting illusion, to be pursued but never attained. I am Lord of Lords, the root of King David."

Rodney's voice then blended with his own words of wisdom, creating a perfect rhythm like a DJ mixing two records. "We, as a nation of people, come from a royal background. Today, I see us treating each other poorly when we should be ashamed of how we raise our children to take school for granted. We should be

93

ashamed of raising them to look up to thug life while frowning upon those who think differently about the crime in the Black community. As for rap music, if you speak negatively and believe it to be true, understand that what you speak and hear will continue to manifest. Please, can we rap with high intellect to inspire our minds and spirits with joy and happiness and to gain wisdom wisely?" Then his voice returned to Haile Selassie's words. "My race of people, if you ever need a place to reside, I have set aside a place for you to live in peace, surrounded by love." A young Black inmate who had been dreaming about freedom asked, "Yo! Where that be?" He asked, believing in his heart that he wasn't ever getting out of prison but was interested in the story Rodney was telling.

Rodney was about to reveal the place, but a C.O. walked into the circle and rudely interrupted. "Alright, break this fucking bullshit up and let's head back inside, now!" Rob's hands started shaking, and his lips quivered. "I'll kill you for disrespecting the king!" he shouted, charging at the C.O. and hitting him with a right hook to the jaw. "Shashamane! Mother fucka!" he screamed, adding more punches. The C.O., a 350-pound gym rat, didn't understand what Rob meant by Shashamane, a place in Ethiopia. The C.O., Haskin, from South Jersey, began to return punches but soon pulled out his stun gun and hit Rob in the chest, sending him to the ground convulsing. Haskin radioed for backup, calling in a Beat Down

(BD). The Warden, hearing of the incident, decided to escalate by sending armed force instead of a regular BD. Guards lined up, gathering their guns and metal shields. They stormed into the yard, masked and shielded. As the guards approached, inmates thought it was a usual BD, but when the guards started shooting, many inmates dropped to the ground. The COs pulled down their gas masks and started spraying tear gas throughout the yard. Inmates were in agony, with snot running down their noses and their eyes burning. They were hog-tied with zip ties that cut into their skin and tossed back into their cells.

The Warden stood behind his desk, contemplating how to handle the chaos. He wanted to make the inmates' lives so miserable that they would wish for death. Five hours later, one head guard proposed a brutal idea. "O.K. men, it's time to get down and dirty. We're going to gas these mother fuckers until every bit of snot runs out of their noses and dries up. Their eyes will burn to the point they want to rip them out of their faces. If any of them die, so be it." The guards, ready to go barbaric, prepared to carry out their plan with deadly enthusiasm. A handful of C.O.s were sent to each pod, opening the doors to the inmate cells and rolling in about five cans of tear gas into each room. The plan was set to inflict maximum suffering on the inmates they deemed inhumane savages.

The minute the inmates noticed what was going on they took, action the best they could. Some tried holding their breaths long as they could before passing out from lack of oxygen, others tried to cover their faces with whatever they could find. The gas had the inmates choking to the point that they all vomited all over each other. Many of their bodies could be found in the corner on the floor balled up in the mix of snot and vomit. None of that mattered to them, at that moment all they could wish for was for the pain in their eyes and the Dry heaving from not having anything else to vomit up would come to an end. The C.O.'s went back to the office room with the other CO's who were sitting back watching and hearing the inmates screaming out. "Mommy! Help me please." An inmate yelled out while others called on the God of their choice. The COs was getting a kick out of seeing the torcher they inflicted on them, it was like music to their ears to be able to hear grown men crying out to their mothers for help. When the cans of Gas ran it's coarse to the end the inmates couldn't help but rub their eyes and trying their best to put a halt to their chronic coughing. They slowly started to get ahold of themselves while noticing the aftermath of the CO's madness. "Benny!" an inmate yelled out as he dropped down to his close friend body that died from not being able to withstand the amount of Gas, he gasped in. He rested his head on his friend body wishing that the reality wasn't true.

"What's next?" a C.O. asked the other CO who came up with the first idea. The CO with the inhumane mind frame name is Peter Smalltree who stood about five foot even and couldn't had been no more than hundred and ten pounds. He had light brown curly hair and he kept his face cleaned shaved. He laughed at the question and turned and looked at the fire hose across the room hanging on the wall. Every section of the prison has this set up just in case the place went up in flames. One by one every CO knew what that meant. The Black CO's had a job to do and they lined up for the job but that didn't stop their guts from feeling a little shameful for what they're about to do to most of the inmates that are their brothers by race. No sooner than the inmates could stop coughing and they could see a little just enough that they noticed the CO's standing in front of them ready for round two. Instantly they turn the fire hoses on full blast causing the water to hit their bodies with a force that pinned them up against whatever the water forced them to. Some Inmates hit their heads against the walls or a bedpost while most of them landed on the floor and it was so much water that the inmates who couldn't swim believed they were drowning. The force of the water that hit the inmates was of the same magnitude of a wasp sting to the tenth power. The water began to feel like it was piercing through their pores like throwing Daggers. C.O. Peter grabbed his CB. "I need special attention on C Pod and more so for Inmate! 35478." The C.O.'s ran down the hallway onto the C Pod in a line armed with firehose's pointing

97

straight at Rodney. Rodney stood there with his head healed high and his chest poking out, taking in all that water for all the Black people who had to suffer from the same treatment over the years. He looked at the guards with a look that showed them he wasn't worried while he scanned the area for the few guards that were Black and those who were cold feel in their guts that something was going to happen, they didn't know if they should be on defensive side or scared for their life. "Full Blast!" the head CO ordered. Rodney closed his eyes and quickly manipulated his mind into believing that he is now one with the nature of water. The more the water hit his body it made him feel as if he was being baptized. His legs were so grounded to the wet floor that the CO's couldn't understand how the mass of water couldn't knock him off his feet. Rodney's face began to shed a tear that blended in with the water being blasted into his face but his reasoning for his tears was because of him hearing his Black brothers screaming out for help in the same manner as those who went through the horror of coming over here on Slave Ships.

"Help! Mom ma! Jesus help me please!" were repeated words shouting out from the crying inmates. Rodney was feeling their pain to the point that he felt that he had to do something. "Have faith everyone, have no fear! I am my brother's keeper!" Some of the inmates who could hear Rodney's voice and knowing in the past that he hadn't stood up for himself over the years in the prison so now they question his word. The water that the inmates were enduring was by the gallons to the point that the water was rising past their ankles. The head CO order for the guards to turn the water off. A guard noticed a CO coming towards him to buzz him in so that he could get to the room to turn off the main water supply. The guard buzzed the CO in and the two of them greeted each other with smiling teeth. "Those pieces of shit got what they had coming to them." Said the Guard. "Well, I can say that we washed the black off some of those Mother Fuckers, or was it dirt I saw going down the drain?" Said the CO and the two of them started laughing at his comment. The CO with all the jokes gathered himself and went over to the wheel on the wall that operated the water by turning it off and on. He started turning the wheel in the formation of the off direction but after he turned it multiple times, he noticed that it kept turning but not causing the water to turn off instead the water started to shoot out from the wheel. Water was flying everywhere landing on top of the computers and the electric box. "Boom!" all the lights went out in the prison and now all the guards stopped smiling and worry started to kick in. They all made it to a small section of the prison. Guards started to pull out their cell phone for light to locate a few back up lantern's and sit there thinking of what to do next. The inmates cell door now became unlocked because of the power going out. The inmates were able to roam freely from Pod to Pod which had many inmates shook by thinking their time of life could be coming to an end for sure if

99

they were some kind of Snitch or for whatever Beef that had them looking over their shoulders.

"This is kind of dangerous for the inmates," one guard said out load for the head lead to hear. "Fuck them all. Have you forgotten that these Mother Fuckers put their hands on one of us? Not once but twice." They all sat there in silence thinking about their Co-Workers who were assaulted. Out the blue an inmate had a radio in his cell that started playing music, skipping station as if it were trying to find one to lock into. The volume started to rise slowly until the beat came in reaching the ears of those inmates and guards that were old enough to know the sound. "Black Cop! Black Cop! Black Cop! Black Cop!" roared out the speakers. Many of the inmates started to recite the remainder of the KRS1 song out loud for the words to stick in each and every one of the Black CO's to hear. The way they rapped out the words to the song as if it wasn't a song anymore, but as far as the Black CO's it felt as if it was an indirect slander. The Black Co's was now getting affined by the song and the inmates kept signing it. "Turn that shit off!" one of the Black CO's order the inmates. The music volume on the radio went up louder on its own while the inmates silenced themselves and just let the music play. Because of the music getting louder the CO's felt that whomever the inmate radio that was playing was trying to be a wise ass on purpose. "Don't make me come find out who's playing that shit! turn it the fuck off now!" the CO shouted.

The music volume went up higher and the CO in rage looked around the room to see what he could grab to bust the radio into pieces and just in case he needed to go upside a Nigga's head. He went over to the wall that mounted an Ax Hammer and he quickly grabbed it off the wall and in the pitch dark he went around each Pods trying to hear were the music was coming from and when he reached the cell, he forgot that the cell doors were open, so he stood in front of the cell and yelled at the inmate with spit coming out of his mouth.

"When these lights come back on Nigga, I'm going to beat the shit out of you and smash that fucking radio to pieces." Inmate 35245 wasn't a person with a lot of muscles, but the brother had his pride and the confidence of Rodney's teachings. He laid in his soaking wet bed wondering to himself how in the hell was the radio still playing after he tried turning it off to keep the Black Cop from acting retarded and that didn't work so he pulled the plug out of the socket, and that didn't work it just kept on playing. The CO angerly kept pulling on the cell door trying to brake in when all he had to simply do was just turn the knob and in frustration the door just open. He paused for a quick second in shook that the door opened. He entered the room like a madman swinging the Ax in the direction of the music until the first swing connected, hitting it into tiny fragments of plastic. After he finished swinging the Ax, he started stumping on it and then kicked it across the room and then looked at the inmate who was looking at him in return like he had stone cold lost his mind. "Now What!? What you going to do about it?" the inmate wasn't sure what the madman was going to do so all he did was kept his lips shut. "I didn't think so" The CO said as he started feeling his way back to the room with the rest of his co-workers and then out the blue another inmate's radio came on by itself and started blasting Public Enemy's Song "Black Steel In The Hour Of Chaos." The members of the Nation of Islam began to lift themselves up to their feet as they could feel the power in the song. Now all the CO's became pissed off while the Black inmates started getting hyped to the point the CO's thought they was plotting on a prison riot so they started putting the clips into their guns and extras on their hips. "Tat! Tat! Tat!" was a sound of what seemed to be some sort of AR rifle. Every inmate hit the floor in their cell taking cover not knowing who and where the bullets resided. "OOH shit! These Mother Fuckers Done killed Stink and Duck." A Black inmate yelled out to the other inmates for them to hear what happen. A voice rang out and by the dialect it seemed to be a White CO that felt the need to say why he killed Stink and Duke. "Hey, it wasn't personal because I couldn't see who I was shouting, but hey! I felt my life was being threatened." The inmates were furious, and they wanted to kill anyone of those CO's. "AWWW!! AWWW!!!" a few inmates were yelling out to free themselves from some frustration. "Black Monk" Rob called out while feeling his way around the Pod trying to find Rodney. "He's

102

over here God." Said an inmate that study the righteous ways of the Five Percenters. Rob held out his arms and the inmates started to reach out in the darkness to grab his arm to guide him to Rodney. Rodney was standing in the same spot where he was being drenched almost to death. His eyes were closed but his third eye was open, open to receive the electrical energy of the unaverse. He tapped into his third eye and could see things happing before they occurred. "Move aside good brothers." Rodney said to the inmates that was help guiding Rob to him. "Yo Bro," Rodney said to Rob.

 Rob made his way over to Rodney and he could tell in Rodney's voice that he was a little ticked off. "Black Monk is everything good?" Rob asked. Rodney waited for Rob to walk a little closer, then he reached out and pulled Rob closer to him quickly causing him to become a bit startled. "Rob, you have walked with me in the yard for some time now blind folded, so this darkness we are in right now shouldn't be a problem for you to be making your way around in the dark. Now I need you to round up the inmates that is ready to unite and get down for some Righteousness." Rob stepped aside holding his head up high with pride. "Attention! If you are of the White race this does not pertain to you, but if you feel in your heart that you will walk in Righteousness with a Black leader then in honor we will step aside and make room for you but in event if fear is to ever enter your heart because of it the price of it is death. All brothers of the Nation of Islam stand in a group over to my left. Brothers of the Five Percent do the same. Nuwaubain's do the same. Israelites procced to do the same and the men that stand alone called RastafarI do the same and all the other men who seeks out for Righteousness do the same." Rob called out all the men of God from all different sets and lined them up. "OK! I need everyone to pull out their paperwork." Some inmates were nerves because this was the first of them hearing of this from Rodney's order. "Why? I mean what's are papers have to do with anything right now." Rob snatched the inmate's papers out of his hand and began to scan over the man's Boi of his criminal record. "Huh! I see why you are asking questions on why the paperwork is needed. It says her you like to play with little boys." Rob gave the man a look as if he wanted to kill him, but he wanted to leave this one up to God and beside he knew that whatever the humans mind thoughts were would become one's reality, so if he was to live in fear then he should die in fear. "Let's make this simple, all the people that are Rapist, child molester or Homosexual's and Atheist step out of line and stand over to the right." Rob said as he walked pass the inmates on the left side taking their paperwork from out their hands and then started pushing the Snitches out the line and placing them with the others over to the right side. "All men on the left side are the followers of Righteousness and the Alpha and Omega of humanity. Those who stand on the right side of us shell be shunned for the remainder of their lives. All of humanity must show one another respect at all times except for the ones on the

104

right." One of the members of the Rainbow coalition was mad at what was taking place and shouted out to Rob.

"Fuck You! Nigga, who the Fuck You think you are? You no better than us, I mean look at us we all in the same place, aren't we?" The Righteous men on the left knew that over the years practicing Rodney's movement that they've become changed men guided by God no matter one's creed. One Righteous inmate replies to the disturbed Homosexual. "All of the men here on the left side of me have a guideline, a book that we live by the ways of Righteousness and those of you on the right side of me have broken the laws of humanity. So, with that being said, Fuck You back for thinking that we don't have the right to believe in what we believe, and you want your way of thinking of this new way of life that we all should except it, and not. Shit! that's why ya'll on that side and were over here." The inmates could feel the tension in the room, but no one wanted to make the first move which would have been a fight amongst themselves. The inmates that were by the door was trying to move quickly out of the way of the massive amount of water that was flowing in from under the door. "Shit man! What the fuck going on? This shit is coming in fast." A man yelled out while they all stood still thinking of what to do. The guards were in the room trying to turn the water hoses off but the more they turned the wheel the more water let out in their room, and it began to flood even quicker. "Make a run for it!" A CO said as he picked up a chair and broke the window in the room and then he climbed through it with using his cell phone to give him little light. The other CO's followed suit and they all headed outside into the yard where they would be safe. Some of the inmates started to panic as the water raised pasted many of the men's waistline. "Lord I'm going to die!" an inmate with very little faith cried out. Just as the water reached their necks Rodney yelled out. "Float! And have faith." Many of the men throughout the prison bodies were floating while a good handful made their way to the bottom taking their last breath sending air bubbles to the top. Floating down the Pods was a radio that was playing the tune of Whodini's rap song "Escape." The song help take their mind off the dead bodies that they had to step on to use the bodies to help themselves stay above water.

Chapter 10

Time to Get Away

At the backend of the prison a good fifty or more men in all black and armed with weapons made their way one by one on top of the roof of the prison. Two of the men that was the most inclined with hand two hand combat was sent to remove whatever guard that was in sight. When the two men made it to the top first, they noticed it wasn't anyone around so one of the men pulled out his binoculars and slowly made his way to the front of the prison by sliding alongside the wall looking around to see what was going on. After scooping the whole seen he ran back and put the bug in one man's ear that spread throughout the rest of the men. "The Worden and the rest of the staff is in the Yard. From the looks of it sorry to say that we probably going to have to make are way pass them if we plan to make it out of here."

The men in black called themselves the S1W's and they knew the time was now being as though the staff is in the yard posted up in the front of the prison. Less than twenty minutes the roof of the prison was taken over by them. A few of the men was caring a box and placed it in the middle of the roof and open it, pulling out a concrete drill and two sledgehammer. The men began to drill into the prison roof until they made a hole that was big enough for Santa Claus to fit in. The Worden and the guards down below could hear what was going on, but they couldn't see what because the men on the roof were in the middle of it, so the Worden and his Staff were wondering what the inmates could be trying to do with the roof. The inmates could hear that something was taking place on the roof, they were hoping that the roof wasn't going to cave them in being as though pieces of the roof was coming down fast and hard on the ones that move out of the way quickly. "Shit man! What's these Mother Fuckers trying to do to us now?" Rob questioned out loud. Rodney ears started to hear as good as a blindman could. "SHwww!" Rodney said while his mind was in tune with the sound that was coming from above their heads. "I feel in my heart that whatever is going on with the roof will be in our favor." One inmate yelled out "Man we can't see." Rodney quickly returned with a reply. "You should be able to see whatever you want with your eye's closed." Some of the inmates was starting to question themselves if they wanted to follow Rodney on his mission. "Man, all this stuff you had us practicing over the years, for times like this and we believed in you but now some of us are uncertain, you have to give us a sign that you should lead." Rodney thought for a minute and then said. "I will guide you and I will use what most of you support." "What's that?" Rodney couldn't make out who shouted that out, but he felt in his spirit that rap and Reggie music at this moment was the clue to making it through his journey. He could hear people talking, doubting if they should trust his word. "O.K. I have sent my thoughts out into the universe and the feedback on it is if we needed light than it wouldn't be anybody better to help us out with that problem and she goes by the name Lyte. Lyte saw to it that the inmates got all the light they needed to make it through this journey just by using her mind knowing her Black race needed her the most right now so she gave them Lyte. Just as they all could see they sure was believers now but that didn't stop them from seeing the dead bodies floating all around them, leaving many of the inmate's sick to their stomach. A few old heads from the Nation of Islam got a little excited and started pointing towards the ceiling. A long Hemp rope that had big knots on it about five feet apart from each other was sent hanging down from the ceiling for them to climb down to help rescue the inmates. They entered a room full of water that was past knee high and about four S1W's kicked the door in that some inmates were trapped in and instantly they were hit in the face and shot back to the other end of the wall by massive water coming out from the room releasing the inmates. When most of the water was out the room the tail end of the inmates in the room started running out the room trying to help the ones that stood still from being in shook from seeing their friends and other men dying in front of them. "I know good brother it's going to be o.k. come on I got you." One inmate said to a young man that lost his friend in the mist of things. He grabbed the young man by his arm and helped him out the room.

The struggle was real while the S1W's helped the inmates climb up the rope to the roof top combining the ones who were set aside on the right side mixed in with the left side, one by one they made their way to the roof top feeling like they were already free. Rodney and Rob were helping the S1W's making themselves the last two to re-night with the others. Some of the good and the bad inmates couldn't make it to the roof being as though the roof wasn't big enough. "Gather around!" Rodney spoke to everyone. "Those brothers who hadn't made it up here it is a duty to make sure that if we get out of this shithole that we must take on sister Harriet Tubman ways of not leaving a passenger behind. I will be the first to take the first step into this Revolution." He took one step forward to prove his point. "I will go down to the yard by myself as a distraction and I need ya'll to have my back. I need - By All Means- the keys to open those outside gates, so in the mist of things I need that to be are number one mission and then will go from there." Rodney walked toward the edge of the roof top to scan out how he was going to make his way down the wall without the Guards seeing him. He looked at Rob and waved him to come over and when Rob stepped forward Rodney put his arm around Rob's neck and said into his ear. "I need you to make sure you keep an I on me and when I point up in this direction that means I want you to send the inmates to the edge of the roof to show our strength. The saddest part about this is that we don't have any guns to fight back with and yes many of men going to be killed but just

110

remember if you think fear of death you die. Oh, one more thing, go tell Knit to go to the laundry room and grab the gear he'd been working on for use over the years and have him pass them out to ya'll." Rodney walked over to where he noticed the rope on the ground that they used to get up there, so he picked it up. "I need y'all to hold this with your life and let me down very slowly." The men did as he said and when he landed onto the ground, he knew his mental had to be thinking straight before he showed his flesh to the Warden and his crew. He slid his way against the wall until he could get a good look at where the Warden and his crew of men moved to. He noticed they were huddled up by the front gate as if they were guarding it. Before walking out towards the Warden and his crew he waited until he felt that the inmates were suited and booted. He walked about ten yards onto the yard with his eye's closed before the so-called guards noticed him. He stopped himself in his tracks the minute his ears heard the guard's guns clicking. Rodney held his hand out for them to halt for a minute. "Before you let loose on my ass, I think you should rethink it again and come up with something different other than them guns, my moma used to say you live by the gun you die by the gun." The Warden couldn't believe the balls this man had to tell his people what to do in his prison. "Who the fuck do you think you are? I can have you killed now." The Warden said to Rodney. Rodney didn't say another word he just slightly turned his hip and pointed up to the roof top. Rob snapped his fingers and hundreds of inmates showed

111

themselves at the edge to be seen in their all-Black Ninja gear. The Warden was shocked to see they had all these men in black staring down at them but to him it was rather funny to see a bunch of men come to a gun fight with a bunch of Shanks. "Kill a few of those Mother Fuckers to let them know this shit ain't a game." Five guards sent at least five rounds into the mist of inmates, killing at the minimum 20 of them.

Rodney waved his finger no, no to them like Brue Lee did after you made him bleed. The Warden took that as a sign of disrespect, so he ordered for his guards to show him no pity. Shots rang out in Rodney's direction, but his mind went into defense mode and before the bullets could touch him a tornado surrounded his body causing the bullets to spit back into the Wardens direction killing the same number of guards as they did inmates. The Warden was a little uneased but determined to prove that he had more power over him. The inmates on the roof couldn't believe what their eyes had just seen. Rodney could feel in his bones that the Warden wasn't satisfied that he didn't kill him, so he held his two hands up to his mouth cupping them to call out the way he needed to. "Cock! Cock! Cock!" he uttered out. No more than a few seconds the roof top and all along the barbed wire gates that surround the prison was now covered by huge Black Ravens. The head Raven landed on Rodney's right shoulder. "I got your back." The Raven said to Rodney. Rodney read in his books that Ravens could really speak but this one was clear like he had been speaking to humans since he'd been hatched. Rodney spoke back to the Raven "How is it you speak so clearly?" the Raven said in return. "Ravens, Crows whatever you want to call use we been in the hood long enough to grasp what a Ninja saying." Rodney had to think to himself that this was kind of strange, but he overstood that the power of the mind is much greater than a bullet. The Warden order for his guards to let lose more rounds at Rodney and before the bullets could reach him Ravens sacrificed their lives for him. Dead corpus of Raven rested all around Rodney and the head Raven eyes turned fiery red and everyone noticed it. "Cockkkkk!" He chirped to let the other Raves know to get ready for what was next. The Raven spoke into Rodney's ear. "What would you like me to do? They killed a good amount of my family." Rodney replied with. "Well, they surely haven't shown respect to nature, and we know what happens if you don't respect nature, it comes back to bite you in the ass." The Raven chirped again but this time he ordered for some more back up. Ravens went after the Warden and his guards, luckily for the Warden he escaped into a little both tower on the ground level. The Ravens were clawing at the top of the guard's heads and piercing their beaks into multiple places on their bodies causing them to wish that they had just died instead of being peaked alive for them to see with their own eye's what was happing in front of them. The Warden knew that he was going to have to call for more back up because he noticed now the inmates were coming down the roof fast looking to kill dressed in all black Ninja gear and by the dozens, they started standing amongst the dead Raven's lying on the ground. After about twenty minutes went by now on the other side of the prison gates are more officers sitting behind their cars with their guns out along with their German Shepherd dogs showing their teeth as if they had been trained for this moment. Rob runs over to Rodney in the mist of things. "Look! what I got." Rob holds out his hand to show Rodney that they got the keys to free all the inmates. "We'll let them be free, except for you know who." Rodney said while waving his hand like Fred Sanford did when he felt something was a little shaky. Rob noticed that the Raven's had put a hurting on the guards to the point that many of them became gun less due to the Ravens fucking their hands up by ripping nice size chunks of meat out of them. To add salt to the womb Rodney manifested in his mind for it to start raining, but this time the rain came down out the sky different, this time the rain came down with a good bit of sea salt. The guards were screaming in pain along with pleading out for help. "AWW! Help me! Please!" was the sounds that echoed throughout the yard. The inmates were coming out the prison one by one out numbering the guards by a substantial amount which leaving most of the guards dead and the ones somewhat alive were being eating by all types of birds like Tuckey Buzzards and Vulture's. So much led was being fired into the yard that the bullets that missed its target decorated the grounds. Rob looked at

114

Rodney. "Man, I saw what you did with them bullets but what you going to do with all of them k-9's." Rodney said. "SHHHH!" holding his pointing finger up to his lips. "You don't hear that growling?" Rodney asked Rob." "Yeah Nigga, I do, those vicious Mother Fuckers over there." Rob said while pointing in the direction of the cops four-legged beast. "No, this bark is one of a kind, listing carefully and listen to the dog bark." Rodney said. A spiritual image of DMX presented himself right in front of their eye's and he spoke. "They got dogs, then my Nigga you got dogs too. Get em boys!" and then X vanished but all you could hear coming from a distance is dogs barking causing the Cops k-9's wondering what was going on. Surrounding the prison gates were a mob of Pitt bulls gamed for action. The Pitt bulls wanted to get at them Shepherds that they were attacking the ones on the outside of the gate and the ones that were inside those gates the Pitt's started to climb the barbed wire gate going over it and some dog's bodies were caught in it which really help the other Pitt's to make it over to destroy the Wardens K-9's. The Pitts were way more out the league of those hairy Shepherds who couldn't take the jaw pressure of any Pitbull's bite. While the officer's dogs were getting destroyed by the Pitts the inmates were attacking and killing officers with Shanks or Mop ringers or their skills of hand-to-hand combat. The prisoners were making their way out of the prison gates while some were still fighting for their lives to get out. Rob and a few other brothers ensured that Rodney made his way out, waiting on the right side of the prison grounds with the Righteous men. Just as Rob was about to exit the gate to meet up with Rodney, Buck sneaked up behind Rob and shanked him in the side of the gut. "That's your Wooden Nickel for you, my Nigga." Rob grabbed at his waist side and slumped over a bit. "Awww," he cried out while looking at his hand and noticing a good amount of blood being lost. He looked up just in time because Buck was moving in on him to finish him off.

Rob and Buck went to war, and neither one of them was going to give up until one was dead, at least that's how it looked from their fighting. Rob realized that even though Buck was gay, he was still a man, albeit one whose balls were a little feminine. Rob hit Buck with shots to the head and body that would have taken most men down. When he realized that wasn't working, he thought fast on his feet before he ran out of breath and Buck started to get the best of him. Rob stopped using his fists and open-hand slapped Buck like he would have done to a disrespectful bitch. Miraculously, it worked because after a few more slaps, the fight was over, and Buck went off looking for his prison hoe. Rob slowly made his way out of the gate, feeling lightheaded as if he was going to pass out. More and more police cars kept arriving while the inmates kept fighting their way out, except for the guilty rapists. Those who were guilty in the eyes of God did not make it out either, dying by gunshot or burning to death. Rob slowly made his way back to

Rodney, who glanced in his direction, not paying attention to Rob's injury. "Rob, go and tell some of the men to get something to burn this motherfucker down because it surely needs to be purified, and fire is for purification." Then Rodney noticed that Rob was badly injured. "Oh shit, you're hurt! You can't do anything; you just stay here."

Rodney panicked for a second, feeling that nothing else mattered at that point in his life other than his best friend's well-being. "Help! Someone help me, please!" Rodney cried out, fearing the loss of Rob. A brother from the Five Percent teachings came forth and began helping Rob by ripping off his own white T-shirt to help stop Rob's bleeding. Rodney's eyes got bloodshot red, and he hadn't even taken a pull on his Happy Blunt. He was far from happy; he was enraged and wanted the place to go up in smoke. He looked over to his right and saw a wounded CO leaning against a cop car, smoking a cigarette while staring into space, having lost a bit of his mind after witnessing the horrific scene. Rodney walked over to the man, snatched the cigarette out of his mouth, and pushed him out of the way. The man looked at him but recognized the look in Rodney's eyes, realizing he wasn't to be messed with. Rodney noticed the cop car was still running with the keys in the ignition, so he opened the door, helped himself in, and drove as close as he could to the prison. He got out of the car, opened the gas tank, and dropped the cigarette into it. Instantly, the car exploded.

"Boom!" was the sound that had many running for their lives. Those who stayed and lived witnessed Rodney walking away from the burning car with fire burning his clothes and himself, but he couldn't feel a thing. It was like his mind was in another place, like a Buddhist monk who had set himself on fire without flinching due to mastering mind over matter. Rodney walked away from the car slowly, with fire dropping off him and hitting the ground, causing bits of the ground to remain on fire. As he moved along, the wind that passed him dampened the fire on his clothes. He walked over to a dead body, put his foot on the body's chest, and ripped the man's shirt off. Then he took a dead cop's billy club, wrapped the shirt around the tip of it, and went to a spot where flames were left behind. He put the shirt up to the fire, catching it on fire. The inmates were watching him to see what he was going to do. A few men who grew up in the eighties started singing out to Rodney, "The Roof, the Roof, the Roof is on fire. We don't need no water, just let the motherfucker burn, burn motherfucker, burn!" They repeated those words over and over until they spoke it into existence. After seeing Rodney walk through the fire like he did, the cops who saw him looking like Michael Myers turned their cars around quickly and got out of the way. The inmates still in their jailhouse uniforms started taking them off and replacing them with the CO's clothing from their bodies. They then started putting them on while tossing the state property uniforms into the fire. The more clothes that hit the fire, the faster it spread. It wasn't long before everyone had to leave the premises, causing everyone to move forward in their own direction, but for the most part, everyone followed Rodney's lead. Those who didn't stepped aside at the last minute.

Rodney noticed them and stopped for a second, looking at them. "What's the problem?" he asked. One of the inmates spoke up for the rest of them. "Sorry, Monk Man, it's just that a few of us are still young and got a lot of Thug life in us. If you respect our wishes, we want some get-back on our oppressors." Rodney didn't want his people wasting their time on revenge, but he understood. "O.K. You're going to do what you want anyway, but know that I still love you. Remember that what one thinks will manifest into reality." The inmates who wanted payback walked over to him one by one and hugged Rodney dearly, feeling bonded despite going in different directions. Rodney went back to get Rob, who was getting very hot from the flames taking over the environment. He picked Rob up from the ground, took Rob's arm, and put it around his shoulder. Rodney slowly walked with Rob and his followers into their new destiny. "Rodney! Hold up a minute!" said Knit as he handed Rodney his all-white gown. The white gown was a way for his followers to recognize him and its blessings that were prayed over by all the righteous inmates. Rodney put on the white flowing gown, feeling immortal and protected. "Forward! Mon," Rob said, pointing in the direction of their freedom.

Chapter 11

War

Right off I95 exit 4 drops you right off on the Ave. where Q was lying in his bed thinking he was dreaming of hearing Bombs going off along with the fact that he couldn't hold his piss any longer and was made to go to the bathroom. He looked over to the other side of the bed and noticed his fly by night had found her way out. He cocked his lips in disappointment at the fact that he was hoping for round two of some more great sex. He struggled his way to the bathroom but quickly lifted the toilet seat and pulled out his manhood so he could release himself. As soon as he shook the piss off his dick, he said out loud "Shit!" he now realized he had to take a shit. After doing so he got up off the toilet and flushed it. He watched his bowel movement go around and around but it never went down, it just kept going around in the whirlpool of water. Q was mad and automatically ready to blame the young lady he had over that night.

"This Bitch! Keeps whipping her ass with Mitten's worth of toilet paper balled up around her hand." He said while trying to flush the water again only this time the water and his piss and shit and many others who lived in the city kept overflowing out the Toilet. He started lifting his feet trying to avoid the filth from touching him. He stood outside the bathroom and tried to wash his hand in the sink but as soon as he turned the water on it started coming out looking shit brown. He turned the water off and stood in his hallway for a second to gather his thoughts, but they were interrupted by the sound of his house shacking and a loud rumbling sound. He went to his window to look out to see what was going on but his window in his bedroom could only see a small part of what was taking place, all he could see was dust and debris, so he grabbed his pants that he had on the night before and put them on and a black T-shirt as well. He went down to the barbershop to look out the big front window. By now his house was feeling like it was going to crumble so he said fuck with looking out the window, so he opens the shop door and looks outside. He couldn't believe what his eyes were seeing, he watched people from his hood running anywhere they could screaming out in rage and fear, many of them was covered in blood of their own or of someone they probably loved. Q noticed a young man running past him fast as hell.

"Yo little homie what's going on?" Q asked the kid. The kid slowed down just a little and turned back to look at Rodney. "We're being attacked, if your Black you better run." Rodney stepped off his step and yelled to the kid as he was still running. "Who is attacking us?" the kid ran out of words to say and ran off leaving a cloud of dust from his feet moving so fast. Q thought about his sister, so he tried using his cell phone but for some reason she wasn't answering so he hung up the phone and now nervous as shit. His mind said go walk and see what's really going on. The rumbling sound got closer to him and through the cloud of dust he notices two army tanks coming down the Ave. "What the Fuck!" he said to himself while walking towards his sister's house. "Yo, I got that Coke, I got that Weed." Said and young black man dressed in all black. His black jeans hung so far off his ass that he had to pull them up a few times after every step he made. Q and the young man were crossing each other's path and again the young man said while looking at Q in the face. "Yo I got that Coke, Weed, whatever you need." Q stopped shook his head at the young brother and said. "Yo can't you see we are being attacked out here, I mean we at war." Q said to the young man. The young man stopped walking to answer the question. "Man, I got four mouths to feed and besides all that we been at war with these Crackers since they came here and stole "our" land and our ancestors from Africa, we just ain't been the ones fighting back, that's all." He pulled up his pants and shrugged his shoulders at Q. Q didn't reply to that but thought about what the young man was saying and then the thought came to his mind that, that's the reality of things. "I'm good young brother, I don't need any drugs." Q said while walking away hearing the young man shouting out. "Yo, I got that Coke! I got that…."

From the looks of everything everyone in the country that lived in the inner city was coming out of their homes due to the water overflowing from every pipe in their house's bursting. People were being forced back into their homes by the law and those who didn't obey the laws order was shot to death on the spot by the Cops or National Guards, Army or an angry scared White man. The word on the streets was that the president stated that the country is under a state of emergency due to the massive breakout of prisoners from every man and women prison in the country. The President's target was the inner city of the country being as though most of the prisoners who had been incarcerated come from there, so it was said that the government didn't have time to figure out who was who, so it was you did as they say or die. It was some Black police officers and enlisted vet's that didn't like what was taking place, so they decided to walk away from their jobs and the people of this country noticed that things were real because they killed their own Blue or Green it didn't matter in the eyes of the government, they were nothing but Benedict Arnolds. Q made it to his sister's house, but she did not answer the phone nor her door.

"Yo Sis! Open the door! You good?" Q yelled at the top of his lungs trying to make sure she heard him. His sister recognized his voice and quickly went to the window and held her finger up at him told hold on a minute. She opened her front door, stuck her head out looking up and down her street and then snatched Q with the quickness pulling him into her house. "Get in here these White people are going crazy out here, it's like some Rose Wood type shit." She said as she picked up her gun from off her kitchen table and popped in a full clip. "Thanks to you my big brother I got this." She say's while holding up the throw away gun he gave her years ago. Q could see that his sister was scared for her life. "Sis talk to me, you over their shaking and all, I never seen you like this before." Q sister tries to calm herself down but the thought of what she just witnessed a half hour before he arrived is a battle. "You know Tracy two doors down from me?" Q was like hell yeah I know her, she the one with the cool ass fat boyfriend that always be sitting on the step." Q's sister started having tears run down her face so Q gently pulls her close to him so that she could receive the well needed hug. After a few minutes she pulls away from him.

"It was a few White men walking up the street and without question they started hitting Kids and Women with Golf clubs and Shelves, but the Black men were shot on the spot or snatched out their homes and drugged into the middle of the street and then shot in the head! You mean you didn't see him in the middle of the street? What are we going to do?" his sister cried out. Q noticed a few dead bodies in the street but all he could say to himself at the time was this was some crazy shit going on. "I didn't look to see if I noticed anyone, my concern was with you. I really don't know what we are going to do other than do what we been doing and

125

that's survive. I can say one thing, this country should be ashamed of itself to have to come down to this." Q's sister placed a Butcher knife in her big purse. "You got your shit on you?" she asks. "Nope, you know I got rid of my guns years ago. I'm surprised you still have the one I gave you." He sister couldn't believe that he got rid of his shit. "So, what you going to do? Go to war with a Spear or Rock in a Sock Nigga?" Q gave her a fake smile but meant ever bit about what he is about to say. "Now you seen me over the years mastering the art of the Sling Shot and don't forget I'm nice with the Razor." His sister really started crying while peeping out the window thinking to herself

"This Nigga on some Nut Shit." Q started to leave, and his sister questioned him. "Where are you going? Please don't go out there." Q stopped at the door and said to her. "Sis I'm going to be fine; I just want to go home and grab a few things and I'll be right back here to make sure your safe." His sister runs up to him and hugs him tight like it was her first and last time. Q kissed her on the cheek goodbye and then open the door and proceeded to go back to his house. When he arrived the smell was so bad in the house, he almost didn't want to enter but he noticed that the door had been broken into, knowing not to ever enter a house that was just broken into was now an afterthought now that it's his place that was broken into. He slowly opens his door and sticks his head in to see if anyone could still be in the house. As he eased his way into his house he glanced into the small opening of the kitchen and became angry at what he saw. When he made his way to the living room, he was even more pissed off that his big blue tooth speaker and Laptop along with the Toaster and Microwave was missing and whatever else he didn't realize at the time. His focused was transformed to the hallway where he noticed someone was in the house and just slid into living room. The living room had two ways to enter and not sure if whomever was in it was holding some type of weapon, so Q stopped and waited for the person to make their next move. The Homeless man named P was hiding out in the living room thinking the person that's onto him may have walked down the hallway passing him, but he was wrong Q noticed him and was mad but a little relieved that it was someone he kinda knew. "Yo, P man what the Fuck! You doing in my Crib?" P looked around the place and looked at Q. "Man all the homeless is taking over some of the homes around here from the people who have abandoned them." Q gave a side eye.

"Man, I haven't even been out my house for an hour and you already trying to take over my shit." P replied to him. "Look around your house, it has shit and piss floating around, and trash dumped all over the place and half your shit got taken from other intruders." Q interrupted him. "Yeah, and who the fuck was it?" P said knowing he was about to tell a lie. "I don't know and I ain't no Snitch no how." Q made his way through the house until he retrieved his weapon of choose. He walked back out the house to intercept some fresh air for a minute. He thought about kicking P out, but he got to thinking that the house was truly ruined, so what would be the purpose of fighting for it until the homeowner's insurance took care of everything. Just as Q stepped down off his step. "Boom!" was the sound of a Brick hitting the roof of a car that an old White man was driving. "OH Shit!" Q said as he started heading back to his sister's house. Q knocked on his sister's door and it felt like she was taking long to answer the door and knowing that she knew that he was coming back he couldn't understand why she wasn't answering the door faster do to the circumstances. He started to worry and went around the back of the house to see if any foul play had taken place while he was gone. When he noticed that everything looked ok, he went back around the house to the front door and just as he was about to knock on the door, he stopped himself from doing so, because just as he was about to knock once more, he heard his sister undoing every lock she had on the door. "God Dam! How many locks you got on the door?"

His sister looked at him like he was crazy and said "Hey" and turned around and went up the steps. Q followed behind her and noticed that while he was gone his sister was gathering her things and she started placing them by the top of the steps. "Nae, what are you going to do with them things?" His sister looked at him like it was a dumb ass question. "What do you mean? I'm keeping this shit. I mean look around this is all that is left, everything else is destroyed." Q couldn't understand her logic. "Look where you going to stash it? and how you going to carry that around while trying to stay alive from these crazy white Folks that have lost their minds." he asked her while the two of them stopped talking and started listening to the sound of dogs barking from outside the house, it seemed as if the dogs were coming up her block, they could tell that they weren't far away as the sound got closer.

"Check every fucking house on this block and if any of them look like a convict, well you know what to do, shot the mother fucker." Said an angry White man amongst the mob of White men who felt the need to lead out this massacrer. "Boom!" was the sound of Nae's front door getting kicked in. Q and his sister looked at each other at the same time. They could hear that it was more than one person who entered the house. "What to do now sis?" Q asked. Nae quickly lifted the Sofa cushion from off the Sofa and picked up her handgun and cock the hammer back so that the bullet would be locked and loaded and then tried to hand it to him. "I guess it's time to get down or lay down and I ani't ready to die so easy." Q pushed her arm down that had the gun in it and held his finger up to his lips. "Did you hear that, Justin? I think someone is upstairs." one of the two white men said to the other. The two men slowly proceed up the steps and Q and his sister could hear them coming. "We got to roll out." Q whispered to his sister. "For what? I'm a kill one of these Crackers." She whispered back. "Look we don't know how many of them are in the house and I'm not trying to lose you." "Pow! Bap!" was a sound of a bullet flying pass Q's head and hitting the wall behind him. Nae grabbed Q's hand and quickly they ran to the next room which takes you back down the steps from a whole different section were the two White were coming up the steps. Nae's house was built in the same time frame when the Blacks from the south were escaping from slavery and now here, they found themselves hiding out in a room inside the wall was once held many slaves during the times of the underground railroad. They could hear the men talking and their feet walking across the hardwood floors. After a good half hour, the sound in the house became mute, so they lifted the door maybe an inch from off the floor and slid it slightly to the right and then gently pushed it forward to set them free. They brushed the dirt off their closes and the two of them started sneezing uncontrollably until they made their way outside the house.

"What now big Brother?" Q hadn't a clue of what they should do so, he started leading them to know man's land while hearing guns shots going off and seeing his Black people wounded running for their life looking for help. As tuff as Nae may come off, seeing the horrific things taking place was very over whelming to her and she started crying and shacking, clinching tight to her brother's arm. "Please Lord protect us." Nae said out loud with all the pleading in her heart. Q went into his pocket and pulled out his cell phone to call his parents. "Fuck!" he shouted outload. "The Fucking Cell phone towers are down; I got no reception." He said while shaking his head at the madness. The night arrived and the air was filled with gun smoke and stale breath from the people running for their life. Q and his sister Nae needed a break from walking and glanced down into a car a couple of feet from them, noticing a Black man in his car upset because he'd run out of gas coming from D.C. The man was in the car with his wife and two kids listening to the news on the radio with their window all the way down and the kids in the back were lying down hiding out while the man and his wife had their seats leaned all the way back like they were going to sleep listening to the breaking news that's taking over every radio station. Q could hear a little of what the news was saying but couldn't make out for certain, so he walked closer to the car. The man and his wife were looking at Q and his sister wondering what they wanted other than what every Black person at that time needed -help-.

"Yo what they talking about?" Q asked the man. The man didn't say a word as his eyes scanned the area looking out for a mob of angry White men, he just turned the volume up so that Q and his sister could hear for themselves what was going on. All six of them was tuned in and one by one tears started to appear in their eye's due to what their ears had just digested. They were hearing the reporter talking about the mass of Black people throughout the country was driving to wherever they thought was safe clogging up the highways and the ones who didn't drive to a destination, it was a good chance they were dead or alive somewhere hiding out for their lives and in the background, you couldn't help but to hear helpless Black children and women and a few men crying out for help by anyone who had a heart of God. "Daddy!" a little girl yelled out crying over top of her father's body who had been shot by a bullet that didn't have a name for a particular person other than a Black man. "This is so sad to see what is taking place here, the Blacks just can't stop killing themselves and now they're trying to put the blame on the White man." Said the White reporter. A few minutes later an old Chinese lady walked over to the reporter and took the mic out of his hand. "Please Mr. President and all the White people who are killing any Nigga that will do, please stop this, you're killing my business and you can't do that you must stop this. Mr. White man you already in dept to us. So please stop this craziness." The little Chinese's lady said over top of her tears of anger. Q and the other five didn't have much time to cry, they had to think fast of what to do next. "Yo man ya'll good?" Q asked the man in the car. The man looked over at his wife not sure of what to say to Q and then he looks at him and say's. "Man, I don't have a clue of where the fuck we are other than Delaware and the fact that we were heading to Philly to my wife's people's house but of course we ran out of gas and the traffic is at a holt and now

132

here we are stuck like Chuck." Q normally would warn a lost person that Wilmington Delaware is the last place to be lost after dark now a days but do to the fact that every Black person seemed to be in the same boat as of now all he could think to say was. "I thought the roads and gas stations wouldn't end up like this, so this is why me and my sis here are walking to see if our parents are o.k. even if it was going to take us until tomorrow this time." Q paused for a second and then continued.

"Brother do you have a Gap for yourself and some food for the kids?" the look on the man's face said it all. Q reached in his pocket and tossed a fifty-dollar bill into the car onto the man's lap. "Sorry bra but this is the best I can do for you." Q thought for a quick second about how through all this mess going on in the country the Chinese restaurants in the hood were still open. Just before Q and his sister started to walk away, he said. "Go down a block or two and you'll see a place to get the kids something to eat." The man and his wife and kids got out the car and started to walk in the direction that Q told them to, but they looked a bit scared. "Can you please take us in the direction of the place until we can see it for ourselves?" the man's wife asked Q. Q and his sister led the way and when they arrived at the restaurant the China man like always was smiling while taking your order and money. After the man ordered the food Q went up to the plastic glass window with the tiny hole in it so you can grab your money. "Excuse me sir I have to ask this question." The little China man behind the glass was smiling the whole time. "O.k. ok how can I help you?" he asked Q. Q looked at the staff in the back stopped doing whatever they were doing, and locking eyes on Q and the five other Black people that just walked in. "Why is it that you smiling so much? And why does it feel like no one in here feels like what's going on, on the outside isn't even taking place and again here you are smiling."

The Chinese man's smile remained pasted on his face. "Well, I smile at you because you and your people have been going through this for many years, and it amazes us that you still do nothing and carry on with your lives as if what is happening is normal. Now, would you like some Duck Sauce, Soy Sauce, and one can of soda?" the Chinese man said while placing the food in the bag. Q found it strange that first, the kid on the block hustling had basically said the same thing. He shook his head and grabbed the food to pass off to the man and his family. The man took the food and said to Q, "Do you want this Pepsi?" He handed out the can of soda to Q, but before Q could take it, his sister Nae snatched it out of his hand quickly. Just as she took it out of his hand, he smelled an unpleasant odor that seemed common whenever he encountered a can of soda from a Chinese store.

"Another thing, what's up with every time I get a drink from here, the can smells like old fish or a case of some funky pussy?" Q asked. The man knew exactly what Q was talking about, but he was trained to just keep smiling and then act a little slow in the brain. "Pussy, pussy good," he said. Q looked at his sister and said, "These Motherfuckers," and then they all walked out of the store.

A mob of Black people was running in their direction. It was like a Black instinct: when you see Black people running, you don't ask any questions; you just follow suit. That's exactly what they did. Once the mob of people reached them, they all ran about five more blocks up the hill until they all needed rest. That's when the questioning of why they were running began. Most of them had been running because they thought it was the right thing to do, with twice as many crazy White men chasing them, not knowing where to go or what to do. The fear of running led them to this place where they were now standing around looking at one another.

Some of the men gathered together along with some of the young kids, while most of the uninjured women cared for the men, women, and children who needed medical treatment. "Oh, Lord Heavens No!" a woman exclaimed as she held her 19-year-old daughter, who was in the middle of having a miscarriage. Blood began to cover her pant leg, and her mother noticed that her daughter's face was sweating profusely, and her body felt like it was boiling. "Water! Please, does anyone have any water?" the woman yelled out. A man had a warm bottle of water in his backpack and handed it to her. "Thanks," she said, taking the top off and giving it to her daughter. The young lady started to choke on the water, pushing her mother's arm aside. "I'm good, Mama." Her nerves were completely shot, her heart beating so fast from running scared that she lost her baby because of it, causing her mind to start to fade away. Her mind was telling her that she wished it had been herself dead rather than her child who never had a chance.

An elder man who didn't know the lady or her daughter put his hand on her back. "Sorry, Miss, that this had to happen, but I can feel in my bones that we must be getting a move on." The lady and everyone else who had taken a seat to rest now got up, ready to move forward. The young lady tried to get up with her mother, but it was a great struggle. "Mama, I can't, just leave me and you go." Her mother wouldn't dare leave her daughter. "Of course not, ask the Lord to give you strength." She tried once again to help her daughter up. "Mama," her daughter said softly as her body went limp. Her dead weight caused her mother to lose her grip, and her daughter's body hit the ground. There was no need for her mother to check for a pulse; a mother's instinct knew right away that her daughter had died.

"No!" the mother yelled, holding tight to her daughter's body, trembling with tears rushing down her wrinkled face. "Come on now, we must go," the elder man said again, this time his words choked up behind the tears he was shedding for the woman. "Go!

Just go!" the lady yelled at him. Everyone but the lady and her daughter kept moving. Many of the men felt a bit cowardly for having to run rather than stay back to help the lady, but they knew if they hadn't kept moving, the danger could have been detrimental to them all.

Chapter 12

The Woods

Rodney and his followers headed into the woods and down the back roads of South Jersey, trying not to be seen. The roads in the direction they were heading were congested to the point that cars couldn't move. If one didn't turn their car off, they would surely run out of gas, trapping other cars from being able to maneuver. Rodney felt that even though the woods would be pitch dark, it would probably still be a lot safer for now. They walked and walked until they couldn't walk anymore, then decided to camp out in the middle of the South Jersey woods.

The smell of mucky water and a faint hint of saltwater lingered in the air, a pleasant aroma for those whose nostrils hadn't smelled the outside of prison walls for many years, let alone the wilderness of New Jersey. Some of the men had a rough time finding their way through the woods in the dark. It was especially difficult for those who had to make their way barefoot or with just their shower shoes from the State Pen, or the shoes they had taken from a punk inmate or a few dead bodies they passed along the way. Many of the men could hear nature more acutely due to Rodney's teachings. The sounds of nature were not the norm for the men who had only been able to hear the sounds of prison life over the years. Now, they keyed in on any sound that wasn't typical, like a blind man honing his sense of smell. Everyone could see each other only by the whites of their eyes or the redness of those who had been smoking some of Rob's and Rodney's Happy-Weed. While many of the men went to sleep, Rodney went through his duffel bag and took out a plastic sandwich bag with herb seeds that Rob and he had saved over the years. He walked around the woods like a blind man who knew where he was going. Every few feet, he'd use the back of his heel to kick the ground just a little and drop a seed into the soil.

"My father, may you bless these seeds for my people forever, for more of these fruits to grow." The minute he dropped the seed into the dirt, a tree began to form instantly. Rodney smiled at the blessing he was receiving. "By morning, they should have budded and dried themselves out, ready to eat, smoke, or however you want to use the herb." When Rodney finished planting all the seeds, he took a deep breath and smelled the greatness of the Sesamilla in the air. Just as quickly, he felt the slightest breeze from flies flocking to the scent of the herb. When the herb trees caught the wind, their seeds scattered everywhere, spreading the herb throughout the country like a vine climbing an old building.

"All my brothers, I need you to understand the importance of what I'm about to tell you. What I'm about to say, I need you all to spread this rule to every man, woman, or child: never, ever kill the seed of these fruits. That means no smoking of the seed. We eat them or plant them in the ground like I did and wait for their fruits to become plentiful." A man spoke out for them all, "Whatever you say, Black Monk."

Rodney had no worries at all, but he knew that through this journey, a few would lose their faith, which meant death. The price of losing their lives for the cause was priceless to them, and Rodney found peace in that. Rodney and a few other men who hadn't fully gone to sleep could hear something walking in the woods. They heard sticks breaking and leaves rustling. "Sounds like we're being surrounded by deer," Rodney said to the men. In the middle of the woods, one could feel the night chill from the waters that outlined the east coast from New York down to the bottom of Florida. The cold men realized that the deer were stacked on top of each other to keep warm, so they began to do the same. Not long after everyone drifted into a deep sleep, Rodney started to feel slight heat and smelled a faint trace of smoke. Other men who were attuned to themselves noticed the same things. "Do you feel that heat and smell that smoke? What do you think, Black Monk?" Rodney wasn't sure. "I don't know as of now, but I'm sure with a little patience, it will be like the old saying—whatever you do in the dark will always come to light."

They started to hear footsteps that sounded like a troop of men coming their way. Rodney closed his eyes and began to meditate to see if he could reveal what was coming. The closer the noise got, the more it frightened the deer from all areas, and they started moving quickly toward Rodney and his followers. The black men could tell it was deer coming by the shapes of their eyes and the sparkling effect they gave off. The light of fire was in the air, moving fast to its destination. Rodney and the rest of the men's eyes started to focus on the flame, which began to form a wide circle. Rodney's and a few others' eyes began to see like night vision binoculars; as long as a little bit of light was revealed, they could see what was going on like an owl in a tree capturing everything down below.

They witnessed men in black and red robes representing the Grand Wizards of the KKK. The men in all white had a staff with burning flames and a long rope that held hostage black men guided to the center of the circle. A wooden cross was already placed in the ground, and the men in white robes began removing the potato sack bags from the captured black men's heads. They tied the first black man to the cross, and the men in red and black robes began to read something that looked like the Holy Bible. Two men in white robes went up to the black man tied to the cross and set his body on fire, starting from his feet. "Aww!" the burning man yelled. The men following Rodney almost couldn't keep themselves from running to rescue the man, but they knew not to move without a plan. Rodney whispered in Rob's ear to pass along to the rest of the men, "Tell everyone to close their eyes so the enemy can't see us. We don't need that to happen since we don't know for sure if they're packing or not, but I'll bet my last breath of air that they are."

Rodney and his followers listened while smelling the brutal and devilish ways of the KKK doing what they do best—killing Black people. After the Klan burned at least ten black men, the night turned into morning, and the morning dew surfaced the earth. All those Klan members were big-time deer hunters, and a few saw deer moving in the woods. Without question, they started shooting their rifles, hoping to hit an eight-point buck. After they saw that it was so many deer close to them, target practice was easy pickings for them but like always a few bullets will get away from the best of shooters and a few of Rodney's followers had been hit by a few bullets hitting the wrong Buck. "Aww! Rodney I've been hit. Why did I have to go out like this? I mean Monk you said as long as we think to live, that we would and look at me now." Rodney couldn't understand at first how they had been found and targeted. He thought to himself that the deer gave them away knowing that those White men could smell a deer a mile away. "I believe Fella's we found our self's some lost Nigger's in the woods." Said a Klan member whose eyes were locked on Rodney and his men. A few Klan members started shooting into the direction of Rodney's crew and the deer that surrounded them were being killed right and left along with a few Black men and Rodney couldn't stand it any longer. "Do what I do!" Rodney shouted out to his crew. Rodney got on a deer's back and all the rest of the deer standing up was ready to carry each member of Rodney's crew to a place of safety. Once the Black men mounted the deer's backs, they darted quickly through the fog until they couldn't be seen or heard by anybody that fit the description of a Klan member. "Brothers, I'm sorry that we had to see that and go through that, but I must say that we must not be too surprised. We as Black people have been traumatized by members of the Klan for decades. Now, what I need us to do is keep moving forward and pray for those brothers we have lost in the past and the present," Rodney spoke to his followers while getting off his deer and bowing his head to pray.

After the men prayed for the dead, they didn't know what their next move was and started to think Rodney didn't either. "Rodney, what now? Where are we going?" asked one of the men, speaking for himself and a few others. Rodney opened his eyes and looked at the flock of men. "My brothers, you must trust me along this journey."

"What if we get lost in this journey? I mean, what do we do if we somehow get split up?" asked a young man. Rodney looked at him and then at all his people. "If that happens, I want you to understand that our clue to bringing us back together, when it's all said and done, is to listen to the messages from the conscious rappers. You have the Teacher, the Blast Master, the Lost Tapes by Esco, the Poor Righteous Teachers, Baldhead Slick, P.E., and YZ who's been thinking of a master plan, among many others. I can't believe that you are still questioning me after seeing the spirit of the great DMX and what he did with those dogs." Rodney noticed the men in the crowd agreeing with his words. "Let's get free!" a man yelled out. Someone in the crowd had an old-school box-looking radio that sounded like a modern-day Bluetooth speaker. The album "Let's Get Free" by Dead Prez started playing, and the beat and words entered their souls. Rodney looked over at Rob, who could tell something was on Rodney's mind. "What up, Star? Everything Ire, Mon?" Rodney was in a complete daze, but he snapped out of it. "I'm okay, my brother, but a young man not too far from here needs me. He's crying out for my help, and I'm going to take care of that. When I return, we must be on our way."

Rob knew that saving the young youth was one of their main missions. "Okay, I'll go with you. Awww," Rob said, feeling the sharp pain from his injury. "No, I must go alone," Rodney said and hugged Rob. "Yo, hold it down here until I..." Before Rodney could finish his sentence, Rob interjected, "Just go, I got it." Rodney felt in his heart that he was going to need the drum that Rob's uncle Wisdom gave him a few years back. He grabbed the drum, slung the leather strap over his shoulder, and walked off, letting his spirit guide him to the scene of a little boy crying out for his help.

This is the moment Rodney appears out of nowhere upon Little A, rocking back and forth on the curb in the prelude of book one, "A Cry for Rodney."

Chapter 13

Surviving the Hunt: A Journey of
Hope and Resistance

Little A grabbed Rodney's arm with a little force. "Wait! Please don't leave me here alone. My parents are gone," Little A cried out, flashing back to the sight of his mother shot dead in her car and his father's lifeless body in the street. "Please, sir, don't leave me out here alone. I'm scared," Little A pleaded. Rodney looked down at Little A and noticed the tears running down the boy's face. He bent over and used the back of his fist to wipe away Little A's tears. "I got you, little homie. No need to worry any longer. You called on me and now you ask for me to save you from the loss of your family, so yes, I will let you tag along." Rodney straightened up and placed his arm around Little A. They walked a long way, maneuvering through the woods and its wildlife with difficulty. "Boom!" The sound of heavy rain came down, making everything a soaking mess, except for Rodney's white flowing robe, which somehow stayed pristine even when touched by mud. Little A stopped. "Are we almost there?" he cried out. "I don't think I can make it anymore; my feet are sore, and the back of my legs hurt."

Rodney understood and stopped to give the kid a rest. He knew that if it were any other man, they wouldn't have lasted through the mental and physical strain of the journey. "Be strong, little man, we're almost there." But Rodney noticed that Little A wasn't looking well and had developed a cough. So, he lifted Little A off the ground, slung him over his shoulder, and carried him along the way. As Rodney got closer to his people, he smelled a strong stench of herb in the air. It was a scent he loved, second only to fresh air. As they got closer to the source of the smoke, Rodney gently let Little A down. Suddenly, they heard a faint sound of dogs barking approaching them. Little A grabbed onto Rodney's leg. "Are those dogs coming to eat us?" he asked, sounding terrified.

Rodney could sense peace in the dogs' barking. "No, little homie, I feel that they're coming our way for our protection." Just as Rodney thought, the dogs arrived, more numerous than a pack of wolves. These dogs were trained, possibly by the military, and they gathered around the men, each growling like DMX. An image of DMX would occasionally appear, vanishing into a star that provided much-needed light when the sun went down.

"Everyone, let's gather our things and move out. The dogs' arrival is a sign that the mob of angry white men must be near," Rodney said to his followers. Little A looked around at the men, who all appeared to have been working out with barbells. Occasionally, an

147

inmate would come up and introduce himself to Little A. "Ayo, Rodney, this here is a cool little kid. What's his story? And what are we going to do with him? He might hold us back from the looks of him." Rodney stood amongst the men and placed Little A in front of him. "This here is Little A, and he'll be coming along with us. Don't worry; he won't hold us back because he is our future, along with the rest of the youth. If he or any other should fall back, it's our duty to pull them up and push them forward. We all know Chin, right?" The men who did agreed. "We will be moving forward to a place set up for us and our youth along with our women."

The mention of women made the men quickly gather their things to head out. After escaping from the Klan's men in the woods, Rodney decided it was time for his men to go into the city, where most Black men come from, so they could maneuver better around people who looked like them and were fighting for the same cause. Rodney and his men followed the riverbanks of the Delaware River until they noticed streetlights to the west and headed in that direction. "Hold up a minute, Black Monk. This old man needs a break. We're going to have to figure out how to get over that bridge if we plan to get to the P.A. side. Maybe we can steal one of those white people's boats along the way," said an elderly man, slumped over, trying to catch his breath.

Everyone stopped and looked at the tragic sight of Black people jumping off the Delaware Memorial Bridge, just like their ancestors who jumped ship in the Atlantic Ocean, refusing to be slaves. They could hear their voices screaming for the last time, and the most disturbing sound was the impact of their bodies hitting the water. Rodney turned away from the sight and looked toward the distance they were heading. He estimated that if they kept moving, they would reach the town just before sunrise. He looked at a few young men, then glanced at the elderly man for a quick second before returning his gaze to the young bucks, silently asking them to lift the elderly man and carry him with pride. They did so willingly. "Forward!" Rob commanded, and they all started walking towards the city's bright lights.

As they got closer, their noses started to squint at a smell that was different from their own. "What is that smell?" someone called out, voicing the thoughts of everyone else. Rodney tapped into his third eye and responded, "Whoever and whatever it is, is feeling neutral about our smell as well." The men noticed a familiar yet fouler smell than what they were used to in prison. Their steps slowed as some men began to feel sick to their stomachs, throwing up the last bit of that nasty prison food. Rob walked around the area, sniffing the air to identify the smell. "It's a prison smell for sure, but it's different," he said to Rodney. Rodney noticed some movement near a building illuminated by streetlights and held out his hand for everyone to stop. "Yo, someone go find Cool C and bring him to me."

A man, not believing what Rodney was asking, questioned, "The rapper Cool C?" Rodney nodded. "Yeah, what other Cool C do you know?" Rodney replied jokingly. "Well, hell, you might as well ask for Steady B." The man turned around, realizing that the crowd had doubled, and figured the best way to call for them. He yelled out, "Oot Ooh!" repeatedly until it reached Cool C and Steady B. "Yo Cool, Yo B, Black Monk wants to see you," said another escaped inmate.

Cool C and Steady B were honored that Rodney wanted to see them, but they wondered why. After a few hours of walking to meet up with Rodney, they finally made it front and center. As soon as they locked eyes with Rodney, they began to shed tears of joy. Rodney opened his arms wide, somehow hugging the two of them simultaneously.

"Why?" Cool C asked. Rodney took a step back and said, "Because I believe in my heart that the two of you have truly asked for forgiveness from your hearts, not just for the government to believe it but more so for the Most High God and yourselves. That alone is why I've sent for the two of you. Oh, and that's not it. I heard over the years you and B mastered the art of glass to the point that old-school reading glasses would be out of business if you two revealed your blueprints." Cool C and Steady B knew exactly what Rodney was talking about. "Well, how can we help you, good brother?" B asked. "Look over there; it's some people, and we don't want to move and be seen and end up in danger."

Cool C and Steady B understood. C opened his duffle bag, and B dug in it, pulling out a pair of glasses they had made from several magnifying glasses cut and pieced together. These glasses provided a more powerful image than binoculars or any telescope. They handed the glasses to Rodney, who placed them on his face. His eyes adjusted, and his vision became as if he were wearing a virtual reality headset. "Oh my," Rodney said, amazed at how clearly he could see men over a hundred yards away, right in front of his face like an HD picture. He held up his fist to dap Cool C and B on their great craftsmanship. "You've done well, the two of you," Rodney said, looking toward the building. "Stand still, and you will really see a difference," C said. Rodney locked in on what he saw moving near the building, standing still like a statue. B asked, "You good, Monk?" Rodney didn't say a word, knowing that speaking would force him to move and taint his vision, and he wasn't having that.

C and B and a few others that were standing close by was wondering what it could be that had Rodney stuck like a deer in headlights so, they all waited patiently for Rodney to give word. Once Rodney saw who and what he saw removed itself from his vision, he took the glasses off and handed them back to Steady B. "Hey Monk, you didn't have one of those late-night imaginary visions that be having your pants wet and sticky did you?" Rob asked jokingly. "I know the look that brother gives when he sees…" Rob say's while smiling and pointing his finger at Rodney. "You think you know me." Rodney said to Rob. "Bredren, I know you better than you know yourself. Don't forget we go way back." Rodney shook his head at Rob letting him know that he was speaking facts. "Tell the men let's roll out." Rodney ordered Rob while he was gathering his things to head in the direction that had his vision on pause for a second. As the men got closer to the building it started to seem like the place was deserted but Rodney knew without a doubt in his mind that it wasn't, but they moved in cautiously. Rodney and about ten men stood under the streetlight looking around trying to see if and what would reveal itself. Walking from out of the darkness with a few others behind her was the face that Rodney's eyes were mesmerized by. Her skin complexion was the glory of Black beauty, the look she gives off is very deceiving, it changes depending on her environment and how much light she receives, It was almost as if she were like a Chameleon blending in for the right cause, but for the most part she stood in front of them about 5'5" in an all-black Ninja gear outlined in white at the bottom of her pants and around the wrists. Her complexion was of every shade of black that one could imagine, her Melanin couldn't be duplicated. Her skin shined the

152

closer she appeared under the light. Every Black man that could see her looked passed her beauty only to see who she had hiding out in the back because looking at her made them want any woman of color but mostly black because they could feel the power from the Black women just from the air that they were breathing in at that very moment. She stood alone under the light with other women waiting in a little distance behind her. Rodney had to interduce himself to her being as though he felt it could be a great chance that one of the men in the back of him would soon want to approach her as well. He steps to her in a kingly manner "Hello I'm Rodney." He said as he held his hand out to her hoping to hit her with the old school kiss her on the hand type of time. "I know who you are Black Monk, we all do." The young lady said having Rodney looking around for who all she was referring too. "Who is we all?" Rodney asked her. The lady walked back in the direction she came from, and Rodney, Rob and a few other men followed. "Them." She said pointing at the image of all the many women who'd broking out of the woman prisons across the country just as they did. "How many of my sister's do I see?" Rodney asked looking out into the crowed of women.

"I estimate over five hundred easy and that's just our Prison alone. We would've had more but most of them got turned out and went Butch on us and the next thing I heard was they're looking for some Rainbow." Rodney and the other men knew right then that they were going to have the biggest task of them all on their hands now. They felt the need to protect the women, hoping to earn their trust back. "I'm sorry what is your name?" Rodney asked.

"My government name is April Jennet Augustus, but over the years, like you, I have inherited a new name: Aja, named after the Orisha Goddess. I am the spirit of the forest and a master herbal healer." Instantly, Rodney thought of Rob. "Oh, my brother over here needs your help." Rodney looked at Rob, and Rob showed Aja his injury. She called out to her friend, a sister from another mother. "Winker, come here with my belongings, please."

Winker was a short, dark-skinned young lady with a low cut with waves in her hair, looking to be in her early 30s. Her body frame suggested she worked out a lot, with muscular legs and arms, but the feminine allure of her chest and hips was an eye-catcher for all the men. "Winker, look at this brother's cut," Aja said. Winker looked at the gash and agreed it was in bad shape, but it wasn't something she hadn't handled before with other women inmates' cuts and bruises. Winker went into Aja's bag and pulled out a big, dried-up leaf that looked like it was once used as a hand fan. She snapped her fingers and sucked her teeth. "Fuck!" she said out loud. "What is it, Winker?" Aja asked. "I forgot the lighter, uhhh," Winker responded, dumping the remaining items in the bag onto the ground. She looked at the aloe plant, oils, dried-up herbs, and a small razor blade.

"I can handle that, that's a small thing to a giant," Rob said, pulling a lighter from his pocket. Winker took the lighter and flicked it to make sure it worked. Then she grabbed Rob by the waist, looking around for a spot for him to sit down. Across from them, she noticed a spot by a broken brick wall that would serve as a seat and rest area. Rodney, Aja, and a few other men watched as Winker prepared to tend to Rob's needs. She picked up the aloe leaf and the razor, slicing the plant open. "Take off your shirt," she ordered Rob. He did as instructed, and Winker applied the aloe all over the area where he'd been shanked. Then she crumbled the dried herbs and placed them on top of the aloe sap. She lit the dried leaf until its tips caught fire, then blew out the small flame, letting the smell of burnt leaves linger in the air. She waved the smoke into the aloe plant covering his gash, chanting words to aid the healing process. Aja joined in the chanting, their words invoking the Most High God within themselves to help Rob heal faster. As they chanted, Rob's cut began to heal. "Aww," Rob said out loud, feeling his skin close together like candle wax cooling and solidifying. Once the gash was completely closed, she gently rubbed hemp oils over it. Winker stepped back, satisfied with her work. "Go ahead and walk around, make sure you don't feel any more pain," Winker said. Rob stood up, noticing he felt no pain at all. "I feel great," he said, putting his shirt back on.

Rodney was impressed by what he had witnessed. Once, he would have laughed at the idea of herbs as medicine, preferring to call a Western doctor. "Aja, you have done well with the ladies. What other tricks do you have in that bag?" Rodney asked. Aja smiled at the joke, which held some truth. She returned the joke, "Look up in the sky, is it a bird or a plane? Wait, no, let's stop playing games and let me show you what I have for you. Wait here a second." She walked back toward the crowd of women ex-inmates. The women moved aside for Aja, who returned with a surprise. The two figures approached Rodney, and he wondered who this man could be, somewhat resembling him but with a lighter skin complexion and long locks that weren't all white. As they got closer, the streetlights revealed the man's identity. Everyone from the tri-state area and those who grew up in the 60s and 70s recognized the free man as Mumia Abu-Jamal. Rodney's face filled with tears of joy, and he hugged the brother whose books he loved to read. Mumia walked humbly to Rodney, embracing him. He knew Rodney was the reason he was free, but he couldn't shake the question of whether this moment was real or just a dream. When he realized it was real, he knelt. "Thank you, thank you. I know you're God-sent. I can feel the God in you. It's like a blessing we never see coming, like yourself." Rodney and everyone else understood what Mumia meant. Rodney helped Mumia up. "You are right, brother. I am God-sent, as are you. Now is our time to shine our light onto this universe," Rodney told Mumia.

156

The men pulled out their spliffs of Happy Herb, filling the sky and surrounding area with smoke. Rob, wanting to thank Winker for her care, slid beside her. "I want to thank you for…" he began, but she interrupted. "I know, I know, no need. You good though?" she asked, smiling. "As long as I got you by my side," he replied, grabbing her waist and pulling her closer. "As long as I can have your hands on my body, I'm good," Rob added. Winker sucked her teeth. "Is that right?" she asked. Rob smiled, shaking his finger. "O.K., I know it!" he said. "Know what?" she asked, smiling. "It's the way you sucked your teeth. What part of the Caribbean are you from?" Winker put on a serious face. "Where do you think?" she asked in her native tongue. Rob knew from the way her words rolled off her tongue that they were from the same island. "What part of my yard are you from?"

"I'm from the Parish of Portmore, how about you?" She replied. "I was born in Kingston." He replied with pride like all Kingston Jamaican's due. "Is that so?" Winker said in a flirty way. He noticed a small cut under her right eye, and he wanted to ask her about it but wasn't sure if it were the right time to ask. What drew his attention to it was how the scare was supposed to tarnish her looks but it did the opposite for her, it added to her beauty in a unique way. Winker noticed him half ass staring at her face. "What! does the little scratch over my eye bother you?" she asked. Rob noticed that her body language went into serious mode. "No, not at all, it's just I was looking at the other women in your bunch and quit a few have the same look. What? were you in a gang up in that piece?" Winker understood why Rob would think that way but felt it was needed to tell what really happen. "You see, the Dike Bitches in the joint wanted to slice a woman face to set the different between them and the straight. So, a lot of these women here that you see with the scar on their faces are Dike's that hadn't found the Rainbow or just want to fight the White man for the cause." Rob gave her a look like he wanted answer's to why she has the scar knowing that the people from there Yard don't get down like that. "So, what's up with the scar on your face?" He asked seriously. "Cool yourself mon," she said just before continuing. "Nah, this Lifer that was put into my room was mad that she couldn't make me her Bitch so one night in my sleep the Bitch cut me for the hopes to make the other inmate's think that I was her property."

Rob could see in her eyes that she was replaying that moment in her mind, and he didn't mean to change her mood, so he gently lifted her face for them to lock eyes. "I didn't mean to get you all worked up, but I want you to know that I will be your protector from here on out if you will allow me to." Winker knew that if she gave her energy to a worthy man such as Rob it would be a great chance, they could accomplish anything together. "All right then I'll hold you to that." She said feeling the sincerity of his word.

Rob's focus was now a little on the angry side after hearing why she ended up with the scar. "That's o.k. because in due time they get what they been waiting for, in due time, Fire will burn the Wicked!" Rob said out loud and then sucking his teeth matching Winkers in return. After everyone started to mingle with one another with the time passing them by so fast that the hours of fun they were having rushed the morning to arrive. Rodney stood before the men and the woman so high from all the herb that he partaken in making him seem as if he was slightly elevated from off the grown about three inches. Rain started to come down causing the smokers to have to put out their medicine. "We have to move out now that morning has come." Everyone began to gather their things to head out. "Pop! Pop! Pop!" was the sound of gun shots into the direction of the crowed of Black people just missing Mumia and Rodney's head by inches. Everyone was ducking down taking cover wondering where the bullets were coming from.

The whole time while they were smoking, drinking homemade jailhouse wine, and engaging in other activities, a few White men followed the smoke hovering over them, mistaking it for a large fire. No fire truck was sent to the scene, so they put two and two together and "Pop!" another shot rang out. "These Niggas can run, but they can't hide," said an elderly White man to the other two men lurking about 150 yards away. They were shooting rounds of bullets at the Black people, feeling justified since the President had ordered the right to do so. The Black people started to run, and many were shot in the back, their bodies left behind. Some men noticed a few were skipping along, and some were running like females. The Dykes were just as fast as the men, and some were even faster. Rodney led the way, even though he didn't lead the pack. Using the power of his mind, he guided the people in the direction needed.

"Yo, do you see this shit? I thought we made it clear that these bundles of sticks had to go their own way, since they want things to be their way," Rob shouted out to Rodney, who was now looking at the men and women who were gay. The rain was coming down fast, but it had lightened up a bit, and the clouds started to hide the sun.

"Okay, we're here, and we're not going anywhere. We are human, and we are all over the world and have a right to be where we want to be," said a gay man, speaking his mind to Rodney and the rest of the Righteous men standing before him.

"This is true, but the place we are going, you can't go," Rodney said to the man.

"What the fuck! We're being treated by you and everyone else who doesn't agree with our lifestyle like the White people treated

Blacks back in the day when they couldn't be in the same places as those Crackers," the gay man argued.

Rodney knew the man had a valid point. "Well, the question I have for you is, why would you want to go somewhere you're not welcome?" The gay man thought about that, his feminine ways kicking in quickly. He spoke without thinking, letting his emotions take over. "Well, I guess you're right. I can't speak for them, but for myself, I won't be going with you guys. Then where should we run to if we can't follow you all?" he asked. Before Rodney could respond, the answer appeared to them all. The sun came out from behind the clouds, lighting the sky with its rays. The heat dried up the moisture in the air, and a big rainbow formed right in front of them. It looked like the rainbow you'd see on a box of Lucky Charms. Not one person could deny it was the most beautiful thing they had ever seen. They may have seen rainbows before, but not as close up as this one appeared to be, still at a good distance.

"Well, there it is," Rodney said, pointing to the sky. "You and the rest of the Rainbow Coalition can follow it until you get to the other side. I'm sure you all can have a gay time in your own world where people like you think alike." The gay men and women only wanted to be happy and have everyone see their lifestyle as okay. So, they saw their calling once they saw the rainbow and started to follow it.

"You best get moving because I've never seen a rainbow last forever," Rob yelled out to the gay family, who responded with the middle finger. All the gays were safe except for the Whites and Blacks who had to worry about getting killed while trying to get to the other side of that rainbow because of the saddest thing this country had come to: a race war.

Along the way, Rodney witnessed many gays coming from Hollywood, some were rappers, and others were undercover, no longer wanting to hide who they were. Some of those men and women were killed by gunshots or firebombings. Even though Rodney and his men didn't see eye to eye with the gays, they still shed a few tears for those dead bodies left behind because many of those men and women were someone straight's kinfolk and, more so, human.

"Yo, check his pockets," Rob said to one of his brothers, pointing at a gay man's body lying in the street's gutter.

"For what?" the young Black brother asked.

Rob didn't feel the need to explain. He walked over, bent down, dug into the dead man's pockets, and pulled out a wad of money wrapped with a red rubber band. "This is why. If I know one thing about those gay motherfuckers, it's that they keep money. Now, let's keep moving," Rob said as the Righteous men and women went on their way.

Throughout the country, every Black person was still running for their lives. This time, instead of heading north, they were going south, hoping the foolishness would end. The men's feet were becoming a problem; their shoes were worn down to the point that the blisters looked like they had been rubbed down to the white meat. Just before they hit the Delaware state line, Rodney looked at the condition his men were in and decided to stop again. Little A. tugged on Rodney's shirt to get his attention. "Where are we? And why are all these people with us? We have White men shooting at us. Rodney, I lost my father to a White man with a gun, and even though he was a cop, he was White with a gun."

Rodney looked down at Little A. for a second, then refocused on the wounded men. "Do you remember I told you that everybody you meet is for a reason? Now is the time to use your eyes and less of your mouth. Start learning the answers to your own questions."

Rodney spoke to Little A. in that manner because he didn't want to put the little guy through more horror than he'd already experienced. Little A. walked over to a huge tree with two roots sticking out of the ground wide enough for him to sit between. He sat there, thinking about how he was the only kid in sight, other than the women inmates who had their babies while locked up and broke out on the same day. Sadly, many of those precious kids born in prison didn't make it before they escaped. He looked at the drum Rodney had given him and realized that it was the only thing he

163

owned right now. He thought about trying his luck at finding his own way home but then had to face the fact that his family was no more. He figured he was stuck with just the faith in believing Rodney would be there for him. From that, he realized he should be grateful and thankful for Rodney and the drum, so he began to beat on the drum without a purpose, and because of that, the sound was just a bunch of ruckus. Rob heard the offbeat sound of him playing the drum, and he was well familiar with the sound of an African drum because back home in Jamaica when he was a child, there weren't many kids who hadn't gotten a drum for Christmas or just played with one that a family member may have had. Rob walked over to Little A. and stood in front of him. "So, you want to learn how to play the drum, huh? Well first, you should—here, give it to me." Rob took the drum from Little A. and then took a seat beside him. "Look, you place the drum between your legs like this. Then you try something like this." Rob beat on the drum, showing him how to do it. "Bap! one Bap Bap! two Bap!" "See? Something like that. Just think of the human heartbeat and go by the rhythm of that, and the soul in you as a young Black man will kick in."

Little A. loved the sound that it gave off and quickly snatched the drum back from him, beginning to beat on it the way Rob told him to. Just as Rob said, the soulfulness in him revealed itself as if he were a natural. "That's it, little homie, I see you. So now, be heard, little bro." Rob was about to go back to being with Winker, but Rodney startled him by being right in front of him when he turned around to leave. "I see you and my son here got a chance to meet one on one."

Rob smiled at the sound of that because he wished one day for Rodney to have a child so that he could be the uncle he always wanted to be. The look on Rodney's face was priceless, showing the love in his eyes for Little A. Rob knew that Rodney was just the man for the little guy. "Yes, and I like the sound of that. I was showing my nephew here how to tap on this drum," Rob said. Rodney was looking at the smile on Little A's face and wanted to cry because he started thinking about how his own father hadn't been in his life, and now here he was, ready to take on this grateful burden. He didn't think about what type of blessing he was going to receive for caring for Little A. He just had love in his heart for his youth; if it wasn't Little A., it would have been another.

"I need you, son, to take the drum and beat it so our Black brothers and sisters who are not with us can find us." Little A. looked at Rodney and felt the love in the word "son" when it came out of Rodney's mouth. He stood up with a question in his mind. "How am I supposed to play when I'm walking?" Rodney laughed. "Just focus on the beat, and you'll be fine," Rodney said, giving Rob a nod for them to get back to the grown folks. When they reached them, Rob and he couldn't believe what they were seeing with their own eyes. It was an all-out orgy going on amongst some of the followers who were not of the Righteous, while others got some rest, smoked blunt after blunt, or were off to the side with one of their books of spiritual guidance.

"Everyone that's asleep, wake the fuck up! And those of you who have found time screwing around and getting high off that Happy, I'm here to tell you the minute we let our guard down is the minute we take our last breath. Now, we all have seen the movie Roots, and if you remember, there was a part that said that when the White man is near, you could smell him because when his hair gets wet, it smells like a wet chicken."

All the Black people knew what the chicken taste like but many of them didn't have a clue of what a wet chicken smelled like, but they got the message. "Aja, come forward and Ladies come forward as well." The women did as they were told. "Now Ladies I've talked with these Righteous brother's over here about how were going to put our life on the line for you all and the children you bring into this world because we understand your worth, but don't think for one second that men are going to stand for any type of disrespect and we don't need a women who feels the need to prove that she can do what a man can do and if not better. It's no need for us to have to compete against one another. If we are willing to put our life on the line for you, then I don't think it's too much to ask for a Righteous Black woman to serve her Black

166

brothers with her spiritual gift of knowing what true love is without the pain unless it's of a loss of your loved one, nothing other than the love of joy."

Every woman was silent and with the men and the women knowing he meant every word he said because when a bunch of women mouths are kept closed, they understood the meaning of Order. The women were being prepped by Aja the whole time already knowing where and what he was talking about, they just let him talk while they figured out the type of men, they wanted to evaluate their Black brothers to their highest potential. By remaining quiet, the women were proving to him that here on out they didn't have to have the last word, they went with the philosophy that they can show you better than they could tell you. They understood that they could truly run the show if they understand to not outshine the Master, not a Master like a Slave owner but a leader, a King that she stands to follow because they trust in the man to lead. Aja stepped forward to Rodney because she chose him, and Rodney took her by the hand and the two of them kissed each other with so much passion that every man and women wanted that true feeling Rodney was referring too. "Ok Ladies and Gents, we have to move out because." Rodney's head started hurting because he could feel that his Black brother's and sister's all over the country were being slaughtered.

"I Feel it's some people close who need our help." Rodney went off to gather his things to lead his people in the direction of 95 south. They walked through Claymont Delaware down into the city of Wilmington and there it was bodies all over the place of people of all color, but mostly Black. Rodney and his followers noticed almost every other block were cars with their trunks wide open. When they walked down a strip called Market Street, they saw a few men surrounding the back of a car with the trunk open. Rodney and Rob and some others walked up to these mid age young Black males. "Yo Little Homie, What's with all these cars with their trunks wide open?" Rodney asked. One of the men turned and looked at them while he held his gun of chose in his hand as he was scanning it over to make sure that it was taped up properly so non fingerprints can be found, and he checked for any kind of engravement on it so that the shit couldn't be traced. "The White man must have felt about himself as being 2% of a Coward being as though if you look around trunks are full of guns, they probably thought that we would take the guns and continue using them on one another, I don't know. Since most of the young Black youth my age along with some elders who had gun's ran out of Amio and the White man and woman and child I guess felt it was unfair so somehow out the blue on every block in the hood one Sunday morning it was a car at the end of each block, with the trunks wide open with nothing but all types of guns in it. Some worked and some didn't." Rodney and the others couldn't believe
168

what they were hearing from the young man. The young men who were taking those guns from out the car was placing the magazine clips into the gun like they had plenty of practice. "Hey, my Youth, do you want to roll out with us? You'll be safe with us." Rodney asked the young men. One of the young men who looked to be the oldest one out of the four of them replied by saying. "Yeah, we know all about you, my brother was in the Clink up state and when he got home, he talked about you and what you were doing and that's all great but when this shit gets even thicker, oh you going to need to pick up one of these guns." Rob's ear perked up to the sound of that. Rodney knew that wouldn't be true for himself but as far as a few of his brother's he knew it would be a few that would flake out on him, and just as he was ready to keep it moving, he noticed a few more of his men and now woman choosing to step aside so they can retaliate, so they started walking over to the trunk as well and started grabbing guns of their own.

"You know this is what they want just so they can wipe us out except for the next few generations to come that will be too weak in numbers to rise up for the cause." Rodney tried explaining to them. "Look grabbing guns and shooting back is the only answer we have, or we just die hoping that these White folks would find some kind of love in their hearts to change the present time? I don't think so," said the young man. Rodney thought about that harsh reality and sadly started walking away and just as he took a few steps the men and woman who stepped away from his mission held their heads down and turned their faces away from him when he tried to give them eye contact. It was the guilt and the fact that they knew that having eye contact with him he could manipulate you into stepping back into line, but they couldn't and wouldn't because they knew their brothers and sisters was being slaughtered and they were willing and ready to die for the cause but understand the need for some of them to step aside and survive so that the Black race here in America don't become extinct. Rodney and Aja, Rob and the rest of his followers moved on and ended up seeing some more Black people in front of them stuck like they didn't have a clue of what to do or were to run to next.

Chapter14

What Else Can Happen?

"I'm hungry," Little A. said to Rodney. Little A. was not just speaking for himself; many men and women were also hungry. Rodney looked at the Black people in front of him who weren't escaped convicts. There were little children, teenagers, and elders begging one another, hoping someone had food. Those who did have some food had very little to eat because the ones who were mad hungry took it from them if they weren't ready to fight for what was theirs.

Two women, from the looks of it, were fighting over a piece of chicken, and a young elderly man was trying to break it up. "Chill! Chill the fuck out!" Q yelled out to his sister and the young lady she was about to fight. Na wasn't trying to hear Q. All she knew was drama was taking place, and she wanted in on it. Na hit the young girl with a right hook that sent her to the ground. "Yo! You don't touch another motherfucker's food; that shit is mad foul." The young lady felt how hard Na hit her, so she remained on the ground, listening to Na telling her about herself. Na hated seeing other Black sisters being bullied, and she loved to put bullies in their place. Q pulled Na back by her shirt just in time before a kick to the face connected with the young lady's cranium. "Enough!" Q yelled at his sister again. Rob noticed what was going on, and the young lady was now picking herself up from off the ground, brushing the dirt off her clothes while standing next to her little ten-year-old son, who wished he was big enough to hit Na for hitting his mother. All she was trying to do was take a piece of the chicken wing to feed him.

Rob kept staring at the young lady because her face looked familiar. He slowly walked over to them, and the closer he got, the more he noticed it was someone he knew. "You gotta be fucking kidding me. Out of all places, this bitch appears!" Rob spoke with anger in his voice. His heart went from love to hatred for this person. Rodney was curious about who Rob was referring to, so he walked over to see for himself. When Rodney saw who it was, he stopped in his tracks and put his hand up to his forehead, spinning around as if he were going to walk back the other way. But he couldn't leave Rob alone with a temper of a killer. The last time Rodney saw that look on Rob's face was the last day Rob had his freedom, the night he saw his so-called baby mother out with his father before Rob killed him. And now, here his ex, Stacy, was right in front of their faces with a ten-year-old little boy.

"This little nigga mine, Stacy?" Rob said to her, pointing at her son. "This isn't your son, and his name is not 'little nigga.' His name is Rob." Now Rob was all messed up in the head, knowing she named another man's baby after him. He couldn't think of a good enough reason for why she did it. "Then why my name?" She

172

had fought with herself over the years, wondering if she would ever have to explain herself to him. But she had come to grips that if she did, then the father and the son should know who the child's kinfolk might be. "I named him Rob because I so much wanted you to be the father. But I was lost out there, having sex because of my selfish ways of needing different thrills of enjoyment by other men, and I ended up pregnant." She paused and took a big swallow before she spoke again. "My son Rob here is the son of the man you killed." She cried, and the little boy began to cry with his mother as well. "Rodney, my son here is your brother," she explained.

Rodney and Rob stood there speechless, trying to process this information. Rodney took a good look at his little brother and could see the family resemblance. Rob, on the other hand, was still mad that Stacy was still in his presence. He noticed she was looking at Rodney admiring his little brother. He rolled his eyes at her, thinking she was all types of bitches back then and now. Rodney reached out for his little brother to come give him a hug. "Rob, this here is my little brother just as you are. So I need you to accept who he is to us, no matter who his mother or his father is. We, as men, have to learn to put some of our differences aside when it comes to caring for our youth or a life-or-death situation," Rodney said, hoping Rob would see the bigger picture. Rob shook his head, understanding what Rodney was saying, but it didn't stop the fact he would be fighting the demon within himself to try and find forgiveness in his heart for Stacy.

"Ladies, if you have children and the father to your child takes care of his kids than what I'm about to say doesn't concern you. Now for the ones whose father hasn't been there for their seed, and you can say within your heart that you didn't run him away with your anger of not having your own selfish ways with him for whatever reason that may be. Now if that's not you and the man is just a no good for nothing Nigga than he should be shunned among us and that goes for the woman as well that refuse the man from being able to raise his child do to her own issues. But I need for every woman to find in her heart time to raise a Black child that didn't come from in between her legs as if it were your own." Rodney finished what he had to say to the women and then walked over to Q. "You and your sister come with us." Rodney tells him as he walks away from them. "Aja, I need you and the women to gather the children up and all the girls and little boys under 12 must stay close to your hips. My son Little A. and my Little brother Rob here will lead the kids with his drum down by the riverside while us men will need our young teenage boys to come right up front, so they don't miss out on how to be an Alpha male." When Rodney finished talking Little A. tugged on his robe once again. "I'm sorry, but I'm still hungry." Little A. said as his stomach was growling to confirm that it was so.

Rodney quickly snapped out of his thoughts and focused on finding Little A. something to eat. A mid age Black man that practices the knowledge of the Five Percenters walks over to Little A. and Rodney. "Peace God, I hear that Little man here is hungry." Little A's face said that the man couldn't be anymore correct. "Black Monk, I made some of that Tuna Bonna and he sure is welcome to have the rest of what I've made. "Little man your, in for a big treat and I know you never had this before." The man said to Little A. and Rodney because you're not getting any Tuna Bonna unless you been locked up or someone who has been and came home and shared the recipe. The Tuna Bonna was about the only decent food that most of them had eaten being as though most of them only had bags full of Commissary, but their biggest problem was the lack of water and many of them were passing out or even dying over not having any at all. After Little A. slopped down his food, he was getting bored and began to play by himself with make believe objects chasing him, so he was running around like a kid on a sugar high. Just as he ran past Rodney one too many times, he became fed up with his energy and quicky grabbed Little A. to stop him. "Hey Son, I think you need to chill because you're going to need that energy for some more walking, we have long travels ahead of us." Little A. started to cry because he was just a kid alone with a bunch of grown people who seemed like all they wanted to do all day to pass time is by smoking, drinking or having sex or talk grow folks' business and here he was just trying to stay

175

sane wishing it were other kids around to play with now. "Hey why not go and get your drum and play it." Rodney said to Little A. Little A. went and got his drum and dipped off sadly a few blocks away at a state park called the Brandywine. He sat on a rock and beat that drum the way Rob showed him. He was loving the scenery of the water running down its path making its way to the Delaware river. He loved the sound that the drum made while beating it by the running water, it was like the beat was bouncing off the rocks and the water was like a pair of Tweeter's speakers that makes your system in your car sounding just right.

Chapter 15

Master Minds

"Yo! Round up the crew J.R. and Zigg and Black Boy, tell them Rock said to get here fast!" Rock said to the young boy Dizzy. Rock was short dark and baldheaded standing in the middle of an Alleyway that smelled like human piss and a faint of human shit from a homeless person that used the place like it was his own privet bathroom. It was dried up Condoms and empty broken beer bottles and trash of paper all over the ground, but it was Rocks place of safety and the place that he thought for sure a White person wouldn't want to be useless they were in town to buy some Dope. Dizzy and J.R. and Rock, Black Boy and Zigg had been childhood friends and now they have come together to hopefully survive together through this war on the Black race. Black Boy walks into the Alleyway wearing a black pair of jeans no shirt and a Pittsburg Pirate hat, tilted slightly to the side. Zigg is six foot, light skin with light brown eyes and his hair was a sandy brown color. He had on a black Jogger sweatsuit with a green stripe going down the side of the pants and J.R. came in seconds later with a pair of Dicky pants and a white T- shirt and his gold Chain hanging from his neck with a charm repping his name on it. Dizzy was just as hood as J.R. and Black Boy but Dizzy was younger and different, he dressed like he didn't give a fuck. His clothes were always wrinkled, and it didn't much matter to him if his clothes matched or not. He had on a pair of Van sneakers that were worn out on the sides of them and his pants were skinny, ripped in its fashion and his shirt was buttoned up to his neck with his hair being Nappy as Fuck. Rock had on a pair of dark blue jeans and a black T-shirt that had a print of 2 Pac smoking a blunt on the front of it. He also had on a pair of ran down "Butter's" Timberland boots that were untied, making sure he had enough room in his boot just in case he needed to tuck away his small handheld 22 pistol.

"Yo Dizzy do you have enough plastic at your crib for that 3-D printer of yours?" Rock asked. Dizzy is a master when it comes to the 3-D printing shit. While others went to college he went out and stole one from out of this person's house and self-taught himself how to use it until he was forced to take classes, on new versions that comes out every so often. "Sure, I do, you know how I get down, why, what's up?" Dizzy asked while placing a Black and Mild cigarette in his mouth. Rock had gotten word that the Black men that felt it was nothing else to do but fight back if they wanted to stay alive had come to grips with the fact that they were being out match when it came down to the gun play, being as though the White People have had much more skills at shooting let alone they had all types of guns and different types of artillery, the main thing was that they had all the Amio. "Look I need you to start making some of them ghost Guns and bullets for us with that 3-D printer, what if you run out of plastic?" Rock asked the question while they all were locked in listening. "It's never going to be a problem, shit it's more than one way to skin a Cat. All we need to do is, if at any time we see anything in the streets that's plastic just grab it and bring it to me and you'll see how I get down for sure." Dizzy said sounding so excited. "Great! Now as for you J.R. now is the time for you to round up your boy's and pull out them RC cars and let's make things happen." J.R. was confused to why the RC cars. "Why the cars? Rock." J.R. asked with the look on his face that was asking for answers. "When the time is right, I'll tell you what and when I'll need you, but in the meantime, I need you to stay close." Rock said and then looked at Zigg and Black boy. "Zigg you already know what I need from you, and as for you Black Boy, I need you to grab up your people that are Black, that went to that school where you learned how to fly them fucking Drone's." Black Boy was cool, so he didn't say a word he just sat back and listened to Rock trying to put together in his mind what and how they were going to plan things out and make it all come together. "What about you, Rock?" Black Boy asked. Rock and Black Boy was the oldest two of the crew and to Black Boy, Rock seemed to believe that he is the smartest of the two and for the most part he was the well diverse of the two, he was very street savvy, and he had a few years of college under his belt. "I got my part." J.R. said. "And that is?" Black questioned back. J.R. smiled to himself on the inside other than revealing a smile on the outside due to the fact this wasn't a laughing matter. "I can show you better than I can tell you, now look I have to go and grab the things I need, and when the time comes, I'm going to call ya'll out by our street call, so when you hear me say "A Yo!" then you know it's me and as soon as the time is right then we take action, oh Zigg make me happy baby." J.R. said while exiting out the alley with his boys following his lead. Zigg was the last one walking out knowing what Rock was asking of him to do without him having too. Being as though Zigg had gone to collage as a Chemist major Rock knew that Zigg is the type that is capable of killing someone silently.

 Later that evening the crew and many others hand come together in a basement of an abandon building. They had gas RC cars and fireworks of all types of explosive and trash bags of recycling plastic and plastic Bullets thanks to the young boy Dizzy. Inventory of Drome's, boxes of them and a plastic body suit for Zigg when he puts together his work that deals with the chemical Strychnine and his concoctions. Zigg was sitting on a rusty pipe at the back wall cutting Bamboo sticks seven inchs long with Duct Tape, a few Ice trays and an ice freezer that was built portable with the capabilities to be re-chargeable. It was about thirty or more Manhole covers placed on the ground along the wall and some of them were being used for the time being to sit down on them to put together their work. Rock stood at the bottom of the steps with his hand under his chin in think mode feeling good about his plan.

The Poor and Middle-class White People in this Country had been killing and dying for the rich White folks, they've become their protectors without even knowing it. Many of them were being killed by those so-called Thug's, but they were just Black people whose backs were up against the wall and had no other chose of the matter. This moment in time was not a laughing matter but as for the White men that had a killer's mind set were laughing among themselves at the thought of any Black person trying to defend themselves because in their eye's the Blacks were in a different class when it came down to War, but many of those White men, women and children who've gotten killed were causing the living White People to end up on their knees in tears of rage and evilness was written on their face's and resting on their hearts, payback was a must on anything that looked black, moved black was to be removed from the face of this earth was their mission until it was completed. The inner city all over this country had dead bodies of Black and White and some Hispanic people lying all over the streets and even though most of those people were Black, it didn't stop the White men from still killing anything looking anything other than white, so every Foreigner who wasn't American born got on the next flight smoking before they all became on shut down and leave us here alone looking foolish. The Chinese were the only ones who were making sure that they were the last to leave and most of them didn't, they stayed back hoping the Blacks would give in so they could keep taking their money, and until the U.S.

Governments dept to them is paid up. They sat back drinking their Tea's watching us fight each other, while plotting at the same time. There are two types of people who were caught up in the middle of this disaster. First you have the Hispanic who some can pass for being White, and some can pass for being Black. The one's who looked Black were being killed or running for their lives' the same as the Black people from this country. Next you have the Biracial children who's hurting more from this than any White or Black person that dwell in this land called America. They're so angry and confused but like most of them when the time comes to encounter with a mad man with a gun pointing at them weather, he is White or Black they would choose sides of race depending on what race was coming at them with the life-or-death matter presented them.

In the hills and the valley's where the rich White People are living their ideal life, having their dinner like clockwork between the times of 5 and 6 and while they were doing so it were men lurking behind there sheds and Garages, big fat tree's or trash cans, but most of them waited in the woods around the housing area if they had any, some slid under parked cars lurking into their windows watching their ever movement until all lights went out in the house. The bunch of men and women that was ready to attack these White People's homes were dressed in all Black Ninja gear. They were some Thugs who wanted what those White folks have, the house the car, the land and their lifestyle. Late, late, night all the White

People had eaten and gotten full and most of the time they went to bed before midnight and by then a spirit in the air felt strange to the people in the Black Ninja gear. By three in the morning all the lights were out in their houses and the Thugs came prepared for the things that could possibly get in their way.

For the dogs that were doing its job, whether it be outside or indoors the Thugs knew that the White People trained their dogs to be nice and they love treats, so these Thugs baked doggie treats, Cookies with a little bit of poison in it. They dropped the Cookies on the ground like the Slave's did with their homemade Hush Puppies treats back in the times of Slaver. Noticing were their dogs liked to hang out they placed them down and with the ingredients in it their dogs couldn't and didn't refuse from eating it. The Thugs mission was to hang two White bodies from their trees in their front lawns and their backyards or down the street swinging from whatever they were strong up to, it was whatever as long as it was payback for all the Black people who had been wrongfully killed by a White cops or by any raciest White person and Zinmer.... is number one on the list. Doors were kicked in depending on what type of Thug intruded into the house, some were master lock pickers, and that's how they made their way in and then you have the one's that could cut glass without making a sound by a special Dimond bit. White men, women and child have been snatched out of their homes and hurtful to say they were hung, the way the

Thugs planned it to be. In the morning just before work the Dew was thick outside and for the White People's homes who hadn't gotten bombarded got up to go to work or if it were the weekend, whatever day it was on the Upper Cholent White folks witnessed what was called "The Modern Day of the New Strange Fruit." Their bodies were hung but nothing as ruthless as they did to the Black people's ancestor here in this country, but you could bet your last dollar that their pockets were empty.

Now that these Thugs were happy to get some get back, they sat back in a distance smoking on a blunt or sipping on their Yack the more they got high and the more they kept seeing the spiritual images of those Black men who they were revenging their death for. Amadou Diollo, Aiyana Jones, Rekia Boyd, Dontre Hamilton, Eric Graner, John Crawford, John Edwards, Maueal Elis, Geoge Floyd, Travon Martin and all the other's that wasn't mentioned. They became really freaked out when the face of Emitt Till and all their other ancestor that had been beaten, burned and brutalize. The horror of seeing this made some of them believe that Rodney's movement was for sure the way to go, so some of those Thug's had a conscience within them that made them leave right away to go seek Rodney. "Man, how we going to find Rodney?" one of the Thugs asked the other. "Follow me." The Thugs saw the vision of Harrat Tubman AKA "Moses" appear. "Follow me," she spoke to them in a very faint voice, and doing as they were told and just before she vanished, she said to them. "Listen for the sound of the drum." The Thugs went on with a keen ear listen out for that drum while the other Thug's moved on to continue their mission. Rich White People were crying out on their front lawns daily and they wanted this to stop at all cause but talking to the other White People who had their minds made up that they would rather die before giving in, they decided to take it to another level.

"Ayo, ayo!" Rock shouted to let his boys know it was going down. On top of apartments and project buildings around the city, at least ten young men stood on the roofs, waiting for the right time to execute their plan. Rock looked out the window, scoping out the street, noticing a cop sitting in his car eyeing the block. Rock went out the backdoor, sliding along the side of the building. He peered to see what the cop was doing from a shorter distance. He reached into the back of his pants, pulled out his gun, and walked up to the cop car.

"Get the fuck out of the car, slowly!" Rock ordered the cop, who had just pissed himself. Shaking like a leaf, the officer raised his hands in the air.

"Please don't shoot, I'm trying to get home to my wife and kids," the officer said.

Rock didn't care about that. "Get on the fucking CB and tell your boys shots are fired at this address. Tell them you've been shot."

The officer looked at Rock in disbelief, stuttering his words. "I don't know what you mean; there haven't been any shootings here."

Rock looked at the cop like he had to be the dumbest motherfucker he had ever met. "Pop! Pop!" Rock fired a few rounds into the street a few feet away from them. "What's that?" Rock asked, pressing the gun to the cop's head.

"Shots fired! I've been hit!" the officer radioed into the station, and just as Rock thought, the call was made. Now, here they came, racing their cop cars down the street, zipping by every block and running every traffic light.

"Thanks," Rock said to the officer before pulling the trigger. "Blap!" The gun went off, leaving the officer's face kissing his steering wheel.

"Here they come," Black Boy said to Rock, showing him what the drone saw coming their way. The cops came down the street about sixty deep. The street had one way going north and the other south, with parked cars on both sides. When the first group of cops arrived, they got out of their cars with guns drawn, watching their own backs and their fellow officers because the scene seemed deserted except for the dead cop in his car. They walked around, looking for any person to serve their justice. About ten officers walked around the building, confused and scared.

186

"Bomb! Bomb! Bomb! And more bombs!" The loudest sound of those manhole covers came down on top of many cops' heads and their cars. Those who weren't hit went deaf in their ears, their bodies pausing for a few minutes.

"Aww!" was the cry of many of those poor cops. Blood and dead bodies surrounded them while the young thugs on the roof looked down, wanting to drop more on them to finish them off. But they had to stick to the plan and save the other manhole covers for the next set of cops, so they waited patiently. The sound was so loud it echoed through the streets, causing more cops to arrive on the scene. When they arrived, their cars couldn't stop fast enough before they got out, guns aimed at the thugs on the roof.

"It's time now," Rock said to Black Boy with a smile, extending his hand for a dap. Black gave his boys the signal. Drones zipped towards the cops, confronting their faces. Before the cops realized the drones were armed with guns, it was too late. "Pop! Pop! Pop!" and more pops were the sounds of the drones shooting at the cops. The cops tried shooting down the drones, but Black Boy maneuvered them, ensuring that if a cop missed, the drone would hit one of their own men. James Snow and his peeps, Jimmy Dollars, kept sticking their heads out of the sewers with their hoodies covering their heads, firing rounds at the cops.

"Let's get out of here!" a cop yelled, fearing for his life. Most got back in their cars and tried to drive off while Rock and Black Boy leaned against a car, legs crossed, enjoying the scene. Cop cars backed out quickly, driving on sidewalks and taking out anything in their way. The officers who didn't make it back to their cars ran as fast as they could, but it was a lost cause. J.R. and his clique sent out their RC cars with bottle rocket bombs and other explosives attached. The sound of those RC cars was like a fast-humming noise, grabbing the cops' attention. The RC cars zipped under the cop cars, crashed, and then blew up, causing the cop cars and others to catch fire. Many burned up while the ones trying to get away couldn't see where they were running due to the thick black smoke the RC gas cars produced. Gunshots went off like a party in Chinatown. Some young black youths, hoodied up, quickly appeared and, at close range, started killing more police officers in cold blood.

Officers of the law were being ambushed, and the sight made many of the black youth feel like they had gotten some much-needed payback. While all this was taking place, Zigg got his gear together, locking eyes on his first victim. He placed a dart into his bamboo blow dart gun, which shot out ice darts filled with strychnine poison. Anyone hit by it would slowly lose their breath and drop dead minutes later. Zigg emptied three ice trays of darts, smiling at his work of art. He gathered his things into his army duffle bag, zipped it up, slung it over his shoulder, and slowly walked off with a cool man's strut.

A few police officers got away, and Rock and his boys knew it. They were okay with it because no man could erase what they had been through from their minds. The thought of the cops living with that for the rest of their lives sat well in their stomachs. Rock and his boys stuck around, feeling like they had just beaten the cops. The mindset of "I wish a nigga would" took over them as they kicked back, knowing it wasn't over. They shrugged their shoulders at that thought, ready for whatever came next.

"Yo, go to the China man and grab me some chicken wings and fries please, I'm hungry after all this killing, shit making me feel like I need to put something on my gut." Rock said to Black Boy who was feeling the same way. The cops were mad at the fact that they had to retreat and now wanted to show their might by fighting back with sending those young Black Thugs a message later that night by sending Bombs by Helicopter's dropping them down on their homes like they did the Move people in Philadelphia in 1985. Every single one of Rocks crew were killed except for Black Boy who went off to go to the Chinese store to get some food with two other men. It was a struggle for Black boy to make it where Rodney was, but by the grace of God it didn't take long.

****

Back at the spot where Rodney and his followers were preparing to move south, Rodney walked off for a little while to chill out alone and think. It struck him as ironic that they were all heading towards the south when the slaves of his forefathers had run north for their so-called freedom. Some of the men were standing around shooting the breeze, joking, and laughing. One of the men noticed some movement coming in their direction, and a few of them stood up, ready to fight the approaching group until they realized the men were wearing the same gear they had on.

"Oh shit! Look, it's Flip, MoJo, and young boy Benny," said one of the men who stood up. Some of the men weren't too thrilled about some of them coming back, given they had already jumped ship once. However, they knew Rodney would check their hearts to see if they were sincere.

"My young boy Benny, are you and the ones with you okay? Do you need any medical help? Or is there anything we can do for y'all?" the man asked young boy Benny, who looked as if he had seen a ghost. "I saw dead people," young Benny told the man, throwing the older man for a loop.

"What do you mean? I mean, there are dead people all over the place." Benny, still in a daze, responded, "I mean, I saw dead people that we all know or heard of before." Benny went on to describe witnessing images of Black people who had been lynched or shot by White People from the past and present. The images were so numerous that they were seared into his brain.

The older man whispered to the man standing next to him, who had heard the same thing, "Go and find Rodney and tell him what we just heard." The young man ran off to find Rodney, who was picking herb buds and placing them in his bag while listening to the message. Rodney started moving faster, sensing urgency because he knew those young men Benny referred to had on the same clothes as his crew, and the White People would likely think they were behind it all.

"We have to go now! Those young men's actions are going to bring white folks here looking for them and us. You know no Black man gets away with killing white folks. We're not O.J., and Johnny's dead." Rodney threw his backpack over his shoulders and quickly gathered his other belongings. "Moving out!" he called to everyone. "Aja, I need you to stay behind us. If we get into trouble and end up separated, take the kids and the women and meet us at the designated spot, listening for the sound of those drums being played."

As the men were leaving the city, Snow and Dollar were making their way out of a sewer a few blocks from where they originally went in. They emerged right as Rodney and his followers were heading towards the Christina River, using the edges of the riverbanks to find a new hiding place. Once the riverbanks ended, the men stopped to rest at the borderline of lower Delaware and Maryland.

The Black men and women from Delaware looked around nervously, expecting danger to come out of the woods. Anyone not from Delaware noticed their anxious glances. "What's up, my brother?" asked a man from P.A. Another from N.Y. stood next to him, also curious.

"Man, we're about to hit these woods back along the way in Elkton, Maryland. If you think we're in Klan territory now, wait until we head down the road to Rising Sun," said an elderly man who stepped into the conversation.

"Look, son, I don't think I can handle that shit, my nigga. I'm not built for this. I mean, I'd die first, son," said the young man from New York.

A few people turned and looked at Black Boy, who started throwing up his Chinese food and couldn't stop. Embarrassed by the smell from soiling his pants, he slumped over, holding his gut. "Awww, fuck," Black Boy said, feeling like he would vomit even more despite wondering what his stomach had left.

He began sweating profusely, worrying the men watching him. "You good, young blood?" Rob asked, handing him some water that someone passed to him. Rodney walked over to see what was happening. "Humm," he said, and Rob noticed.

"What's up, Monk?" Rob asked Rodney. "Chin spoke of this, and if I remember correctly, he said this would happen all over the country to people who eat their food, especially the meat." Rob thought to himself, "That's why I don't eat that ish."

"Black Boy, can you make it? We have to go now," Rodney asked. Black stood up as best he could, convincing himself he could move along. Rodney, all the men, women, and a handful of children had to move at night, taking baby steps along the way. Going through Elkton, Maryland, and sneaking through Rising Sun, Maryland, they faced nothing but Klan members and Trump supporters who happened to hate Black people.

Many Black people from the area or passing through had already been killed, and their bodies were left to be eaten by buzzards, malnourished dogs, and flies, leaving maggots behind. The smell of those dead bodies would be embedded in the lingering air for eternity. Rodney started noticing that it wasn't just Black people being killed; there was a young White male hanging from a tree, with a Black person—couldn't tell if it was a man or a woman— swinging right beside him.

"Yo Rodney, what do you think the deal is with the Black and White bodies hanging next to each other?" Rob asked.

"I'm not sure, but I bet the message being sent here is that this town doesn't take kindly to Blacks and Whites getting along," Rodney replied.

Rob thought about that for a second. "Seems like you're talking about the whole fucking country in general."

Rodney replied, "We can't stop here for too long because these White boys around here love to play in the woods at night. We must keep it moving until we get close to Silver Spring, Maryland. The next spot after that will be B-More and then D.C."

Tagging along the way, they started to notice an old run-down house off to the side, alone, missing two pieces of wood that were once attached to it, leaving the small house to welcome birds, squirrels, and whatever else wanted in. Some of the kids were curious about what the inside of the house looked like. They walked over to it and entered the house. The only thing left in the house were five orange buckets stuck together in the corner. The buckets looked new, and just for the sake of taking something, one of the kids decided to take them.

"Man, why are you taking that shit?" one of the kids asked the boy who was gathering the buckets.

The kid really didn't know why but he replied, "I don't know, maybe someone would need to carry something in it."

They all walked out of the small house that was now the wildlife's home. Little A. was looking around and could see that the men and women's minds had become stressed; it was written all over their faces. He stepped out of the crowd of people and started beating his drum the way Rob taught him. The people were moving a little better, but their spirits still seemed down. It was like a DJ playing music at a party, but the playlist wasn't making the party jump. A kid from New York was bobbing his head to Little A.'s drumbeat. He looked around to find the boy who had gone into the old run-down house with him and grabbed a few of those buckets.

"Yo! Come here for a sec," he said to the boy with the buckets.

The boy stopped and looked at him. "You were right, I need them," he said, taking the buckets from the boy, who didn't care as long as they were being used and taken off his hands. The young man from N.Y. had a number 2 pencil and an ink pen in his back pocket. He pulled them out, stepped out of the crowd, and walked back over to stand beside Little A., holding his hand out for Little A. to stop moving for a second to let the men and women keep going. He placed the bucket on the ground and then used his pen and pencil to start beating the buckets the same way he would back home in Times Square, earning some spare change.

The men and women, especially the elderly, smiled and walked much faster. A teenage boy from Philly, who also played buckets on late nights on South Street, came over to join in. He wanted everyone to hear him as well, but he didn't have anything to use to beat on the buckets, and it was eating at him. He smiled when he saw a tree a few feet away. He quickly walked over to it, searched for a limb or two, broke off a branch into two pieces, and removed the excess bark. He ran over to Little A. and the boy from N.Y., stood in front of them, holding his two twigs in his hand.

The boy from N.Y. was now sitting on a bucket while playing another. He was so good at it that he stood up, took out another bucket from under him, and handed it to the boy from Philly without missing a beat, causing the people to move in better harmony. A couple of kids who were capable of doing the same thing wanted to partake, so some of them started to pat their hands on their knees to the beat. Now all five buckets and Little A.'s drum were going to work, and those young men felt the love from the people enjoying what they were doing for them.

Three of the young men ran to the front of the crowd and led them with their beat, while three others went to the back and did the same. Little A. stayed in the middle of the crowd, beating his drum so they could feel the bass it was giving off. This made the walk to D.C. much easier and faster for them. Black paused for a second with sweat dripping down his face. His body went limp, and he fell hard to the ground. Everyone stopped what they were doing to see what was going on with Black.

196

"We need help! Fast, we have a man down," a man yelled out. Rodney, Rob, Aja, and Winker came over to Black to have a look at him.

"Don't look good for him. He has that white shit coming out of his mouth," Winker said.

Rob, standing beside her, had seen many Kung Fu flicks on TV to know that to be true. Black's body wouldn't move, and his eyes looked dilated. Winker checked his wrist for a pulse. Everything had stopped working in Black's body. Winker turned and looked at Rodney. "He's no longer with us."

Everyone who stood around went into tears, killing the happy vibes that once surrounded them. People stood around wondering why this man died so young and from what. Rodney stood over Black's body, hand on his chin, thinking about why and how. He closed his eyes, took a deep breath, and then slowly exhaled. After five long minutes of meditation, he opened his eyes and spoke.

"It's happening all over the country. Black people are dying from eating the China man's food."

The people around started shaking their heads at the thought. "Man, first it was the White man, now we got to worry about those slanted-eye motherfuckers," a man said angrily.

The closer Rodney and his followers went down south, the more they walked towards the belly of the beast. The south was brought up with racism and heartless killings of the Black race, causing the spirits of the old to linger in the air while the present moment was taking a page out of the old good book of Revelation. Rob couldn't take it any longer seeing everyone down when only a half-hour ago they were in great spirits, despite the harsh war going on.

"Yo! I know this young man died, and many of you are sad, but let's stop with the old tradition of crying over death when we should actually be partying for his homecoming to the Most High God. Can you dig it? Yo! The way I see it is, the young man is blessed right now, and we should understand that. Now let's all get up and change the vibes! Yeah, mon," Rob said and then gave Little A. a look and a nod toward the drum to signal him to get back to beating on it. One by one, they all got up and started partying, enjoying themselves the best way they knew how all over again.

Many of the men and women made some jailhouse wine that they set aside for a special moment, and now the time had come. The ones that smoked didn't need a reason because they understood that the herb is for good vibes, so smoking took place almost twenty-four-seven. They all celebrated until most of them passed out from partying too much. Little A. and the kids who were beating the buckets never went to sleep.

"These old heads can't hang," a young boy said to another kid standing next to him.

As morning arrived, they could hear hound dogs barking and heading in their direction. Jam Master Jay's spirit was in the atmosphere, with an image of himself standing in an Adidas track suit and his famous black derby resting on his head. "Run, run, run, run!" people were saying when they noticed who he was and what his sudden appearance meant. Many of them got the message and started to run so those bloodhounds wouldn't get them.

"Pow! Pow!" "Yee-haw!" were the sounds of guns being shot into the air by a mob of drunken White Men running towards them. After running for a while, a few men stopped, causing some of the others to do the same and wonder why.

"When are we going to stop running and start fighting back, Monk?" asked a man who looked to be in his early twenties. He was young and now feeling like a sucker because he felt that all his mother had told him about running away from his problems wasn't the answer. "Is running the answer, Monk?" the boy asked Rodney.

Rodney could see that everyone was getting tired of running. "There will be a time when all the hand-to-hand combat I have taught you will be needed. If we choose to fight now, the women and the kids will be subjected to the same, and I'm trying to prevent that at all costs. Right now is no different than when our ancestors who didn't commit suicide coming over on those slave ships because they understood that if you are alive, you still have a chance to procreate life for a better tomorrow."

"Bap! tap! Bap, bap tap!" Was a faint sound not too far from where Little A. was standing. He started to listen carefully to where the sound was coming from. He looked around to see if the other young men who was beating on the Buckets without them knowing. When he noticed that they all were chilling making small talk amongst each other he knew then that it was coming from somewhere else nearby. Little A. walked about ten yards to his left where he looked down a hill where he could hear the sound more clearer coming from that direction. He started to walk down the hill by himself. He wasn't afraid because he was smart enough to know that the sound of the beat came from some people who had soul, so he figured that they had to be of the Black race whoever it was.

"Yo A, where you think you're going all by yourself?" Rob asked. Little A. kept walking down the hill. "Come, I hear someone playing a drum like mine." Little A. said while Rob followed behind him. Just as they reach the bottom of the hill Little A. noticed some kids get up and start running from them because they weren't sure if they were friend or foe. As the kids tried to get away, they looked back at little A. to see if they lost him, or he was coming after them while they pleaded in their hearts that he didn't. Rob cut them off before they could get away and snatched one of the boys up by the back of his shirt. "Get the fuck off me!" the boy shouted out. Rob looked around to see where the boys were trying to run off to and he noticed an old Park Ranger Hut that looked as if it hadn't been used over a hundred years. He looked at the kid and noticed the kid looking over in that direction. "Cool out kid, you in good hands." Rob told the kid hoping that he would chill the fuck out. Once the other kids that were trying to run noticed that they weren't being taking away that maybe Rob and Little A. were ok.

"Why are you two here?" one of the kids asked Rob and little A. Little A. answered back with. "I heard the drum you guys were playing and I came to see who it was." The kids didn't think that they were playing to load for anyone to hear them and they were wrong because in this present time there living in now Little A. could hear the sound of a Drum a mile away. "You guys need to be careful because the Snatcher's are out looking for us and if they see you, they'll snatch you up to." The boy said to Rob and Little A. "Who's the Snatchers?" Rob asked. "It's a midsize White man and a tall Black man. The Black man snatched me up and brought me here in these woods and took us to this place here to meet up here with this White man." Rob thought that to be strange being as though Whites and blacks are killing each other now. "How long ago did this take place because for a few months now Blacks have been killing Whites and vice versa." The kid didn't hesitate to say "I was snatched up a week ago, and I know about what's going on outside these woods but Mr. I think it's something bad happing down here in these woods. Me and" he points at the other two kids that was with him. "We got away before we were locked in that shed over there." The boy points to the shed that was about 50 yards away. "We came back here spying on what we could see." Rob asked the boy "What did you see?" the little boy said. "We saw a Nigga and a Cracker exchange money while locking the door behind them leaving in different direction." Rob looked at little A. "Go get Monk and tell him to come fast and to bring the old head Luther, he'll know who I'm talking about." Little A. ran off to do as he was told. When Rodney and Luther got word, they rushed down the hill until they noticed Rob and the kids. "What's going on?" Rodney asked Rob. "This young man here says that he was snatched and almost placed in that shed their but luckily these four got away somehow." Rodney was looking over at the shed, it looked very small and low to the ground almost only reveling most of its roof top. He walks over to it with Rob and Luther right behind him.

When they reached the shed, the first thing they noticed was a big padlock on the door. It was an old-fashioned padlock.

"Hey Luther, do you think you could pick this lock? I mean, I don't want to insult you by thinking that you couldn't," Rodney said.

"Well, don't then," Old Head Luther replied. "From the looks of the lock, it's very old, and the type of key it takes is that old-school antique type. I can pick it, but it could take all night, perhaps."

Rodney was wondering if it was worth sticking around for something he had no clue about inside the shed or if he should take the few boys with him and just keep moving. While they were standing there, they heard a noise coming from inside the shed, so Rob placed his ear up to the door and could faintly hear people crying out for what seemed to be help.

"It's people in there, alright," Rob said to Rodney.

Luther had a look on his face like he'd come up with something.

"What is it, Luther?" Rodney asked him.

"I'm looking at the lock, and I thought to myself, if the lock is on the door, how is it attached? Then I noticed that the lock's hinges are attached to the door by screws," he said while pointing at the lock. "If I can get these screws off, the lock will just drop to the ground."

The plan sounded like it was coming from a true pro.

"Well, what are you waiting for?" Rodney asked him.

Luther pulled out of his pocket his pick that he used to pick locks. It was flat on one end, just in case he had to unscrew something. He grabbed the rusty lock and went to stick the pick into the screw, and as he turned it, the screw caused the wood to crumble. This was a good thing, so he tried the other screws, and they did the same. He smiled.

"Hit the lock," Luther said to Rob, and Rob hit the lock hard, but it wasn't really necessary because it was so old that a little force would have sent it to the ground.

They opened the door and entered a small room that was pretty much empty except for some old rusty-looking tools in the far corner. The noise was sounding much louder to them now, as though they could tell that they were standing over top of it. It wasn't hard to notice the wooden door with a metal handle on it leading to something. Rob walked over to it and opened the door, and a foul smell hit his nose. It was so bad that he didn't even notice what was taking place behind that door.

Rodney and Luther got a whiff of the funky smell, but they knew they had to look past that, so they held their noses and peeked in, noticing young men and women, Black people, and their youth crying out for help, looking like they hadn't eaten in months.
204

Rodney and the others started to help the youth up out of the filth one by one. It was hard trying to help those who hadn't yet been washed up from lying around in their own urine and feces before they were sent off.

"Thank you! Thank you!" a young girl said on her knees in prayer form right at Rodney's feet.

"Where are you from?" Rodney asked her.

"I'm from D.C. Most of us in here are from D.C."

Rodney looked at all twenty of the captured youth and asked, "Who all is here from D.C.?"

Sadly, every single one of them but two raised their hands. These poor young teenagers, little boys, and girls had been snatched up for the purpose of sex trafficking. This place had been a holding spot for slaves in the past, and now, to this present day, it holds the unexplained 29,782 missing Black kids in D.C. and abroad.

"May God be the Glory," Rodney said, with tears coming down his face from the sad scene and knowing what was going to happen to them if he hadn't stumbled across them.

"How often is someone being brought here?" Rodney asked, looking for anyone to answer.

"A child or a teen comes every day, and whoever has been here the longest most likely will be leaving that day. So, when one comes in, one goes out. Straight like that," said one of the older teenagers in the group.

"How many miles is D.C. from here?" Rodney replied.

The young kid looked around him, and all he could see was woods, so he wasn't too sure of his whereabouts. "I have no clue where we are; we're in the middle of the woods. I take it maybe a little more than half an hour. I know that because I kept checking my watch for the time."

Rodney knew from the highway signs that he was at least 30 miles outside of D.C., but when you're on foot, it could seem much farther.

"O.K., well, everything is going to be closure, and we need to get out of here now before those kidnappers return," Rodney said, and then a thought came to his mind. "Didn't you say that one man was White and the other was Black?"

The young man nodded at him to confirm those words as facts.

"Pop! Pop!" were the sounds of two rounds being fired in the area where Rodney and all the youth were. The shots came from a White man wearing a trucker hat and a Confederate flag on his overall shirt, covering his fat belly and a pair of worn-down blue jeans being held up by black suspenders. Two of the youth were hit by the bullets, but luckily, none were dead—one was hit in the leg while the other young man was hit in the foot.

"Run!" Rodney said, taking off in the opposite direction, and everyone followed him until they felt out of harm's way for the meantime.

Chapter 16

KKK

No more than two miles away, Mason and his four friends were sitting around in his barn-type shed, drinking and smoking their choice of Marlboro cigarettes and old Michelob beer. Mason pulled his pack of smokes from under the shoulder part of his white T-shirt, smacked the bottom of the pack a few times, pulled one out, and placed it in his mouth. He then picked up his bottle of beer from off the card table that the five men surrounded, sitting down and talking shit to each other. Mason took a healthy swig of his beer and then let out a big hillbilly burp that was so loud it caused the other four men to start laughing at the way he cocked his lips to the corner of his mouth while making the burp erupt.

One of the men sitting at the table was a longtime friend of Mason named Joe. He was laughing so hard that he spit the mouthful of beer he had across the table. "Aww shit! Dude, what the fuck!" Mason said to Joe. Joe was getting himself together while wiping up his mess. "I'm sorry, brother, but you're a true fucking hillbilly, you fucking redneck." All the men were in laughter. "Fucking right I am!" Mason said with pride while pulling on his Confederate flag suspenders and kissing them.

"Say Mason, why'd you let off with those niggers? We could have killed a few, but instead, you held us back. Why?" said Ray, whose face went from laughter to serious, and Mason could see it written all over his face. Without any hesitation, Mason replied, "Those niggers? Oh, they headed in the direction of more of our brotherhood. The Klan is strong, and them niggers are heading down south, and the deeper they go, the more of those White Knights will hunt their souls as they witness with their eyes the massacres being done to their own kind. So I ask you, Ray, why should we have wasted our fucking bullets on running dead niggers?"

Ray wasn't trying to hear that shit, due to the fact that the only way he saw fit now was if you see a nigger, now you don't, because all niggers must die. Ray gave Mason a smirk as if to say, fuck that. "While you are letting them get away, those young thugged-out niggers are killing our sons and raping our women! My cousin David and a few of his friends were found in their homes murdered, their skin on their faces peeled off, and their eyeballs blasted out by a fucking hand power wash machine that they left behind. Their bodies were nailed to whatever they were next to at the time. It looked as if they were nailed down by being shot and hit with nails from fucking nail guns. To top it off, my family down in VA said it's happening all over the place, and it's starting to feel like these niggers are winning, even though I know they ain't. But killing one White person is an unforgiven threat." The men at the table were digesting his words with the desire to fetch revenge on a nigger. Mason knew what was going on in that aspect of the matter because he himself had been informed of the killings the Blacks were doing from his own cousins in Texas.

"So, what do you want me to do? If you wanted to kill them, then you should have done it yourself, and I wouldn't have faulted you. But don't fault me because I chose otherwise to do things my way." Mason said, hoping that his friends understood that he was down for the cause and that he wasn't starting to have a soft spot in his heart for the Black race. One of Ray's friends that was sitting at the table felt that was well said, so he held his beer mug high in the air with some of it pouring onto the table and started to sing his song that he came up with for his brothers to chime in. "Kill me a nigger and the White race will be richer, and thanks to us great White Americans, America is great again…. Thanks to me, I will kill a nigger, which means one less nigger. White power! White power!" He slowly went on with the song as the other four men were loving the lyrics and chimed in on parts they felt in sync with. They sang and sang, drank all they could, and buttered their noses with a little white powder, leaving them one by one drifting off to sleep from being so drunk and high.

Forty yards away from the shed were three Black males in the woods looking into the shed, noticing Mason and his friends dozing off. One faintly whistled to alert five other Black males in their early 50s. All eight of them stood hiding behind a tree and a parked old-school pickup truck that had a few things in the back of the flatbed. All together at once, they went snooping into the flatbed of the truck, finding a long rope, a few gas cans full of gasoline, chainsaws, shovels, and a green ten-gallon bucket with nails and a hammer resting on top of them.

"Yo, Man Man, grab that can," said Man Man's best friend Tuck while he grabbed two gas cans of his own. The other six men grabbed whatever they could out of that truck to defend themselves if need be. Tuck nodded at Man Man to follow him. Tuck slowly moved his frail body around the truck to get a better view of his plan. He slowly duck-walked as smoothly as he could, and Man Man mimicked him as he tagged along. It was easy for them to do so because their pants weren't hanging off their asses. The other six men crept over to them with shovels and hammers in their hands, and one had the chainsaw ready to go to work.

Man Man and Tuck began splattering gasoline onto the shed until they couldn't take the smell of the fumes any longer, and the entire shed looked like rain had hit it. All it took was for one to pull out a blunt to smoke, ready to get high, and then they all pulled out blunts from their pockets or from behind their ears, a joint or a pipe or some edibles. The green smoke that hovered over their heads became thick with a strong odor to it, and the wind was blowing the chow into the shed, causing the White men's noses to start to quiver. Mason started to wake up, and he could tell that someone around the area was smoking that good happy. He stood up from the table, causing the other men to become a bit startled, and they woke up as well. One said, "What's that smell?" Ray looked over at his friend and said to him, "Are you that dumb?"

Tuck was peeping through the doorway jam and snapped his fingers for the other brothers to know to step the fuck back. He took the last pull off his blunt and tossed it onto the shed, causing it to instantly go up in flames. The White men in the shed tried to make a break for the door but were met with the presence of hammers and shovels clobbering them upside their heads, causing them to remain put. "The roof, the roof, the roof is on fire! So let the motherfucker burn, burn motherfucker burn!" Tuck and the seven other Black men sang as they watched and listened to the screams of those White men burning to the ground with the shed tumbling down on top of them. "Let's roll out before we be the ones getting fried," Tuck said as he started to run away with the others following behind.

After Tuck and his friends were done taking a break by resting their overly worked feet, they faintly heard the sound of the drums being played by Little A and some others. They were told by other Blacks to listen out for the drummers and that D.C. go-go swing, as our forefathers were told to follow the North Star. During Tuck and his friends' journey, their lack of food and water was becoming their biggest problem, not just for them alone but for the Black race especially. Between the heat and real hunger kicking in, anyone who said or did one thing wrong was heightened in the eyes of the hungry Black man, causing mad confusion and total chaos.

"Tuck! Look, I see Black people. I guess listening out for the drumming was on point," Man Man said to Tuck as he walked towards Rodney and his followers, who were packing their things to move on. The party was over, and Rodney and Rob were standing aside, watching the humbleness in their people. They had just finished a conversation about how, despite the Black race being slaughtered by those who run the country, they were saving souls, and that was all that mattered. However, by doing so, the people who ran the country didn't like that crime numbers had gone down tenfold.

Tuck, Man Man, and their boys were out of breath, noticing everyone around them looked ready to move on. Rodney and Rob were leaning up against a big fat tree with their arms folded across their chests. Rob noticed some people coming towards them looking lost, so he tapped Rodney on his arm. "Look, Monk, I think we just got our wish. Looks like a good handful of them are coming our way right now." They smiled at the sight of Tuck and his friends. Tuck and his boys dropped to their knees, weeping tears of thankfulness that Rodney had forgiven them for their sins.

"Stand up with your heads held high, men," Rodney told them. The men did as they were told, and Rodney and Rob walked over to greet them. "Did you men see anything strange on your journey here?" Tuck spoke for his homies while trying to think. "Nah, I can't say other than how it seems so easy for men to rape another person, male or female. It seemed like the devil has taken over their flesh."

Just as Tuck finished talking, an older ex-inmate came up to Rodney and whispered in his ear. "Yo, the word on the street is that you can't even trust your own Black brother because they're out there fighting, shooting, and killing each other just as fast as the White men, if not more." Rodney's mind tapped into what the old man was saying, and he could envision everything the man was talking about, so tears of sorrow began tumbling down his cheeks. "Shit!" Rodney said in anger, and Rob looked at him in disbelief that he used another curse word.

"Tell me something I don't know. The Black people have never stopped killing each other, so what now? Because we are blatantly being attacked, are these niggas going to wake up? I wish, but the chances of that seem slim to none." Rob nodded his head at what Rodney was saying. "Monk, you're right on that, and you know

214

what I hate? I hate the fact that most of it is over money or bitches, and at the top of the list is the self-hate. It kills me that a Black man will kill another Black man on 'GP' General Purpose but will turn the cheek to a White man who has killed a Black man for no reason other than White superiority beliefs. I have to question myself at times and ask who do these niggas work for, or are they from their past life coming from those cotton fields not knowing any better of how to love themselves or the ones who look like them." Rob said as he thought to himself, Fire burn the wicked. Rob snapped his fingers at Rodney so that he wouldn't keep focusing on the horror story. "Monk! You good?"

Rodney snapped out of it, "Yeah, I'm good, my brother, but there's going to be a time when we'll be apart for a minute. This was just revealed to me by my third eye." Rodney said while walking away, and everyone followed along until they hit the streets of D.C. The city was deserted when they arrived, like a scene from an old western. The sound of Rodney, the inmates, and other Black people who tagged along had been heard miles away by residents, which let the President know that they were nearby.

Rodney and some of his crew slid over to the side, standing still, trying to figure out why and what was going on. Out of the blue, from every block, they were surrounded by the FBI. A blacked-out Suburban raced down the street that Rodney and Rob were posted on and came to a screeching halt. Rodney held his hand out for

Rob and some of the other Black men who weren't going to let anything happen to him or any other Black man. "Wait, this is what I was referring to. They want to talk to me; they're just going to try and play me, dumb me down, and hope I say yes, sir."

Two big White men jumped out of the truck, dressed in all black, with their guns out, ready to kill. They snatched Rodney up, and they couldn't believe he wasn't putting up a fight. It was almost as if he wanted them to kidnap him. When they grabbed him, it was with so much ease because Rodney made himself feel light as a feather. They threw him in the truck and drove him to the White House to meet the President.

When they arrived, the two guards got out of the truck and tried to manhandle Rodney, but by him being light as a feather, it made it impossible for them to do so. It felt like their arms had become weak. It sure wasn't like when Rodney hit the State Penn and he was digging his toes into the ground because of his fear. But not now; he walked up to the White House like he should be the rightful ruler of the place. The minute he walked into the building, he started to feel as if he was Benjamin Banneker himself.

They escorted Rodney to a room off to the side on the first floor, not too far from the main guest rooms. When they opened the door to the room, Rodney noticed how huge it was, his eyes widening as he saw five more White men standing in their positions protecting the President. Three of them stood around him while the other two had their hands full, with one looking out the window while the other stood outside the door. The President himself sat at a desk that was big and wide and made from Black Onyx.

"So, if it isn't Rodney," and he started to snap his fingers as if he had forgotten Rodney's last name. "My God! For Pete's sake, what is your last name?" Rodney looked at the President and said to him, "I have no one particular last name." The President looked at him with a little anger in his face, thinking Rodney was trying to be a wise ass. "How is that?" the President wanted to know. "Well, I have the last name of every Black man that your people have encountered at some point in time." The President smiled and leaned back in his chair, which was so big it made him look like he was sitting in a bird cage. "Oh, I get it. You mean like your people, the Johnsons, the Smiths, and the Williams. Is this what you're trying to tell me?"

Rodney knew that the President was trying to be sarcastic and was glad he asked that question. "Them too, as well as Abara, Abebe, Judah, and Ezra, and all the other last names of my race of people." The President looked at Rodney and became a little uneasy because he knew Rodney wasn't the Rodney of old; he had become an educated nigga of self, Public Enemy Number One. The President threw his files onto the table, opened them, and started pulling out pictures and paperwork on everything they knew about Rodney, now staring him in the face.

"So, we know just about everything we need to know about you. But what is it that you call yourself doing? And what's the reason for this foolishness? I mean, who the hell are you?" the President asked. "I am the son of God, and I'm here to lead my people to a place where they are safe." The President looked at Rodney as if he had said something wrong. "What do you mean, a safer place? There is no safer place than the United States of America, bra," the President said with a smirk on his face.

Rodney looked at the President as if he were the one who was crazy. "Black people here in this country are being killed by your law enforcement, and the guns and drugs all come hand in hand. It's funny to me that Blacks don't make guns or have the capability to bring in the mass of drugs that enter this country every minute of the hour, sir, but my race of people seems to fill your jails all across the country because of it." Rodney was ready to keep talking, but he had to at least give the President time to hopefully think and then respond.

The President uncrossed his legs and got up from the table to fix himself a half glass of brandy. "Okay, what is it that we can do to help you? Because all this no crime and taking a walk to this so-called safer place is hurting the country. We need more rebels out there killing like they do best so that we can make some more money off someone doing hard time in the State Penn. I mean, don't take it personal and disrespectful because it's all just about business."

Before Rodney replied, he wanted to have a seat. "May I?" he asked, pointing to the matching chair of the President. The President nodded, and Rodney sat down at the table, going into a deep trance-like state for a good three minutes. He snapped out of his train of thought, looked the President in the eye, and began to speak his mind.

"So, first things first, I would like to talk about how the game here in this country has been so one-sided, and this is why we are on a mission to do for ourselves and to live righteously in the eyes of the Most High God who looks like me." The President looked at Rodney as if he already knew that, and for those who don't know, they are still blinded by the facts of who they really are.

"Mr. President, from the times of our forefathers to this present time, the pay has been unfair when it comes to the race of people. Whites versus Blacks, paying the Blacks way less money on jobs, and to add salt to the wound, you hire your own kind whether his skill was credible or not. But his skin color alone stamped that he should be hired over any minority." The President was trying to fix his lips to chime in, but Rodney wasn't ready for his response, so he continued talking.

"You see, the Black man, woman, and child had all the skills to do hard labor in this country and were forced to do for ourselves. Then here comes White America taking the hard-working jobs and making their rules and regulations on what can and cannot be, pushing our race of people to believe that the ways of W.E.B. Du Bois, Booker T. Washington, and all the Black Boule ways are now the only way to make a good, honest living and establish one's self-worth. I didn't even talk about how one had to get degree after degree, which meant years of debt. We had to prove over and over again that we could play this game, even if it meant changing our tongue as far as our speech just so that one wouldn't pinpoint that they're of the Black race. Oh, let's not forget that many have not chosen the surnames of their forefathers who are Black for the hopes of a chance to work for a company that will only hire as many Blacks as one could count on their hands and feet just to seem that their company isn't racist, while Whites will be employed by the hundreds."

The President couldn't help himself from saying another word because the truth Rodney was speaking was tormenting his ears. "Enough of all that. My family and many other White families came over here and had to struggle just as hard as you Blacks. Look at them now and look at the Blacks here in America who have done well for themselves. Well, shit, if they can do it, so can the next Black man." The President gave Rodney a look as if to say, "What do you have to say now?" while stirring his ice cubes in his glass, waiting for Rodney to try and come up with some excuse for why the Black man can't get ahead in this country.

Rodney gave the President a little snicker and spoke his mind. "Mr. President, you are so right. We can, and we have been able to make it through this rough war over decades, and we've been moving at a rapid rate despite the circumstances of our setbacks from the storms that have been placed in front of us. But to me, Mr. President, I understand that I can't keep asking for you to change how you feel about our race of people. In the meantime, we want peace so that we can change the minds of our children who have lost their righteous morality to the ways of the Western world that the Pale man has been ruling for over three decades, led by the Catholic Pope."

"Whatever! Whatever! Look, what is it you want from us?" the President asked, his tone laced with disgust, clearly uninterested in continuing the conversation. Rodney thought to himself, why ask what we want and need when all he has to do is ask himself if he would trade his shoes for an average Black man's shoes here in America.

"Well, Mr. President, I would like to start by asking what it is we want in this present time, or are we talking about where me and mine are headed?" Rodney waited for a response. The President threw his hands up in the air and said, "We're in the present time, so let's talk." He took a sip of his drink while locking eyes with Rodney. Rodney quickly responded, "Okay. Given that our forefathers had their rights to education taken away and with today's youth not being taught proper education that can benefit their near future, I would ask for reparations of free education of any kind. Anyone who has paid for it in the past will be refunded with interest, and no taxes whatsoever. That's a start."

He paused for a second, staring at the smirk on the President's face, which seemed to say, "Nigga, please." "After all that's said and done, how about we break down every citizen to be economically equal—no man greater than another, and no more being superior over a woman other than her own will of submission. Another thing we would like is to take the land here in this country and divide it up, favoring the hot climate areas for us to control. But we'll rotate every so many years with you so that the sun doesn't kill you sooner." Again, the President gave him the same smirk, but his eyes showed that he disliked what he was hearing.

"Anything else?" the President said sarcastically. Rodney thought long and hard about whether there was anything else he wanted to say. There was much more he could have spoken on, but he knew that asking and complaining wouldn't move his mission any sooner. However, something came over his spirit, and he spoke his mind. "I don't like how every White person hates the fact that O.J. got off on a murder charge even though he was found not guilty. I guess you all see how the Black race has felt over the years when a White person kills a Black person and gets off knowing the person is guilty."

One of the President's bodyguards couldn't help himself from speaking, even though he wasn't supposed to meddle in other people's business. "That's because we all know he did it, and I don't give two shits about a glove not fitting. He did it, point blank!" The man was truly irate, causing his face to turn red and a bit of spit to dangle from his lip. Rodney waited a second for the man to compose himself a little better, so he could snag his attention as well as the President's and anyone else in the room.

"I can sadly say that we can all Google years of Black men being killed in this country by all types of racist organizations, such as the Klan, Skinheads, and many others who hate the Black man's skin color. The saddest part is that those doing the most are the ones we've been told would protect and serve the young Black youth, but the reality is that the young Black youth have been murdered in cold blood in the days of yesterday. The present time mimics yesterday's sorrows. And the end result of those lost souls equals White men getting off on murder due to some kind of foolish judgment, leaving generations of Black Americans hurting in their hearts from the loss of a loved one or the outcome of the verdict with all charges dropped, making the Black race question their place here in this country."

Rodney wanted to see if the President had anything to say, but he didn't. That didn't mean his thoughts weren't screaming, "A nigga should stay in his place." The President waved his hand quickly at Rodney to finish what else he had to say because he was fed up with Rodney not complying with what he thought would be best for the Black race in America: to stay dependent on them and learn new survival tactics among each other in this unfair playground called the U.S.A.

Rodney understood that talking and protesting with signs, marching up and down the streets, hooting and hollering wasn't going to change anything with people who would die before sharing their inheritance. He stood up from his chair, looked around, and thought to himself that there was one other thing he wanted to say before leaving the room. "Another thing, I don't like the way your courts or anyone who had something to do with Bill Cosby going to prison. Here is a man who had the image of what White people and many Blacks would say is a great role model for the Black race. But now, to kill his image and make him out to be this rapist in the eyes of the new generation of kids to come. What is it? Was it because he was trying to do too much with his money?

Or was it that you wanted some of his money, or was it truly to sabotage his image forever?" Rodney asked these questions softly, in a cool manner, waiting for the President to respond, but all he got was the President staring at the open doors to his office, indicating for Rodney to let himself out.

Rodney turned to walk out the door, feeling like nothing was going to change on their end, but he held his head high, believing in his own purpose and mission. The President opened his box of cigars that rested on the edge of his table. He held the cigar up to his nose and smelled it quickly right after he ripped the plastic off of it. "Oh wait, Rodney, and whatever your last name may be, I hope you grow two eyes in the back of your head." Rodney stopped and paused at the door without turning around to look at him. He laughed to himself on the inside and said to the President, "No need for that."

The President looked at him as if he didn't understand. "No need for what?" he questioned Rodney with a bit of attitude in his voice.

Rodney slowly started to walk away but not before having the last word. "You holding up your middle finger at me behind my back. That's what." He walked away, feeling the President's bodyguard breathing down his neck to make sure he didn't make a beeline back into the room to murder the President. They couldn't believe a man could be so divine and peaceful despite all that had been done to his race. But vengeance was not a thought in his imagination. He understood that love and the works of his father, Jah, meant that everything would manifest in the order of what's rightfully due to come to those of the humble and of the wicked of all men and women in this day and time.

Chapter 17

Still in DC

Rodney's journey to find his followers was a lonely and strenuous walk. He stopped about a mile from the sound of the drum that his ears had picked up. He paused to look around for any FBI, CIA, or anyone else he needed to be wary of, ensuring they wouldn't know where he was headed. He found it strange that none of his people were out there, ready to come get him, to protect him from the killers lurking in the woods and streets, ready to take a man's life. He thought about smoking a blunt, and just as he was fumbling in his pockets to retrieve his lighter and the Corn Husk prewrapped with his Happy in it, he suddenly heard a noise over his right shoulder. It sounded like an old metal trash can being kicked around. He turned to see if his ears were right, but all he could see was a building, the trees, and the grass surrounding it. Then, he began to hear a woman trying to scream something, but her words became muffled and muted soon after. Rodney stood there, feeling deep in his heart that something truly bad was happening, but the question of what lingered in his mind at that moment. "Stop!" was the word that escaped the troubled woman's mouth, sounding as if she was crying out for help. Rodney began to walk in that direction, and the closer he got to what his ears were hearing, he stopped in his tracks because one of the metal trash cans had been kicked in front of him, letting him know that some kind of ruckus was happening on the other side of the building.

"Help!" the woman cried out, desperate for anyone to rescue her from the devilish actions of two black males trying to silence her and prevent exposure of their wrongdoing. Rodney's instincts urged him to move faster to help this woman, not caring about the color of her skin, only that she was in need of his help. As he rounded the building and saw what was happening, his eyes widened in shock, much like the great Bernie Mac. He witnessed a middle-aged black male holding a knife to a young black woman's throat while forcing himself on her, bent over a rusty oil barrel. While one of the men was raping the young woman, the other was doing his best to cover her mouth. Rodney couldn't stand what he was seeing, and a fiery rage ignited in his heart. He started thinking about how to defuse the situation, determined to stop the rapist from ever harming anyone again.

As the rapist continued to force himself on the young woman, suddenly, due to Rodney's mind power, the man pulled out of her, stepping back to look down at his penis, which was slowly melting off his body. He frantically tried to stop his flesh from falling off and hitting the ground. "AaaaHhhhh!!!" he screamed, bewildered by what was happening.

Rodney seized the moment, leaping into the air and kicking the man in the ribs, causing the predator to buckle down to one knee. Wasting no time, Rodney attempted to gouge the man's eyes out, digging his two fingers into them. The rapist grabbed at his face, clutching Rodney's wrists as if trying to kill him with his bare hands. Just as Rodney freed his wrist from the man's grip, the other rapist sucker-punched Rodney in the jaw, sending him crashing to the ground. His head spun as if he had been twirled around a thousand times like a dreidel. The assailant, who had landed the punch, was confident that no one could withstand his right hook and was certain Rodney was down for the count before he even hit the ground.

The young man stepped over Rodney's dazed body, pulled out his dick, and began to give Rodney an unwanted golden shower. The other rapist gathered himself and started laughing at his partner's actions, especially at the thought of trying to take a shit on Rodney as soon as he could muster up a few drops. Rodney tried to say something, but he couldn't; all he could do was taste the salty urine on his lips.

"Tat! Tat!" A loud sound, like that of a .45 caliber gun, rang out. As quickly as the bullets fired, the two rapists' bodies hit the ground, their heads blown to pieces. Rodney struggled to clear his head and saw someone taking off their shirt and trying to hand it to him to wipe the dead man's piss off his face. "Rob?" Rodney questioned once he recognized who had come to take care of business.

"Wa Gwan! Rasta!" Rob said as he stood over one of the dead men, wanting to unload the clip into him some more, but knowing he had to save the remaining rounds for a greater cause.

"You have a gun? I thought I taught you how to use your bare hands to kill a man if you had to. Why the gun?" Rodney asked, trying to figure out how, when, and where Rob got the gun.

Without hesitation, Rob replied, "What the Blood Clot, Boy! They came to a fight with a little knife, and I, on the other hand, wanted them to know you don't bring a knife to a gunfight, so I used my machine to dead them Pussy Holes."

Rodney understood what Rob was saying, but the fact that he used a gun bothered him a bit. "Where'd you get the gun?"

Rob sucked his teeth at the question, but he had never lied to Rodney before and wasn't about to start now. "I picked one up along the way. I mean, all those people who've been living by the gun are now dead, lying all around, so I borrowed someone's for the time being."

Rodney just shook his head at Rob, and then they started to head back to where the others were camping out. As Rodney and Rob struggled up the hill, they thanked God when they finally reached the top, which felt like a hike in the mountains. The first two people they saw from the crew were Old Head Peg Leg and his friend Butchie. Rob started smiling from ear to ear at the sight of Old Man Peg Leg talking shit—everyone knew he was a true shit-talker.

"Peg, yo, you're crazy as fuck!" Butchie said, while the two men standing around, shooting the shit with them, joined in with laughter.

"Hey, Peg, you remember when that boy Scratch was messing with you? He came up wanting to try his luck at beating up a one-legged man. And as soon as he got within arm's reach, you snatched that right metal leg off your hip and smacked that poor man across the face. That's why they still call that Nigga Scratch now." Everyone laughed out loud.

"What's so funny? I want to laugh too," Rodney said as he and Rob approached the group.

"We're just talking about this crazy Nigga right here," Butchie said, pointing at Peg. "Check it, this Nigga has gotten to the point where he's playing golf and using his metal leg as a putter." Everyone started laughing again, as if Butchie was telling a joke.

"I'm serious! This is some real shit. I've seen him do it with my own eyes." The men kept laughing, but they understood that anything was possible, especially for a black man walking in the footsteps of Rodney's teachings.

One of the men got up and walked over to the big fat tree about five yards away to take a much-needed piss after drinking some of the homemade wine they'd made. Just as the man pulled out his manhood and began to take a leak on the tree, two other black people, not far from him, were lurking, watching what he was about to do. As soon as the first stream of piss exited his dick, the man and woman, dying of dehydration, ran over and dropped to their knees with their mouths open wide, trying to capture the urine before it hit the tree or the ground. The man taking the piss tried to stop, because this was some strange shit for him to deal with, but he couldn't hold it back. The pain of trying to stop was unbearable, so he thought, fuck it, drink up, as he closed his eyes to the sight of it.

Rodney and Rob were watching the scene unfold. They looked around and noticed the man and woman weren't the only ones dehydrated; their lips were chapped, with a white ring forming a circle around them from the salt residue of dehydration.

"Yo, Rob, go find Old Man Lenape," Rodney said. Rob didn't hesitate on going to find the old man, but he wondered the reasoning for Rodney asking for him. Lenape was an old man who was doing time back in Jersey with them for stealing food from a store at gun point but he felt that it seemed to have been one side when it came to the things that he does vs White America. To him he was named after his great great grandfather who was Chief Lenape of Delaware whose land was stolen at gun point and at the same time rules of bias stipulations against all his people, so old man Lenape felt he wasn't stealing from something that belong to him already. Lenape and Rob made their way over to Rodney. Lenape like always had on his Native Charm around his Neck and his brown soft leather Moccasins he made while being locked up over the years. He spoke soft and slow since he was almost around the age of Chin before he died. Lenape was a short man and very wise. "Rodney" Lenape said quietly with a slight bow showing respect and his old age. Rodney was happy to see that Lenape was holding on better than some of the younger men of the crew. "Lenape, I called for you because I've witnessed with my own eye's many of days you called on our father in heaven and asked for rain and he gave it to you. What is it my Elder that we can do to get water so these helpless people can stay alive?" Lenape closed his eye's looking back in time when he was a younger man in prison dance in his traditional form calling on his father in heaven to bless him with his needs more than his wants. "This is not a problem; you must come with me, and I will show you my family's traditional dance we would do when we needed water." Lenape said to Rodney in a calm manner. Rodney and Rob walked slowly beside Lenape as he leaded them to his belongings. When they reach Lenape's area where he had his belongings, they noticed things hanging all around what looked like something that would ward off evil spirts. Lenape slowly started to do his rain dance but at the speed at what he was doing the dance wouldn't have seen a dropped.

"This is how you do it, along with a prayer that we chant in the process. But the dance must be much faster and with more people, with a rhythm that will speak to God's soul." Rodney and Rob practiced the dance until they got it right, along with the native tongue of the rain prayer.

"We have to gather the others before more of our men and women die," Rodney said to Rob.

"Who do you suppose will be the best for the job?" Rob asked before heading out to find dancers.

Rodney already had in mind who he was going to call on. "Go round up all of those Black Greeks who love stepping anyhow."

Rob shook his head and chuckled. "You mean like the Q's, Alpha Dogs, and those pretty boys in red and white?"

Rodney winked at him to confirm. "Exactly!"

Rob went around to the men he knew and asked every man and woman who was a friend or knew a friend or kinfolk in a Greek Frat to step forward. Men and women from all over proudly came to see what Rodney asked of them. When they all gathered in front of Rodney, he looked among the people and noticed their pride.

Without saying a word, Rodney began to display the rain dance moves that Lenape had taught him. The Black Greeks, men and women, were watching him but didn't understand the meaning of it. From the looks on their faces, it seemed as if they were feeling disrespected. Many of the Greeks were whispering to one another, and the tension in the air was thick, as if a fight might break out. Rodney and Rob could see and feel the vibe of the people and knew something needed to change for the better before black people started turning on each other.

"What's wrong, my brothers?" Rodney asked the crowd.

"What's up with all this dancing and chanting? You trying to play us out like we're suckers or something?" one Greek questioned.

Rodney thought for a moment about their reaction and then asked himself, isn't that what they do?

"Not at all, my brothers and sisters. It's just that we need water desperately, and in numbers, we can make it happen."

The crowd got quiet for a minute, thinking about what he just said, until someone shouted out, "That Nigga trying to play us like we some Stepin Fetchit type motherfuckers!"

The crowd instantly forgot Rodney's purpose for gathering them and was now on edge, ready to fight because one man said the wrong thing. Rob thought quickly and began to do the rain dance and chant as if he were a Greek man, and seconds later, Rodney fell in line. The sky above them turned gray in an instant, responding to the energy of the prayer chants and earth-stomping, sending a message out into the universe. The crowd watched Rob and Rodney, and they could feel the energy in the atmosphere, causing them to sense the power in the dancing and chanting. One by one, men and women started to follow what Rodney needed them to do, and within a second after they all came together as one, the rain began pouring down— but only in this one area where a thousand black people had gathered for the cause. This place would now remain raining for eternity. Some men and women drank God's water and bathed in the mud, feeling anointed and protected by God. Rodney, Rob, Lenape, and some other nearby men were doing something impossible in the eyes of most: they were smoking their Happy, and for some reason, despite the heavy rain, not a drop put out the spliff.

"Ayo! Does this shit work for anything we want?" a Greek Frat asked, looking to Rodney or Rob for an answer.

Rodney nodded at the young man. "Yes, you may ask the Gods for whatever you want because we are the Gods."

The young man looked at Rodney as if he was crazy for thinking so highly of himself and his people. The proud Greek said out loud, "Well! Shit, I want to dance for money," and he stepped even harder, making a statement that he would stomp a mud hole in the ground for some cash.

Rob watched the young man dancing hard in hopes of money falling into his lap. "Why do you want money that's not yours?" Rob asked.

"Shit! Once it hits my hand, it's mine," the young man replied, being funny while smacking five with his Greek brother standing next to him.

"So that will be at the sake of whom the money comes from, other than your own? Why not have your own? Brother, is what I'm saying going over your head? If so, please ask anyone who does understand to explain."

The look on the young men's faces showed they understood that this mission wasn't a joking matter. Everyone got the message and straightened up to listen because they could tell Rob had more to say.

"That paper you're referring to holds no value to you but for sure keeps you in debt. Where we're going, all you need is to love God and appreciate the smallest things God has blessed us with, which provide everything we need all around us."

"Yeah, ok. Well, if that's so, then why are Niggas out here hungry and shit?" said a young man from the crowd.

"They are, young one, because we don't believe that we can do for ourselves, which brings us wealth. They put the value of money before life, which means they have set themselves to believe that money is greater than themselves, and that's insane."

The young man heard Rob's words, but because he was too young to have lived in the times when the black race lived in this manner, he couldn't grasp what Rob was talking about. To make matters worse, here they were, somewhere in the middle of the D.C. area, and out of nowhere, walking into the crowd of Rodney's people and others tagging along with the rest of their race, came the young man Q had run into in Wilmington when all the chaos first started. Q had asked the young brother if he understood that they were at war, leaving Q scratching his scalp, confused about what the man was saying about having to do whatever it takes to feed his kids. Now, here he was again, repeating the same thing all over. "Yo, I got that Coke and Got that Weed."

Sadly, a few dope fiends tried sneakily to cop some, backsliding into their old habits, trying to escape the madness. Nothing gets past Rob's eyes when it comes to selling narcotics. He noticed what was happening out of the corner of his eye, and he became angry, feeling that all Rodney was doing for his people was being disrespected by the Devil himself right in front of them. "Hell no," raced through his mind.

The young brother selling the drugs felt that as long as he only showed the product, people would walk away from the righteous crowd and follow him behind the building, around the corner, or behind a tree, depending on where he could make his quick sale and gain that person's spirit for a little bit of cash that the white man prints. Just as the young hustler looked around to see if any of the righteous men and women were watching, he thought the coast was clear. He passed off the drug to the junkie, and just as the junkie turned to walk off to do his business, he stopped in his tracks at the sight of Rob standing in front of him. The junkie took a deep swallow, looked Rob in the face, and then bowed his head in shame. Rob shed a tear, rolling down one side of his face, with the thought that he needed to put an end to this. He quickly pulled out his gun from behind his back. "Blow!" he shot the junkie in the head while talking to the dead body. "Only the strong will survive, and the weak shall die."

The young man who sold the drugs tried to turn and make a dash for it, but as soon as he turned to run, he couldn't outrun the bullet that caught him in the back of the head. "No more selling this bad business around here anymore," Rob said, walking over to the hustler's body, tears streaming down his face for what he felt he had to do. But what hurt his heart the most was knowing it wouldn't be long before another hustler would be born.

It all happened so fast. Rodney saw what went down and rushed over to Rob, looking down at the two dead black men. He cried at the sight of it and looked over at Rob. "Why did you have to kill them? They were our brothers, and they could have changed their ways. This killing in you is all wrong, brother. It seems that after the first time you killed, it's still in your heart," Rodney said to his best friend, hoping to change his heart.

Rob sat there for a second and thought before he spoke. "Nah, disrespect my brother, but we are moving forward from all this, and we don't need this to set us back. This man was very sick—he was sick before he came with us, and now he's sick again. So, like some patients in the hospital who are so sick that there's nothing more to be done, it's best to let the family prepare for funeral arrangements. And this sellout over here," he pointed at the young hustler, "what!" He shrugged his shoulders. "He's giving our people poison, and he's working for the man, and the sad thing is, the sucker doesn't even know it. I know we sold some of that Happy, but that's given to us from God, and no man should be able to tell I and I if I can use it or sell it."

Rodney walked over to his best friend and hugged him. "It's your heart that needs to change. If you feel the need to use a gun to protect yourself with violence instead of using God's energy within yourself, maybe you've forgotten your self-worth and your own capabilities. But I know you will soon come forward again in using your heart."

Rob thought Rodney might have a point, but he still felt the need for zero tolerance of any wrongdoing among them. "Look, I overstand what you're saying, Black Monk, but something inside me is saying that this Tupac Thug Life thing is coming over my soul somewhat." In Rob's mind at that moment was Tupac's song "All I Want to Be Is a Soldier." Rodney said to him, "Don't you understand we have to be one?"

Rob thought this would be a great time to pull out a spliff and spark up. He took the blunt he had placed behind his right ear, pulled out his lighter from his pocket, and lit it, taking a hefty pull. As he let out a cloud of smoke into the air, he said to Rodney, "Brother, I have never forgotten that we are one, but the way I see it, I am I, seen? And you yourself are I, I self-brethren. You, I, and everyone are different, my brother, but as we move forward, I believe we're going to need this here machine." Rob said, holding up his gun to show Rodney he was ready to get down.

Rodney didn't agree with Rob's new mindset, but he understood Rob's intentions, so he just nodded his head, accepting it. What saddened his heart was knowing that Rob knew the rules of this spiritual revolution—the warfare going on is all mental, where you manifest your thoughts into reality. Rodney put his arm around Rob, and they started to walk off when someone in the crowd shouted, "So, it's okay for us to have guns now?" Within seconds, half the black people revealed that they were packing.

"Well, it's about time," a young man in the crowd said.

Rodney looked at Rob and said, "See what you started."

Rob looked back at him and said, "Where we're headed down South, everybody's packing, and things are going to pop off more than a Chinese festival. And trust and believe, we're going to need it in places where white people can kill a Nigga and say they feared for their life."

Rodney gave Rob a look. "I'm not here to fight with you, my brother. We're going to move forward together."

Rodney started looking around to see how many D.C. and Baltimore black people were going to follow him in his way of moving forward, but he noticed only a few. Rob tapped Rodney's arm. "No worries, Rasta, they're right over there." He pointed to a crowd of black people from D.C. and Baltimore, looking like straight-up gangstas and some for sure rebels. "They're with us, but you know a lot of them like to play with those machines. Don't worry yourself, mon, they just feel the need to die for the cause, and if need be, in a different way, my brother."

The two of them started to move along with all their followers and many more tagging along to their next destination.

Chapter 18

Shattered Sanctuaries in VA

Gusty winds were making trees wave hello to those who lived in Jamestown VA. Massive flooding was coming up from the ocean shorelines causing many people to leave their homes and go live with other family members or friends and many went to stranger's homes for help if that were their only hope. A few days after Halloween a family of ten White people showed up to a resident's trailer home. A Red Neck man in his mid-fifty's stepped up to the Trailer home and almost was for sure that the resident's owner was of a White family due to mostly Whites resided and he believed in his mind that most Black people lived in the City Projects or if not, they owned something most likely to be somewhere in the country in a ran down house. The short pot belly man with a baldhead and a trucker's hat on his head with his all-white scruffy beard hanging down off his chin looking like a young Santa Claus took a few knocks at the door pounding on it like he was the fucking Cops. He startled the family inside the home and a young lady in her early 20's opens the door on a slight crack looking out at the family of ten wondering what they could want being as though they weren't any family of hers. "Can I help you?" The man smiled at her. "Yes, me and my family here" He turns and looks at his family. "We need a place to stay for a few days if you don't mind. We been washed out of our homes by the sea, and we lost everything except for our bullets and guns. We even lost our dog Trigger; God bless his soul."

The young lady looked at the man and felt a little sorry for him and his family, but she knew she'd need to let her father handle this matter. So, she closed the door and went to her father, who was sitting down watching TV.

"Dad, it's a family outside asking for help."

Her father got up from his recliner chair, struggling with his skinny frame and old age to the front door, with his little lap dog barking alongside him. The old man opened the door wide.

"How can I help you?" he asked, repeating the question.

The white man standing outside gave the old man the same smile.

"Look, brother to a brother, my family and I need a place to rest. Our home and everything we own is gone."

The old white man thought about it.

"I only have two bedrooms as it is, and I share this with my daughter, granddaughter, and her two kids. I don't think I'll have any room for your family, sir."

The Santa Claus lookalike didn't feel loved or welcomed, so he got a little angry and spit down onto the trailer's porch, looking at the old man. He peeped past the old man to see what was going on inside the house and noticed a little boy in pampers whose skin looked as if the child had a tan. Coming from out the back room was a mixed child of the black and white races. The boy was no more than 13 and had his face planted into his cell phone, not noticing anything going on. He had curly hair, and his skin revealed that he was indeed a mulatto. The man at the door kicked the door with his foot in anger.

The old man looked at the man like he was crazy and then closed the door in the man's face, but he didn't lock the door and the man forcefully open the door letting himself in the man's home. "Get out!" the old man's daughter yelled while punching the man on his back, neck and head or whatever she could hit. The other family members of the intruder rushed into the house to defend their family. As soon as they came in, they started swinging on the girl and the old man as well until two men of the that family noticed, the young Mulatto standing in the middle of the room in shock standing there like he was frozen ice. The two men started smiling at him and then those smiles turned into the looks of hatred across their faces. One of the angry men pulled out his gun and lifted it up to the young man's head. The 13-year-old boy pissed his pants and dropped his cell phone to the floor. "Please I didn't do anything." The boy cried out wondering what was going on. The boy's mother cried out. "Oh God for heaven's sake, please don't kill my." The man with the gun turns and points the gun at her. "You Nigga loving Bitch, You're the problem. "Boom!" The man shot the young lady in the chest not caring if she died or not, he just felt that if anything that had love for the Black man must die. "You should have kept your legs closed or screamed rape Bitch." The young lady's fathers' heart was torn to pieces and wanted to kill those people in his house, but he was old and couldn't defend his family. The man with the gun turned back to look at the 13-year-old boy name Bobby Jr. Wilson. Bobby asked the man over his crying voice. "What have I done?" The man with the gun looked deep into the boy's eye's so he can feel the hatred in depth when he tells him why. He smirks at the boy as if the answer couldn't be any simpler.

"Because your daddy is a Black man who has given you Nigger blood. And your daddy isn't any kin of mine."

That took the young man by surprise for a second, and he quickly said, "Isn't the color of blood of all men red?"

The man with the gun was beyond mad now. "You see, that's the shit I can't stand, a smart-ass Nigger."

"Pow!" The man with the gun shot the boy in the head and then looked over at the young man's grandfather. "Come on, Pops, you should know better." He shrugged his shoulders at the old man.

"Don't worry, old man, I'm not going to kill you; we just want a place to rest our heads."

The old man was shaking and trembling, not knowing what to do, but he knew with his family gone, he had nothing else to live for. Not wanting to live anymore, the old man went to grab the butcher knife that was on the edge of the kitchen countertop to try his best to kill the gunman. Just as he took his only chance at stabbing the gunman, he wasn't fast enough with the knife and found out real fast that you don't take a knife to a gunfight. He found himself shot dead with the rest of his family.

"Search the house!" said one of the family members.

The men searched the house and found a few other young kids hiding under their beds. When they got caught, they were snatched up and escorted out of the house by being pushed. "Get the fuck on!" the man yelled at them.

"Well, I guess we got a place to stay now," the man said to his family members. The men took over the house, kicked up their feet, and started watching TV without caring that the dead bodies were lying on the floor, leaking blood onto the once-tan rug.

****

On the other side of town, not too far from where the scene just took place, was a Black family home being used as a holding place for many Blacks who had run to them for help and shelter. In the small home, five different families were trying to live and fight together until all this craziness in the country passed over. One man in the family and a few others were standing outside the home, looking out onto the road that passed by the house. "Zoom!" was the loud sound of a person on a dirt bike flying by so fast you couldn't tell who it was on the bike. Joe looked at the others standing outside with him. They all knew that the last time someone came flying through, it was because a mob of White people was coming to kill more Black people. "YO Chuck! Go get the rest of the people and tell them to strap up again and take their positions."

"Help!" was called out in rage by many other Black people running in their direction. Quickly, Joe went into the house, lifted the sofa cushion, grabbed his gun, and checked it over to make sure that it was locked and loaded. "Move now!" he shouted out for everyone in the house to hear. Just then, he opened his kitchen drawer, grabbed a brown paper lunch bag, tucked it into his back pocket, and then headed back out the front door, seeing a Black woman and her children, covered in blood, sweat, and tears, falling to the ground on his front lawn, trying to stay alive. He walked over to them with his eyes locked on the people coming out from all angles, everywhere, screaming for help. He grabbed the lady and lifted her off the ground while she held onto her children's arms.

"Butch! Take them to the safe spot in the back," Joe said. Butch took the lady and her two kids to the old barn right behind the house. He sat the lady and her kids down on the clean horse hay inside the barn and then went to the back window of the barn to look out and see if anyone was coming from that direction. For the most part, up until now, it was the safe place for them to hide out because they had dug holes in the ground surrounding the place with homemade bombs in them. They took old soda bottles and filled them with gasoline, then dropped the cut ends of extension cord wires into them, ready to be plugged into the outdoor socket hooked up about fifteen yards away from the barn, connecting to the house.

Joe started helping many Black people by allowing them to go to the barn in the back. One by one, he passed those through who could only pass the Brown Paper Bag test. He stopped every last one who was lighter than the brown paper bag and held them up along the side of the house. Everything was happening so fast that no one was paying attention to what he was doing as far as color was concerned; all they knew was that, at that moment, they felt safe being around Black people.

The sight of White people now coming out of the woods, firing their guns in Joe's direction, caused him to think that he was going to have to make a break for it. However, he and everyone else heard a humming noise that sounded like a thousand bees. Within a flash, they noticed some young Black men who had put their lives on the line for the cause of many Blacks to live. They came down the street, with kids and young adults jumping off their dirt bikes, sending them right into the mob of angry White men. Some of those men on the dirt bikes stayed on, going out on a straight suicide mission. The dirt bikes caught fire instantly, and the yelling started when the fire began burning everyone.

Not long after, Butch came out from the barn and noticed Joe alongside the house with the rest of the people. He ran over to him quickly. "Joe, you good?" he asked, trying to seem concerned. "Yup, I'm good, but not too sure about these Niggas right here." Butch looked at Joe like he didn't have time for his bullshit. "Not now, Joe, with this dumb shit." Joe quickly glanced at the Black people with envy in his eyes and spoke. "You're right." But in his mind, he was thinking this wasn't the time or place, but he felt helping light-skinned Niggas was a waste of time. "Come on, let's get back to the barn now while we have a chance," Butch said. Joe and the Black people standing there were now trying to figure out what was going on and whether they should trust the two of them or not. They didn't have much time to figure it out because more White men were coming out of the woods fast. "No! These Niggas ain't going nowhere with us," Joe said to Butch. Butch wanted to reply but knew they didn't have much time before more White men got close enough to come and kill them. So, he started guiding those that he could to the barn while Joe held the ones he could back at gunpoint.

"Man, what is this all about?" asked a light-skinned man with light green eyes, and it's a good chance that he didn't smoke herb because his lips were pink. Joe walked over to the man and stood in his face. Joe was a little shorter, but that only made matters worse with his little man syndrome. "What's what, motherfucker?" Joe asked the man standing in front of him while looking him up and down, checking him as if he were a soft Nigga. "I'm talking about us and this brown paper bag and this whole light-skinned shit." Quickly, Joe replied, "Because I don't like you pretty boy motherfuckers, nor those light-skinned bitches thinking they all that. You and the rest of y'all can go and side with those crackers. Shit, some of y'all can pass for White anyhow." While saying it, his eyes were looking at a mixed child who was clearly from Black and White parents. "Man, tell me how you really feel," the light-skinned man said sarcastically. "I did, motherfucker! What, you need me to elaborate?" Joe said, staring into the man's face.

"Man, cut this shit out!" said an older light-skinned woman. "Shut the fuck up, bitch!" Joe told her with so much anger in his voice that he was spraying it with spit flying out of his mouth. "Bop!" The light-skinned young man had tears in his eyes because he was hurt hearing how his own Black brother felt about him. So, he punched Joe hard on the left side of his ear, causing him to become a little dazed. "Man, what did I ever do to you? Man, we're all Black people! What the fuck is wrong with you?" he asked Joe. Joe heard every word, even though for the moment everything seemed slow. "That's why I'm going to do what us real Niggas do best!" Joe said to him once he gathered himself together. The light-skinned man looked at Joe with a crooked eye like he didn't understand what Joe was referring to. Joe, without a thought or care, lifted his gun up and shot the light-skinned brother in the chest. Joe looked at the other four light-skinned people standing there in shock at what had just happened. Joe didn't care about them one bit because, in his mind, they were all sellouts because they had less melanin than he did. He checked his revolver to see how many bullets were left in the gun. He started counting, "1, 2, 3, 4." Then he pointed the gun at the rest of the helpless Black people, counting out loud. "1! Pop 2! Pop! 3! Pop!" was the sound of three rounds Joe shot, killing the remainder of those who once stood around him. Then he checked the smoking gun to make sure he had ammo and began shaking his head yes to confirm that he should have three more bullets left. He looked over his shoulder, checking to see how many more White people were coming. Then he stopped himself in his tracks and noticed the leader that led the mob of White men was holding his men back while they watched him kill his own light-skinned brothers and sisters. Joe stared at those White men who were smiling at him for a brief second and then turned his back on them without shame in his heart for what

253

they felt. Those few White men went back into the woods because they felt Joe had everything under control as far as him doing their killing of his own, just like the gangsters who had been killing one another for decades. It never crossed Joe's mind that he was being a sucker for doing that to his own race of people because, over the years, his envy of wanting something that those light-skinned brothers had that he didn't, thinking they had it better than himself just because of the color of their skin. Joe was so jealous of his light-skinned brothers that he had the nerve to look down at the dead bodies and spit on them. "Sellouts!" he said to the dead bodies and then took off running away to the back of the house at the barn with the rest of them who he would call his Niggas. He opened the barn door just enough to get in, hoping no one White saw him.

Butch was standing in front of the socket with an extension cord ready to be flicked on just in case he needed to. "Check the back window one more time!" Butch ordered Joe. Joe checked the window like Butch said and ducked down quickly. "Fuck! Flick the switch now!" he shouted. Then he ran over to Butch. "Man, they're about 20 yards out with guns and sticks with fire on them, with their arms extended holding onto a long leash that held a few dogs tagging along." Butch knew if he went to look for himself, they could all be bombarded and slaughtered to death. So, without hesitation, he quickly flicked the switch just in time for the White men who were just about to come past those bottles to feel the wrath of fire shooting up in the air, catching them and a few dogs on fire. All you could hear for a quick second was the screams and yelps of those who had been set on fire until those White men stopped in their tracks, seeing what was happening to their loved ones. This caused them to start shooting into the barn. Screams were yelled out that were so horrifying from that barn from Black people that echoed out to God to help them. Butch was now throwing hay off to the side and then started digging to the top surface of the ground that revealed the door they used for safety at times like this. Just as Butch opened the door to the hole in the ground that could easily hold about sixty people comfortably, they all jumped in before he could help them down because the White men were sending so many rounds into the barn that if you didn't make it in the hole, you would have been left behind dead or wounded without help.

Joe was the last to get in because he knew how to close the trap door properly and used some of the wounded men as a shield while dropping down into the hole. "We should be safe down here until those Crackers think we're burned up or filled with lead," Joe said to Butch as he dusted the dirt off himself. Butch was happy to be alive, but anger was written all over his face. "Where are the other Black people, Joe?" Joe gave him a faint smile. "Who? Them light-skinned Niggas? Oh, I took care of those pretty motherfuckers." Butch stepped up in Joe's space, glaring at him. "What do you mean, Joe?" Joe took a step back to regain his space. "I put their heads to bed, it's as simple as that."

"Why?" a lady shouted out because one of those men was her son. "I'll kill you with my bare hands!" a man yelled out because his brother was killed as well. The man charged at Joe, but his face met the sight of the .45 revolver Joe still had in his hand with three bullets. Butch held one of the men back who didn't give a fuck about Joe and his gun at the moment. Butch never took his eyes off Joe. "I did all y'all a favor. I know at some point in time them pretty motherfuckers are going to come back in style, and then they're going to start looking at us brown Niggas like we ain't shit. It's bad enough the White man thinks of us like that now, and our women." Joe stated his words as if they were facts. All the Black people in that hole were looking at Joe, wondering if they themselves thought and spoke about their own brothers and sisters in the same manner.

"Fuck that bullshit! I mean, how long is it going to take for dark-skinned Blacks and light-skinned Blacks to understand we're the same people, even with this foolishness of self-hate among one another!" Butch yelled at Joe. Joe wasn't trying to hear that. "Man, every brother ain't a brother; they can very much be undercover," Joe said, giving him a line from one of Public Enemy's rap songs. Right then, Butch thought about what Joe had just stated and figured Joe was right about that. One second later, he pointed his

256

gun at Joe's face, making his nose smell stale gun smoke. "Oh, and a dark-skinned brother such as yourself can't be? You're the sellout, undercover, or whoever you think is light-skinned is a sellout. The problem is you and your fucking mindset!" Joe's eyes widened at the sight of the gun in his face, and he took a slow step backward.

"Oh, so now you're going to point your gun at me, my Nigga? What, your wife or mom or somebody in your family must be one of them high yellow motherfuckers, that's why you're sticking up for them pretty boy Niggas." Everyone listening to him speak seemed as if many of them had heard this type of talk before, but now it was different because it was one of their own family members being accused of being a sellout because their skin was a few shades lighter than a darker-shaded Black person or a brown paper bag. Butch had all he could take of Joe. "Well, I guess you're out of luck," Butch said to Joe.

"What do you mean by that?" Joe said, feeling disgusted that the rest of them weren't trying to understand his mindset. "I'm trying to catch up with Rodney and his followers and live righteous. Brother Rodney preaches to never point a gun at your brother, and you, you have killed who you think is not your brother. But the truth is, you're not the brother you are referring to," Butch said. Everyone nodded their heads in agreement.

"I guess if you take a look at most of your so-called Black leaders, they just so happen to be lighter than your damn brown paper bag foolishness." Joe sat there for a minute and thought about it, scanning through his head what his so-called Black leaders looked like. For the most part, he realized that Butch may have a point. "I never thought to see it that way, but what is your point?" Joe asked as if none of this mattered to him anyway. For the most part, he felt some of those so-called leaders were sellouts anyhow.

"Well, I guess you will never be able to see." Butch said. "Pop!" Joe's head received an unwilling bullet to his dome, causing his body to hit the ground with his blood oozing out of his cranium slowly like a funnel being used for an oil change.

Butch's heart felt heavy for having to kill one of his own Black brethren, but his gut told him he did the right thing. "After the fire burns out and those crazy murderers leave, we can be on our way. I don't think we will be safe here any longer," Butch told the people among him who were standing there, glad that Joe was dead and now feeling safer without the worry of being shot because of their skin color, unless it was the White folks outside waiting on them.

After a few hours passed, Butch peeped out all the windows in the barn to see if it was safe for them to move to their new destination. "I suppose it's cool to leave now. I don't see a soul in sight, and I don't smell anything that smells like wet chickens." A teenage boy looked confused at what Butch said. "Mister, what do you mean by you don't smell anything that smells like a wet chicken?" Butch looked around and could tell a few other young people didn't understand as well.

"Who else doesn't know why I said that?" Men and women of this generation were looking and pointing at each other. "Okay, if you are lucky to be around a White person who hasn't washed their hair in days, and you stand around them, then you'll understand what a wet chicken smells like. Now, for those who have never smelled a wet chicken, you'll just have to take my word for it."

Butch opened the door to the barn, and one by one they crept slowly out the door, not having a clue of which way to go. Butch had heard months ago that Rodney and his followers were heading down south, so he started leading the way towards the Carolinas. Town after town, the air was filled with the smell of gun smoke and death, while the grounds they walked on were littered with empty bullet shells and many dead bodies. Most of the people who were still alive and walking among the dead started picking things up from the bodies, like money, water, candy, and some type of weapon, gun, or knife. The oddest thing they found were more and more Chinese throwing stars and bows and arrows stuck in some of the bodies.

Everyone started getting tired and wanted to stop to rest. Butch looked around and started noticing that quite a few men, women, and a handful of kids were coughing every so often and slowing the pack down. Butch thought to himself—does he leave the sick behind so they don't contaminate others, or should he carry them along until they reached Rodney so he could heal them? The thought ran through his mind, but Butch was ready to keep moving. He didn't want to go off on his own, especially not knowing where and when he would link up with Rodney.

"Oh shit! Oh! Oh!" a young lady said, pointing her finger in front of herself. A few people around her ran over, asking what she saw because when they quickly tried seeing what it was, she was pointing at, they didn't see a thing. Tears were in the young lady's eyes until they started rolling down her face. You could tell these weren't tears of worry; they were tears of hope and love. "I just, just saw 2Pac," she said, stuttering her words.

Because of the trauma they all had been enduring, many of them believed she was going a little crazy, out of her mind. Many slowly walked away from her, disappointed. Just as they had enough of what they thought were lies from the young woman, a young man in his mid-40s widened his eyes at what he just witnessed and tapped the man's arm next to him. "Did you see that?"

The man next to him looked at him as if he too was going crazy. "See what, my man?" The man started pointing in front of him about 10 yards away behind the other man's back. Then the man turned around and all he could see was the morning dew misting in the air and green smoke from the herb people were smoking. "Man, I don't see shit! What did you see?" The man was in disbelief that what he saw was no longer there.

"Biggie," the man said, starting to think he was going crazy. The other man sucked his teeth at him. "Biggie who?" he asked, having a good feeling he already knew who he was referring to. "Notorious B.I.G." The man spoke his truth, but since the young lady stated she'd seen 2Pac, the other man thought for sure he was full of it. The man started to walk away from him, giving him the rapper Jadakiss's laugh.

People started talking about who was going crazy or who had become ill and handicapped. A few people were going up to Butch, asking him about the people he had with him and their condition. "Butch, what are we going to do with these people who are starting to become delusional?" said the man who had just walked away from the man who saw Biggie.

"My man, I believe we ourselves are going to see things that a man's eyes had never seen before us."

"Look at what this country has come to right now. If you think for one minute that we have seen it all, my friend, it will be a rude awakening for you," Butch said, waving his hand for the man and everyone else to move along with him as he led them in the direction the young lady and the man who saw the images of two of the greatest rappers of all time had gone. Butch's mind was all over the place from seeing horrifying events of people being killed and fighting for their lives, but what was gut-wrenching was the smell in the air—it matched the awful stench of crack cocaine being smoked along with a crackhead passing gas.

Butch stopped for a few seconds to vomit, causing others around him to do the same as if they had gotten seasick. People were dying from sickness and disease; White or Black, it didn't matter because everyone walking through the thickness of God's plague put upon America was suffering. Butch and a few others following him reached the tip of the Carolinas and their bodies began to shake as they noticed more Black people in sight. Most of them were gunned down by skilled White countrymen who had been hunting since childhood. To top it off, these men controlled all the gun shops and weren't selling bullets to any Black person. It was unfair, but that's the outcome of war.

Most of the Black deaths in the South happened at night because God used the sun to burn the skin of all mankind, but only in America. For Black people, the sunburn simply darkened their skin, making them look burnt. This enraged many Black men and women who wanted to lighten their skin tone to the point of taking their own lives in shame. For White people, it caused them to die of skin cancer overnight. Big red bumps formed all over their bodies as if their skin was boiling, resulting in blisters with pus oozing out. They preferred doing their killing at night, hoping not to get bitten to death by mosquitoes that now targeted anyone showing signs of sickness or open wounds. The Ninjas in black suits were masters of assassination with impeccable skills, but they were also dying in high numbers. Meanwhile, the White people's barbaric ways carried them on until they felt victorious. Even though the White race was killing off the Black race more than ever in history, they were still stunned by the sight of new strange fruit hanging from trees right outside their front doors.

All over the country, the police force, National Guard, and military were all White American troops, except for a few White Puerto Ricans, White Mexicans, and a few Blacks who thought they were different from other Black people and stayed, thinking they could make a change. The White people in these departments had come together about the matter of still seeing their race being hung like the countless Black people in the South in the early 1900s. Every officer of the law and the National Guard were going around taking down the strange fruit that was appearing all over the country. It seemed that for every Black person killed, the Black Ninjas charged the White race with two of their kind to add to the trees of strange fruit. While the troops were cutting down the dead bodies from the trees, they often found notes in the pockets. Each note read, "For every one of ours, becomes two of yours."

The men began looking inside the uniforms of the dead Ninjas to see where the clothing was made. "Hey Jed! What have you gathered so far?" asked a tall, slim, clean-shaven officer named Matty White. "I've got nothing other than the norm—Black faces and the Ninja gear they're wearing, which is for sure government-issued state property." Matty broke down and almost cried a river because of all the White men, women, and children whose lives were taken.

"Yo Matt, you okay? What's with all the tears?" Jed wanted to know because they had done this before, and Matty had never broken down like this. "Man, look at this shit!" Matt said, pointing at the dead bodies. "Is all this worth it? I mean, what are we going to do? Kill them all?"

Jed's mind went right to thinking about his own family he had lost in the last few months. "Hell yeah! If that's what it takes, we'll kill every one of those Niggers if we have to. Brother, we lost a whole lot more men to the Redman than what these Niggers are doing to us right now."

Matt understood what he was saying but still wanted to know if it was all still worth it. "Okay, Jed, but is it worth it?" Jed gave him a look as if the question was the craziest thing he'd ever heard. "Is standing like a man and defending what our forefathers have stolen and built for us as far as this empire is concerned worth it? Then fuck yeah! I will die to keep our race above all and to carry on to our children the stature of White privilege throughout this country and to the rest of the world."

Matty didn't say a word because those were his thoughts exactly, but at that moment, he felt he needed to be reminded and brought back to their reality. Jed held his hand out for Matty to give him a handshake. "You good, brother?" Matty shook Jed's hand and nodded that he was good. "Cool, now let's get back and report these bodies to the chief and hope to get some get-back by hopefully seeing an unlucky Nigger along the way."

The two of them got back in their cars and slowly drove over dead bodies until they found an open path that had been cleared by a bulldozer at some point, pushing the dead bodies off to the side of the road. Butch and a few survivors finally made it to Rodney and the rest of his followers. Butch looked around, trying to remember what Rodney looked like from the "America's Most Wanted" signs posted all over the country. When Butch didn't see Rodney nearby, he started asking around if anyone had seen him. Many were busy reading the Bible or the Koran, preparing spiritually for the war within themselves. Butch dared not interrupt those deep in their books.

A young man walked up to Butch and looked him up and down. "Present your papers, my nigga!" Butch looked at the young man, confused. "Who, me? I think you've got the wrong person." The young man repeated, "Papers!" Butch thought the young man meant rolling papers for herb. "I don't have any papers." Now the young man was suspicious, thinking Butch might be a snitch. "Nigga! You ever been to jail before?" Butch shook his head. The young man was incredulous. "Not once? No overnighters either?" Butch kept shaking his head. "Nope," he said. The young man, still suspicious, warned, "If you're the cops and you're trying to bring us down, I'll kill you myself with my bare hands." Butch appreciated the young man's dedication to protecting Rodney. "Young man, I'm here for the same reason you are. Now please help me find Rodney fast because there are a few sick people over there." He pointed to the sick people he brought with him. "They need his help before more of them die." The young man honestly replied, "I don't have a clue where he is."

Butch could tell he was telling the truth, so he walked through the crowd with the sick tagging along, glancing at Rodney's photo in his pocket to make sure he didn't miss him. When Butch finally spotted Rodney, he saw Rodney alone, seemingly meditating, but with a look of weeping on his face. He approached Rodney, unsure

266

if he should interrupt. Rodney didn't move, but he slowly opened his eyes. "Butch, am I correct?" Rodney asked, already knowing but wanting to be sure. Butch was amazed at Rodney's perception. "Correct!" he said excitedly. "May I ask what's wrong?" Butch asked, concerned. Rodney's tears vanished in seconds as he gathered his thoughts. "It's the things I can see that you and the others haven't witnessed yet. Humanity has really lost its way. People take lives to prove some point. A dog gets more love than a Black man. What happened to the days when love between a man and a woman kept the world going around?"

Butch knew what Rodney was talking about but felt torn between siding with Rob and his rebels or following Rodney's non-violent path. He asked, "The tears, it's the tears that had me concerned. Please don't mind me meddling into your thoughts." Rodney faintly smiled. "No, you're good. The tears are because I see where we're heading. Blacks are killing their own mixed-blood children, fearing they'll side with the other race in life-or-death matters. The White race is doing the same, leaving mixed-race kids feeling they have no choice." Rodney stood up from his meditative stance and opened his eyes, with Butch right where he had envisioned. "We out!" Rodney said, signaling everyone to move on.

Butch noticed Rodney moving quickly and called out, "Rodney, what about the sick and crippled ones I brought to you?" Concerned for their well-being, he followed Rodney. Without breaking stride, Rodney replied, "I have healed them all. The crippled are no longer, and the sickness has been removed from their bodies because I know their hearts, just as I know yours, my brother."

Butch looked at Rodney as if he were crazy. "You are an angel that I have sent for years before you changed your heartless ways to understand true love, and that's why I sent you to come to me." Butch hadn't a clue what Rodney was saying, but he never doubted much because he knew the power of the mind is real. Rodney walked past his followers, and they took notice of the seriousness on his face, causing them to gather their belongings and quickly start to follow. Out of the blue, Rob made his way to the front of the pack to meet up with Rodney. "Where's the fire?" Rob asked sarcastically, noticing how fast Rodney was walking. At that moment, Rodney thought to himself, if he only knew.

As they walked along the shoreline of South Carolina, the midday heat caused many of them to drink seawater, especially those who had just joined and hadn't been locked down with Rodney to learn his proper teachings of fasting. When night came, it was still hot, as if the sun had never set, and the beach sand of Myrtle Beach blew into their eyes and ears from the strong wind, making it feel like they were in a desert. Rodney held out his hand to stop Rob. "I had a mental conversation with Aja, and she informed me that our Black mothers and sisters are extremely stressed and, worse of all, angry." Rob knew what that meant. "Look at the sea," Rodney said to Rob, pointing to the ocean. Rob and the others tried to cover their eyes from the sand to see what Rodney was pointing at. They all looked at the ocean, and some saw what was happening right away, while others took a minute because they had become seasick from looking at all that water. It seemed as if the ocean wave had surpassed its max height, as if it were a tsunami.

"What the bloodclot!" Rob exclaimed, noticing that the ocean was starting to boil, and the waves turned into bubbles. The mist from the burning hot ocean reached some of the people, causing many of them to jump back like hot kitchen grease popping onto their skin. A few minutes later, the ocean slowly began to turn pink and then dark red. The ocean turned red because it was killing off the top layers of fish like sharks and whales. Dead fish began to surface until their corpses melted and vanished into the bloody sea. Creatures from the deep, such as dragon-like monsters and fish large enough to swallow a whale, began to jump out of the water and come onto the beach, covering miles of it. They all stood there, unable to believe their eyes.

"It talks about this in the Bible, in Revelation," a proud Israelite shouted for everyone to hear. "The time is now! I told my mom and some of my friends they had better get right because the time was coming, and now look." After the man said that, he went down on his knees and began to pray. All the righteous men of all religions followed suit and started to do the same. The more they prayed, the more things surfaced from the bottom of the ocean. The last thing that twisted everyone's nose was a funky odor coming from the sea. In the ocean, a few different colors sparkled throughout the water, resembling mermaids. Half-woman and half-fish creatures were popping up and down in the ocean, protected by the deep-sea monsters, as mermaids were considered the goddesses of the sea.

"Man, I knew I smelled that fishy smell before. I had this chick back in my day whose pussy smelled just like that," said an old man who looked to be in his early 70s. "The question is, did you fuck that stinking pussy, or are you trying to tell us you fucked one of these here mermaids?" said the old man's right-hand man, causing every man around to laugh their asses off. "No time for jokes. We need to move on before many of these men lose what little faith they have," Rodney said as he turned to move along but was stopped in his tracks by the sight of at least a hundred white men with guns pointing at them. It seemed as if they were just about to attempt to kill everyone who had lost their faith until Rodney noticed the white men were scared shitless by what they were witnessing.

"Shit, these niggers doing that voodoo shit again! I'm out!" a White Man shouted, and many of them felt the same, turning and running back to their houses in the hills and valleys to fight another day. Rob was about to chase after them with a good number of brothers who wanted revenge, but Rodney stopped him and spoke. "Don't you see, brother, that this is turning into more of a spiritual warfare? The combat skills we learned will be of little use." Rob tossed Rodney's arm away from him. "Nah, I see it like this. When you meet someone, it's for a reason. This is just the same thing. We learned hand-to-hand combat, and I believe we're going to need it. If you ever saw the movie 'Shaka Zulu,' he said if you leave your enemies behind, their children will rise and come back to haunt you." Rodney agreed somewhat with what he was saying. "Man, we need to get a move on, but the bottom of my feet are turning purple," Rob said, looking at the bottom of his feet.

"Yea ha! Yea ha!" they heard, along with a sound that resembled a thousand horses racing towards them. "Yo! See, my brother, they're coming back," Rob said to Rodney, thinking the "yea ha" sounded much like a white cowboy or a drunk redneck. Rodney stood still, waiting to see what was coming, while Rob and a few others went into a fight mode, grabbing their guns just in case Rob was right. Everyone saw that the horses were being ridden by a bunch of Black men with cowboy boots and big hats. Some of the Black men were tagging along with some untamed horses. As they got closer to Rodney, the horses started to tame themselves, becoming horses of honor. When the men on horses made their way to Rodney, they made some of the men and their horses gallop

271

aside to create a pathway for the horses they had set aside for him. When presenting them to him, the horses were the most beautiful creatures they had ever seen in their lifetime.

It might seem to those who heard about it that this beautiful white stallion was no different from any other, but this horse's eyes were red, its hooves looked as if they were marble, and its hair was as silky as that of a newborn baby. "This here white horse is for you," said one of the cowboys on his black horse. Rodney had never been on a horse before, but when he mounted it, he felt as if he belonged there. "And you bring me this gift with all these Black men on horses. What do you call yourselves?" The man on the black horse smiled and then spat some chewing tobacco onto the ground. "We are what you think we are. That's right, we are the first and true cowboys. Every man on these horses is a Black cowboy, coming all the way from Texas, which we all know is truly Mexico. Nobody knows they are taking their land back, slowly but surely." Rodney had read books about the Black cowboys out west, along with a few from Philadelphia, PA, and other places. Right then, he thought about the man saying that the Mexicans were taking their land back. He recalled Chin telling him that things would seem to repeat themselves but in a good way, and that it must get worse before it gets better.

"Do any of you good brothers have a few extra horses for my brother here, Rob, and a few others?" The man gave him a look that said it wouldn't be a problem and then whistled. Three more beautiful horses came forward. One had red hair with bright black spots and, when it sneezed, it revealed a gold crown around its tooth. The other horses were various shades of brown, very elegant looking, and the third was a mix of silver and black. Rob looked over all three horses and realized it was a hard choice, but he chose the red one because he felt the name Fire was just right for that horse. Rob got onto his horse and began to make it dance. Rodney couldn't believe what he was seeing. "What is this? You already know how to ride a horse?" Rodney asked. "Yeah, mon. Back in my yard, my grandfather had a few of these, and he taught me how to control them before he passed away and we moved to foreign." Rodney smacked his horse on its backside with a switch from a tree, causing the horse to take off in the needed direction as if he had given the order. The truth was that they were so in tune with nature that every animal knew its purpose. All the animals that lived on land were heading south, and the south became congested with people and animals from every part of the country.

The Black people became scared of these animals and wanted to run, but Rodney told them, like many men before him, not to run when a dog is chasing you. Many who lost faith in his words said "hell no" and ran off in fear, which lined them up for the White people gunning them down where they stood, adding to the remains of all the dead bodies of each race. The Black people's backs were against the ocean, forced there for safety. If pushed further, they would end up in the boiling ocean water and the blood of the fishes. If they moved a little west, they would end up dead or wishing they were due to the evilness of the ongoing race war. "No! You don't have to run from the animals any longer. To us, they are no longer beasts; they're here to help us," Rodney spoke to the people. "Put your guns down, brothers," Rob called out to those ready to shoot anything that looked harmful. "We'll stay here until I feel the animals think it's safe for us to move on," Rodney told the people. He wanted to have mental telepathy with Aja to know if the women traveling behind were okay and to check on the young children weighing heavily on his mind.

While Rodney and everyone held back for a day or two, most of the animals went down south, hunting the hunters by killing all the people who ran every zoo or anyone who looked like a circus keeper. But now, the so-called beasts were in need of food and became vicious, killing only White people because they always felt threatened by a White man with a gun. The only thing that tried to help the White race from being killed or chased away by the aggressive beasts were their own dogs, but for the most part, the dogs were being killed and chased off to make way for Rodney and his followers. Rodney looked as far as his eyes could see and thought about how angry the Black woman must be at this country. Within those few days of rest, Rodney had many mental telepathy talks with Aja. She shared that the sisters were doing great, respected what the Black men were doing for them, and were learning that when they let the men lead, they could focus on the world's needs. Right now, they knew the Black man's back was against the wall, so they stepped up to help by tapping into their inner god and using nature's elements and wild beasts to fight off their enemies.

What devastated Rodney, his woman, and the Black race the most was the young Black youth, especially the boys who didn't care much about life because they didn't know which way of righteousness was correct. They were disobedient to the women, running off to fight, but mostly running to their own deaths. Many women cried out for this to end so they could have men in the household because they now understood the importance of the balance between man and woman. In the last mental conversation Rodney had with Aja, she told him to look into the sky. He remained looking until it became dark without stars. Then, there was a quick flash of white light that blinded everyone momentarily. In the blink of an eye, it was gone, and the sky began to clear up. The clouds hovered closer to the ground, and then a loud thunder sound shook everyone's insides, causing many elders to die from it.

While the White man was shooting and killing anything Black, and the animals as well, except for those who ran out of bullets, some

275

White people were game enough to knuckle up and fight. However, their skills didn't match the Black race, who used to fight hand-to-hand. The youth of today figured it was wiser to pick up a gun like their enemies. Because of this, the White people turned around and went to a place they felt safe: the country woods, until they could figure out what to do next. Rodney got the sign that it was safe to move on, but he noticed that some of the normally happy and upbeat men now looked as if they had just lost their best friend. Rodney went into his pocket, pulled out some herb because he knew it was good for uplifting one's spirit, crumbled it in his hand, looked for a dried-up leaf, and held it up to his face. He said a blessing over it, then rolled the herb and set it on fire. He took a good puff, held the smoke in, and then passed the spliff to one of the men, who passed it around to hundreds of others. Word got out that the spliff never went out; it was everlasting.

"What's wrong, my brothers? Why the sad faces?" Rodney asked, wondering why they were down when they hadn't lost any men to the White man's killings this time. One of the men lifted his head and began explaining. "We can see, at times in the sky, that rainbow and people I love along with the rich and famous. I couldn't believe the ones that were making their way over the rainbow," the man said with sadness in his voice. "What is it, Monk? Here it is that some men don't even want to be men, and then you have women who want to be men. May I ask what the Black man did so bad to the point that they were hated and used?" Rodney understood their pain from seeing a loved one or friend who decided to take the route of the rainbow. "Well, the way I see it is that we shouldn't put all the blame on ourselves due to the fact that many Black people today are European-minded to the point that if the White man says it's okay, then it's okay."

The western ways of homosexuality 50 years ago often led to questions about whether the person was of God or the Devil. Many hid in the closet, ashamed of what they had become or worried about what others thought of them. Today, Black men and women have accepted aspects of Roman culture, feeling more ashamed of their race and more inclined to embrace the Devil's work by loving those who have colonized them." The men looked at him, trying to understand. "The sad thing is that they don't see that with their way of life, life cannot go on. Even if a gay man sleeps with a gay woman and they have children, the lack of true masculinity of an Alpha male will cause society to crumble. I know it hurts when it's a loved one, like a child or family member, but we must respect their wishes of self-destruction and live on."

Rodney blanked out for a second, tapping into his past life and remembering when he was in the motherland. He had witnessed a man being stoned to death and two women caught carpet munching each other, who were subsequently shunned by the straight community. Rob walked up to Rodney, looked at the men, and asked Rodney what was going on. Rodney explained the men's concern, and after listening, Rob sucked his teeth and said, "That's an easy fix, you hear? Fire burn! the Wicked Mon!" He pulled out a lighter, sparked it to make a flame, and held it up in the air. "Fire is for the putrefaction of all things, so burn! More fire on the Botty Boy! Gawn them a go!" he said, pointing his finger to the sky as if the rainbow were in sight.

The men started to get themselves together, their ears catching the sound of that D.C. Go-Go beat being played by some people from D.C. Everyone began moving along, dancing further south as if they were doing the Soul Train Line dance. People from B-More started to do the Krunk Dance, subconsciously adopting old African dance styles. They zipped through VA, and when they reached the end of South Carolina, the partying didn't stop. They found themselves deep in the woods, feeling safe and getting closer to where Rodney was taking them. A few men made a huge circle around everyone, with a couple stepping aside to be on the lookout, while others gathered sticks or anything that would catch fire. They made more than one fire pit large enough to burn pounds of herb growing fast and wild all over the place. They burned and inhaled all the smoke they could until some passed out asleep while others felt so high, they seemed to be floating in the air, feeling invincible because the herb protected their flesh and faith.

The light from the fire was so intense that they had no problem seeing anything around them. The heat from the pits was overwhelming, but the high they received from the herb made it worthwhile. The smoke hovering over them rose high into the sky, making White men nearby think it was one of their own, so they never ventured into the woods that night. Rodney and Rob vibed with everyone, feeling like a change was surely coming. They went into a deep meditation for a quick second to grab what energy they could from the universe. Rob tapped into the music of conscious rap and cultural reggae. He keenly listened to every word, soaking in songs by Black Star, Killer Mike, Philly's finest Black Thought, and later, the great Garnett Silk. Rodney, on the other hand, opened his eyes, looked at the ground, and in anger, kicked a piece of a brick next to him. The brick hit a tree, making a noise that broke Rob's meditation. He noticed Rodney was upset about something. "What's wrong, Monk?" Rodney turned to him quickly, anger in his voice.

"First, it was the young Black youth running out to fight back against the people who declared war on them. Now I can feel Aja's worries, so I tapped into her mind to understand what was wrong. When I connected with her feelings and mental state, I felt her pain." Rodney stopped talking for a second, overwhelmed by the pain he was about to share. "Her worries are about all the young Black boys and girls with autism or Down syndrome who have run off to only our father in heaven knows where. Many parents, family members, and friends tried to stop them, but the strength God gave them was unstoppable." Rob didn't understand and scratched his head. "What do you mean, Monk?" Rodney looked at Rob. "The kids told their parents that love is the only way and that they needed to find me." Rob shook his head, saying, "What's wrong with that?" Rodney continued, "The problem is they feel the need to be amongst themselves, and no one knows where they are." Now Rob understood why Rodney was concerned. Rodney foresaw almost everything. "Everything's going to be crisp, mon. Don't worry yourself, mon. Jah will guide them on their journey to wherever he wants them to be."

After Rob said that, he thought about how powerful and merciful Jah the Almighty is. He always knew those kids were special to the world. He smiled at the thought, a slight tear running down his face, and then he let the beat from the ongoing party take over his soul, starting to dance. Rodney joined in, and they partied for the remainder of the night.

Chapter 19

Mr. President

The White House's rooftops and ground area were guarded by top-notch Navy and Army men, guns in hand, ready to do what they were trained to do. Inside the White House, the President and others from the Tea Party, along with undercover Trump supporters, sat at the President's massive desk in the East Wing meeting room. "Mr. President, I'm a reporter from the New York Times. I'm here, of course, for the cause, but as a reporter asking questions, is there anything you would like to say to the citizens out there fighting or to anyone?" asked a short, slim White American man with a Rainbow Fanny pack bag across his chest holding his personal belongings. His black hair was pulled back into a bun, faded on the sides. The President sat at the table, every man in the room waiting for him to answer.

"Well, my main concern right now is the dead bodies we keep finding of our families and friends in states where we've run those coloreds out. I find it strange because I don't see them coming back to kill our people when they can't afford to be separate from each other, let alone come back to kill our loved ones. I've gotten word that when those men in the black ninja clothing were killed and left to rot for what they've done, I sent men to investigate. They checked the tags of those dead bodies to see where the clothes were

281

made. It said they were government-issued, meaning those Niggas were ex-cons. But I also got word that some clothing without bodies in it had tags saying they were made in China, just like everything else." Everyone in the room was shocked to hear that last part, wondering what it meant.

"What? Oh no!" were the words of the men in the room, wanting to hear more about what the President knew. "What are you going to do about that, Mr. President?" asked a man from the Tea Party and head of the Elk Lodge in Maryland's Rising Sun. The President looked the man in the eyes. "I have special forces looking into it as we speak, and you best believe we will get to the bottom of this." The New York reporter thought now was the right time to share the updated news he had received a few hours ago. "Mr. President, I'm sad to say that I have more news to add to your concern." The President waved his hand for the man to continue. "I have parents calling for our help to find their autistic and Down syndrome kids who have run off." The President didn't understand. "What do you mean they've run off? Run off where?" he asked. The reporter began making his way through the crowd to get closer to the President. "Mr. President, from what I gathered, the kids range in all ages, but those 13 and under are being led by elders who are also autistic and have Down syndrome. The parents said that when they tried to stop their kids from running off, their kids turned on them, wanting to fight back. Their parents tried to fight back and make them stay, but they were no match for their kids' natural strength that God had blessed them with. When the parents asked why, the kids all said the same thing: 'You all truly don't know what love is when it comes to the humanity of people.' They were very angry but sad at the same time, knowing they didn't want any part of what was going on in this country. Rumors are going around that the parents heard the kids might be looking to find that Nigga Rodney." Everyone in the room was speechless; you could hear a pin drop. "I can't believe he just said that!" a man in the room said with a smile that revealed his cigarette-stained teeth. They all laughed together, and one man said out loud, "You couldn't be more racist, could you?" again, they all laughed more at the reporter, who replied, "What do you mean? I didn't call him a Nigger. I simply called them what they like calling themselves. Hey, I could have used another word, one they seem to call themselves nowadays—Savage—but?" The reporter chuckled for a quick second before finishing what he had to say. "Our forefathers used that term many moons ago. Isn't it funny how our words have mystical powers over the minds of mankind?" Everyone went silent and serious for a second, thinking about what the reporter had said.

"But! Hey, look at what those great words we've created have done for us and, for God sakes, look at what it has done to those Niggas!" The reporter started dancing around like he was trying to dance sarcastically as if he was some kind of B-boy about to break dance. Everyone in the room went into laughter and tried busting out their own dance moves. It was one of those good Old Boy parties going on in the White House for the remainder of the night as they drank their tea, snacked on their cheese and crackers, sipped on their yak, and smoked top-notch cigars.

The next morning, the men in the White House had hangovers from too much partying, but they still knew that playtime was over, and it was back to setting things straight. They made a few phone calls to the poorer class of people and asked them to pull out those white sheets and march on top of the dead bodies of Black people to ensure they instilled fear in anyone who witnessed them. They carried torches of fire to burn the dead bodies. It was the Georgia Klan members walking down the streets of Atlanta, pulling out their dicks and pissing on the burning bodies, kidding around to see if they could put the fire out. Every so often, they would get the shits and giggles because, glancing out of the corner of their eyes, they would see a gay Black man running for his life like a lady. The only ones in those sheets who didn't find humor in the gay Black man running were those living on the down-low under them sheets.

While the Klan was walking up and down the streets, they were gaining members by the minute from onlookers of white people who needed protection from the Blacks who had been showing up every so often, killing anybody who looked white. Five members of the Klan approached a group of white people standing outside on the porch of an abandoned house. They all looked as if they needed a bath, but what drew their attention was a middle-aged white man appearing to manhandle a white woman who was trying to stop him. "Hey son, you don't need to be doing that to your lady in times like this. Shit, you need to sign up with us and get rid of all that hostility built up in ya." After saying that, the Klan member walked over with his boys, slid the sheet covering his head off so that the white people on the porch would feel safe and proud to see the face of their own kind.

The young man on the porch continued to have his way with the young lady despite what the Klan member said. The Klan member grabbed the young man's wrist with force, holding it tight to get his attention. The young man looked him in the eyes with anger and disgust and then snatched his hand away. "Man, this bitch isn't white. She's fucking P.R., man." The Klan member looked her up and down slowly. "She sure does look white to me," he said, trying to see if he could spot any signs of her blackness, but it was hard to notice anything past the dirt on her face and the streaks of tears rushing down her cheeks. "Man! I know she is because she used to be my cousin's girl before all this shit went down."

The Klan member and his friends stepped up on the porch and got close to the man and the young lady. "So, what you're saying to me is that you're sure she's P.R. and not white, and if so, why haven't you killed this nigger bitch yet, if what you say is true?" The young white man had no problem explaining. "Well, just before you all came, I was just about to have my way with her." The Klan member knew what he was referring to. "You mean without her consent?" He asked, now thinking to himself that the young lady might just be P.R. He snapped his fingers at his boys and pointed to her bag that she was holding onto tightly by the strap along her shoulder. Two of the men took her bag away from her even though she tried not to let it go easily.

While they rummaged through the bag, the Klan member grabbed the young lady's chin gently, moving it around as if he was checking for something other than her skin tone. "Well, well, well, look at what we have here, Luke," said one of the Klan members who just removed the young lady's driver's license from the bag. "It says right here that her last name is Santos. I believe the young man is right about this one." The young lady had a look of no worries on her face until she looked into the eyes of one of the men who went into her bag. She felt now that her African descent could be what she always thought it to be, a downfall for her life. She dropped down to her knees. "Look! I'm white," she said, trying her best to plead her case while pulling up her sleeve to show the man her skin color is no different than his own. The young lady was shaking in fear at that moment. "Relax, will you?" The man said, trying to help her from off her knees onto her feet. "You're not going to kill me, are you?" she asked. The man looked her in the eyes and, with a straight face, told her, "No," while kicking at his friend's foot without her noticing. "I'm not going to kill you, but I think my man was onto something as we were walking up to you all, and since you already like being on your knees begging and shit..."

He started counting out loud while pointing his finger at his friends along with the young man who was trying to take advantage of her before they arrived. The man forcefully grabbed her long hair, wrapped it around his hand, and led her into the house, looking for a place to rape her. He went from room to room while his friends were looking around to see if there was anything or anyone left behind they might have wanted to keep. With a quick glance and their minds stuck on getting some pussy, they didn't notice anything. One of the men went into the kitchen to check the sink to see if the water was still running, and it was. He quickly went looking for his friend Luke from room to room until he went into the last room, finding Luke about to undo his pants and have his way with the young lady lying on an unmade bed with a dirty mattress with old piss stains on it.

The young Puerto Rican girl was ready to be sadly used but wanted badly to be accepted and thankful to be alive. It was a feeling inside her at that moment making her feel like trash, but she was ready to toss it into the back of her mind forever just as she has done with her African ancestors. Luke's friend grabbed the young lady by the arm, lifted her off the bed, and walked her to the bathroom with the other men following him. He turned the shower water on and threw Miss Santos into the shower, then roughly ripped her clothes off her body. The men watched the dirt rush down the drain, revealing that she had a nice clean bush of hair over her kitty cat. Once her body ran off as much dirt as it could, Luke had enough of just standing there with a hard-on, waiting to rearrange her insides.

He quickly and forcefully yanked her out of the shower, took her back to the room, tossed her naked body onto the bed, and then snatched her legs open wide. He rammed his hardness inside her with all the force fueled by deep hatred and anger behind every stroke. The young man, who was about to become a Klan member, was next and pulled out his erection. "Flip that bitch around so I can hit her in the shitter!" he ordered his new friend. They began taking advantage of every hole her body had to offer. Now she had three men with dicks all over her: one man's dick was in her mouth, deep-throating her, tapping her tonsils. When they were ready to climax, they pulled out and shot their load onto her face, causing their semen to run down her chin like a scene from a porn movie. At first, the young lady wasn't enjoying it, but her mind went crazy to withstand being violated. The more they violated her, the more the smut in her came out, and she began to show that she was enjoying it, smiling at the white men as if she appreciated being smutted out by them. She began licking off the salty sperm that touched the tip of her lips.

Luke's best friend was the last to get at her. He stood over her with his pants still on, having her stare at him, wondering why he didn't get the memo. "What's with you?" she asked, smiling and pointing her thumb at him and then at his boys. Luke's boy unzipped his pants and pulled out his dick, careful not to reveal the pistol he had resting on his ass cheek. His dick wasn't erect, and the lady looked at him, then back down at his limp dick. "Well, it looks like you don't want to play," she said, now feeling like playtime had changed. She tried to get up from the bed, but the man pushed her back down, holding his dick out for her to give him head. Just as she hesitated, he stopped her. "Beg to suck my dick first," he ordered, wanting her to know that the white man is superior over her because of her African blood. "I don't know what to say," she said. "Say, 'I always wanted to suck a pure white man's dick. And I would love for you to let me. Oh, and I love my white skin that your race has given us Latinos who have the same skin color.'" She looked at him as if he were a sick individual who didn't understand that their skin was the same color. She did as she was told, and just as he was about to cum, she felt his dick pulsating in her mouth, ready to explode. Just as he began to cum, she started slurping up all her spit from his dick. He quickly pulled his dick out of her mouth and, before she could close her mouth, shoved his pistol in, making her gag on the steel piece. "One thing you should know about us pure white people is that when we say we're going to do something, we mean it. Luke over there said he wasn't going to kill you, but I didn't." The young lady started crying, tears running down her face. She tried to speak, but the man held the back of her head firmly. "What part of Spain are you from?" he asked, removing the gun from her mouth so she could speak. "I don't know," she said, shrugging her shoulders. "What part of Africa are your people from?" he asked, knowing she wouldn't know that either. "Hurry up! Who are they? And where are they from?" he shouted. "I don't know," she said. The man looked at her and slowly placed the gun next to her temple. "What do you know?" he asked as he cocked the hammer on the gun. The young lady urinated on herself, knowing if she said the wrong thing, her life would be over. "All I know is I'm white. See, if it wasn't for white Europeans enslaving my people, I wouldn't have this skin color, so you must understand that I'm white as well." She pointed at her skin color, trying to plead her case. The man spoke. "Then you're sadly mistaken." "Pop!" he shot her in the head, causing a big hole to appear on the other side, blood oozing out onto the bed. Her body lay there, stiff as a piece of plywood. Not feeling a bit of remorse, Luke looked at the young kid and asked, "So, you following us, or are you going to sit around here waiting for more pussy to come by?" The young man looked around, realizing he better make up his mind quickly because the four Klan members had zipped up their pants and left the house, ready to move on. "Wait up!" the young man said, picking up his pace to catch up with them. Luke's friend handed him a black trash bag and gave the young man his freshly cleaned white sheets. The young man opened the bag, pulled out his new attire, and felt part of something for the first time. It helped that this group of Klan members were the lowest of the barrel; they too were cut from the same cloth— poor white trash.

Luke and his friends kept walking, hoping to find more members to join them and a few more "niggas" to kill along the way. Later that night, they were walking down a street. Under any other circumstances, the streets would be filled with street niggas living the street life, but now the town and the surrounding blocks were deserted. Luke walked the streets with pride that he was part of the White Knights. He joined many moons ago to fill his void of hate and need for power. He quickly stopped in his tracks and held back his friends with his arm. "Wait a second, I see a nigger over there eating watermelon," he pointed across the street where they saw two young Black men chilling out on a stoop of a house at the end of the block. "Luke, I'm looking at what you're looking at, and those niggas don't look like they're eating watermelon." Luke looked at the young man who had just joined them as if he were stupid. "That just means the niggas are chilling." Luke said, scoping out the area as best he could. All he could make out were two Black kids. One of the Black kids was standing up, leaning against an oak tree in front of the stoop his friend was sitting on. He had on black pants, a black hoodie, and a black ski mask that was open-faced.

The other young man was chilling on the stoop, and he as well had on all black, but he was wearing a pair of black shades instead of a mask and his hands were covered with black leather gloves that held a black 9mm. "Let's kill those Niggers!" The young man said to Luke and the others trying to fit right in with his new way of life. They were about to make a move on them to try their best to kill the two Black boys until Luke held them back once again. "Let's wait and see for a minute. One of those Jig a Boo's might pop out of nowhere, it could be a set up for us." The other men were grateful of Luke to be in change because they felt like they must have been some dumb Fucks for not thinking that for themselves. They waited for at least a good half hour and thought -what the hell if any other Nigga's pop up will just kill them as well-. Out the corner of the young Black kids' eye who was sitting on the stoop noticed a little short Mexican walking down the block who appeared to be alone. He started approaching in the direction of the two young Black men. "Oh shit!" Said the young Black man standing up against the tree. "Yo! What the fuck, we gotta off this

SA or what?" His friend sitting on the stoop cocked his trigger back without losing sight of the Mexican. The Mexican had on a big white cowboy hat, black and white Cowboy Boots and a big silver belt buckle and from the way he walked you could tell that the little man had a gun on him half his size. "Chill Home's, you ok with me." The Mexican told the two young brothers. "You sure? Because I'm from L.A. my Nigga and we been warring with ya'll for a minute now." Said the young man that now stepped away from the tree and started to walk over to the Mexican. Luke and his friend thought it would be a great time to kill the two kids, but they didn't even notice the little Mexican standing there because he was in front of a Tan Pick-up Truck that hid him from Luke and his boys.

They started tiptoeing towards the two Black men and getting close as they wanted while at the same time, they quickly pulled back the trigger on their guns catching the two young brothers off guard causing them to become startled, while the short Mexican was seeing everything taking place, he remained calm. "Oh Fuck!" the one that was on the stoop shouted out pointing up his gun at his victim. "Pow" he shot Luke's Best friend right in the middle of his head. Luke watched his lifeless friend's body hit the concrete; he immediately pointed his gun at the young Black man with rage of anger. "Pow!" "Pow!" was the sound of two more gunshots going off leaving the two young Black men wondering what happened

while they started checking themselves to see if they had gotten hit by a bullet. "Pow! Pow! Pow! Pow!" was the sound of the gun going off quickly after taking the lives of the four other Klan members. That little, short Mexican was so nice with his gun that he shot the other four men so fast that you would have thought he'd been in many one-on-one duals and remained standing. The two young Black men was so happy that the little Mexican saved them. "Thank you, my friend, that's what we supposed to do, stick together against them White Mother Fuckers." Said the young brother that killed Luke's friend. The Mexican smiled at him and walked up close to the kid and spoke softly but stern. "I didn't do it Because we're brother's Home's, I did it because we want are land back because those Puta's stole it from us." The two young Black men looked at the little Mexican and didn't know what to say to him, so they just watched the little man blow the smoke away from his gun and stuck it back in his waistband. The two young Black men looked at each other and one said to the other. "Shit all this time I thought Mexicans were Black people just like me and you." Said one that was from California. "Well with colonialisms taking place and they wanting to praise a White Virgin Mary and a White Jesus, what do you expect." Said the young brother that stepped away from the tree and the two of them nodded their heads at each other walking away hoping that the little Mexican man don't meet up with a young White man who will remind him quick that he's still a Nigga, but just one that speaks
294

Spanish like a drown skin Dominican. "Yo Bro, I think if we keep heading down south, we'll be heading in the right direction, hopefully meeting up with Rodney. I've been told to listen out for the sound of some type of drums being played." Said the young man named Cid. His friend G was tucking his gun away in his black Boot and then he pulled his pant leg down over it and stood up looking at his friend Cid. "You know that's all cool and shit, but for real for real I feel you on that Rodney shit but Bro after what them Crackers did to my mom's and little brother." G starts to cry for a second as his mind ponders on the last moment when he'd seen his mother and little brother. It was only a few months back when all this happened.

A mob of older White men came into a home in George that a few young Black men took over from a family that left the house behind. The Mob of men ram shacked the home not caring if anyone was in the house or not. They took their chances that most Black women are single with the probabilities of having a young teenager running around trying to find himself to be a man and that was G, the teenage boy who was pinned down to the grown by three White men while the other three grabbed his mother and his little brother and took them out the back door and all G could her was his mother screaming please don't do this. His mother thought she was going to be raped it was like she could feel it in her bones but her words of saying no! not little Keem, G's little 9-year-old brother's name out over and over. The sound of hearing that, his mother trying to fight herself away free from those men holding her back while the other men tortured little Keem by using a long Dill Dow Dick to rape the poor boy. When they finished violating Keems rectum, it was bleeding out like a young lady who's on the first or second day of their monthly period. Keem passed out and his body rested on the ground as he was slowly dying. The screaming sounds again of his mother became louder shouting out No! again until the men in the house dragged G out the back door to see what they had done to his little brother and was about to do to his mother. G looked at his little brother on the grown with a bloody Dill Dow Dick sticking out of his rectum. G tossed his food onto the ground and looks at his mother who is reaching out for him thinking the sick fucks were going to try to have their way with him the same way they had done his little brother. "Shit, we going to really Buck check this one here." Said one of the White men holding G at the time. G's mother was screaming so loud that the sound of it would never leave a living soul's mind that heard it. The men holding her were getting tired of holding her back because they were dealing with a mother fighting for her kids and that's when they took his mother to the end of their backyard that had a little creek with running water flowing down it. "Look" Said one of the white men to the other. He points to the creek, and they notice a few Gators' hoping for them to leave a few dead bodies behind for them to eat but they decided why wait and took his

296

mother over to the edge of the creek and in a laughing matter they tossed her body out to the Gator's and G was made to watch every bit of her body being devalued until there was no remains of her. The White men were so fascinated by how fast she was eaten that they lost focus on the hold they had on G that he snatched himself away from them, almost leaving his arm behind, but his escape led him to this moment of thinking. "Yeah, and with that being said Bro I think I rather go out dying for my revenge." Cid knew what took place that night so he understood how G could feel that way. "I got your back on that to Bro and shit I ain't forget about my cousins who lost their homes in Louisiana do to them bursting those Levees open so all that water would come in to wash out those Nigga's out for good along with their homes. You heard what President Bush said. What you think he meant by saying they were going to build it back up into a new New Orléans? The meaning behind it meant, out with the old and in with the new, Blacks lose their homes and then they make new homes and over price them so high that they won't be able to afford them for generations and then the White young generation come in buying up the land and start taking shit all over again through ownership." Cid said and then they dabbed each other up and kept moving along down the Delta with their ears open listening for the sound of the drums they were hearing about.

"Yo Bro, What up with all this Pedophilia shit? Why a sick fuck wants to fuck a little kid bro? that's some evil shit yo." Said G. Cid thought about it for a quick second and couldn't muster up any reason why. "You know bro, they really pushing this Ho Mo shit off as well, and man they seem to let it be known that a lot of Black men and women have feed into the bullshit by placing it on T.V. and I don't know about you, but I'm tired of seeing a so-called man wanting to be a Bitch you dig me?" Cid was agreeing with G. "It's the mother's Cid, it's the mothers. They love their kid so much that they'll overlook the ways of God and feel guilty inside about bringing a child into this world believing that they don't need a man, especially a Black man such as himself. Man, they be power tripping over their own ego. One thing is for sure is that I heard that the boy Rodney don't play that Ho Mo shit." They started to look around as if they weren't sure which way to go. "Oh, shit, look over there," Cid said to G while looking over G's shoulder. G turned and looked, and the two of them saw what looked like a slim person trying to maneuver around sneakily in a clear bubble. "It can't be," G said to Cid, feeling like he knew who that could be.

"What?" asked Cid.

"Man, who's the only person you know ever in a bubble?" Cid started thinking about it but still wasn't putting two and two together.

298

"Bro, look at the man's shoes; the shits are black and sparkling and shit." Then it hit Cid. "Oh, fuck! Mike Jackson!"

Michael Jackson heard him, and he feared everyone, so he tried getting away, but G and Cid ran over to him to make sure they weren't delusional. When they got up to Mike, they could tell he was scared and could hear Mike crying like a little boy.

"It is him," Cid said to G while they were standing in front of Mike in his bubble, up against the wall in fear.

"What's up, Mike? Why are you scared of us? We're your fans, and look at us, we're black just like you. There's no need to be afraid of us, Mike," G said to Mike.

Michael Jackson tried getting himself together, but he was still nervous. "The fans are why I'm here in this bubble. I've been scared and always running."

"Running from who, Mike?" Cid asked.

Mike just shook his finger at him. "I told you all about those people who like little boys. They tried to make it out to be me, but only the truth will cause a man to want to live in a bubble and almost get killed."

Cid and G looked at each other like they couldn't believe Mike was alive.

True Reparation

"And my black brothers, I'm afraid of you all here in America because I don't feel safe around people who seem to have no problem doing harm to their own kind, to the ones that look like themselves." Cid and G understood what he was trying to say.

"You guys can go down this way, and you'll see the Artist and his symbol carved out in trees all around. He'll tell you which way to go to find Rodney," Mike explained, still unsure if he could trust them but hoping he could.

"Yo, Mike, how is it you're not dead and the whole world thinks you are?" G asked.

Mike hadn't been asked that question yet because they'd been the only two who'd talked to him in years, so all he could come up with was the truth of the matter. "Oh, the power of money, and no one can touch me in my bubble. Yeeh he!" Mike Jackson said, looking around to see if those people of the Illuminati were still looking for him.

"Mike, yo, you good. You need to relax, calm down a bit. And where can I get that bubble?" G asked.

Mike wasn't trying to hear what G was saying because he felt that only the people of the elites with fame and money would understand his worries. "Rodney will show you everything you'll need to get out of this hellhole, and not to mention that he will introduce you to…"

300

Mike, for some reason, couldn't finish what he was trying to say, as if a cat had gotten his tongue.

"Introduce us to what?" Cid asked.

Mike put his head down. "I cannot say. Oh God, I'm saying too much now." Mike pointed in the direction they needed to go. "You must go. I'm getting too emotional right now. Please, just go. I love you all."

He blew them a kiss goodbye as they followed in the direction he sent them. G and Cid had been walking for hours, not knowing which way to go because they were looking for a symbol of the Artist, and it didn't seem like there was any sign of any kind of Artist symbol to show them where to go next. They stood still for a few minutes in the middle of nowhere.

"Fuck! Bro, we've been walking back and forth this way and that way, and now where the fuck are we?" G said out loud, being pissed off, frustrated, and hungry. Cid was hungry himself and past frustrated.

"I mean, what fucking Artist symbol is he talking about? We have been looking for some damn symbol, and now here we are in the middle of fucking nowhere," Cid said, as they both held their hands up to their heads, wondering what to do.

"God! Please send us this Artist symbol," G called out for God to hear him.

"You called for me?" G and Cid looked around them to see where the voice was coming from, and out of nowhere in the mist of darkness, they started to notice a very short person whose height resembled a little leprechaun. The closer the image got, the more they noticed it was a man with high-heeled boots on, adding a few inches to his shortness. He also had long earrings dangling off his ears. By the time the little man met up with them face to face, Cid and G started shaking because they really started thinking that they were going crazy. First, they believed that they'd talked to Michael Jackson, and now they had Prince, aka The Artist, staring at them in their faces. They were speechless. Prince could see that they were having a hard time believing what their eyes were seeing.

"Young men, I'm so happy that you have chosen this path," Prince said, feeling that they must be on the path of righteousness, finding their way to link up with Rodney.

"Prove to us that you're the Prince that we're thinking of and not a look-alike fraud," G said with a straight face, causing Cid to snap out of himself being star-struck for the moment.

Prince sang a two-minute verse from one of his hits called "Little Red Corvette," and instantly they knew for sure that it was him and only him because not a soul on Earth could sing a Prince song the way he could.

"Oh shit, Cid, it's him for real," G said.

Cid looked at G as if to say, "No shit." Now Cid had to ask a few questions of his own. "Who else is out here with you? You seem to be all alone," Cid asked while looking around to see if anyone else was going to pop up out of the blue.

"Well, Rick James and John Fletcher, aka Ecstasy, were not too long ago right by my side, but they're out there looking to catch those fucking predators who like messing with little kids." Cid had a look on his face that asked why Rick James and Ecstasy.

"Why Rick James and Ecs.?" Cid asked.

"Because Rick and Ecstasy could find a freak anywhere." Cid smiled at the comment, and then he had to ask his last question. "Yo Prince, what is it with you liking to put on girl clothes?"

Prince looked at Cid with a serious look on his face, leaned up against the tree next to him, crossed his legs, and pulled out a joint of reefer from behind his ear. He then dug into his pocket, retrieved his lighter, lit the joint, and began to take a hard pull, causing a buildup of smoke to enter his lungs. He then let out little bits of smoke through his mouth and nose.

"I'm the closest thing you're going to see when it comes to a real pimp. The only thing that's different with me is that I don't send women out into the streets to sell their pussy and then have them return to me with my scratch. I myself have the gift that those beautiful young ladies want; they want to fuck me so bad they just pay me upfront for the hopes of it. So many of them want to give me their money because they feel it's the right thing to do, you dig? Even though they know I don't need their precious money because..." He paused for a second, looked down at the ground, then looked back up at them, giving them a quick snicker. "What can I say? They all talk about wanting themselves a tall basketball-playing man, but they for sure love to be fucking with this little man right here! If I choose to fuck one of those ladies, they'll leave me a little gift behind, and those clothes I wear that are of women's clothing are the gift..." Prince continued to say, "What I'm trying to say is I hope what I choose to wear one day isn't one of your old ladies' belongings," he said while brushing himself off to let it be known that he is the shit.

"Enough with all the questions. If you're trying to find Rodney, keep going south that way," he pointed in the direction in front of him. "Near the shoreline and listen."

Cid and G cut him off and at the same time spoke, "Listen for the sound of the African drum, and the sound that it gives off will stand out like no other."

Prince was at the end of his joint and flicked it into the grass. "Well, go on, young brothers, and don't forget to tell Rodney I sent you."

Cid and G thought to themselves that Rodney must be that guy if he had connections with M.J. and Prince. Prince remained in his stance until Cid and G walked out of his sight, and then he felt the need to take his shoes off because the high-heeled boots he had on were taking a toll on his feet.

 In those backwoods, it had a damp feeling with a slight breeze in the air, causing Cid and G to cool off a bit from walking over twenty miles. The wind was blowing the trees a tad bit, causing the fresh smell of the earth's fine greenery to make them feel at ease for the moment. Their ears, on the other hand, couldn't shake off the constant screams of those in rage shouting out to the predators and the cries of the victims being slaughtered. Cid couldn't take it anymore and held his ears closed with his hands, trying to stop hearing the madness.

"Yo, this shit has to come to an end," Cid said to G. G heard him, but he was past that point and remained silent, keying in on the faint sound of the drum he was hearing.

"Shh!" G said and pointed to his ear for Cid to catch his drift. Cid was trying to make out what he was talking about, but his mind wouldn't let go of the horrific sound of the American people killing themselves. The sound of the animals fighting each other began to take over the sound of the death of the humans who were being killed. The sound of it made Cid and G's eyes widen like the image of the Old Sam Bo Nigger.

G took off running, and like most Black folks, Cid followed him, running until they couldn't run anymore. "Man, where are you running to?" Cid asked G, with his hands on his knees, breathing like he was about to take his last breath.

G stopped himself in his tracks without paying Cid any mind as he began to hear running water from a little distance. Then he started to walk toward the sound and waved Cid on to follow along. The closer they got to the sound of the water, the more the sound of the drum bounced off the water, traveling through the air and reaching their ears.

"I'm starting to feel the beat in my soul, Cid." Cid's mouth was too dry for him to say a word because he didn't have any water to drink other than the dirty creek water. He tried speaking but couldn't, and he thought to himself, what on God's green earth is he going to do? Then, out of the corner of his eye, he saw something big and slightly green. He couldn't make out what it was, but his curiosity sent him to go see. He took a few steps, looked down at it, and noticed it was a wild watermelon patch. He quickly grabbed the first rock he saw close to him and used it to try and crack it open. As soon as he got enough of the watermelon open, he drank the juice from it.

"Oh, that's how we're going to do?" G asked him while watching him gulp down the sweet watermelon juice. Cid ignored G and kept on slurping down the juice while pointing at the multiple amounts of them all on the ground. Little ones, big ones, were also surrounded by crops of corn. G grabbed a few melons, then started ripping off the cornhusks from the corn and stuffing them in his pocket.

Cid stopped slurping and dropped the melon onto the ground. "Why are you putting that cornhusk in your pocket?"

G pulled out his bag of herb and started to crumble it up into tiny pieces, placing it into the cornhusk, and then began rolling it. "Look, we ain't got any papers or blunts or any type of pipe to smoke our shit, so this is what one of my dreadlock friends back home showed me how they did it where he comes from."

Cid liked the sound of that. "Then roll it and smoke it then, my Nigga."

"Nah, Bro, it doesn't work like that. You got to let the husk dry so it can burn properly."

Cid shook his head okay. G started sniffing the air like he was a basset hound.

"What the fuck? Cid, you smell that?" Cid had the faintest idea of what he was referring to.

"Nah man, what you smell?" he asked G.

"You don't smell that loud, Bro?"

Cid laughed at G and spoke, "My Nigga, you got the herb in your hand." He laughed at him harder.

"Bro, I haven't even lit the L yet for you to be smelling what I'm talking about. I smell it in the air, and look over there where the smell is coming from. The air is thick with a tint of greenery lingering around," G said while pointing in the direction of the smoke rising up to the clouds with a somewhat skunk and seawater smell to it.

They started to walk down the hill, getting closer to the sound of that drum they had been listening out for. Their eyes started to burn from all the smoke in the air from the buildings burning down and the large population of herb smokers. Rubbing at his eyes, G asked, "Isn't today 4/20?"

Cid thought about the days that passed them by so fast. "Yes sir, why?" he asked G.

"Because I bet that's our people down there smoking, waiting on us, and if that ain't it, I bet with all that herb in the air it has to be nothing but peace among the people. And in this country in the time we're living in, that's hard to come by, my Nigga."

Cid followed his nose and slid slowly down the hill, smiling the whole way down because he knew right away that they'd made it to their destination. G took a little longer to get down the hill because he was scared, but once he reached the bottom, he let out a few tears of joy.

"Cid, we made it, Bro!" They began to dance to the rhythm of the drums that were rocking that D.C. Go-Go swing. There was no need for the little spliff G rolled up for the two of them because at the bottom of the hill were the people of Rodney's camp and other Black people. The amount of herb stuffed in a bonfire would have made it into the world record book for the biggest bonfire, stuffed with crops of the best herb God blessed them all with. If anyone were to walk within a hundred yards close to it, they were sure to get a contact high, and anything closer would have likely caused them to pass out.

"With all this smoke lingering in the air, G, don't you think those White killers will know we're down here?" Before Cid could reply to G, Rob came out of nowhere, walking through a cloud of herb smoke, and reached out to grab a handful of smoke and began to cover his face with it.

"You don't have to worry yourself with that; the herb will protect the I. The only problem we have is these." He swatted at a few pesky flies that loved the smell of the skunk weed lingering in the air. "You've made it, my brothers, so now I will introduce you to many of the other brothers." Cid and G followed him.

"Where is Rodney?" A woman from a distance was asking while waving off the smell of that herb lingering in the air. "Where is he, that no-good Nigga?" she ranted while men standing around pointed her in his direction. Not one person knew who she was; all they knew was it was an angry Black woman asking for Rodney. She looked like she hadn't eaten anything in a few days, and her lips were dried up like a woman's pussy that can't get aroused. She needed water badly, and a few men offered her some, but she refused to take it from them, which they felt was strange. She gave it a quick thought, then stopped herself in her tracks and snatched the water bottle out of the man's hand who offered her some.

"Give me that!" she said as she gulped down the water like it would be her last. She tossed the empty container onto the ground, then started pushing her way through the men. Word got out that an angry Black woman was looking for Rodney. The news reached Rob's ears, and he wanted to know who this woman could be, so he made sure to find her before her eyes and Rodney's eyes could reunite.

"Hold the fuck up! Who do you think you are?" Rob asked as he took a step back from the unpleasant odor her body was giving off.

"You're not Rodney, and if you won't take me to him, then move the fuck out of my way," the lady said.

"What is your purpose with him?" Rob asked.

"I'm the woman that birthed that no-good Nigga."

Rob looked at her and had a flashback from when he used to live near Rodney and his mother, and then said to himself, "It sure is his mother." But it was something a little different about her, and he couldn't make out what. He instantly changed his mannerisms to wanting to treat her like she was some type of Black queen.

"Miss Brown, I'm Rob. Do you remember me?" he asked her while looking her up and down in disbelief at her appearance.

Rodney's mother looked at Rob real hard, trying to make out who he was without the long dreadlocks that looked like shitlocks to her. "Oh, I sure do remember who you are; you're the one that killed your best friend's father." She spit on the ground with an attitude and continued to speak. "You did a good deed by killing that other no-good Nigga, and the best of all was when the cops came to lock your ass up and never let you out again. But I see you made your way out anyhow, but I hope and pray you don't give any of these Nigga Bitches any more babies because the world could for sure do without them no-good motherfuckers!"

At that moment, if Rob could be a white man, his face would have turned red hot. He was boiling on the inside and wanted to kill her with his bare hands. "You're so lucky," Rob said to her.

"And why is that? Shit, I would say that it seems you're lucky as well. I'm really surprised that another Nigga hasn't killed you yet, and that's probably because in jail, you Niggers didn't have a gun to shoot each other with." Rodney's mother went into a demonic-like laughter. "That's right, I said it. And what is it with you?" She looked around at the Black men. "With your hair looking like a fucking mess? You Niggers sure do look like you're two minutes out of the cotton fields." She said this while holding onto her stomach from the laughter that had her abs hurting in a good way to her. "O.k., now take me to see Rodney, Nigga." She ordered Rob without any politeness whatsoever.

She left a bad taste in Rob's mouth because he couldn't understand how any Black woman or Black person could be so hateful to their own race. She went as far as to bleach her skin so that she could remove the Blackness from herself the best she could. Bleaching her skin had her looking like an old white lady with a bad skin disorder. She even went as far as to put sky-blue contacts into her eyes, and her hair was thinning out from all the perm and hot combing she had done to it over the years. She shook her head at the sight of all the Black men in her view because she hated the sight of them not being behind bars, where she felt deep in her heart that every Black man should be.

As they walked through the crowd of people, one ex-con who was crazy over light, bright, and almost white-looking women had his eyes on Rodney's mother as he noticed her from a little distance away. She noticed him as they made their way closer to him. The man quickly changed his thoughts about her, and now the look on his face made him wonder what the hell happened to this poor lady.

"What the fuck are you looking at?" Rodney's mother asked him while making sure their eyes locked. The man didn't say a word as he looked away and looked at Rob, and he could see that Rob was beyond frustrated with the lady.

"Oh, that's not like a Nigga, you gave up too quick. What, the cat got your tongue?" She laughed and proceeded to speak some more. "It's best that the cat got your tongue because I don't fuck with Niggers no more. You see, the only Nigga that ever ran up in this here pussy is fucking dead because of this Nigga right here." She pointed at Rob. Rob quickly stopped in his tracks and turned to hit her, but he stopped himself for the grace of his friend, his brother from another mother.

"Come on!" Rob ordered her as he slowly began to walk to where she wanted to go, but he made sure he took the longest way he could in hopes that she would give up and leave, or better yet, drop dead.

When Rob and Rodney's mother were getting closer to where Rodney was, Rob noticed about 50 yards away a handful of Black men forming a circle. Rob thought instantly that it had to be two brothers fighting. The closer they got, he could see that the crowd of people wasn't in a violent state, so now he really wanted to see what was taking place. He put a little pep in his step, and the closer he got to them, he couldn't believe what his eyes were seeing. He saw about twenty men who looked as if they could die for a chance to take a shower, let alone with hunger and dehydration written all over their faces. But one man stood out from the rest. He was a tall, slim, brown-skinned, bald-headed brother dressed as if he were from some big city, showing off his urban wear. His clothes looked as if they had just come out of the cleaners, and the shoes on his feet looked like he had just taken them out of the box.

Rob noticed the man looking at him coming towards him, and he gave Rob a smile, revealing his gold fronts, hoping that Rob was coming to participate in his way of life. Rob knew from the looks of the man that he was some type of hustler because, to him, a hustler can spot another one like a pimp knows a pimp. The man turned back to the man participating in the game they were playing.

The man dressed as if he were the player of the year was standing up with a magazine resting on his arm and hand, which was held out like he was trying to slap five with someone. He used his right hand to maneuver something on top of the magazine, but Rob wasn't close enough to see what was really going on.

The closer he got, he could hear the man speaking to the crowd of people. "I'm slow at this game, and I'm trying to see if I'm starting to slip in my old age." The man had to be no more than 50 years of age, and the look of worry had never rested on his smiling face. Rob got close enough now to see the man was moving three plastic soda bottle caps with a little red sponge ball under one of them. The man dug into his pocket and pulled out a wad of money, spreading it out in his hand for everyone to see the twenty-dollar bills all the way down to the singles.

"Bet twenty," the man said to the man in front of him playing the game. "There are three caps here, and one of them has the red ball under it. If he doesn't pick the right cap, I will allow someone else to choose, but it's going to cost them fifty for the try."

Onlookers were checking their pockets for cash while others were trying to put their money together because they felt they knew where the red ball was. "Alright, my man, which one is it? This one or that one? Go ahead and pick." The man that was an ex-con was about to pick the cap closest to himself.

"No!" A few shouted out to him, making him rethink his decision. He hesitated for a minute and then chose his gut feeling anyway. Just before the man lifted the cap to reveal if the red ball was under it, he asked, "Are you sure? Does anyone else think they want in on his pick?"

One or two people felt that the man playing the game was going to pick the right cap, so they raised their hands to let the hustler know that they wanted in. "O.k., let me see the money." The man said to them while he placed twenty dollars into their hands to confirm their bet. The ex-con pointed at the cap, and the hustler lifted the cap to reveal that the red ball was not there.

After watching those who lost their money have the look of disbelief on their faces, he nicely removed the cash from their hands. "Ok so now that we know that this cap doesn't have the ball under it who is willing to pick one of these two caps right here to try their luck?" quickly about ten more people wanted to try their luck, raising their hand up that they wanted a piece of that wad of money he was holding in his hand. The hustler smiled at people with a devilish grim that was so deceiving he knew he had them right where he wanted them. He looked at the crowed of people gathering their money up watching who had what to lose and in his mind, he wanted all that loop, it was the feeling it made him feel inside having them feel defeated, the pain they had in their guts without him having to lay a hand on one of them.

The ten people had their fifty dollars out, ready to try their luck, and the hustler placed a crisp Ben in their hands to finalize the bet. "Everyone here is sold on this same cap, am I right?" he asked the participants. They all nodded yes. The hustler knew he was going to lose this bet, but it wouldn't be a hustle if he didn't, so he asked again, "Are you sure?" They all said yes, confident in their choice.

Out of the blue, someone nobody knew came up from behind the hustler and tapped him on the shoulder. The hustler turned around, looked at the man, then blew him off and looked back towards the crowd of players. He asked the man who tapped him on the shoulder what he wanted. The young man said, "I want in on the bet, am I too late?"

The hustler asked, "Where's your fifty?"

The young man responded, "Fuck it! I got a beam, bet the hundred for your two hundred."

The hustler placed the magazine on the ground and went back into his pocket for more money. He pulled out nothing but crisp hundreds this time. He placed two hundred in the man's hands and asked if anyone else wanted to up the bet for a chance at getting one of those crisp hundreds. Just as he thought, a few more wanted in, and he placed more money in their hands. The hustler knew exactly how much he had put out and how much he was going to make.

"Ok, y'all want this cap right here, right?" he asked, and they all said yes, anxious to see the results. The hustler turned the cap over and, with a straight face, sat back for a minute to see their reactions when they noticed the ball wasn't where they thought it would be. Again, the hustler took the money from them, neatly placed the bills in order, and put them back in his pocket, feeling like a job well done because once again he broke the pockets of the Niggers. Once he placed the money in his pocket, a smile reappeared on his face to show the people that it was all fun and games, nothing personal.

He started to walk away as he heard many of the people who lost their money getting a little angry, realizing they'd been hustled. He walked away slowly with a cool strut. Rob ran up on him from behind and grabbed him by the shoulder to stop him. The hustler was ready to fight, thinking it was an angry loser ready for beef. He looked at Rob once he realized Rob didn't approach him with a hostile demeanor.

"What's up?" he asked Rob, eyeing him suspiciously.

"What's your name and your angle?" Rob asked, his face serious.

"People in the streets know me as Chi-Town, and my angle is," the hustler said, chuckling, "I just let the world know that the hand is quicker than the eye."

Rob nodded. "Is that right? Chi-town, what is your purpose in coming here? We're on a mission that seems to be out of your league from the looks of you."

Chi-town smiled and replied, "You may be right because all this fighting, killing, and shit is beyond me. I'm like a true pimp, it's all about the money. That's the bottom line. Y'all Niggers and the White Crackers are fucking shit up. My great-grandfather was from Alabama and mastered this game using walnuts instead of soda caps. He passed it down to his son, who was chased out of the south and forced to move my father and his wife to Chicago in 1944 because of a poor loser looking to kill him. My father worked as a shoeshine man as long as I could remember, but after adding other siblings to the family, he had to do what he knew best. That was what his father had taught him. Years later, I learned the game, and I've never worked a job in my entire life. I have four children that I put through college with the art of this game."

Rob found it strange that the man lasted this long without someone harming him over losing money like rent or car notes and food for their kids. "Brother, I ask you to stop what you are doing. I believe you have done well for yourself and your family, but I'm saying this for your own good."

Chi-town, being from the streets, took that as a threat. "Look here, I haven't sold any drugs to my people, and I haven't laid a finger on anyone because I never had to. But don't think for a minute that I will let anyone get in the way of my family business. I will die for my struggle, no different than you will with yours. Now pardon me." He turned his back on Rob and walked away, leaving him standing there, thinking to himself that Chi-town made his point. He hoped Chi-town realized that in the near future, paper cash wouldn't hold any weight.

Rob watched Chi-town walk away, passing a cornfield. A kid with Down syndrome ran out of the field, up to Chi-town, and pulled on his shirt, saying out loud for everyone to hear, "No more fighting, no more fighting!" The kid then ran back into the high cornfield. Rob made sure to tell Rodney what he saw. He started walking to find Rodney and looked at Rodney's mom, who was laughing again.

"What's so funny now?" he asked her.

"Once again, a Nigga has taken advantage of another Nigga. You see, those Niggers have been had." She held onto her gut while the happy pain bounced around her abs.

Rob sucked his teeth at her and continued moving along with her, still going on about how the Black race keeps knocking each other down. Rob had to stay humble and bite his words once again but wished she didn't have that state of mind because she was missing out on her own son's mission to put all that foolishness behind them.

Chapter 20

Spiritual warfare

Rodney was chilling, sitting on a humongous rock that could hold about six people without a problem. He was on his second blunt, high as a kite, letting the sun's rays enter his eyes so that the energy could hit his cranium. He didn't stare at it for too long because he knew his eyes could only take a few minutes of the sun's rays before damaging his retina. He was all alone until he could feel the presence of Rob coming his way. Rob told Rodney's mother to stay put for a minute while he went to make sure Rodney was okay with seeing her.

When Rob approached him, Rodney sensed something was wrong because the look on Rob's face suggested he had some news. Rodney took another pull on the blunt, and as soon as Rob was face-to-face with him, he passed the spliff off.

"Wa Gwan?" Rob said to Rodney as he took the spliff and began fixing it so it would burn correctly.

"Tell me something good," Rodney asked him.

Rob passed him back the spliff and spoke. "I wish I had good news for you, my brother, but what I do have is news that's going to make you scratch your head."

Rodney looked at him, wondering what it could be. Most of the time, he could see things before they happened, but once again, when it had to do with him personally, it was much harder for him to see.

"Ok, let me have it," Rodney said, prompting Rob to spit out the info.

"OK, first thing first, I witnessed a kid with Down syndrome run out of the cornfields and yell for everyone to hear that we should stop fighting. Then, just like that, he was gone, back into the cornfield somewhere."

"That could mean for us as a race as a whole to stop fighting each other, or it could refer to the race war itself," Rodney said, thinking it was strange. He'd been overly concerned about their well-being, so he started pondering on it, putting his hand to his chin and going deeper into thought.

"Don't get too deep into your thoughts about them because I believe you have more to worry about, my brother," Rob said to him.

"What do you mean?" Rodney asked, with concern written all over his face.

"Your mother is here, bro."

Rodney looked around to see where she was, but he couldn't spot her, so he asked, "My mother is here, bro? Where is she then?"

Rob pointed in the direction he had just come from. "She's over there waiting for me to bring you over to her."

Rodney couldn't believe what he was hearing, but it didn't matter—he had wanted to see his mother for a long time. He asked Rob to please bring her to him.

"Are you sure, Monk?" Rob asked before doing as he was asked.

"Yes, I must see her.

Without another word, Rob walked off to get her. As Rob and Rodney's mother started coming toward him, Rodney noticed that her clothes were filthy and her skin was brown from dirt. Despite this, he could see that her skin was much lighter than the last time he had seen her just before he went to prison. Even though her skin was lightened from all the bleaching she had used over the years, she still couldn't hide her wide nose and her nappy hair, which she had permed or hot-combed to mimic the looks of a White woman.

His mother laid her eyes on him for the first time in a few years, and a look of disgust took over her face. Rodney was happy to see his mother, even with the unpleasant smile she was giving off. He went over to her to reach out and give her a hug that he had longed for. She stepped back and pushed his arms away, frowning even more.

"Nigga, please. What, you thought I came here to show you some love? Please, that shit went out the door when you and that nigger bitch Michelle got together. Oh, you know that Black bitch is on baby number three, and if I had to bet my last fucking dollar, I'd bet she's got three different baby daddies to add to it."

At that very moment, Rodney didn't have any concerns about Michelle whatsoever, but what was hurting him inside was the cold rejection from his mother when he wanted a simple hug. He tried to think of something to say to her that would at least make her come to grips with showing some type of love to him.

"Nigga, what do you think you're doing with these niggas other than wasting y'all's time? The White man is killing you niggas one by one. Just look, the cops have been doing that shit forever. What are you and your niggas going to do about it? Not a damn thing. Yup, I said it—you all are going to die."

She began to laugh at her own words, and from the sound of her laughter, Rodney could tell that her soul had been taken over by some type of demon. His mother looked into his eyes and could tell that she was getting to him with her hurtful words. She loved the fact that she was making a Black man feel unwanted, unloved, and shameful. She felt like she had his dick tucked between his legs like a dog that had been badly broken by an abusive owner.

"Look at your hair! It looks like that nigger Buckwheat—you know, from the Little Rascals."

Rob and Rodney looked at each other and then back at her, making a fool of herself.

"All you need, nigga, is some white ribbons tied up at the end of them shits."

Rob couldn't take it anymore without saying something to her.

"Look at you out here in eighty-some-degree weather with a long fur coat on that looks like an old rug from out of someone's basement that's been flooded."

Rodney's mother removed all smiles from her face and looked Rob dead in his eyes.

"Don't look at me crazy because I chose to never leave this coat behind. Yes, I may look strange and out of place, but have you looked at them young niggas who be out in them streets with hoodies on or a fucking ski mask all fucking summer?"

Rob didn't reply, knowing he couldn't win an argument with a woman, so he kept his mouth closed and looked at Rodney.

"Man, that's the same coat Jim got her for her birthday years ago," Rodney said to Rob.

"Bro, it looks like it too," Rob said, and then they turned back to Rodney's mother, catching her scratching her ass and digging into her nose. She looked at her finger and flicked the booger onto the ground. Rodney shook his head at his mother and began to walk away.

"Rodney! Nigga! Don't you walk away from me. I'm your mother! I'm not done talking to you yet."

Rodney stopped for a second and turned to face her.

"Why, Momma? Why do you feel you needed to come seek me out just to talk down about me and our Black race? Why, Momma?"

"Oh, because Little Nigga you and the rest of them Nigga's need to hear what I have to say."

"Well, Momma, didn't you teach me at a young age that if someone didn't have something nice to say, they shouldn't say anything at all?"

"That's correct, but Nigga, I'm only going to speak the truth, and if the shoe fits, so be it." Before he could respond, she laughed out loud and continued flapping her lips. "What, you think you're going to save the Black race from the White man's oppression?

Nigga, please. Just look at the hopes of your youth today. Their dreams are inedible fragments of their imagination. The young Black males have woken up and finally decided that working for the White man is their only option. Without knowing their capabilities and self-worth, they'd rather focus on fast money or, for some, not working at all and just taking what the government offers. These types of niggas are what young winches glamorize when they're young and hot in the pants, ready for a young, dumb, and full-of-cum nigga to come along and give them a baby. Oh, then reality hits the woman in the face when she looks out into the world that surrounds her, feeling and seeing the struggles that her race must face at the mercy of the White man's power in this country. When she gets older and has learned to fend for herself, she starts to despise the Black man, just as I have, because he starts to feel hopeless, helpless, and powerless to compete in this country among all the other races. The Black woman has been fed up with her Black man because she feels like a woman who has a man fighting for her protection needs to show that he can by protecting her. May the strongest man win, and her hope for that was lost long ago. She won't say it to his face, but damn it, I will. She looks at him like he's a coward unless that nigga's got some money for her. That's right! I said it, nigga—all you're good for is the little bit of money in your pocket and maybe some good dick. Oh, and for those niggas who think they've got it made because they have a little more money than the next nigga and some good old White friends, thinking they've got it going on because of money and all the material things they've gained over the years. They don't realize they've been had because, for one, they don't have unity within their race or, more importantly, family unity. Without the Black woman lifting him up and another Black man telling him to keep his chin held high, he has and will continue to give up on himself and continue killing himself. Now, for the Black winches, they really are lost mentally because they want to be the leader when they know the man is supposed to lead, but her trust in him has vanished. She claims niggas ain't shit and all she feels she's good for is getting an education or anything that has to do with sex because she knows sex sells. That no-good-for-nothing bitch will fuck you good until she's finished with you. Whatever it was that she once wanted from you is gone, she will replace you and blame you for her leaving your ass. Ask me how I know—I know because I'm that bitch that the shoe fits. You show me a Black winch that is all about her so-called king, and I'll bet I'll be sitting here waiting all fucking night."

Rodney's mother saw tears running down her son's eyes. Hearing how she really felt and thought she was speaking the truth was digging into his gut, causing pain.

"Aww, nigga, what's with those tears? You mad because of what I said? OK, let me sing you a song. 'Cry me a river, nigga, cry me a river, my nigga. Oh yes, I love to see you cry, my nigga!' Or should I sing 'Rock-a-bye Baby on the Treetop?'" She started laughing at Rodney, pointing at him and holding up her other hand to her mouth to hold back some more laughter.

After everything Rodney's mother said to him, Aja could feel that he was stressing over something, so she tapped into his mind. When it was revealed to her what Rodney's mother was saying to him, she wanted his mother to see that so-called Black bitch who had her man's back. Out of nowhere, she came out like a true ninja and spoke. "I'm right here, you lost woman."

"Who the fuck are you?" Rodney's mother asked.

"I'm the one that's going to remind you that the same thing that makes you laugh will make you cry." At that moment, Aja used her mind power to make Rodney's mother's skin start to turn back to its natural complexion. Seeing her bleached skin start to turn light brown, Rodney's mother got really upset.

"This bitch is a witch!" she yelled out loud, pointing her finger at Aja. Aja was loving every bit of it, even as Rodney's mother started to claw at her own skin, trying to reach the white meat in the hope that it would stay that way.

"You winch! What have you done to me?" Rodney's mother yelled at her.

"Blap!" was the sound of a Colt 45 bullet hitting Rodney's mother's head, causing her brain to splatter all over the ground she stood on. Tears blinded Rodney's vision for the moment, so he didn't see anything that took place, but he knew it was probably his mother who had been shot because her voice went mute. Seconds later, right after the gunshot went off, Aja's voice was loud and clear to him.

"I got your Black winch right here, you black piece of shit!" Aja said while Rodney watched his mother's lifeless body for the last time, noticing that her skin was still turning to its natural complexion. He cried out, "Aja, Aja, why?" He asked, already knowing why inside.

Aja hugged him and warmed his heart with her touch. "Because, my love, she didn't love herself. Just as she spoke of the Black man and how they're killing themselves slowly but surely, I just rushed hers a bit. Sorry to say, my love, but the bitch had it coming. And look, if she was rolling with us, she wouldn't have been able to die so easily."

"Yes, Rasta," Rob said, while he and Aja helped Rodney move along so they could gather their horses, leaving his mother behind to rot alone. Rodney started thinking about the night Rob killed his father, hearing the gunshot ring out and his body hitting the ground, taking his last breath. Now his mother had died in the same manner, and he knew one thing for sure: his parents' lives were taken away from him because of someone with a gun. Quietly to himself, he said, "Guns don't kill people; people behind the gun kill people."

"No more guns! Please, Rob, Aja, no more guns, please." Rob looked at him, then down at his own hip that held his gun, and thought more about what Rodney was asking of them.

"My brother, go and ask that to the men of the NRA and all of them White people out there with their guns smoking from killing one of us." Rodney wasn't trying to hear that, especially since he lost his parents because of a gun, along with most of the Blacks killing each other all over the world because of it.

"I can't take it anymore. It has to stop before we're all dead, White or Black—it doesn't matter because a bullet doesn't know shit about color." Aja understood what he was saying, but she was a stern believer in fighting fire with fire.

"My love, I'm sorry for the way your family had to go, but in the times we're living in, most killings are done by someone with a gun. Murder is murder. Back in biblical times, a man killed another man with the jawbone of an ass. Point is, murder and death are all the same if you ask me." She looked at Rodney the whole time, and she became saddened to see the tears rolling down his face. They mimicked her tears during many nights behind prison walls, hoping for her moment to be free, free as the Black race cries for every day. She started thinking about what she could do to take his mind off everything going on. She snapped her fingers at him, but he didn't respond. So, she started snapping her fingers in front of his face, and still, he didn't budge. She looked at Rob, and Rob looked at Rodney, wishing that his friend would snap out of whatever was taking over his mind at this very moment.

"Yo, bro! You good?" he asked Rodney, but he still didn't respond. Aja tugged on Rob's arm and said to him, "Give me a good while with him alone, and I believe I can bring him back." Rob nodded his head in agreement and then asked, "Do you want me to go find Winker?"

Aja smiled at Rob and said, "Not at all. I can handle this on my own." Rob said, "Well, okay," and started walking away to find a place to chill out. Aja took Rodney by his hand and started to lead them to a grassy area with a few trees shielding them from the sun. A slight gust of wind caused the leaves to swing back and forth, giving off a nice breeze. Aja stood in front of him and began to undress slowly. Rodney cocked one eye at her and began to watch. Aja dropped her panties to the ground and then stepped out of them, slowly moving closer to him. She kissed his lips softly with so much passion that his body flinched at the feeling and then instantly became at ease. Aja grabbed onto his pants, undid his button and zipper, and then whipped out his manhood. She

333

couldn't believe how soft it was as she caressed his thick shaft. The two of them had been locked down for so long that they started to become overly heated, turning into two whoremongers whose bodies couldn't wait to be ravished by one another. Rodney's erection seemed as if he'd popped a few of those blue pills, but the truth was that the sweet smell of Aja's pussy lingered in the air, hitting his nose and causing his mind never to forget that scent. He reached down to touch her between her legs, and his hand slipped off her leg quickly from her juices flowing like a woman who just can't control herself from squirting, and that's exactly what she was doing. She couldn't wait any longer for him to stand there and just look at her, so she grabbed his dick, turned around, and slightly bent over, sliding his manhood inside her. The moan she gave off the minute he entered her body was a sound of love any man would yearn for. Rodney busted a nut three quick times inside her, and the two of them felt an electric energy coursing through their bodies, like they were going to be grounded together for life. Rodney snapped back to reality and pulled himself out of Aja, looking at her and then down at the ground.

"I greatly appreciate what you just did, but you must put your clothes back on because we don't have much time." Aja didn't ask why or where, she just did as she was told. Rodney loved that he didn't have to explain himself, knowing full well he didn't have time for all that. The two of them tried to wipe the essence of sex off themselves the best they could and then went looking for Rob. Rob noticed them first and started to put a little pep in his step so that he could catch up to them.

"Yo! Hold up," Rob called out. Rodney turned around, saw Rob with a big grin on his face, and started smiling himself. The closer Rob got, he could smell that the birds and the bees had taken place, and he thought to himself how he couldn't wait for his time to do the same when he got back with his lady—a small chance with this revolutionary war still going on.

"The horses are not far from here. I tied them up about a mile that way," Rob said to Rodney, pointing south in the direction they were headed. "What's next, Star?" Rob asked with his Jamaican drawl.

Rodney's third eye revealed to him what was going to happen within the next couple of months, but his tongue had a lock on it, like the Lord up above didn't want what was revealed to be shared with everyone. "Well, my brother, what I will tell the two of you is that what we are about to witness will almost seem as if one were dreaming. I must say that when the Lord has a blessing for his people, we never seem to see it coming in the manner of how the blessing comes."

Rob and Aja tried to think of what type of blessings he was referring to, understanding that just waking up is a blessing. Still, their minds couldn't fathom God's plan for them, so they could only use their imagination. Rob pointed at the horses and the two other brothers who had been caring for them. Rodney was so happy to see how well-kept those horses looked. He smiled at the fact that when his people put their love into doing something, only greatness comes from it.

"Look at the shine on their coats," Rob said aloud as he picked up his pace to see his red stallion. When he got close to his horse, he noticed the young man Junior and his uncle Cee smiling at his return. Rob returned the smile, but then his face changed as if his eyes saw something out of the ordinary. His horse was so happy to see him that it started to dance the way Junior and his uncle had trained it. But what surprised him was when his horse smiled back at him, showing his big white teeth with one in the front having pieces of gold that sparkled.

The horse raised up on its two back legs and made a grunting sound to show it was happy. "What is going on? Why does my horse have gold on its tooth?" Rob asked, not taking his eyes off the horse's teeth.

Cee felt the need to explain. "Well, you see, your horse must have had a bad tooth. It was hurting him to the point he wouldn't eat or want to move. He just stood all day with a sad face. So, when I checked on him, he let me check his teeth, and that's when I saw a few big black holes in his front right tooth. I'm not a dentist, but all I could think of was trying to find a way to get the bad parts out and do what our old heads in the South used to do before dentists today put that silver stuff in our mouths."

Rob shook his head, trying to wrap his mind around what Cee did to fix the problem. "What did you use on the tooth to get rid of the bad parts?" Rob asked him.

"Well, I had a box of Arm & Hammer baking soda, some apple cider vinegar, and some jailhouse toothpaste. I applied that for a few weeks, then asked some of the brothers if they had any gold chains or rings they could donate for the cause. Without a fight, they turned over their gold and silver for you, my brother. So, I took the gold and silver, melted it down, and quickly applied it to his tooth. To my surprise, he didn't even flinch, and a few days later, these are the results."

"Well, thank you very much, Cee. When we all finish our mission, I shall pay you threefold," Rob said while mounting his horse. Rodney and Aja greeted Junior and Cee, then the three of them got on their horses and trotted off slowly to gather the rest of their followers to head further down south.

Chapter 21

Is Color Really A Thing.

One summer later, the Black and White races had nearly killed each other. Up to this point, the Black race was losing the war due to a lack of guns, ammo, and men. The White men and their children made it their business to gather the dead men's guns and ammo whenever one of their men died. Every road in the country and all the land of the countryside were covered in the blood of men who felt they were fighting in honor of their race. Some died from sickness, some took their own lives after witnessing their loved ones being tortured or murdered, and others couldn't bring themselves to kill anyone. It was kill or be killed, and some said they wanted no part of it any longer. So, some took pills to overdose, some took a blade to their wrists, while others jumped into the deep ends of rivers and oceans.

Word got out that Rodney was headed toward Miami, so everyone started heading in the same direction. However, they all came to a halt because the Black race had no more guns or bullets to defend themselves in Texas, Mississippi, Alabama, Georgia, and all of Florida. The White people were bragging and taunting the Black people, who now felt utterly defenseless. The White men didn't care about the fight being unfair until the night of Juneteenth. A dozen Black men were dying rapidly, and onlookers couldn't take it any longer. In the middle of Florida, a Black man had seen enough and called out the White men who were still shooting down unarmed Black people.

"Cracker, don't be such a coward! You can see we can't win this fight when you all have the guns and all the bullets. How about you put your guns down and fight with your bare hands like a man?" The two White men he was talking to thought it was a joke.

"What do you mean? Nigger, you're asking us to use our bare hands because you don't have any more guns or help from DMX and OutKast's dogs. We shot them bitches dead. You Niggers don't want to fight us bare-handed. Haven't you seen most of our hockey players? They ain't got no teeth for nothing, and the Irish have been bare-knuckling since it existed. How about you Niggers take my spare gun and do what y'all know best: kill a Nigger that looks just like you. Shit, the Klan has been able to kill fewer of you motherfuckers since you learned how to pull a trigger."

"Pow!" The White man talking had just gotten socked in the jaw, causing him to stumble back a bit. The ordinary person would have been knocked out cold, but when a White man has booze in him, it's hard as fuck to knock him out. The brother who hit the White man waited for his reaction.

"You talk too much!" the Black man said out loud.

Word got out about the Black man's request to fight hand-to-hand, and all at once, all over those five states, every White man started putting their guns down on the ground with pride. All at once, as if they had planned it, the White men rushed the Black race. One by one, many of their men were getting knocked out by the older Black men. The young Black youth looked around mad as fuck that the guns had been taken out of the equation since many of them had never been taught how to fight with their hands, except for Rodney's crew of escaped prisoners. The young Black youth caused the score to be even when it came to hand-to-hand fighting because they didn't know how to throw hands.

As the all-out brawl took place in these states, every so often a White man or a Black man would try to walk away without killing each other. They never wanted this race war to happen in the first place, feeling that fighting over color is a foolish man's game. But every time someone stepped out of line to run off the fighting battlefield, an old White man would pick up a gun from one of the dead bodies and proudly shoot them down. The bare-knuckle fighting became three times worse than an MMA fight out of control because the result was death 99% of the time. The hand-to-hand fighting made the war more personal, like being killed by a knife versus a gun.

Months went by before Rodney and his followers ended up at the tip of Florida. After coming through South Carolina and Georgia

340

and seeing the ruthlessness of the dirty South, its old history of hatred was no longer the way of southern hospitality. The Confederate flags were being hung just about everywhere by White people who loved the old ways of the South, especially the power they had over the scared old Black people. The street curbs were occupied by Black and White Americans' blood running down its drain. The climate seemed to change overnight, and the daytime lasted for 30 days of light. Three months later, the nights lasted 30 days of darkness. The animals started to sense the change in the local area, causing the snakes, rats, cats, dogs, and anything that crawled or crept along the earth to travel back up north, except for the ravens who stayed and waited in the trees for Rodney and his followers to make it to their destination.

The mermaids of the sea started leaving the ocean and surfaced on the land, placing their fishy-smelling selves anywhere they thought they could grab the attention of any lustful man or woman. The mermaids didn't talk; all they did was sit still for a second while trying to look pretty on the land for all the angry men fighting to see them. They would flap their fish tails up and down, revealing to the men their bald pussies, causing every so often a horny Black or White man to try and screw the fish's pussy hole. People whose minds hadn't faded totally into that level of sin couldn't understand what their eyes were witnessing, seeing a man fucking a fish.

"Stop fighting! Stop fighting! Stop fighting!" was being shouted out, but no one could figure out at that moment who was shouting out to them. Every state that held the remaining people still fighting noticed a bunch of autistic kids marching around them.

"Stop fighting! God is using us to warn you all!" said a handful of autistic kids. The men fighting paid them no mind and continued fighting until someone was dead.

"AHH!" a White man in Florida shouted out loud just before he took his last breath. His body hit the ground, and other White men standing around noticed a quick puddle of blood leaking out of the man's body. They couldn't understand what was going on because that man wasn't in the midst of fighting at that moment. A few White men stood over the dead body, noticing that the man had a black Chinese throwing star pierced into the back of his neck. This started to become the norm all around them, and they noticed every so often a man would drop dead right beside them with a star lodged into his body from the waist up.

****

In Texas, a group of four Black teenage girls had an old White woman on her knees, begging them not to beat her to death. The reading glasses the old White lady had on her face had been knocked off, causing them to break and scratch her nose. Her face looked red from being smacked, and the tears running down her face weren't from the pain inflicted upon her but from knowing this day would come. She never believed she'd live to see it or become a victim of this race war. A Black man, who loved being on TikTok, noticed what was going on from a distance and walked over to see if the four young Black women had it in them to kill the White lady. He had so much hate built up in him that he wouldn't have had a problem doing it himself. When he got close to them, he said, "Y'all been bullshitting, what's taking y'all so long to nab this bitch?" One of the Black women, thinking the same thing, pulled out a razor blade from between her tits. She raised her arm and was just about to swing the razor across the White lady's face and then her jugular, but her arm was caught mid-swing by the Black man.

"Hold on a minute," he said, looking the old White lady up and down, trying to figure out where he'd seen her before. "Where do I know you from?" he asked.

"I'm Miss Jane Elliott. I'm not your enemy. I've been teaching all over the country about racism and how, if things didn't change, America would come to this." It started to click, and the Black man remembered seeing her on TikTok.

"Yes! That is you. I'm so sorry that it's come down to this, but..." Miss Elliott cut his words short.

"You don't have to explain. Remember, I'm Miss Jane Elliott, the teacher." The man shook his pointing finger at her.

"Yes, your class should be taught all over America. But Miss Jane, if you want to be safe, you have to get out of here." She looked at him and said, "Where to? If I run to my White race, they'll think I'm a sellout because I speak the truth. And if you hadn't just saved my life from these young girls, they would have killed me."

One of the young Black girls stepped forward and said, "I'm sorry, Miss Elliott. We didn't know who you were, and you're right, you would have been killed if it weren't for this man right here." The young lady pulled out a pill from her pocket and handed it to Miss Elliott.

"What is this?" Miss Elliott asked.

"I'm a lab tech. I invent drugs for the government. Every day, I try new things, and this pill I've been working on is supposed to turn white skin darker every six months, trying to preserve the White race. The sun has already been doing damage to your race, so that's why I've been working on this pill." Miss Elliott took the pill from her, opened her hand, and looked at it.

"Go ahead, Miss Elliott, take the pill and see if it works, because if not, who knows what will happen to you." Miss Elliott sat there contemplating what to do.

"Come on, guys, we got to move on!" said a Black man, urging them to leave Miss Elliott to her own demise. The sky suddenly turned dark gray; seconds before, it had been hot like a blazing fire. The dark gray sky had a shine to it that made the people in those states fighting see a dim reflection of themselves throughout the sky. The ravens in the trees with red eyes seemed to give the people a small amount of light. A rumbling, sounding like an earthquake, echoed throughout the country, causing everyone to pause and back away from each other while staring into the sky. The sound grew closer, and the sky slowly changed to a smoky orange color. The Black race of people looked at the orange smoke overhead, thinking it was the same thing the government had been spraying over the ghettos in America for years. Suddenly, a whistle-like sound flooded their ears for a second, and then the grounds of those four chaotic states felt like a massive volcano erupting. Men's body parts were blown to pieces, mixed together by a bomb.

The surviving men in those states pulled themselves together and went out wondering who dropped the bomb on them. The problem was that the bomb blew up into nothing but ash particles as thin as sand grains. Many men were killed that day, but the Black race had no choice but to fight to stay alive, while the White race had to defend themselves or die, carrying the weight of figuring out who dared to drop the bomb on this country. From that day on, the country was under attack, causing the White race to become very weak and stressed, fearing their dynasty was in jeopardy. However, the fighting Irish and the great African-Armenian warriors in this country felt the need to keep the race war going. This was the only time in this country that money wasn't necessary. The value of a man and his wealth in these times were measured by his health, strength, food, loyalty, and word.

With all the fighting and bombing of unknown origins, the President was still safe and sound, sitting at home in the White House with his feet kicked up on his desk, leaning back in his chair, smoking a Herf Heads cigar.

Back in Washington D.C., the place was deserted except for the army tanks that surrounded the White House. Instead of wrought iron black gates, a stone wall now encircled the grounds, reaching the top of the windows with broken glass on top, ensuring anyone contemplating scaling the wall would think twice. Covering the top of the White House was a bulletproof glass dome surrounding the stone wall. Handheld drones were sent miles out to scan the D.C. area by men in black. About fifty Secret Service men stayed close to the President.

"I need to talk with that Rodney kid once more. For that young man to want to walk away from this country now while we're being attacked by Lord knows who, I have to question if he's somewhat behind this sneak attack," the President said to one of his Secret Service men.

"I can snatch him up once again for you and bring him back here if you like, Mr. President," said the short but stocky Secret Service man.

"I think that will be a grand idea. I'll go as well; I need to get out from behind these stone walls anyway. Have five good men tag along, and I'll be waiting out front in ten minutes," the President said. The Secret Service man gathered up five of who he thought were the best out of the fifty men, and ten minutes later, they pulled up in a blacked-out Lincoln Navigator with the doors open for the President to get in.

They used the drones to search for Rodney and his crew miles out, so they wouldn't enter harm's way. Some of the drones were being shot down by White police officers who thought they were like the ones that killed many of their colleagues, controlled by young Black people in the past. Within four hours of searching every state under D.C., Rodney and a large number of his followers were seen. The President took back roads and underground highways that everyday citizens didn't know about. He remained put until he felt the time was right to nab Rodney.

"We'll sit here and watch him until I say move in," the President said to the driver and the other four men in the truck.

347

"Yes sir! Oh, and sir, Mr. President?" The President looked at the driver.

"Yes?" he asked.

"Do you want the Nigger dead or alive?" The fact that the President had to think about it for a good minute said a lot about how he really felt about Rodney and why this race war was taking place.

"Dead? Shit, no! I mean, at least not now. I need to look into his eyes to see if he's who we have to worry about. A man who doesn't talk much has a plan, and I'm about to find out something before we kill him. So, no, I don't want him dead." Right after the President said that, he felt the need to make the moment into a joking matter. "Just make sure the Nigger is clean before he enters the truck, and if not, give him this." He held out some baby wipes, reminiscent of Trump's gesture with paper towels to Puerto Ricans when they were hit by a storm that almost wiped out the island. The six men in the truck laughed at Trump's actions and now at the former President's mockery.

Rodney, Aja, Rob, and Winker stood around in central Florida, watching the changing weather. The only constant was the rainbow that occasionally saw a happy gay person skipping up to meet and greet others from the LGBTQ family. Many men and women, preferring to live their truth rather than die in a senseless battle, found solace in this symbolic display.

"Yo Rob, what do you think is causing those people to want to reach the top of that rainbow?" Rodney asked.

Rob thought about it, often coming up with different reasons, some considered insane by conventional mental health standards. "They are taking the seeds out of the fruits and crossbreeding the male seed with other male seeds and vice versa with the women. That might have something to do with it. Also, I've been saying to watch out for that water; I bet it's got something in it," Rob laughed at his own joke about the water turning people gay.

Rodney chuckled a bit but pondered the potential truth behind it. "No matter what, in the end, they will be judged and handled without being able to explain anything. The sad thing is that I believe some of them are good-hearted people with a lot of love in their hearts. But having a good heart doesn't get you into our kingdom of glory, which is about to come." Aja and her friend nodded in agreement.

"Fire burn the wicked, mon!" Rob shouted, his face contorted as if he smelled something foul.

Rodney closed his eyes for a few minutes, and the others assumed he was praying, leaving him alone to talk about how many days it would take to reach Miami. Ten minutes later, Rodney said, "They are here. I knew they would come back to get me again."

Rob knew who he was referring to, but Aja and Winker were uncertain, though they had an idea. "Who, my king? Who thinks they're going to take you away from me?" Aja asked, her voice full of concern and determination to protect him.

"Uncle Sam," he said. "I will be fine. They just want to have another talk with me. I don't know if you've noticed, but something fishy is going on. White people are getting killed by someone other than our race, and our people are slowly dying after eating the Chinese food they've been feeding the hungry in the ghettos."

Rodney walked away, hurting inside from having to leave Aja. She ran over to him. "What's the matter, Monk?" she asked.

"Don't come looking for me. I don't want my Queen to be in any more harm's way," Rodney said. Aja respected his wishes but resolved to stay back unless she sensed danger, ready to use her inner spirit to shake the Earth if needed. Rodney appreciated this about her but hoped she wouldn't have to cause more drama in the universe.

Rodney took a deep breath, gathered a few of his things, and walked away from the group, knowing the President's people wouldn't approach them directly. "I'm going to walk away from y'all because they're not going to come over here. They think we're going to catch one of them and do lord knows what. Now isn't that some shit?" Rodney said as he waited in the open, in the middle of the street, with his bag on the ground. He took a blunt from behind his ear and a lighter from his pocket. After several failed attempts to light it, he became angry but caught himself, deciding not to let anything control his emotions. He cleared the lint from the lighter and finally got a small flame. He adopted a meditative stance, closing his eyes, waiting for the truck to arrive.

"There he is. If I didn't know any better, I'd think that Nigger is waiting for us. Go get him now; we don't have much time," the President ordered his Secret Service men.

Rodney grabbed his bag, tossed it over his shoulder, and opened his eyes as the Secret Service pulled up. His piercing gaze made the two men who stepped out of the truck reconsider their aggressive approach. Rodney helped himself into the truck, and the two Secret Service men got back in, checking the area before closing the doors.

There were two Secret Service men in the back of the truck with Rodney in the middle, and two others up front. Not a single word was exchanged during the entire ride back to the White House. When they arrived, Rodney noticed things looked different. The grounds were surrounded by military tanks and armed soldiers, with two big black Cane Corso dogs guarding the front gate. Their master held them back as the bulletproof door slowly raised to let the truck into the parking hideout. Seconds after the tail end of the truck entered, they were in a bubble and quickly sent into a dark road leading to an underground tunnel. The President wanted them to go there to avoid being spied on from above.

The truck stopped, and all four doors opened wide as if someone had opened them from the outside. They were in front of a secret wall door, behind which the President was waiting patiently for their return. Nobody in the truck moved, and Rodney wondered what the holdup was. He remained seated, waiting to see what the four Secret Service men would do. They all looked at Rodney simultaneously, causing him to get the message. He slowly got out of the truck and stepped onto the ground. Within two minutes, his body had been scanned, and in a flash, he was inside the underground part of the White House. The President greeted him with a wide smile, his hands outstretched as if he had forgotten their last conversation.

Rodney walked into the room with his hands behind his back, his stride that of a king who did not extend his hand in return. The President's smile faded, so he took a seat and gestured for Rodney to do the same. This time, he didn't have his glass of scotch or his big cigar. Instead, he had two cone-shaped blunts on his desk with a lighter and two glasses of ice water. He lit one blunt and took a

352

hard pull, trying to show off as if he were a pro. A smile appeared on his face at the thought of Rodney doing the same, so he waved for Rodney to join him.

Rodney looked at the blunt on the table and then at the President. "What's with the herb? I mean, I know why I partake in it, but what's your reason for all this? You do know I got into some trouble over herb, right?" The President was happy to exhale a healthy cloud of smoke before almost choking to death.

"Yes, Rodney, we know everything about you. I just wanted to share some of this nice Blueberry Kush because I know you Nig—" He caught himself about to say "Niggers" but checked himself for what he thought was the greater cause. "I know you Blacks or Rasta men like to smoke your weed, joint, spliff, or whatever you want to call it."

Rodney wanted to call out the racist undertone but refrained, knowing better. "I don't smoke any of those things you're talking about. I don't smoke herb; I eat herb, drink herbs, and burn herb. You know, my Happy."

The President looked a little surprised, thinking that Rodney was bullshitting him. "Isn't your Happy herb?" he asked. Rodney nodded, giving a fake smile in return.

"I said I eat and burn the herb, but I don't smoke, especially not yours. I mean, after all these years of locking people away because

353

of this beautiful flower, now you're saying it's going to bring us peace and you want to make it legal? Nigga, please."

The President didn't fully grasp Rodney's point but took it as wordplay, though being called a "Nigga" was a first. "OK. Well, it's just business. No need to beat around the bush. Do you know why you are here?" Rodney looked at him and quickly responded.

"Yeah, because you think you are above me and feel you can kidnap me at any time and not face charges like anyone else would." Rodney stared into his eyes, trying to see if his words had sunk in.

"Very good, boy. You are an intelligent one. I sent for you once again to stop your people from carrying on like savages before your whole race gets wiped out. I believe this country has a bigger problem now. We have noticed that some of the killings of my race are not just done by you Blacks. Together, we need to get to the bottom of this before we all end up dead."

Rodney pondered what he just heard, especially the part about ending up dead. He wondered if the President meant external forces or the White race's past mindset of pushing the button for mass destruction, the atomic bomb. He looked up at the ceiling, hoping for the Most High God to give him the right words to say.

"The way I see it, the problem this country is having now is your problem. When have my people ever had any say in this country other than before you came here and took it from us?" The President's face turned red, veins popping out of his forehead. He was about to lash out but stopped himself.

"I have no clue what you're referring to. We all know you people came from Africa."

Rodney quickly replied, "Along with the Africans who inhabited this land many moons ago, later called the Indigenous people." The President knew Rodney spoke the truth but played blind to the facts, like those White people who claim not to be racist but turn a blind eye to blatant racism.

"Look, if you don't help us, we can't help you," the President said, sounding like a cop trying to bust someone.

Then the President asked, "Rodney, do you and your so-called people call yourselves Americans?" Rodney's throat jammed up, and his body became numb. When he finally spoke, his voice changed into that of El-Hajj Malik El-Shabazz, echoing through the President's ears and the building.

"I can't call myself an American. If you and I were Americans, there would be no problem. The only Americans I see are the White race. It's a shame that we have been here for many years and are still looked down upon. My race has been sitting at the table, waiting to eat the fruits of this country, given scraps, expected to feed our youth. The youth is tired of their stomachs growling and has had enough. Do you get my drift, Mr. President?"

The President was too young to recognize Malcolm X's voice but was freaked out by witnessing a spirit enter another. Before he could say a word, Rodney continued.

"I and the other 22 million Black people born in this country don't feel American because if we were, we wouldn't need amendments to the Constitution or the NAACP. Yes, my race is a victim of Americanism, democracy, and hypocrisy. With these eyes, I see my people as victims of your American system. You see, I don't see an American dream; what we are all witnessing is America's nightmare."

The President and every man in the room were speechless for a minute, and then the President said, "Yeah, yeah, yeah, we get all that, but we need this war to end for the greater cause of the country. I mean, this here thing is bigger than me and you—Black or Right, I mean White. Again, how can we help you?"

Rodney seemed to be in a trance, as his body was being manipulated by multiple spirits of different people. His words transformed into the voice of H. Rap Brown. "This is your stolen property, based around politics, and the only politics for my Black race is one of a Revolutionary. You have given our race no other choice but to defend ourselves against the people who have been oppressing us. You made us believe our problem is unemployment, and Mr. President, I must say this war taking place will surely solve that, for no man will have the need for money but for my people, their freedom."

Rodney saw the look on the President's face and snapped his fingers at him, trying to bring him back from being in a daze. In his own voice, without knowing what was going to come out, he spoke the words that popped into his mind from the powers of truth that rimed the atmosphere at that moment. "Oh! Before I forget, put Pete Rose in the Baseball Hall of Fame before the man passes away, stop it with all the BS."

The President had a look of disbelief, wondering what the hell that had to do with anything. "What does that have to do with anything?" he asked.

Rodney hadn't a clue why he said it, as he had no idea who Pete Rose was, but his mind spoke truth to all matters at the present time. "I reckon because it's a change that needs to be made, just like the change that awaits us in this land."

The President jumped up from his desk, leaning over with his hands choking the desk. "That's my point. If you just tell your people to be like Rodney King and ask for everyone to get along— and again, do you want your race to be wiped off the face of the earth?" He paused, waiting for Rodney to respond. When Rodney didn't, he continued. "Look, if you do this for me, I will make sure myself that you will have everything your people ask for before this country gets bombarded by whoever is behind those black ninja suits."

Rodney held his head up high and spoke, "You can't give me and my people what is already ours. You and yours have, let's just say, borrowed it. Fire burns the wicked! If your heart isn't right with the Almighty and you are of the wicked, then fire will blaze upon you and remove your wicked energy from the face of the earth. If you are of the Almighty, you will witness the greatness from the Most High's chosen ones rising to the highest point of humanity. So, I ask you, are you of the wicked or of the Most High?"

The President didn't care to answer the question. "I guess I would have to say of the Most High because I want the best for this country. God bless America!"

Rodney quickly responded, "Wrong! Allowing God's will to unfold, no matter the circumstances, allowing His spirit of righteousness to lead the way rather than a man and his man-made reality of his own self-conscious."

"So, what do you suggest we, the people of this country, do then?" The President asked.

"The only thing I can say, Mr. President, is that everyone on this earth reaps what they sow. If you come from good soil, you will

358

harvest good fruits. Ask yourself, have you been a part of the bad apple that has spoiled it for the bunch?"

The President was beyond frustrated that Rodney wasn't complying the way he wanted. "Reap what you sow, right? Just like how you Blacks feel about never being slaves in the cotton fields again is the same way we feel about not giving up on this country. It would be over my dead body first."

Rodney nodded. "Then you're a part of the Revolution, and I would say we're on the same page when it comes to that."

"I guess you're right. So, I guess you must be going on your merry way before your peeps come looking for you."

Rodney didn't let the shade thrown at him rub him the wrong way. He stood up, and out of nowhere, the spirit of music took over all the sound systems in the building with just the hook and the beat of the song "Looking at the Front Door" by Main Source. Rodney felt the song was right on time, so that's just what he did. The President pushed the button to let the door rise so Rodney could leave, and just before it closed, Rodney said, "Many of my people have been dying as well, and when we ran through some of their pockets, we found notes saying 'Ancient Chinese Secret,' and I don't think it's a coincidence that they've died after eating the Chinese food from the hoods all over this country."

The cage-like gate closed behind Rodney's last word, leaving the President in a room full of agents. "Those Niggas sure do have some peculiar ways about them, I would say." They all nodded in agreement, and someone shouted out, "What's next?"

The President had to humble himself and almost choke on his words. "Die like men and be the proud patriots we are, and have the poor Whites fight for us." All the men in the room understood that kings move pawns the way they want them to be moved.

"Maybe we just need to go into the hood and grab one of those slanted-eyed people and get to the bottom of this," the President said.

"You mean we are going to find out what's behind the killing of the Blacks eating their food?" asked one of the agents.

The President looked at him like he was some type of dumbass. "No, you asswipe, I don't give two shits about them dying. I'm talking about our people, Brad."

Agent Brad stood there wondering why he didn't know that. "Well, I say let's go out and get one of those Bruce Lee look-alikes," said Brad.

The President gave the nod for him to proceed. "I want at least two owners of a Chinese restaurant from every state. I don't care if they own a spot in Maine where the population of Blacks is probably 10 percent."

Chapter 22

China Man

In East Asia, in Hong Kong's Chinatown, down in the basement of an underground gambling house and brothel, there was a secret room. Beyond the gamblers and prostitutes was a door that only the leaders of the top eight Asian countries could enter—China, Japan, Vietnam, the Philippines, both Koreas, and any other country where the people had slanted eyes. The wooden door was guarded by a short but muscular Asian man wearing a white ninja suit. The eight men at the round table also wore ninja attire, but the leaders had different colored outfits—some red, some black, some gold, yellow, or purple. Their faces were covered so that each one wouldn't know who was who, because all that mattered to them was the greater cause of taking down the greatest empire. The other thing they all had in common was their love of drinking tea from little, tiny cups.

The man in the red ninja gear had something to say after sipping his tea, so he grabbed his phone and sent a group text to the men at the table, communicating through AI to translate his message into their respective languages. "I hear the white men in America are going around the country grabbing a few men from East Asia. They've been pressing hard with questions about why the Niggers over there are dying after eating the food we've been cooking for them, and why white men are being taken out by Chinese stars." The men all looked at their phones, read the text, and laughed together before taking big sips of their tea.

The man in the black ninja gear sent a reply to the group text. "I guess we can attack now and show them who is boss." The others read the message, and then the man in the gold gear responded to the one in black. "From the aggression in your text and the arrogance within yourself, I would think you are the man who leads the nation of Japan or maybe Korea. But I'm not going to call out who's who, but I will say that attacking now would be a big mistake. If we do so now, I believe the Niggers over there will stop fighting the white man to get at us. I think it would be wiser to let the white man kill most of the black men off first, and then we attack while the white men are vulnerable, feeling victorious over the black race. Then we shall show them the way of East Asia."

The men at the table read the text, and on the right side of each man was a gift—a box of the best hand-rolled cigars from Cuba. They all took one from their boxes and began smoking together, signaling their agreement with the dialogue. The man in yellow felt the need to send one more text for all the men at the table to understand the importance of winning the next world war. "We must win this war because if not, if one more woman has a child to add to our country, the next man would end up in the ocean due to overpopulation. We must change the times of the new world and make East Asia's morals the way of the new world."

More was said through text over the night after the tea party, along with late-night sex and small amounts of rum. The last text that went out to them all was from the man in red once again. "So, when do we know when to attack again?" He asked making sure that they weren't too drunk to understand the importance of winning this war, it was now or never in his eyes. one by one, minute after each one replied to the same text that stated when almost all the black people are dead and the white man vulnerable because of the so-called victory." That night the eight men slept in their beds believing that their time has arrived for them to rule the world.

Back in Washington D.C.

Rodney walked out into the middle of the street, feeling the earth's ground shake, causing dust to blow in his direction. He walked about three miles away from the White House, barefoot, so that he could become grounded with the earth until he couldn't walk anymore. He thought of the long journey ahead of him and wished for someone to come his way to help him get back to his people who were waiting for his return in central Florida. Rodney's feet started to bleed, and he was about to give up on walking for the rest of the night, thinking he'd wake up in the morning and head down south. But just as he was about to head into the woods to find a safe place to sleep, Aja rode up beside him on her white horse. The horse was so happy to see him that when Aja pulled for him to slow down, the horse stopped, raised its back legs, paused for a minute, and then slowly rested on all four legs so that it would be easier for him to get on. Aja held out her arm and helped Rodney onto the horse. As soon as Rodney was on and stable, the horse slowly got up and started heading back down south to central Florida. Within three days, when they arrived at the same location they once were, they noticed that most of the men, women, and children were gone. The ones who stayed behind were mostly drug addicts or snitches that no one wanted to be around.

Rodney and Aja stood in the middle of Florida on his horse, wondering where his people could be. "I trust that Rob sensed the need to keep moving toward Miami because he must have felt that they were in danger and needed to move along, or the black people deep in the Dirty South really need our help," Rodney said, hoping to ease Aja's worried nerves.

"How would Rob and the rest of your people be able to help the masses of black people when they all need help at the same time?" she asked Rodney.

"I feel many of our people will not be saved, but those who will be saved are the 144,000 who will see the world of tomorrow," Rodney replied.

Aja smacked down the reins that steered the horse. "Faster!" she shouted, and in a day and a half, they started noticing that they had found the tail end of his followers just about to reach the tip of Miami. The men and women were slowly coming to a halt while the few in the front were moving forward at a slow pace. Many of the men, women, and children were being killed simply because they were outnumbered in that area. As the black race got closer to Miami, the more the white race populated the grounds with the heart and spirit of their forefathers, who held the mindset of the Confederacy. The blacks in other states were keeping the war on an even plane when it came to the death rates. The closer the two races got to Miami, the more the white race started to diminish, thanks to the help of those ninjas from Asia and the great mindset of guerrilla warfare from the black race. Their style of guerrilla warfare was impeccable. The way many of the black men who had been locked down in prison for many years learned to make do with what they had for survival was the same way they manipulated their strategy of guerrilla warfare. Along with the everyday struggles that the black race had to endure from generation to generation, their struggle made them wiser and stronger. They put two and two together and started to take over as if the spirit of Shaka Zulu had taken over their mind, body, and soul.

Rodney got down off his horse and helped Aja down as well. "We must go and find Rob. I know that brother needs us like we all need each other." Aja could feel the spirits of black women throughout her body as their minds started causing the planet to shiver with rain and thunder, bringing tears to their eyes from all the killing and the injustice of the past, along with the inability to express their true nature of love. "I'll be right by your side the whole way there, my king," Aja said, looking directly into Rodney's eyes, revealing that her truth for him resided in her gaze. He could feel his mind overflowing with the reality of the future and the present. He held his head with his hands as sweat ran down his arms until his armpits felt like a river that had come to a halt.

He began seeing images in his mind of Native leaders like Geronimo, Chief Joseph, Sitting Bull, Black Hawk, and many more, all with war paint on their faces. Their faces would fade in and out, one replacing the other, each showing what to expect in the coming months. Rodney also saw children and adults with autism or Down syndrome speaking to a blurry image. If someone blinked, they would miss one by one as these individuals reached out their hands and vanished into the universe. Rodney wondered if they would be safe wherever they were being taken. He then recalled what Chin had told him long ago about questioning the things revealed to him but remembering that the spirit of God within himself was all the protection needed, so there was no need for him or his followers to worry about unexplainable events.

Aja walked up behind Rodney and grabbed him by the waist. "My love, is there anything I can do for you?" she asked, hoping to lighten his burden.

"As a matter of fact, there is. I need you to take all the children under the age of 13 and keep them safe down at the beaches. Have your women over 50 look after them, and when they are settled and secure, you can leave them with someone you trust to take over your teachings of wisdom."

Aja had no problem with finding an answer to that. "I will let the spirit of Shahrazad Ali guide the minds of all the women over 50, directing them with her philosophy," she said, thinking it would be a grand idea, as she had gained much wisdom from Miss Shahrazad before she passed away.

"Okay. Then I need you to gather all the little boys and girls and the grown women who are ready to use their minds to help us survive this war by controlling what women gods have to offer, which is Mother Nature. They will channel that power and tap into the spirits of the dead, bringing them back to life seeking revenge."

When Rodney finished telling her what he needed, Aja could feel her body starting to change, as if it was preparing to cause havoc

368

in the universe. "Okay, that's not going to be a problem," Aja said, her voice choking up as she tried to hold back her tears. Rodney noticed her eyes getting watery.

"Why the watery eyes, my queen?"

Aja wiped the tears from her face. "Because I'm going to miss you, and I don't know when I'm going to see you again."

Rodney knew what she was thinking before she even said it, and as calmly as could be, he said to her, "Every hour and every minute of the hour, we'll be together. We'll never be apart; I need you by my side through this battle."

Aja looked confused. "How, my love, can you ask me to be elsewhere when the time of bloodshed arrives?"

Rodney raised his voice at her on purpose. "Can you hear me?" Then he softened his tone after noticing Aja jump at his intensity. "You will hear my every word and become my eyes in the back of my head, and your woman's intuition will know my every move."

Aja stood there, still looking sad and somewhat doubtful of his words. Rodney could see in her whole demeanor that she had little faith due to her love for him blinding her for the moment. So, Rodney gently pulled her close to his body and gave her a warm hug that felt so breathtaking, as if her body had just entered into his own, causing her to become warm and stiff, as if she had no control over herself. Rodney grabbed her two hands with his and held them tight, then bent his head down just a little bit so he could blow his warm breath into her ear, causing her white creamy precum to fill the crotch area of her panties. He released her hands and gently lifted her chin so she could look into his eyes. "I love you, Aja." The way he said it, she knew in her heart he was something like a god. Her legs trembled as if it was the best sex she ever had. She closed her eyes to embrace his words, and right then, she could see herself in his body, walking every step of the way, knowing what's on the other side of the mountain without ever being there. She felt bad at the fact that she had just gotten herself a quick release and didn't get to return the favor.

"My love, may I please you once more before you go off?"

Rodney wanted to, but he also thought about what Chin had told him. "I'm sorry, my love, but I must turn you down because I have a long journey ahead of me, and I'm going to need my legs." His heart started to soften because he was going to miss her as well, along with his lustful mind that was telling him he was being a sucker for not having one last time. He wanted to change his lustful thinking so that his erection would loosen up and his hard-on would go down. "You must go now," he told her, then slowly turned his back on her because it was the only way he could let her go without shedding more tears.

Aja walked away, feeling more in love with him; it was like every minute they spent together, her love for him grew even deeper. Rodney stood there looking ahead and noticed an old-looking man in the distance. It seemed as if the man had locks on his head and was holding a walking staff like Moses had in the Bible. Rodney could tell that the man was probably blind by the way he was walking and trying to feel his way around his surroundings. The man could smell a human from miles away and hear sound as clearly as Dre's beats.

"Looking for brother Rodney, looking for Br—" the closer the man got, the more Rodney could hear that the man was referring to him. Rodney walked towards him, trying to figure out why the man looked somewhat familiar.

"Sir, do I know you?" he asked the man. The man turned to look at him and smiled because he recognized Rodney's voice right away.

"Yes, I and I are looking for the I."

Rodney immediately knew who he was because there was only one other person who spoke to him in that manner, and that was Wisdom, or Rob.

"Wisdom!" he shouted. "Is that you?" The man nodded in confirmation.

"How did you find me? And how did you get here?"

Wisdom kept the smile on his face. "I gave you that African drum years ago because I knew today would come when that drum would be needed. That's why I told you years ago to never stop beating it. I knew what I was doing. I knew that everyone, including myself, would be able to hear it, feel the beat, and follow the rhythm to move forward. I walked here like I walk everywhere else, Monk. What, you think I paid someone to drive over other cars and dead bodies to get here? I took one step at a time, and I never let what we call time control my mind, nor did I let the words on paper activate their spell on me. Yes, Star, I know about the spell the alphabet brings upon people."

Rodney hugged Wisdom tightly, looking around, hoping Aja was still nearby so she could meet him. "Unc, let's go and find your nephew."

Wisdom, supported by his staff, stood up completely upright, proud and strong. "I'm ready, Monk. I've been waiting to see him for years now, and I knew this day would soon come." Wisdom's smile never left his face, fueled by the knowledge of how the story of the black race would unfold.

Rodney put his arm around Wisdom, and the two of them walked in the direction in front of them, feeling the heat from the black people ahead as they got closer to Miami.

372

"Be aware, Monk, that you're about to see things with your own eyes that will make you believe what you're seeing is impossible—true events of reality taking place," Wisdom said, now with a straight face, letting Rodney know he was dead serious.

"I wish I could say the same for you, but I can't lie. I've seen things that already make me question if I'm dreaming or not. In a way, I'm glad you won't and haven't been seeing what's going on out here."

Wisdom understood what Rodney was trying to say, but he also knew that just because a man is blind doesn't mean he can't see what's on the other side of the mountain. "Rodney, I've seen more being blind than you have with sight. Being blind is a gift and a curse. While you see clearly with your eyes open in the present, for me, it's as if I'm always in meditation mode, seeing things before they unfold in the dark. And we all know what happens in the dark comes to light. I live my life one chess move ahead."

The two of them continued walking straight, and Wisdom tapped Rodney on the shoulder. "This way, Monk, it's a lot quicker." Rodney looked at him, wondering how he would know, but then he remembered what Wisdom had just told him and decided to trust him. Sure enough, Wisdom was right—they made it to Miami a day earlier than expected.

Rodney and Wisdom were exhausted from walking through the crowds, speaking to everyone they could. By the time they reached Rob and the other ex-inmates waiting for them, it had taken four days to pass through the masses of people. Rodney hadn't eaten in two weeks, and the hunger was just now hitting him as he looked around at people eating whatever food they could find, mostly from fast-food dumpsters, and most of that food had already been picked over by birds, rats, or other hungry black people who were more focused on surviving than on finding food. Every man who followed Rodney's teachings was grateful for learning how to properly fast; they didn't worry about food like those who hadn't yet adjusted to his way of life.

"Rastafari!" Wisdom shouted as soon as he saw Rob. Rob's back was turned, talking to two other men, but when he turned around, the first and only person he saw was Rodney.

"Wa Gwan! My brotha, I see you made it forward," Rob said to Rodney. Then, out of the corner of his eye, he noticed someone behind Rodney and thought his eyes were playing tricks on him. He had to take a double look.

"Uncle! Uncle! Jah! Jah Bless! Oh, my goodness! Lord have mercy!" Rob recognized his uncle and began crying his heart out. He started bowing to his uncle Wisdom, knowing that the Rasta man was a king, so his uncle did the same, and then they hugged each other tightly, holding nine years of lost time from being apart.

"Look at you, Star. You look good, Mon. I can't believe I can put my hands on you. I knew this day would come, but now that it's here, it doesn't feel real, Mon." Rob's sad tears turned into tears of joy.

"I know, Unc. It doesn't seem real, but it is. And just like you said, this day has come. So, what else have you had a vision of that you care to share with us?"

Wisdom thought about the question, and everyone around them was eager to hear what the elder had to say. Wisdom laughed on the inside at the question but thought about what would be the best thing to say without saying too much and nothing at all, but his words would speak volumes. The grin that spread across his face had Rob shaking his head.

"Aww, shit, Unc. What is it? I know that grin when I see it."

Wisdom turned his head from side to side as if he could see the people standing around. "Change is going to come," Wisdom said, reminiscing about his past vision of what the future holds for his people.

An old head who looked to be around the same age as Wisdom finished what Wisdom had just said by singing the last words of

Sam Cooke's "A Change Is Gonna Come." "Yes, it is," the man sang, thinking about the struggle the black race went through in the '50s and '60s and how they had now come to this.

"Okay, brothers, what are we waiting on? Why are we not moving along?" Rodney said, mentally ready to embrace his destiny because the freedom he wanted to provide for his people couldn't come fast enough.

Rob pulled out his two guns from the back of his waistband and checked to see if they were loaded.

"What are you doing? Put that thing away. I see you haven't learned yet that we don't need that, and besides, the white people have put their guns down and are fighting us like men."

Rob wasn't trying to hear that. "Right until they start losing, and then you can bet your life that they're going to pick those guns up again."

Rodney began to look around and noticed that everyone was almost doing the same thing after seeing Rob check his gun.

"Yo, Monk, like I told you before, everyone ain't like you. You're talking about some spiritual war you've got going on, but you're not killing the people who are killing our people. And yes, I witnessed your voice changing into another man, but…" Rodney could tell Rob was second-guessing his calling to lead the people.

"And what more do I have to show you?" Rodney asked Rob, and he could see that Rob had no words because he wasn't paying him much attention.

"Wisdom, come close to me, please," Rodney asked, catching everyone's attention. Everyone around was paying attention to what was happening. Wisdom approached Rodney, and then Rodney put his hand over Wisdom's eyes.

"Look at me!" Rodney shouted at Rob. Rob looked up from his guns and noticed Rodney's hand covering Wisdom's eyes. Rodney removed his hand from Wisdom's face, and Wisdom fell to his knees because Rodney had made him able to see.

"Oh my God! Rastafari! Jah!" Tears of joy flowed down Wisdom's face, and everyone around him who had forgotten that Rodney had special powers from God now witnessed it once again. They all got down on their knees, tears of joy running down their faces, asking for forgiveness from him.

Rodney let his heart guide him to make Wisdom see once more, but just as quickly as he gave him sight, he took it away again, showing the people that he could give or take, and it was up to the individual if they wanted what he had to offer. Rodney began to cry as well because even though everyone had seen what he could do, more than a third of them still didn't put away their guns.

Rob looked at Rodney and said, "Monk, the only way to get rid of those crackers is to beat them at their own game. Besides, half these young brothers, all they know is how to bust a cap in a Nigga's ass." Rob's resolve to keep the guns never wavered, knowing that, from the looks of things, it would be suicide for his people, who would rather die with pride and honor for the cause of the revolution.

There was one elder man who wasn't an ex-con or a follower of Rodney; he was just a Black man like many others who ended up at the same place because, for some reason, when one black person runs off, they all follow and ask questions later. "Who the hell are you supposed to be? And you as well?" the man asked as if he had a problem with Rodney and Wisdom.

Rob didn't care; he was ready to go over and go upside the old man's head, knowing that the man was his elder, but no one disrespects his uncle. He was about to confront the man until his uncle Wisdom held him back with his arm, stopping his body from moving as if his arm had turned into a metal rod. "I got this," Wisdom said to Rob.

Wisdom had a feeling that the man didn't love himself or his race and that his faith had never existed. "I and I am a Rasta man. I and I am not a perfect man, but I and I am an Ethiopian warrior of the King of all Kings and the Lord of all Lords. I and I humble myself to praise and bow to the King Jah Rastafari! King Haile Selassie I. I and I deal with peace and love for humanity and set fire on the wicked. I and I know that I am no better than any man, just as no man is better than I because he can see with his eyes, and I can't. I and I don't ever want to fight with my brother. I and I know that at some point, you and I are going to need somebody to lean on, and I, my brother, might not be able to watch your back, but I have two good shoulders you can always lean on."

For the first time in his life, the man's heart felt that black love that every black person wishes we could have toward one another. The words from Wisdom entered his soul, making him feel what black power is all about. The man started to cry, holding his arms out for the hug he needed. "I'm sorry, my brother, I'm sorry. I just started to hate who we are as a race, or should I say the ones who have lost their true nature of God and are out here killing one another and hating on each other because of what one has that the next man doesn't. Man, I'm just fucking sick of it."

Wisdom hugged the man while Rob and Rodney stood there watching, thinking to themselves that it wouldn't be long before that old man saw the way of Rodney's path.

"It's all good, my brother. I'm here to help you, and tomorrow, if we're still here, we'll do the same for the next man who needs a hug, an ear, or whatever," Wisdom said.

Just then, all three of them turned around, their eyes widening and their mouths dropping open at what they were seeing—a tsunami coming in their direction, miles out as far back as South America. The waves were so high you would have thought the sky and the ocean had reversed themselves. Rodney quickly glanced over at almost everyone he could, trying to save as many souls as possible by using the power of his mind. He knew that many people were going to die soon once the tsunami hit, especially those who lacked faith in whatever God they chose to believe in. No one God was better than the other, but what saved people's lives was the faith they held within themselves that only their God could remove them from the face of the earth if need be.

"Oh my God! Oh, Jesus have mercy! Jah! Rastafari! Allah!" were the words of many of the men shouting out as they saw the wave coming their way. Many of the people with little faith were running, looking for a place to hide, while others were holding onto objects like telephone poles, old blue post office mailboxes, and whatever else they thought was nailed to the ground. The mist from the water in the air from the tsunami had everyone drenched in seawater, even though it looked close yet was still countries away.

Men, women, and children who were afraid of being killed took the quicker way out, picking up guns and giving the Devil and the white man their wishes by shooting themselves or slitting their wrists with box cutters. Rodney did nothing to stop them. He was,

380

for sure, sad to see them go after making it this far, but the black race didn't have time to focus on the weak-minded; the revolution needed only the strong to stand firm and prevail.

If only those who didn't have much faith had waited a few days before the wave was actually going to reach them, they would have witnessed the miracle that took place before the eyes of the true believers in their Gods. The tsunami wave started to make its way to the American shores of the Atlantic Ocean, but before the wave collapsed onto the land, flooding the lower lands of the country and causing the water levels to rise quickly, which led more and more people of all races to become suicidal, the wave split open like the Red Sea. One part went west into the ocean, and the other east.

Rodney and Rob looked at each other, knowing that was their sign to enter the middle of Miami. They knew that if faith was going to be needed, now was the time. Even though the black race was holding its own in fighting the white man, the continued killing of each other and the self-hatred among the black community was causing them to be outnumbered in the middle of the pit in Miami.

Rodney knew he wasn't going to pick up a gun to kill anyone, but he also knew his body was marked with a bullet to the head. Posters with his face on them, declaring him wanted, were plastered on telephone poles, houses, and cars that had been lost in the war. The white men didn't want money; they just wanted to be the one known for catching the Nigga who had caused all the other Niggas to get out of line. Many of them kept a picture of him in their pockets, while others had his face embedded in their minds, so if they got the chance to catch him, he would be alive but not for long before they had their picnic with him.

"Brother, at some point, can you escape this madness and check on the women and children?" Rodney asked Rob. Just as Rob was about to answer him, they heard what sounded like a herd of horses coming their way from behind. Aja, Winker, and about a thousand of Aja's black sisters who were ex-cons stood behind her, making their presence known to the black men, letting them know they had their backs and were ready to throw down and fight.

Rodney and Rob didn't have time to argue with them about what he had told them because they knew God was within them as well, and if He sent two to a thousand of His best women for this mission, then who were they to question it?

A platoon of white men was coming toward them with all types of weapons that weren't guns, charging at them with killer intentions. They all started fighting. Wisdom was fighting with his bare hands like he was that old master with long white hair in a kung fu movie, beating and killing people gracefully. His style was that of a master of blind kung fu. Rob and Rodney were trying to make sure that

Wisdom was okay, given that he was blind, but seeing him handle himself was one thing. What amazed them was when they saw him fighting two big white men. One of them grabbed him from behind, and as the other one approached from the front, Wisdom took his hair out from where he had wrapped his dreadlocks around his head, swung his head around in a circle, and his long dreadlock lassoed around the man's neck like a cowboy in a rodeo show. He quickly snatched the man towards him and choked him out with one hand while using his other hand to take the knife out of the man's hand and backstab the man who held him by the waist. He stabbed the man in the gut, turned to face him, and then twisted the knife inside the man's stomach clockwise before letting go of the knife to let the man die slowly while he swiftly moved on to his next victim.

"That's the Nigger right there!" a white man shouted as they killed whoever came in their way of grabbing him up. Rodney was being guarded by his people at the time, and when many of the black people who had never seen him but only heard of him noticed him for the first time, something came over them. At that moment, they felt he was God-sent, and they all started killing and defending themselves, saying out loud, "This is a cry for Rodney!" to psyche themselves up to kill someone for the cause of kill or be killed.

The white race had the black race trapped with their backs against the ocean. Many of the black people were stomping on white people's faces and running to help the next black person in need of help. But the sad thing was that, despite what seemed like the black race winning this fight, they were sadly mistaken. The black race couldn't afford even one death among them because they were already outnumbered.

In the midst of the battle, Rob shouted out to his uncle, "Toss me the machete so I can chop off a couple of these heads to show them how we do at the Yard".

Wisdom did a Kung Fu roll out of the way of the battle for a quick second, reached into his backpack, and tossed Rob the machete. "Don't cut yourself now, hear!" Wisdom said as he keenly focused on a young black man who was being beaten unmercifully by three young white men, almost to death. Wisdom didn't run; he walked calmly, like Jason from the Halloween movies. Just as he got close enough to help the boy, the machete he had given to Rob came flying through the air, hitting one of the men in the neck. The blade stuck, with blood slowly oozing out, waiting for the man's body to hit the ground. Rob yanked the machete out of the man's neck and started swinging at the next one. Wisdom's hearing was so sharp that he knew Rob had joined him when he heard the machete strike the second white man on the back. Wisdom thought to himself and said to Rob, "Well, I'll be damned. I guess you never forgot what I taught you many years ago." Just as the man's body hit the ground, Rob was right on top of him, retrieving his blade once again.

"You thought I forgot," Rob said to Wisdom, continuing to fight. Every so often, he would glance over at Rodney, noticing the river of tears flowing down his face. This worried him, but now wasn't the time to ask why Rodney wasn't fighting to help his people.

Rodney's mind wandered back to his childhood, thinking about how his own black brothers had treated him and each other. Then his mind shifted to his current mission, wondering if his race was ready for what most people fear—change. As he watched America reach this point, he often found himself stuck, trying to figure out his own trials and tribulations, which were difficult for him to foresee and test his faith.

After days and weeks, from sunup to sundown, people were still fighting and dying by the minute. "Boom! Boom!" Everyone paused once again, wondering if the bomb had landed nearby. Once they realized the bomb had hit an entirely different state, causing the ground to shake from state to state and polluting the air with dust and debris particles from the fires it caused, they carried on killing each other—the American way.

"Fuck this bullshit!" a white man yelled to his people. He couldn't stand watching his race die from attacks on two fronts. Even though he had skills with his hands, he felt they could only take out one person at a time, and he wanted the war with the black race to end. He understood that the ones sending bombs were the bigger problem, so he picked up a gun from the ground and went on a shooting rampage until his gun was empty. One by one, all the other white men started doing the same.

"Turn that Nigger Rodney over to us now! Let's get this thing over with! We want him because he's the one who got your people all riled up, forgetting how to march for what you people want." Every black person who reached down to retrieve a gun was shot to death, and those who made it without getting shot were likely hit elsewhere, becoming crippled.

Rodney couldn't take it anymore and gracefully slipped through the crowd of people guarding him, allowing the angry white mob to grab him. From a distance, a white cowboy on his horse lassoed a rope around Rodney's neck. You could tell the cowboy was a pro by the distance and accuracy with which he tossed the rope. The man yanked the rope as tight as he could, not caring if it cut Rodney's head off, and then tapped his horse, causing it to run in a big circle, away from the battle. Many of the white people, eager to see Rodney's death, tagged along after the cowboy and his horse, which now had Rodney's body dragging along the ground, just like what was done to James Byrd Jr. in Jasper, Texas. The word was out that if they caught Rodney, they didn't want to be late for the "Nigger's Picnic" they had planned.

386

The white people from Miami directed the cowboy to string Rodney up on an old tree that was infamous in the area, known among both blacks and whites for bearing strange fruit many times over the years. Rodney's body was forcefully pulled up the tree by his neck, and he didn't move, as if he was already dead.

"Shit, the Nigger seems to be already dead. You think you killed him already?" All the white people who were already there waiting for this day started laughing. A young white teenager picked up a broken brick and threw it as hard as he could at Rodney's head. The brick hit Rodney, but he didn't flinch or cry out in pain. They quickly learned that he must have run out of tears because he didn't shed one, refusing to give them the satisfaction ever again.

A young white lady holding a skinny twig she had carved for this day couldn't wait to be part of the torment. She took the twig and jammed it into Rodney's left nostril, moving it back and forth, left to right, until his blood stained the stick. Afterward, she pranced around, showing off the blood to other white onlookers. Some would grab her hand, lick the blood from the stick, and laugh. "Look, he must be too poor to buy shoes!" they mocked, noticing his bare feet.

A white man with black hair and a skunk-colored beard approached Rodney's swinging body and stopped it by grabbing one of his feet. The man was smoking the tail end of a cigar. He

387

took two big puffs to ignite the cherry red and then, with malice, pressed the cigar against the bottom of Rodney's foot. Despite the burning, Rodney gave no reaction.

"Say something, Nigger!" shouted an angry old white lady. The torture continued, with each white person taking turns inflicting harm on Rodney. They switched out from person to person and then returned to the war, murdering other black people. This went on from sunrise to sunrise the next day. Rodney's body was leaking blood, his face and body severely swollen. If you looked at his face, it would make Emmett Till's appearance in his casket seem almost pleasant in comparison. Everyone was standing around, cell phones out, recording what they had done to Rodney, with people worldwide watching.

"Oh yes, he's dead as fuck," a white man shouted. Despite the ongoing war, the white people didn't hesitate to bring out kegs of beer, drinking with no reason other than it was early—6:30 in the morning. Some people woke up from the fire pit going out, feeling a slight chill in the air. The tree Rodney's body was hanging from had thick, trunk-like branches, barren of leaves. Everyone's attention was drawn to a huge black crow that flew down and perched on a branch above Rodney's head. The crow was the biggest anyone had ever seen. Its eyes were so large that the redness in them looked like the sun in the sky on a hot summer night.

388

The crow looked down at Rodney as if it recognized him, and then two other crows landed on the branch next to it. The big crow seemed to be instructing one of the other crows to do something, but the crow hesitated, undecided. After contemplating for a moment, the crow flew down to the branch with the rope around Rodney's neck and began pecking at it with its sharp beak.

"Get out of here!" a fat, drunken white man shouted at the crow. He quickly picked up his rifle and proved to everyone watching that he was a bird hunter by shooting the crow out of the tree. The big crow, devastated that it had lost one of its offspring, cried out, summoning three more crows to the tree. The large bird was determined to get Rodney's body down, so it ordered another crow to continue the task. But before that crow could reach the branch, the white man shot it too, sending feathers floating down to the ground.

The large crow, now furious, decided to do it itself. As the white man shot at it, the crow barely flinched, as the bullets felt like nothing more than BB pellets. The crow leaned close to Rodney's ear and whispered, "I got your back." It continued pecking at the rope until it started to unravel. Rodney's body was just about to hit the ground when the large crow, filled with lead from the man's gun, fell out of the tree and died.

The remaining crows in the tree called out in anger, summoning more crows to witness what the white man had done to their king. Within moments, a flock of crows descended, covering the tree and the surrounding area. The white people didn't like what they were seeing because anything resembling the color black was something they wanted removed from their sight. The other men began shooting at the crows, killing many, but for every one they killed, three more appeared, fighting for the death of their king.

Suddenly, the crows started flying in circles, attacking the white people with their sharp beaks, injuring as many as they could before being shot down. Rodney's body hit the ground, and a handful of white men tried to take it away, but the crows wouldn't allow it. They began pecking the guns out of the men's hands and ripping their eyeballs out with their beaks. Rodney lay face down in the dirt as the crows covered his entire back with their claws, trying to lift his body away. The crows were so strong that once they got Rodney up from the ground, his body never touched the ground again until the crows ascended into the sky with his body, searching for the right place and time to bring him back down to land.

The crows dropped his body in the heart of the war, and the black people were heartbroken and angry, along with being sad at the sight of him, but they still had to fight. The white people were not humbled in the least, and to add salt to the black race's wounds, they taunted them while killing them off, making sarcastic remarks about what they had done to Rodney. The minute Rob noticed what they'd done to his friend, and Wisdom could hear the people whispering about the horrific display of Rodney's body, they tried their best to keep Aja from finding out about his condition. But her woman's intuition was spot-on, and when she saw in her mind what they had done to him, she cried out to the spirits and souls of the dead that inhabited the surrounding area.

The crows were still protecting Rodney's body but were shot down one by one, making the ground look like dead fleas on a white carpet. Aja mumbled under her breath, but no one could make out what she was saying until her words grew louder as she called out the names of the spirits into the universe to bring her words into existence. "Tribe Ais, Tribe Apalachee, Tribe Creek, Seminole…" Aja called out, along with the other nine tribes that once inhabited the Florida area before the Pilgrims arrived. The spirits of the dead bodies lying on the ground were released into the universe, and the tribes of the Natives were being reborn, causing their souls to feel like they were having déjà vu when they saw the white men fighting the dark men.

Their spirits wanted revenge for what the Pilgrims had done to them, and each time Aja called out a tribe's name, the spirit and soul of a person from that tribe entered into the dead bodies of every black person who they had once been in their past lifetime.

391

Then their bodies began to rise up from the ground in full tribal Native American war attire, complete with feathers in their hair, war paint on their faces, bows and arrows in their hands, along with tomahawks, spears, and guns. The white people couldn't believe what they were seeing, but they felt no fear because they believed they had beaten them once before and could do it again.

The white race was being targeted and killed by bows and arrows, bullets, Chinese stars, bombs, and the hands of black people, while the rest of the world watched on the news, witnessing God's work taking place in America. The biggest problem for the white people came around midday when the heat was unbearable, feeling like slave heat. They wore layers of clothing to ward off the sun's rays that were burning their skin, while the black race was going back to their African roots, fighting in nothing but panties and boxers, revealing the men's chests and women's breasts.

A significant number of black people who weren't following Rodney's teachings started looking at him as if he was the cause of the white people declaring war on them. Some of those who saw his body on the ground kicked dirt on him in disrespect as if he were already dead. Wisdom was fighting, backing up until he reached Rodney's body. He couldn't see Rodney's injuries, but the wounds had an odor that Wisdom knew all too well from when he was a kid working in an old folks' home with his mother. He touched Rodney's body to feel how badly he was hurt and concluded that he needed to seal his open wounds quickly before death or devilish spirits entered his body.

Wisdom dragged Rodney's body off to the side, away from the fighting. He reached into Rodney's white robe and felt a few small items in the inside pocket. Wisdom could feel and smell a bag of "Happy" and a piece of a plant with sharp edges on it and a tube with something in it. He twisted the cap off the tube, took a whiff, and recognized it as Preparation H, which he used when his hemorrhoids flared up. Wisdom wanted to clean off the blood from Rodney's body, but there was too much for a blind man to manage. He had nothing but his hands to apply the ointment and the aloe plant.

Rodney wasn't in physical pain because he was in total control of his mind, using the full capacity of his brain to focus on not giving the pain any attention, but his body was so severely beaten that he could barely move. Wisdom sat there with tears in his eyes because of what they had done to Rodney, but the most painful tears he shed were from having to rescue Rodney by pulling him away from some of his own race.

Rodney's body began to heal quickly with the aloe plant that Wisdom applied to his cuts. Rodney had studied the aloe plant and knew about its great healing properties. He understood it was good for both the outside and the inside of the body, so he peeled off the skin of the plant and ate the whole thing. Then he reached into his pocket and started eating his "Happy" as well, causing his body to get stronger, like Popeye eating his spinach. Once he finished, he rose to his feet and took a few steps forward, and all the blood and dirt on him was removed. He bent over and helped Wisdom up from the ground.

"Get up, Unc." Wisdom used his hands to feel Rodney's body where he knew his cuts had been. When he touched Rodney's arm, he quickly pulled his hand back because Rodney's skin was so soft and smooth, unlike any human he had felt before—slick like an eel coming out of the water. Wisdom couldn't help but wonder if Rodney was an alien or a god.

Rodney and Wisdom started walking back into the battle, and for the first time, Rodney began to use his mind to kill. The first to go were those he felt had betrayed his race, the ones who had kicked dirt on him when he was down on the ground. Then came all the racist white people who were fighting to survive, trying to save their selfish pride. Rob noticed what Rodney was doing, and a smile of joy came over him, not just because Rodney was killing racist white people, but because he felt it was about time Rodney finally stood up and fought back.

"Big up, Rasta!" Rob yelled out to Rodney, firing two shots into the air. Rodney looked around, seeing oppressed people and

Africans getting a second chance at revenge. He knew Aja had called on the spirits to help their race. He noticed the white people's fears turning into their reality, and as Rodney walked forward, he looked into the sky, seeing the sunrise slowly, its rays opening a pathway for him and his followers to walk through. As they did, their bodies were lifted off the ground by bombs exploding all around them.

"Oh my goodness, we got to get out of here!" shouted an undercover gay man, his voice trying to sound like a woman. The sky turned gray quickly, and a heavy shower of rain started pouring down like it does in Florida almost every day. It lasted for a good half-hour, and then the sun came out, with steam rising from the ground. Shortly after the storm, a big rainbow appeared in the sky, and gay people ran to the top of it, trying to make it to the other side where they felt they could live happily. More undercover gays, both white and black, slid out of the battlefield and ran up to the rainbow, skipping their way over the colors. This made Rodney's stomach turn, and he couldn't take it anymore, so he asked his inner self to fix the problems the country was going through. Then he started to smell smoke, seeing it rising from behind the tall buildings in front of him. Trees and bushes all over the country were catching fire, and people were dying from the smoke that traveled everywhere, causing the rainbow to dissipate. Some of the gay people who didn't make it across to the other side started falling out of the sky, screaming like a bunch of scared children until their bodies hit the ground, staining it with their blood.

Everyone who witnessed this couldn't believe it, but that didn't stop them from continuing to fight. The white people went back on their word about not picking up guns anymore, and Rodney had had enough. He held his hands up high to the sky with his eyes closed and began to utter words that most people couldn't understand because it sounded like he was speaking in tongues. The white people who saw Rodney again couldn't understand how he was still alive.

"This man must be of the devil, or he must be God himself in flesh, because that Nigger was hanging from a tree and left to die, and not many have lived from that. I'm out!" an older white man said as he turned and ran from the war as fast as he could.

Over everyone's heads, they could hear airplanes zipping through the sky like jets. The planes circled the air a few times, causing both whites and blacks to look up and see what was coming next. Within minutes, the planes started flying faster and lower toward the ground, shooting their guns, killing any American they could see, white or black. Everyone tried to run away while shooting up at the jets, but hitting them was like a kid throwing a rock at a mountain.

The Asians stopped shooting at people so they could focus on landing, and the minute they did, the white Americans began shooting at the jets, hoping to kill anything inside. But when they reached the planes, they realized it didn't matter what kind of bullets hit them because it wasn't people flying the planes and killing on sight—it was robots that the Asians had created, so they didn't have to worry about losing their own men. The most that happened to the robots were sparks from bullets bouncing off them. The white race, along with a few black people who still wanted to be Americans, joined forces and started fighting side by side against the robots. Slowly, one by one, members of both races decided they couldn't win the war against the robots. The brave Americans had to become turncoats and run off, trying to hide somewhere. Those cowards from both races went their separate ways, hoping to escape the robots.

Rodney and his people, who kept their minds focused on never dying, survived. Nothing could harm them, not even the robots, but they couldn't do anything to them either unless they had a stick of dynamite to blow them to pieces.

The president sent one of his agents out into the battle, telling someone to spread the news that they were considering pushing the button of mass destruction—the atomic bomb. The Asians were monitoring every move the country made through monitors installed in every robot. They noticed the white people vanishing without being killed and realized that the white race was likely looking for an easy way to win the war, so they watched closely from their desks in Asia, observing the monitors.

"Ha! Ha!" an Asian man laughed out loud at the thought of American white men trying to hold onto the land they had stolen with their lives depending on it. The men at the table burst out laughing when they noticed the president trying to set off the bomb, but they had hacked the system over two years ago without anyone knowing. After several failed attempts, the president sent out another order for his race of people—not thinking once about including the black race—to get out of the country before things got worse. Every state in the country had a secret underground exit, known only to those in the inner circles of the government. The word was passed around quickly in whispers about the president ordering his race to find a way out. They began running, making their way to those tunnels and one by one leaving the country, while the majority of the black race stood in the middle of Miami, wondering what to do and where to go.

"Oh God!" "What the fuck!" "What is it?" were the words of many of the black people who were standing around the banks of the ocean, noticing the ocean waves moving back out into the sea in a circular motion, like someone had thrown a huge rock into it. Most of the top surface of the water was being covered with something metallic but flat, as if they could walk across it all the way to

Africa. It started to slowly rise from the ocean, and the more it emerged, the more it looked like a wall being built to hold back the water that surrounded it. The black people were amazed at what they were seeing, causing many to run off, not knowing what was coming out of the ocean, while others stood still, waiting to see what would happen next.

"Run, Nigga! Run! You know if the white man is running, then it can't be safe," said a scared black man, grabbing his little boy's hand in the midst of running off to no man's land. By the time whatever was coming out of the water finished rising, it was now hovering over the water about ten feet high and was somewhat wide in a circular shape, as if it were impossible for it to have fit into the waters it came out of, covering the sky completely. Rodney, his followers, and everyone else who stuck around to see what this thing was noticed that this big metal object had no windows, no lights—just a big round circle.

Rodney's focus was no longer on the thing in the air that looked like some type of UFO to him. He pointed his finger out towards the ocean to his followers and Rob to see what was sailing in. It was three old-looking ships in the front and many more behind them. One had a flag hanging high from the top, flapping in the wind with its red, black, and green colors. The flag was three times bigger than the one Betsy Ross made for the United States in 1777. The other ship had a flag with the Star of David on it, but the print was of a whole different color—it was white, purple, and black. The third ship's flag was waving the red, gold, and green, and the names of a few of the ships were The Black Star Liner, King Negus, and Yeshua.

The black race felt it was about time someone from the motherland had come to their rescue, except for Rodney and those who followed him because they knew he was the rescue they had been waiting for. The ones who could run to the ships did so, while those who couldn't walked alongside Rodney. They noticed smoke rising from the tops of the ships, and the closer they got, the stronger the smell of "Happy" became—but not because someone was smoking it. The purpose of the smell was that the ships were being run on hemp oil.

When all the black people reached the ships, one man yelled out with tears of joy in his voice, "Take me home!" Rodney stood still, holding his race of people back from boarding the ships because he wasn't sure if they were sent by other white Europeans to enslave them in a new world somewhere over in some foreign land with more people who looked like their past oppressors. "Hold up a minute!" Rodney said, holding his hand out to keep the people back. Just then, the big UFO opened a door right in front of all the black people, and an image of a man stepped out, looking just like Rodney. He was tall and dark as night, only revealing the whiteness of his eyes. The only difference between Rodney and the man coming out of the spaceship was his hair—his dreadlocks were much longer. He wore the same white gown, causing Rodney to scratch his head at the sight of his own twin. He couldn't believe it, and then he noticed the man waving at him, signaling for him alone to come towards him.

The man never spoke any words because words were made up to place spells on people, so he and the other Gods that were like him communicated with their eyes through mental telepathy. Rodney remembered what Chin had taught him about how to read people's eyes, so he walked up to the man, who then lowered some steps for him to come up into the spaceship. The steps were made of gold, and no other man would have been able to walk up those steps because the gold was so pure it was very soft. The one who could step on it would have to walk lightly on their feet, as if they were floating.

When Rodney entered the spacecraft, he noticed that it was almost filled with all the black women and children that Aja and Miss Ali had cared for. Some were people they thought were dead but weren't—they were the ones who had found the ship by mistake before many others, with the understanding that death was just a mindset. Rodney had tears streaming down his eyes, but they became tears of joy when he saw that everyone had happy and pleasant looks on their faces. Rodney looked at his twin, and the man nodded yes, indicating that it was okay for his people to go and see what the ships that sailed in had to offer them.

Rodney wanted to impress his twin by showing how close he had gotten to being a God within himself, so instead of using the steps to get back down from the ship, Rodney floated into the sky until he landed among his people. Rob had never seen this from him before, and his mouth was stuck wide open. He already knew Rodney was on a different level, but this took him by surprise for sure.

"This ship here is for all those Hebrew Israelites to get on and go home to Israel and stay there if they choose to," Rodney said as he pointed to the ship with the flag of the Star of David on it. "And this ship here is for any black person who believes we're the people of Africa and wants to go and live anywhere there if his black brother from the motherland welcomes them. And this ship here is for those Rastas who want to go home to Ethiopia," he said while pointing in the direction of the flags with the red, black, and green, and the red, gold, and green. The people entered the ships of their desire, while those who felt they had never been to those places and wanted to stay back to see what America had to offer now that most of the white people had left and gone back to Europe for the time being remained.

Rob and Wisdom were the first to get on the ship heading to Ethiopia and wanted Rodney to step on as well. Rodney stood still and didn't move. Rob looked at him as if he didn't understand.

"Monk, you're not coming with us?" he asked Rodney, tears appearing in his eyes because he felt it might be the last time they would ever see each other again.

"No, my brother, I can't go with you this time. I must go my own way, but don't worry yourself. I'll come forward to Shashamane to visit you and Unc. in the near future. Don't be concerned with me not being allowed to come see you and Wisdom because the land of Africa is ours and has always been ours, and nothing and no one will be able to stop me from doing so," Rodney said as they shared tears with each other. Then they hugged before he turned to go back to the UFO ship to board it.

The white race who stayed behind, or who never got out of the country, mostly because they were poor and didn't know the right people to help them escape, felt they would stay and fight for what their ancestors left behind for them to be privileged, even if they felt they didn't have a chance to survive the war that the Asians were bringing to America.

Chapter 23

Brothers in Blood: America's Last Stand

The white men who bore arms against the Asian people took cover in military spots that allowed them to see who and what was trying to enter the country, but that didn't matter because the Asian countries were sending ships, planes, and tanks to America to cause havoc. They didn't need to come in fast with guns blazing because they outnumbered the white Americans three to one, and the white men could no longer handle the force of tanks and robots. Now, they were starting to feel what it was like to run out of bullets and be unable to properly defend themselves.

"I'm going to die!" yelled out a white man who had just seen the man next to him get destroyed by a robot. Just before the robot could get to him, the white man took his own gun, held it up to his head, and fired. "Bap!" One shot to his head was all it took for the man to take his own life. The robot, angered by what the man did, kicked dirt on him in disgust and then started jumping on the man's dead body. "Coward! Coward! Coward!" the robot shouted as it turned its head around in a full circle, checking to see if it could find more white people to kill. This continued until nearly all of the 15 percent of the white race that stayed behind were killed.

The robots, by the thousands, searched every state, trying to see if any of them were left behind to be killed. The last place they were checking was the projects in the ghettos because they still had an eye on the black race from the people still running the Chinese restaurants.

****

Rodney got on the spaceship and didn't turn to look back at his black brothers and sisters that boarded those ships heading to Africa because he had cried enough throughout his journey. The fact that he knew that the Pan-African movement they put together while being locked up would ensure it was just a matter of time before they linked up once again. The door closed behind him, and just as fast as things would disappear in the Bermuda Triangle, the spaceship vanished from the sky, and not one person could say if the spaceship went back into the ocean or if it vanished into the sky. All anyone could say for sure is that it was no longer there.

Rodney's twin and the other people that looked like them and weren't part of Rodney's followers gathered around Rodney, looking him over, wondering to themselves why more of them hadn't turned out like Rodney and what it would take for them to. Rodney started to use his mind to tell them that in a few months, he was going to have to leave the ship to go see how their race of people who stayed back in America were going to make out. The men that looked like him already knew this because the God in them knew things beforehand just the same as Rodney could do. Rodney started to notice the ship in another part was holding all the ancestors of the indigenous people of America and the spirits of all the black people who have been killed by white cops or any type of person that thought they had authority over them because of the mere fact that they felt they were better because of their skin complexion.

After months went by, the black race of people that stayed back were no longer hiding. They were walking around trying to see what was going on because they knew most of the white men had made their way out of the country, and Rodney and some of his people went on those ships while others stayed back. It seemed as if they were having to fend for themselves at all costs, and many of them were very scared of the thought of having to clean the country's mess up, rebuild it, and start all over again. It was strange to them that the robots would notice a black person and not dare lay a hand on them now, but if a white person popped out of nowhere, they would be killed with fatalities like in the game Mortal Kombat by a robot. This started making the black people feel that the robots were sent to come and rescue them from the oppressions of white America, so they began talking amongst themselves about what state they wanted to go and live in or what house they wanted in the hills where some white person used to live.

"Man, I'm so glad that them crackers are gone, man. I ain't got to go to work no more and act like I give a fuck. Man, fuck all that, I love who I be. I'm from New York, you know what I mean, son? I'm a true hustler, and I'm going to get mine, son. But these taxes these white people were making us pay, son, is for the birds, my dude. Well, goodbye to that," said a young black man to his friend from the Bronx.

"Word, son, I feel you. Look, peep this—all this shit is our fucking land, my nigga, and it's just us, son. Just us niggas." The young man laughed at the thought that just ran through his mind. "I mean, until I start fucking all these bitches and populate these grounds with my seed all up in this motherfucker."

The two friends smiled at the shit they were talking while they were smoking on some Happy. The Happy had others come around and share their inputs on what they wanted, but most of them were referring to cleaning the land up and growing food since most of them were dying every day from hunger. The blacks that thought a little differently were planning on how to own the big corporations that they never encountered except by working for one.

A man across from the two young men from the Bronx was with a group of men in blue and white clothing. Some were looking really mean and serious, while some were dancing and laughing, having fun, but there was one slim brother who had thoughts bigger than most.

"Yo Jigg, my nigga, you know how we've been taking over shit, and we're the largest gang out this piece. Man, we could have all this shit turn blue and white and add the brothers with their red and white," the young man said to his homeboy, who was dressed like him.

"What you talking about, my nigga?" his friend asked, thinking seriously about what their gang could achieve, being as though they are 35,000 strong.

"What, my nigga, you don't see it? Look, this shit is empty, my nigga. Yo, what I'm trying to say is if we can come together to fight these white folks, then why can't we all become white, blue, and red?" His homeboy looked at him like he had a question.

"That part," he said, questioning his boy to make himself clear. "Look, them Bloods had our back just as much as we had theirs, and those niggas are about 20,000 strong themselves."

"I hear you, my nigga, but what about all the other black gangs?"

His boy stepped to him and backhanded his chest gently. "Peep this—those niggas are deep as well, but we need them to come on board, and every man would need to play his own position so that we can take over this whole motherfucking country." His Homie shook his head yes at him with a serious look on his face. "You talking that real shit my Nigg, I feel you though." A thought quickly came to his mind. "Whats that shit you smoking that got you talking that shit?" his friend quickly replied. "That Happy that Nigga Rodney blessed us with." They gave each other dap by tapping their fist together. Some of them went over to some of their other friends' houses to run the game by them so they would be able to have a head start over the other blacks that had their mind frame sold on some type of politician or lawyer or Judge or just a Nigga that thinks because they once had money and thinks it still hold its own wait or they had made some money in Crypto Currency. It was a divine spirt in the air because all the street gang members all came together in peace once the word got out about taken the land over. All the leaders of each gang came together like five fingers into one solid fist, coming together as one playing their part in the mission under the same principles for the cause under the color's Blue and white, and Red. "Well Cuz, we hear you talking about the colors and shit but what we going to call ourselves my Nigga?" One young kid asked. "We can come up with some type of shit but I'm thinking the shit got to have some real meaning to it, not saying ours don't but this one has to rep all this land, shit if we plan to take it over and run shit. Shit I was thinking to call us the Indigenous Brothers. I mean something like that." Some of his Homeboys were feeling it but it was some in the back that didn't even like the fact that he felt he had too much say so in everything and a tab bit of jealousy was kicking in for some. "Ok I hear you my Nigga but most of the country is under water what the fuck you suppose to do with that?" the one from the back hating asked. "Any land above ground we control, simple as that." The slim O.G. said to the man that was an undercover hater and then he starts smacking at some mosquito's that were fucking his neck up. "Look my Nigga's, if you look around, we lost a lot of brother's but together we gained a nation, a notion of million that can't be held back." Other brothers except for the hatter were agreeing with him and they all were dapping each other up. "Say it loud I'm black and I'm proud!" Someone in the crowd just felt the need to yell it out and the next thing you knew was all the gang members started doing their signature dance of their gang they repped before coming together as one.

The whole time this was taking place, the Asians were watching the Black people's every move. The men in Asia, sitting at a big table and looking into a monitor, discussed the situation. The one in the red Ninja suit said, "Look at those Black people. Our problem won't be those uppity Blacks; all they care about is controlling the smaller things like money until they feel all the hard work is over, and then they try to come in and take over things. But it's those Black men right there who have realized that they're stronger in numbers and that two heads are better than one."

The Ninja in all black replied, "Well, look at most of them—they are weak from hunger. How do we expect them to clean up the mess over there?"

The Ninja in yellow added, "Good thinking. Let's drop off some rice, cabbage, and plenty of chicken—you know the Black man loves some chicken and watermelon."

The next day, six months' worth of food supplies was dropped off in the middle of Miami and some other parts of the country. Hungry and thirsty Black people bombarded the supply of food before it even hit the ground. People were trying to snatch it out of the air before the next hungry man could get it.

"Look at them fighting over the food. Don't they know how to share? And it seems that they have forgotten the old saying 'ladies go first.' I guess that went out of style way back then," said the Ninja in red.

"I see, and it's been almost a month, and they haven't even tried to clean up around themselves. They keep shitting and pissing on top of piss and shit," the Ninja in white added.

The Ninja in all black had to add his input to the conversation. "The way I see it, they're doing what they must to survive. I don't see them as savages like the white man or themselves. They're true survivors, and they've been through a lot, withstanding all that the white man has put them through. I think they would be just great for what we need of them." They all nodded in agreement.

"There are still some well-trained, fighting white men who just won't leave with the rest of them. I wonder how the ones that got away managed without the robots killing them?" the Ninja in red asked.

The one in black, who was a little more versed in American history than the others, replied, "I believe they used those underground railroad tunnels that the old Negroes used when they thought they were escaping from slavery to the North." The other men looked at each other, realizing they hadn't known that but understanding the possibilities. "Once they got out of the tunnels, they most likely went into a submarine heading back to where they originated from—Europe."

The men kept their eyes on the monitor, watching the Black race trying their best to figure out how they were going to rebuild what had been destroyed and continue to regulate the things that weren't destroyed. The Black people who followed the order of gang life formed an alliance among themselves regarding how they were going to run the country, while the Black people who thought they had been on the upside of being stand-up Americans felt they should be the ones in control, being as though many of them had some type of education with a degree. They looked down upon the gangsters because they felt they would only run the country through crime and extortion.

They all came together to try and figure out a way to seize control of what they were trying to do, regardless of their morals, because they felt their needs and wants were more important than what any thug could ask for, even though they didn't even try to hear out what the gangsters were trying to put in place. They sat back and waited, hoping that the young and old gangsters would start fighting each other so they could move in and take over while they were doing so. But the gangsters had done all the fighting and killing of their own in the past, and many of the leaders had a new mindset of "been there and done that," so they didn't want any more parts of it. Now that a year had passed and not one of them had killed anyone for the sake of being cool or because they didn't like the colors one repped, one of the leaders of the Black Gorillas was having a conversation with one of those uppity Blacks who went to college for law about their differences.

The gang leader was getting angry at the man for only seeing things from his perspective and only wanting the ways of the old. "My man, this is a different time and a different day, and we are here to show everyone what we know how to do best, and that's uniting, my brother. And here you are, standing here telling me that we need to continue with the ways of white America's agenda."

The young Black lawyer sucked his teeth as if he knew he was right about what he felt. "How so?" he questioned the gangster, with an attitude in his voice because he felt he was a little wiser due to his Widener College degree.

The young gangster looked at the young Black man in front of him with a look that made it clear he knew the brother thought his intellect was superior. "Man, you're so smart you're stupid." The man looked at the gangster like he was crazy. "Why is that?" he asked, sucking his teeth with sarcasm.

"Because, motherfucker, you and the rest of those niggas think we're gonna need money, but who makes it? And what's it backed by? In your mind, money has always been the way to solve all our problems. I used to think like y'all until now. What will that money buy you now?" The man stood there looking at him as if the question was only relevant for a short time. He felt that a few years from now, the white race would resurface in this country, take it back, and make things happen all over again, just like they used to.

While he stood there, looking at the gangster with his lip cocked to the side, he took out a pack of smokes, placed a cigarette in his mouth, lit it, and took a deep pull. He then let out a cloud of smoke that briefly obscured their view of each other. The one thing they both knew was that they would have to pick up a gun again to defend themselves. Many were already checking the dead bodies lying around for guns still in working order, especially if bullets came with them. The lawyer could see that the gangster was packing, noticing the gun resting on his hip.

"I can see the thug in you hasn't changed; you're still carrying that hammer. And God forbid if all you gangsters get ahold of guns, it won't be long before you niggas start killing each other again," the lawyer said, waiting for a response.

"What! What kind of bullshit is that? I know you just can't wait to see us start killing each other so you and the rest of those who think like you can sit back and think you're smarter and better than us. But what you fail to realize is that we've been there and done that. We're moving along in the same manner as Malcolm X, while you blue-collar niggas try to prove yourselves to each other, thinking MLK's philosophy has come true for you when dealing with other niggas. You think you're different from the other Black people who might be gangsters or uneducated, but by far, I know there are two types of gangsters: the one with the image of a grimy street thug, and the other in a suit and tie, maybe clean-shaven, ready to show the corporate side of what a gangster is. We're no different, other than you thinking so."

415

After saying his last words to the lawyer, he turned his back on the man and went on to have a conversation with another gang member, ready to talk more about their plans to come together and what it would take to make peace with niggas like the lawyer who think they're better than them. The lawyer walked away, thinking it would only be a matter of time before those types of niggas did what they do best—kill another nigga.

****

Back in Asia the men were sitting at the table still looking into the monitor seeing how the blacks were getting along and they noticed that the confusion going on from the ones who once had it going on as far as being black in America with a little cash and the ones who did what they had to do to survive the best way they knew how. The Asian men felt the black people would have killed themselves off by now but not at the fast rate that they would have hoped for. The man in the yellow Ninja gear laughed out load for a second. "I see why the Robots hadn't killed or found some of the little bit of white men that was coming back to the country, or the ones that never left." He points to the monitor that was revealing some white people taking out a few Robots. "I can see little more grain of salt sprinkling into the country amongst the black pepper." Replied the man in all Black "These white men are using metal detectors that people use at the Beaches to look for metal objects from the ground and look now they are blowing the Robots up with

416

M80 cherry Bombs." One of the men felt that was a little funny. "Which one of you guys are still importing them the fireworks?" they all laughed and turned around looking at the one dressed in Yellow.

"Ok you guys got me, but that little shit will be all gone in no time and then what will those Crackers do?" The man in the Red said "Pause, did you just call a White man a Cracker?" they all burst out into a load laughter. The one at the table in Purple went straight into serious mode. "I think it's time to make are move now while some parts of the country is above water and other parts of it don't burn up from them Nigga's not being able to put the major fires out." With the looks of them ready to get down to business they put their hands out in front of them and planted their hands one over top the other like kids do in little league baseball just before the game starts. "Has those ship with the tanks on them arrived over their yet?" asked the one in the purple for anyone to answer. "The ships have been there for three days now waiting for us to just say when." Said the one in all Black. "Ok then, let us gather all we need and recount the money and who's going to be the one that wishes to be in charge of that?" the one in the all-white stood up from the table.

"I got it." The man in the purple went under the table and pulled out a black briefcase and handed it to him. They all got up from the table and flew back to their country so they could let everyone back home know what was about to take place. They sent out a mass text through TikTok to all their countrymen about what was going on without Black Americans knowing because they look at totally different things on TikTok than the Black race of people who prefer to see women twerking and anything else that has drama going on.

The next morning in the middle of Asia, those men at the table were ready to enter their Jet plane. In the air flying over the top of the United States were five jet planes circling around the country, lowering their altitude with each lap they took. The Black people who were still alive were looking and jumping up in a happy and begging way in the hopes that those planes were there to drop more food and water off to them. One Black man who was waiting to see was standing next to his family looking up into the sky.

"Those planes aren't here to give us food," the man said to his older brother.

"How you figure Nate?" his brother questioned because he didn't understand why his little brother said that when all this time the planes in the sky have been dropping food down to them ever since the white men left.

"Because Kurt, just think they cut down on sending us food for the last six months and now they haven't dropped anything in the last month. I think they're here on some other shit," Nate replied.

"Like what?" his brother asked sarcastically.

"I don't know, but I bet you it's them motherfuckers from over in Asia somewhere, Mother Fucking China somewhere," Nate continued. His brother really got confused and discussed it with Nate.

"Why man? Why the Chinese? What did they ever do to us?" Nate was younger than his brother, but he was a bit wiser just because he thought somewhat outside the box and being as though his brother was old school and his mindset had him stuck in the past because he thought everyone was going to try and do the right, Godly things in this cruel world.

"Man, those motherfuckers won't give a Black man a break if he's two cents short for a candy bar, let alone if their shit they sold you was fucked up; you can't even return it or exchange the shit," Nate explained. His brother Kurt crossed his arms against his chest in more disgust.

"What the hell does that have to do with what we're talking about?" Nate replied to his brother calmly, "Nigga, don't you read where the food's been coming from out the sky? Are you so dumb to think the shit just appeared out of nowhere and just dropped out the fucking sky? Man, the shit says it's coming from China and I would bet you some money, if I had any, that those niggas are coming here thinking that we owe them for that fucking food and

419

shit." Kurt stood there with nothing else to say but thought in his head why he hadn't thought of that himself other than just seeing it as the food just dropping out the sky. He knew his brother was a little wiser than himself and the thought of it made his face have a smirk on it, revealing the slight jealousy within himself because of it.

A good amount of Black people that were in Miami or walking somewhere else as far as they could, trying to find a place to live, but the bulk of the people was still in Florida, all around the Miami area and its outskirts. Some Black people who were camping out living on what used to be the airport runway were grabbing all their things they could and then started running and jumping as fast as they could out of the way of those five jet planes landing, causing the runway to become hot and smoky until they came to a complete stop. Some of the people were on the ground looking while some were standing waiting to see who these people are getting out of those jets.

The planes opened the door to let down the stairs and out came from each plane ten robots, and they stood in a single file, five on one side and five on the other, and then each man came out in their ninja attire of the colors they repped. One holding a black briefcase and one holding what looked like an envelope, and then they all walked towards each other, greeting one another. The black people were looking at these men bowing to each other as if they were kings.

The Asian man in yellow turned over the briefcase to the man in red. "How much is in here?" the man in red asked as he took the briefcase from the man in yellow and then opened it a crack to take a peek inside. "I think it's no more no less than a million; I counted it once again before getting off the plane, do you think that's enough to give them?" the man standing in black chimed in. "Ha, for them? It's more than enough because they are not going to spread it amongst all of them because of their greediness for money, and that, my friend, goes way back to Africa. Just like everyone else, the strong will inherit the money from the weak and keep it for empowerment over the next man," the one in red opened the briefcase and quickly glanced over the money. "He's right! Those niggas think the world of money. Now let's sit back and wait and see." The Asian men pulled out Cigars and started smoking it trying to kill time to see what black man was going to come forward as a leader trying to see what they wanted and had to offer. The Asian men were getting tired of waiting on a so-called leader of the "black" people. The black people sat back never taking their eyes off the men and one Ghetto woman from New Orleans stood out in the mist of everyone and shouted out too many of the black men who were waiting to see if they were going to have to fight those men from Asia. "I know them Nigga's don't want know smoke because we can do this!" She went on and on at the lips getting the men worked up and ready to fight. "Oh shit! one is walking over here now! It's on! Bring it my Nigga!" she shouted out once more. Three black men looked at each other and without hesitation they came together not knowing one another at all. "Let's see what this dude wants?" said the one that's the oldest of the three black men. He had clothes on his back but most of it were torn to pieces and the shoes on his feet could tag along with them and hold its own conversation because the bottom back of his shoes were talking. They walked toward the Ninja in the red and the black men eyes were locked in on the briefcase and in their eye's the only thing that could most likely be in it would be some money or guns. "What you think is in the briefcase O.G.?" ask the young man. The man was man enough to step forward and see what the

Asian people wanted without fear in his heart. "We going to soon find out nephew." The old man said looking around to see if any other black people were going to come and join him to somehow show some type of power in unity. Before anyone could open their mouths to say a word the Ninja handed the old head the tan envelope and then said. "Who is your leader?" He asked the O.G. The old head looked at him as if that were a great question. "What you mean a leader?" He said to the Asian man with an attitude. The Ninja just looked at him as if he'd delt with his kind once before. "I'm taking about who is the one you all look up to now within your race to speak for your people. Is it Dr. Umar or Young Pharaoh or we noticed at one time you had this Rodney man looking like he had things looking promising for your race of people and then out of nowhere he bounced on you all, I take it he's a fraud." The old head and the two other men heard what he said, and they got to thinking to themselves that the man had a great point. He left them with no food or water or anyone that could protect them and tell them what they should do for themselves. The only thing he left them was for them to keep their faith and learn how to come together as one and save the land. "I would have to say that us black people don't have a one per say person that we call are leader, but why is that your concern?" the old head asked.

"We just wanted to make sure that the money gets in the hand of the right person and since you came forward first, we felt you must be the one in charge." The Ninja said looking down at the man because he was judging him by his appearance. Money was all the old head and the three others needed to hear and the old head cracked the briefcase open. "What's this for?" The old head asked with a little stutter in his voice. "This is for your people for the Reparation the white man didn't give you all." The Ninja said with a slight laughter in his voice as if he were doing the black race a favor. The young black man tapped the O.G. on the side of his leg. "But the money isn't U.S. money, man how much that shit worth?"

The old head didn't think to question that at the time because all his mind could think of at the moment was out of all the black people that are there standing around wasn't going to see a dime of that money other than the other two standing there with him. The Ninja in the Black said out loud for the one in the red to hear him. The Ninja in the Red understood the langue he heard shouted out and looked over to his left just as the Ninja in the black shouted out to him. He noticed about a good hundred black men coming his way. He stood there and gave his men a look and then they came over to him while they wondered in their mines were these black men going to go along with their offer or was things going to have to get ugly not knowing that the black men thought they were there to help them since they've been doing so in the last year. The black men coming towards them had been watching them the hole time with a pair of Binoculars and now they were interested in what was in that briefcase. The old head tried to quickly pass the money to someone he thought could hold it for them for a second until the time would be right for them to walk away with it, instead of the group of men walking over o the Ninja's first they quickly moved in on the old head and the two other men. When they got to the old head, he could tell by the look on their faces that they weren't about any games. "What did those Ninja's give you?" the man with a crew of black men behind him asked while the old head acted dumb. "What the only Nigga's I see is the one's you with and the one's here with me, you talking about them Ninja's
424

right?" The old head asked knowing he was on some bullshit. The man looked at the old head and tried looking past his shoulder because he noticed the old head didn't have the briefcase anymore. He signaled out to one of his friends to go and find the briefcase. The man went looking as he told and when he got to the person that had the briefcase, he saw the man trying to hide it under an abandon car.

He saw the man under the car and grabbed the briefcase out of his hand, then bent down and smacked the man upside his head just to let him know he was on some bullshit. The man grabbed at his head because of it but didn't want any problems, especially since the man who retrieved the briefcase looked as if he'd eaten weights for lunch, breakfast, and dinner. So the man just looked at him as he watched him take the money back to his friend who told him to retrieve it. "Here you go, Big E," he said while handing over the briefcase to him, and then he walked over to his boy and stood beside him, waiting to see what was in it.

When he opened the briefcase and noticed that the money wasn't American, their faces twisted up at the sight of it. "What the fuck is this supposed to be?" he said out loud, questioning himself, and then his boy starts to walk over to the Ninjas while all the other black people sat back and watched them. The two of them stepped up to the five Ninjas and noticed they were being smiled at by the Ninjas. They couldn't see their faces, but they could feel the fakeness of the smiles behind their masks. Now the two black men approaching them put aside the thought of them being there to help them.

"What's the meaning of this money?" the younger brother asked the five Ninjas.

"Are you the leader of the black race?" the Ninja in the white asked.

The brother looked at them like, why do you care. "I'm an O.G. who once gangbanged but now I'm here with others behind me that are black men who are leaders of themselves."

The Asian men thought the same thing about that statement: that in their eyes the black race has no structure, and they were happy with that because, in the end, without structure there is confusion, and with confusion comes self-destruction.

"The money is for you and your people; you all deserve it. We want to offer this to you all so that you have another option," the Ninja in white explained.

The two black men looked at the man in the white Ninja gear, wanting him to elaborate on what other option he was referring to. "What might that be?" he asked.

"Well, you see, you can take the money and try and make out the best you can here with it, or you all can do what we've been doing

426

for the U.S. for decades, and that's working cheap labor for next to peanuts," the Ninja proposed.

The young brother looked at him as if he had the black race fucked up. "So let me get this straight, you want the black people to take this money and do what we want with it or work for you, and who the fuck are the five of you?" the brother asked.

"We are the ones here that are going to take over this place and keep you all here because it was yours in the first place, but we figured the money will give you all a good start on serving, so what do you say?" the Ninja asked, holding out his hand for a handshake.

The brother looked at him and then down at the briefcase because the Ninja was eyeing it for him to open it. He opens the briefcase and peeps into it once more as if the currency had changed. "What the fuck are we supposed to do with this? The shit ain't worth two cents of Chinese money."

The Chinese man in the yellow Ninja gear got a little offended. "The American dollar is no more, and the Yuan, my nigga, is your new currency so you all either take it or just simply be our broke slaves."

Everyone could tell the two black brothers were getting heated but the black people standing back didn't have a clue as of why because they still thought they were there to help them. "Over my dead body will I take that bull crap money and I'll die first before I become anyone's slave," one brother declared.

The four other Ninjas knew what the outcome was going to be if that was the answer they got. The Ninja in red did a Kung Fu roll and rolled about three rolls in front of the Ninja in white and handed him a small handgun. The Ninja in red all in one motion grabbed the gun without anyone seeing it and then quickly rolled in front of the black man and stood up in front of him face to face. "Blap!" was the sound of a bullet coming out of the gun, hitting the black man in the middle of his forehead. "Ahhh!" was yelled out by many of the black people who saw what just took place and they started rushing after the five Ninjas, but the one in red wasn't going anywhere because the other black man that was with his friend grabbed him by the neck with so much force the Ninja dropped the gun and slowly went to his knees while his breath was being choked out of him until he died in the man's bare hands.

The Ninjas' robots were coming to their rescue, but it didn't matter; they were outnumbered and the black people stomped on them, breaking them into pieces and then picked them up to fight the other four Ninjas, but those four were very skilled in Kung Fu and they kicked and punched their way back onto the jet they flew in

428

on and then they got the hell out of the country as fast as they could. "Hell yeah! We chased them slanted-eye motherfuckers out of here," shouted out a middle-aged black male who felt like they have solved their problems now that they're gone.

Later that night around 9 pm a bright light was covering over the entire country that caused the people to not be able to see the person next to them let alone be able to see what was in the sky causing them not to be able to see. "What is going on?" A black woman shouted out for anyone to answer. No one said a word because no one had an answer until the black people started to hear others screaming out from being killed. "The robots are back! Run!" Multiple robots were being dropped out of planes with parachutes and the second they hit the ground they started shooting and killing the black people, not caring if it were women or their children; they were just programmed to kill anything that moved and wasn't a robot.

The four Ninjas sat on the plane watching the robots destroy most of the black race of people, very happy they didn't have to get their hands dirty while the robots did all the dirty work. Rodney was in tears because he was meditating and could see what was taking place, and his heart was in so much pain because seeing how the black people were handling themselves seemed as if they didn't have a fair chance.

It was very hard for him to sit there and watch his race of people being killed, but he wanted to see just what they were going to do: either be a slave or die fighting like many of their ancestors had done. Or would they do as the old generation of black people who felt like marching down the streets asking the killers to please stop? Or would they continue noticing that the Robots were stepping around the dead bodies like they were part of a black Greek fraternity, and the saddest thing to see was the Robots using the legs of the dead bodies as if they were Kappa canes, tossing them in the air and catching them before they hit the ground. If one were to drop a leg, they would start stomping the ground in anger like the Q's and waving their hands in the air. Black men that were Frat, seeing this, were falling into the trap of the Robots by understanding that the Robots were being utmost disrespectful, so they started running up to the Robots trying to take one down to destroy it with his bare hands, without a care in the world if he were to die because of it, because they would die in honor of their Frat.

Rodney was thinking to himself how his race of people could come together to form some type of gang, or Frat, or some type of political party or religion, and be quick to die or kill over it if anyone disrespected it. But in the past, his race of people would rather talk about the injustice being done to the black race or march down the streets with signs saying "This has to stop!" or, if they have been blinded by White America's media, they'll start asking the victim questions about why didn't they do this or that as if they were the ones in the wrong, blaming his own race for the actions of his oppressors. Rodney just started shaking his head at the thought of that and then he looked around and noticed that the people around him that looked like him were looking at him because they knew what he was thinking at that moment, and they were giving him the look like don't turn your face up towards your people like that because he shouldn't forget that he once was like them many years ago before he realized the blessing of being of Myelinated people, which they all knew is God.

The people Rodney was around started to communicate with each other and then it reached him, questioning him about when he was going to stop crying and help his people the way they came for him. Rodney just looked at them and questioned himself, "What am I waiting for?" But his mind didn't know how to make his body be removed from his flesh into his immortal being because the tears that were falling down his face blocked his vision and focus of when was the right time. Rodney went down to his knees, holding his stomach in pain. He closed his eyes and tapped into his mental, and Aja's thoughts were sending him a message saying that if he didn't go back out there and help his people, there would be none. And if he just opened his eyes and looked in a different direction, he'd see that he isn't alone. Rodney opened his eyes and became dizzy for a moment because it seemed as if the men in the room with him were standing right in his face, making him feel like he was looking at himself through a circus mirror. He shook himself out of the daze, only this time they slowly opened the door to the ship, and then Rodney walked over to the ledge of it looking down all around the country, smiling when he noticed the Marcus Garvey ship docking, and the Harriet Tubman ship, along with all the other ships that his people had left out on and now have returned to help out the cause because they could feel that Rodney couldn't do it alone and they wanted to practice what they preached by uniting and coming together in the time of need the way he taught them.

Rodney saw them getting off the ships in their Ninja gear and then he looked at a few Robots surround a black woman who was giving birth to her baby. The woman couldn't help but scream out in pain because she was giving childbirth at that very moment, along with seeing those Robots surrounding her.

The baby's head was protruding out of her vagina, and her screams became louder until a Robot grabbed her up from the ground by her neck, choking the life out of her, causing her legs to dangle with blood dripping down from them. The head of the child was locked in a chokehold around its neck by the tightening from the mother being tensed just before her life was snatched away from her. The Robots were programmed to have the killer's mindset of

432

a white slave master in America. The Robot held the woman's body over its head with one hand and used the other to grab the baby by the head and pulled the body out of the vagina, then tossed the Black woman's body aside while holding onto the baby as it waited for its brain to register what it should do with the baby. Not long before it met up with the lady giving birth, the Robot had just killed a Black cowboy and had taken the cowboy's lasso, which it had wrapped around its arm, causing its brain to register.

The Robot took the rope and wrapped it around the child's neck, pulling on it a bit to tighten up the noose. The baby was crying out in horror. "Aaaaa!" were the screams of the baby, and then the Robot started to swing the rope and the baby over the top of its head like he was about to lasso the rope out into a rodeo event. The Black people standing around hiding out so they wouldn't be killed were watching what was going on from afar, like a slave scared, watching another of their kind being whipped to death.

Rob and other Black men who came off those ships were coming onto land in Ninja gear, and when the Robots and the Black people watching saw them, they became confused. The Robot that held the baby didn't know if it should be happy to see those Ninjas and toss the baby, or should it stop and wait for a command, but it made the mad Robot swing the rope around faster the closer they came towards him. From the distance where Rob and all the others were coming from to rescue the child and the Black people, they were still too far out to help, so Rodney let loose of his flesh and floated out of the ski with his bare toes hovering over the land like a feather falling out of the ski until his spirit hit the land area where the child had just been lassoed and released into the air.

Rodney wasn't like most people because he was at the right place at the right time instead of the wrong time. Just before the baby's body was about to hit the ground, Rodney stopped the child from doing so by using his soft pillow toes to safely stop the child from hitting the ground. Rodney picked the baby up from off his feet and held him high up to the stars in the sky like Kunta Kinte's father did in the movie Roots when he was a child. "Behold, no one greater than yourself." Every Black person that wasn't part of his crew cried out loud, "Oh my God!" They felt like he had to be some type of savior and redeemer for them because they were looking around, and the Robots' brains started to malfunction, and they began to stop themselves in their tracks and then started to fall over, hitting the ground with little bits of smoke coming out of them.

The Black race of people started believing they didn't have to worry about those Robots any longer. The Black people started to get on their knees and began to praise Rodney as if he were the new Jesus of this time frame. The five Asian Ninjas noticed what was taking place through the Robots' monitors that were still standing and wanted it to stop, so they got back into their jet and made sure to have landed right where Rodney and now all the ex-cons in Black Ninjas' gear were standing strong and firm behind him. The Asians landed the plane with a few things on their person like throwing stars and smoke bombs they used to make it hard for them to be seen moving around.

It wasn't hard to figure out who was who, being as though they had on Ninja gear of different colors except for the one that tagged along with them in his all-black, and he was very effective in killing the Black people in their Ninja gear because he blended in with them so well that he killed many of them before they noticed his eyes were slanted and that they were about to take their last breath. They got out the jet fast and dropping the smoke bombs out all in front of them causing the black people to lose their vision of them. The people were hearing a choking sound coming from some others standing around them because one by one, someone was holding onto their necks with their hands and their eyeballs were halfway popping out of their faces from being hit by throwing stars. Once they were all used up, they moved in on them and started beating and killing any Black person who chose to die rather than becoming a slave for the Asian race. Rodney didn't like what he was seeing, and he had to dig deep in his heart and summon all the power in his mind to bring this to an end quickly because the Asian men were so swift with killing the Black people. Rodney stood toe to toe with those Ninjas like he was Bruce Lee's teacher Ip Man and held out his hand in front of him for them to come to a halt. "Stop this madness before I have to humble the five of you," Rodney said to them, while they didn't pay him any mind and kept on killing Black people with their bare knuckles and swift kicks.

Unlike Rodney, he didn't want to kill anybody because he strongly believed that if a man could rise out of bed once again, then the human has a chance to change his heart to the right place, which is love, and love is God. Rodney wanted to do something that the five men would understand who he truly was and not the fraud they thought him to be. Rodney began to use his mind power, causing the air to become dry like a desert and hot like a sauna. The five Asian men started to gasp for air, but the more they gasped, the drier their throats got. The Ninja in all white was the first to drop dead onto the ground, leaving the other four Ninjas' eyeballs to start drying up as they feared that they were going to die. The only words they could get out of their mouths at the time were "God help us," said in their Asian tongue.

Rodney knew the words they were crying out because he was tapped into his Godly being and his third eye that made sure he knew everything that was created in the universe. Rodney could feel in the hearts of the four men that they no longer wanted to control America or the rest of the world because they realized that they would do anything to not die at that very moment, and silently their hearts cried out for forgiveness and another chance at life if God spared them seconds from now before they took their last breath.

Rodney stood in front of them while they were on the ground looking up at him, wondering what he was going to do to them, being as though they were weak and had killed hundreds of his people. Rodney opened his mouth and sucked in a good amount of the dry air. Then he walked over to the dead Ninja in white, bent down on one knee, and squeezed the man's lips like he was going to proceed to do mouth-to-mouth resuscitation. He softly blew into the man's mouth and instantly his body woke up from the dead, and the four other Ninjas couldn't believe their eyes. Then Rodney closed his eyes and kept his hands straight out in front of him like he was still trying to hold something back, but instead, he let his hands stay in front of him so they could suck up the energy surrounding them, causing the power of it to go straight into his mind and right into his blood and through his veins that ran all throughout his body.

He held his hand out in front of the Asian men's faces while focusing his mind on saving their lives to prove to them that he isn't a fraud. The four men began gasping for air, holding onto their throats trying to catch their breath. "You! You! How do you know the ancient Chinese secret? You must have stolen the Master's paperwork because only..." Rodney cut the man off and finished what the man was going to say. "Chin," Rodney said. The five men looked at Rodney and asked, "How do you know Master Chin?"

"Master Chin was my master, and he taught me everything that a human should know to heal the sick and help others that need to learn how to love themselves enough to know that they can't begin to love anyone correctly if they don't love themselves, let alone understand their purpose in life, and without that, how would one know where they are going tomorrow?"

Then Rodney used his mind power to raise the men up from off the ground to their feet. "You must be some type of God because some of the things you have done with your mind, Chin hasn't even accomplished. I guess you're not a fraud after all," said the Ninja in Yellow.

"You and your race of people are of color, and with the right teachings, you would love to understand the truth that the Black man is God."

"Preach!" was yelled out from a New Yorker, a person of the Five Percenters, who was from out the back of the crowd that stood behind Rodney.

"We are so sorry!" said the Asian man in black as he started bowing in tears because the truth of Rodney being God was gut-wrenching to him, being as though the man never thought he would

438

witness the day of judgment in the manner of life and almost death at the present time.

"I have given you a second chance at life, so now what are the five of you going to do about it and your race of people?" Rodney asked them.

"You have created every living thing and this here land is yours, and you and your race of people should have it and dwell in it in peace, but remember the white man is gone now, but as long as he is still living, he's coming here or to our place ready to conquer and take control over the land, but us Asian brothers have your backs."

Rodney loved what he was hearing because he knew their hearts at the time were genuine. "You all may leave here in peace, but make sure you take those that never left the Hood with you," he told the Asian man in Purple, who questioned, "Who may that be?" He asked because where he's from, not many of them have anything tied up much in the Hood. "The ones who've been cooking their food and giving it to us with feathers on their chicken wings and selling us knock-off clothing." From that alone, the Asian men knew just what he was referring to. "Yes, my Lord, yes," the five of them said while bowing and walking backward, never taking their eyes off him to let Rodney know that they were going to back off humbly and make their way to their jet that was waiting for them.

The Ninja in Yellow went into his secret pocket and started feeling around in it, and Rob noticed what he was doing and lifted his eyebrow at the thought that ran through his head. "Yo, my man, no no, no, we don't do that around here. When a Ninja digs in his pocket after there was some beef, then my Ninja, we were taught growing up in the hood to not let that hand come back out of that pocket because of the chances you may have something in it to harm me with," Rob said while he ran up on him with a serious look on his face that said he didn't trust anybody that wasn't down with Rodney. Then he grabbed the man at his wrist and held it tight and then started patting the man down the way one of the brothers from the Nation of Islam taught him. The pat-down he gave them was quick and swift, and when Rob felt that the only thing on the man's person was what the man was reaching for, he slowly started pulling the man's wrist out of his pocket revealing that the man was trying to pull out his keys, but Rob thought, wait a minute now, is this some type of sneaky weapon being as though he's a real Ninja. "Why the heck!" He said but stopped himself because he was working on trying not to use curse words any longer. "Why are you pulling out keys, my Ninja?" The Ninja in yellow stood there wondering why Rob was so concerned about his keys. "I'm about to start the plane up." He pointed the keypad towards the Jet and started it up by the push of a button. Rob looked at the jet plane. "Well, I'll be damned, first this Ninja surprised me with the fact that he could speak English all along and now pushing a freaking button to start the plane, I'll be damned." Rob waved his hand at him for them to proceed on making their way onto the plane.

All the Black people stood together, waving them off goodbye as the jet zipped down the runway and off into the sky, then vanished out of their vision in a matter of seconds. Rodney walked out in front of everyone and stood there waiting for everyone to become silent. He stood there looking out to his race of people, watching them gather themselves up to listen to what he had to say. Rodney looked over to his brother from another mother, Rob. "My brother, come stand here next to me on my right side for you to represent the meaning of what a right-hand man should be to our race of people." Rob, with honor, walked over to Rodney, and the energy of love made the crowd of Black people feel the vibe of what Black power stood for. "You are my brother, and I am that shoulder you can lean on," Rodney said to Rob with his eyes scanning the crowd of people. "Aja, my Queen, please come forward." Aja made her way through a handful of people and stood on the left side of him. "You and every Black woman that is alive is the heart and soul of this world that surrounds us. We are your children, which means you are the mother of human creation. You bring life into the world

441

and are blessed to be able to bring a boy into the world who will become a king who will soon have a queen, which means you come from royalty. Aja, my Queen, you will sit on any throne beside me as many will mimic who we are as kings and queens sharing this land of our ancestors, which are called indigenous people." Rodney stopped talking and leaned over a bit to kiss Aja on the lips with so much passion in front of everyone to sense the power of love.

The people got a feeling that wasn't expected, like the norm when it came to seeing two people kissing each other with so much passion that the norm would be some type of sexual desire entering into the minds of the lustful humans, but instead, the Black people felt the passion of that kiss was so powerful that they felt the bond between man and woman that the kiss was stamped and notarized as the love symbol for Black people. The symbol of that kiss was etched in stone from the looks of Aja's thick full lips that looked as sexy as the rapper Eve's lips, and Rodney's lips weren't as big but the shape of them was impeccable, the curves and edges of his lips were so defined that they looked as if they had to have been the lips of God. Rodney looked back into the crowd of people. "I and I am a man. I and I also a king, and most importantly, I and I am spirit while my flesh is the image of God. We no longer need to see our brothers as Black or worry about being all Black or pro-Black, for we are the leaders of humanity only because our Black sisters have created us all, all to be one, one blood. I need every one of you to look at your hands now." Every Black person did as they were told, and all in the crowd, you heard ows and ahs from people in disbelief because when they looked at their hands, Rodney made everyone have one long sharp fingernail that stood out from the rest, and they all looked up at him wondering what's the meaning of it. "We must understand who we are as a people with the mind frame of the old when we the human race understood that humans are truly just a powerful energy of the mind and the inner spirit of love, which is God. For us all to be one we will do as my brothers from the old has many years ago. Now take your brother's arm next to you no matter if it's a woman or child and use that sharp fingernail to slice your brother's arm with it until your blood runs down your arm like the Nile River and then I want you to rub your blood together so that we all will become one blood." Without question many of them did it with pride while some hesitated do to the fact that some of the people they knew at one point and time had some type of blood issue that they weren't trying to receive so they backed away and gave Rodney a look and a person out in the crowd shouted out.

"Wait, how do I know this guy ain't got AIDS or some shit?" Rodney understood the lady's questioning what the facts could be. "I have healed all sickness and diseases from every human here. The only thing that our people must remember is that our minds control the universe that surrounds us. So, I and I must say for those who have faith in the spirit of goodness, knows the fact that no wickedness against us shall prosper. And if a brother is so much as to do one of his brothers wrong, he shall be shunned to the utmost by us all, causing one's mental to go haywire, going off the deep end, causing psychological suicide until they reach their own death." Rodney noticed the people getting more comfortable. Some were kneeling on one knee, and some made their way up in trees, sitting on branches to hear more of what he had to say.

"When us Myelinated people realize this, we will receive the blessing of our higher self, which is the inner light that shines bright within us like a star from up above with a grateful heart for the love of all humanity. We shall all attend school again, only this time we will focus on building our inner self. Our youth will learn their relationship between the trees and the wind that causes the breeze, and where it comes from, and flow like the water that surrounds us all. Nature will be taught by our Queens because she is mother nature. Our job as men is to protect our Queens and bear more fruits to our race of people and raise the youth up to be walking images of Gods and Goddesses using our Chakras to their fullest capacity, coming forward as men and women of one blood and one big spirit of humanity. We will love our skin whether it's fair-complected, blue-black, or earth green because when the skin is so dark that the night gives off a greenish color to the skin, giving an illusion of the body's skin from the green foods we eat that feed the body the oxygen our bodies need to keep our temples at a high vibration. No more bleaching of our skin, lightening our melanated complexion because of being ashamed of our skin color. No darker-skinned man should ever feel because he is so black that he must stay back, or if one is so light that he won't have to worry about his own brother calling him out to be a 'Whiteboy.' We have the land, and I have planted the herb that is the healing of all nations, and now we must till the land to harvest our food. Clothing will be a choice, for our nakedness will be the only clothing that will be needed, for our humbleness of our minds won't allow our nakedness to cause lustful thoughts of each other because we must understand that the skin is only the beauty of the outside of a person, not within. What is mine is all of ours, for we all are one, and all we have is each other's as brothers. So, with that being said, there is no need for us to keep trying to get over on each other, trying to be one up on the next man, nor do we have to worry any longer about money and what the power of having it can do for you, like trying to mimic the white race of people who were living their best life while we tried our best to keep up. We will have nothing to prove to anyone, only to ourselves, seeking out the highest point of our purpose here on Earth. Again, we will give our Queens the world, and she will fill our hearts with respect and true love and bear our children so that we can rule the world once more as we did in the past and hand it forward to her so that other races of people around the world will honor our race of people for their master minds of their creativity of what they have brought to the table of life other than being what we have been in most people's eyes around the world, and that's being America's greatest entertainers. Now let's all reap what is rightfully ours and understand that what has happened here is our true reparation for our people, not being backed by the American dollar but yet understanding that God's plans for us is how we received our reparation, this was written way before the black woman had given birth to the first black man. I have taken what's yours and now I have given it forward to you all once again because it's like the old saying goes - out with the old and in with the new - waiting for us to show the world a new Dynasty of the greatest people of humanity that ever walked the face of this Earth." The power of those words had the Black people feeling powerful like the Black Panther Party did in the 60's, they threw their arms up in the air, pumping their fists while screaming out loud, "Power to the People!" Rob was loving the vibe that was taking place and he started pacing himself back and forth, biting on his bottom lip because he was so proud to be alive and be a part of this great moment. The dream of Tupac's mission of Thug Life seemed to have become a true reality and not the dream he once wished for.

The End

Questions to White America and Black America

First and foremost, I want to make myself clear to everyone who reads this book. I wrote "A Cry for Rodney Part 1" to open the eyes of the Black race to consciously think about the shameful spirit of self-hate. I wrote Part 2 for every American of the United States to hopefully open the eyes of the American people to understand that racism will be the downfall of this country if it persists. I hope the book opens the readers' minds to understand that if we are believers in some form of a loving God, then we must know that everything that has and will take place here on Earth is God's work. He knows and sees everything, so I must say that we, the people of this country, the United States of America, and the world, must humbly submit ourselves to God's love and accept everything. Because in the power of the Most High, all is possible. I also want everyone to know that by no means would I ever want to see this country come down to a race war or any kind of violence whatsoever. I wholeheartedly believe that what we put into the universe, whether positive or negative, will manifest into our reality.

Dear White Americans,

First, I would like to start off by informing you all that when you hear of a Black man being "Pro-Black," which many of you may see as being rebellious, it does not mean that we are anti-white. A Pro-Black man has become a proud man of his race, just as Europeans feel about their own ancestors and what they have done for your race in this present time. I know it must feel good to live a life of "White Privilege." I understand that many White Americans live in poverty and face challenges just like any other person in America. However, one thing that the poor, middle, and rich White Americans can relate to is the fact that 90 percent of things related to controlling this country, from the filth of poverty and its drugs to the highest points of command that oversee this country, are dominated by whites. With that being factual, a struggling man standing on his own two feet can feel that the color of his skin in this country can always keep him in a first-class stature against all other races of people who will be nothing but second-class citizens to White America. With this mentality, I would say the majority of you exhibit narcissistic traits of mental and physical abuse. What I'm trying to say is that you have been the abusers of the Black race from the time the two have encountered one another. The Black race of people here in America is like a woman being beaten by an abusive man, and all she can do is cry out for help and hope for a better tomorrow.

Now I have a question to ask White America: why is it that you can steal something and not be charged with a crime? We all know that if a man of color got caught, he would be charged in a court of law. This is certainly the case for a Black American. If that Black man finds himself in the courtroom, guilty as charged, and starts to say he's sorry for what he's done, the judge is going to say he is sorry, but the state needs justice, and the Black man goes off to jail, and life goes on. So, let's ask why America is not being charged with the crime of stealing this land when everyone knows about it all over the world and everyone wants to reap the benefits of it.

I must ask you this: do you think the Black race wants to hear that you're sorry for what your ancestors have done to our ancestors? Sorry will not change the struggle and oppression that is set upon the Black race here in America due to the injustice of the White race, who think they're superior, both economically and intellectually. If you do not believe this to be true and feel we all have equal rights and opportunities in this country, then I have to ask you all, "Would you want to add to the small percentage of White people who wish for the lifestyle of a Black American's struggles?"

On the flip side, we have many Black Americans whose mentality is so American that they don't even realize they're Europeans in Black skin. Their way of thinking is programmed to believe in money, materialistic things, and accepting the European ancient ways of homosexuality, which has never been the Black race's way of life. But as the great Don King once said, "Only in America." Many Black Americans want better for themselves, which is understandable, but if they are basing their standards on the dreams of living life as good as most of White America, it tells me that they understand the scale of fairness in this country is so one-sided.

Again, for those who feel this is a bunch of crap, ask yourself if you would honestly change your hearts to love and tell the powers that be to change everything so that every man who bleeds red will be, now and forever, equal in humanity and economically. The spirit of shame in racism should lead to punishment for anyone who turns a blind eye towards it, and they should be shunned so that this country can somewhat move forward in these days of time in some kind of human harmony of Jah's love.

For those of you who are not too arrogant and not afraid in your hearts of the Black race getting it in their hearts and minds to get revenge for what your ancestors have done to our people, I can say that even if we wanted to, we don't have the unity or the power of weapons of mass destruction that White America has. Our mentality has never been and never will be of such a barbaric spirit to kill in the manner of what has been and still is being done by White America to Black Americans. What will happen is up to the Most High Jah, and what will be will be. When that day comes, I hope that White America will find in its spirit the ability to change its ways on how to treat the Black race with the utmost respect. Because when the rest of the world comes after this country in war, you'll be able to sleep at night knowing that Black Americans would be proud to have your backs in the midst of battle. But if you keep oppressing us and killing us, then all we can do is sit back and let Jah do his work. May God bless us all.

P.S. If you find what I have written offensive, I'm sorry, but I would have to say that if this doesn't pertain to you, then so be it. But if the shoe fits, then wear it.

Dear Black Brothers and Sisters,

I want to say first that I love my Black race of people all over the world. I am the utmost proud of our race of people who have conquered struggles over the past decades and put our race at a level of high expectations in such a very short time frame, causing our race today to be greatly thankful for what little we have. But I'm ashamed of the killing that is among us, and this goes from Africa to America. My American Brothers and Sisters, I have to say that we as a race can and need to change our ways morally for the betterment of our people. The violence due to self-hate is because of one not loving themselves. If this doesn't stop, we'll wipe ourselves off the face of this earth.

Now let's talk about a small part of politics here in America—not government politics. I want everyone to think of the main reason how this country was formed. For example, let's say you and a friend went into a store, and you only had enough to buy yourself a candy bar. You go to the counter and purchase the candy bar, and you go outside the store and wait for your friend to get the things he wants. When he leaves the store, he comes out with way more than he could afford to pay for. You eat your candy, and he eats all that he robbed the store of. The next time you two go to the store, the difference is this time he enters the store with no money and comes out with damn near the whole store's merchandise. You see all he has and ask him for some, and you just might get lucky for him to share that one time. But the next time he takes his time to steal and you don't follow suit and start asking for some of his stolen goods, he's going to tell you to go and get your own the same way he did, or you just sit there and watch him continue eating in front of your face.

So, I ask why, as a race of people, do we think that the people who stole this land are going to give us a fair share of the pie in this country when many of their pilgrims or patriots lost their lives over this stolen land? You can run towards your poli-tricks if you want to, but understand that the people who run this country have an agenda. If you don't meet their expectations while you're in office, then slander will be brought up against your name, and if you're unlucky, charges will be brought upon you. Behind it all is that "American dollar" that we all slave for. That's right, I said slave for. "In God We Trust" is on every hard day's worth of work and more work chasing that money in hopes of making one feel as if he's doing better than a man less fortunate, and some tend to look down at their integrity. This money has controlled us to the point where many of us judge a person based on how successful they are in life by the amount of money in their bank account.

Many of our women look at the Black man in these times to only bring our seed of life into this world, but in the end, base his manhood on the money he can bring to the table. My brothers, if we want our women and other races to look at us with respect, then we must demand it among ourselves first. If we don't, why would they? Why would our women trust us with protecting them against this harsh world we're living in if we keep killing each other and kicking a brother down when he's at his lowest point instead of lifting him up so tomorrow would be better for us all?

Why are we blaming our kids' education today on the government's school system instead of teaching them the importance of wanting to learn all they can, no matter if it's something that doesn't seem relevant in the outside world? We must understand that a person who looks like you will give more love and have much more patience than someone of the opposite race. Many of our youth in the inner cities, and some who are not but want to be followers, have adopted the mindset of glorifying criminal behavior, calling each other "nigga" and "bitch," or "savage." This behavior can only do one thing to our race: set us back further in the respectful eyes of others and, more importantly, ourselves.

We talk about the cops killing Black people all over this country and how inhumane it is, yet it's even more so when you do it to your own kind. Now, one of the biggest questions I want to ask at the table when we're at home breaking bread with our family and friends is, "Are we afraid to do for ourselves as a race of people and not mistake that for meaning selfish doings of one's own greed? When are we going to ask ourselves where do we move as a Nation of Black people, morally, spiritually, and without the cloudiness of religion?"

If we continue to fight each other and chase the dreams of this American high-class standard, we'll never be able to tap into who we really are. By losing out on that, the God within our souls feels trapped in bondage like slaves wanting and begging for equal rights and justice. We must unite and talk about where we're going as a race of people because moving in life without direction means you don't know where you're going, so you're probably lost, stuck in the same place.

We all know racism is taught, and it most likely happens when families are home with the children at the dinner table, absorbing all its philosophy while breaking bread with each other. Let's not just come together and march up and down the streets with bullhorns, pumping our fists in the air, and making threats about what we won't stand for. I question, "What is that?" If the Nat Turner spirit isn't in your blood, then I suppose talking, pleading, and selling wolf tickets with a lot of hopes and prayers that the people you're protesting against will somehow say they understand they've done you wrong is ineffective.

Let's talk about moving forward with money taken out of the equation, and then we'll see man's nature of love and how money is most likely the number one problem in our realm of Black America. It's either you have it or you don't, but just remember, money doesn't make the man.

I have to say this again: I'm proud of our race of people who have been slaughtered, stripped of their natural tongue, and programmed into generations of ignorance due to the enslavement of the most barbaric and inhuman system in world history. Within a short duration, our race has accomplished way beyond our expectations. No matter what the stumbling block is, we will rise, and that's because what doesn't kill you makes you stronger. So, with the help of the oppression White America has set upon us, there shouldn't be much that we can't accomplish. Our race should be very proud of itself because much has been done through us, even though many of our achievements have been stolen or sadly overlooked and underappreciated.

"WARNING!!!"

My brothers and sisters, if we look around in the inner cities of urban communities, we see businesses owned by Koreans, Chinese, or other Asian descent that we support wholeheartedly. I'm from a very small city called Wilmington in the state of Delaware, with the nearest big city being Philadelphia, PA. In just those two states alone, I can say that the business of nail technicians has, for the most part, become extinct among Black and Hispanic entrepreneur women within the last 30 years. This shift is largely due to Koreans, who have played on our own inability to unite with one another, show loyalty, and exhibit much-needed patience. Noticing our weakness among ourselves, they opened nail salons all over the country in Black communities, offering their services to the same people who once owned such businesses. Now, Black and Hispanic women support people who are truly foreign to them. I bet this is happening all over the country, and if it hasn't yet, it's coming if we allow it by continuing to give them our money.

****

To My Brothers Who Are Barbers in This Country

I understand wanting to help people who want to learn how to cut hair by showing off your skills through social media, but now what you have done is enable the greatest copiers in the world to learn our craft and its style. I'm a professional barber with over 30 years of experience. One afternoon, I was lost in West Philly and had to pull over to figure out how to get unlost. I looked across the street and saw a huge sign in a wide window advertising five-dollar haircuts. I thought to myself, "Who the hell is getting a five-dollar haircut and could possibly be satisfied with the work?" When I tell you, my brothers, that the haircuts were coming out of that shop looking like top-dollar cuts, I was shocked.

Curious, I got out of my car and walked up to that big window. What I saw saddened my heart: a barbershop with more than 50 Black people of all ages waiting to get cuts from Koreans or another Asian ethnicity. This type of activity hasn't reached my small city yet, but if it's happening in Philly, which has a high population of Black people, other major cities will soon feel the same effect. If you start to see this forming, I hope our people can unite and reclaim our businesses. Remember, they are not going to hire a Black person to work in their shop, and if they do, I bet he'll be watched like a hawk and underpaid. My answer to that is for them to stay in business in Chinatown.

To the People of the United States of America

Last but not least, I want to address a problem that affects everyone, yesterday, today, and tomorrow. We must understand the importance of what we eat because we are what we eat. Here in the U.S., houses are being built every minute due to overpopulation, which means less farming and more meat eating. This meat-eating lifestyle has subconsciously adopted a suicidal mentality. When an animal is stressed out and killed for food, the energy within you will adopt a beastly persona, while you think you're perfectly fine. Look at the obese people in America and how they carry themselves; whether they are White or Black, they still walk on two feet with some resemblance to a savage beast. White America loves war, killing Black people, and poor innocent animals. Black people rob and kill each other, exhibiting a lot of hyperattention. The two biggest things they have in common are the lust for all kinds of crazy, wild sex, whether with the opposite sex or the same. If you eat food out of a can, expect to start thinking with a canned attitude, which can come off as rude.

I bet that if we all tried to cut out the meat and farm more with fewer chemicals, we would become much better thinkers, be more physically in shape, which leads to better health, and most

460

importantly, be more loving to one another without that "Thriller graveyard" feeling in your stomach. Just something to think about: If something is running away to avoid being harmed or killed, doesn't it make sense that you shouldn't be eating it?

I know people are not going to like my opinion, and I may be wrong, but I have one more thing I need to mention because it needs to be dealt with like yesterday. I strongly feel that anybody who feels they are not the gender they were born with needs to stay out of the restrooms of their chosen gender. This is in no way the same as when Black people were made to use separate restrooms because any race of people cannot change their race even if they wanted to. If you are saying you are part of the LGBTQ+ community, then why not post that up on a restroom door with a big rainbow symbol on it, like how there's an image of a man or woman for those born with natural body parts and not a mental state of what one feels is correct? I don't think it's cool for a woman to witness a trans man pulling out his manhood in a woman's bathroom just because his mental state tells him it's okay and everyone should accommodate him. Nor is it cool to see a butch or stud woman trying to sneak into a man's restroom to feel like a man. I bet they even try pissing standing up. I vote for LGBTQ+ people to have their own restrooms. I really don't think this should be a problem, as I'm sure the LGBTQ+ community demands their choice of independence. So, there you have it: a restroom sign at large stating "LGBTQ+." Don't be mad; be happy to put a stamp on what you believe you are and take it up with the Most High Jah on the day of judgment.

A Cry for Rodney II

463